GUNS IN THE DESERT

In the 1920s the Senussi tribesmen of Southern Libya need modern weapons to help in their fight against their Italian masters.

They approach American soldier of fortune, Clayton Andrews, asking him to negotiate the purchase of arms from the famous gun-runner James Martingell. When Clay reaches England he finds Martingell is dead, and has to deal with his successor, Richard Elligan, and the adventuress Sophie von Bernhardt who is now married to Richard.

The deal is done, but Richard falls ill, so Sophie and the faithful servant Ned Carew, set off for the Sahara. As they fight to survive on their epic journey, relationships begin to change...

GUNS IN THE DESERT

GUNS IN
THE DESERT

by

Christopher Nicole

Magna Large Print Books
Long Preston, North Yorkshire,
BD23 4ND, England.

British Library Cataloguing in Publication Data.

Nicole, Christopher
     Guns in the desert.

     A catalogue record of this book is
     available from the British Library

     ISBN   0-7505-1561-9

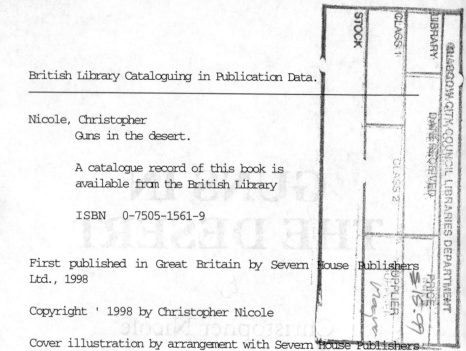

First published in Great Britain by Severn House Publishers
Ltd., 1998

Copyright ' 1998 by Christopher Nicole

Cover illustration by arrangement with Severn House Publishers
Ltd.

The moral right of the author has been asserted

Published in Large Print 2000 by arrangement with Severn
House Publishers Ltd.

Magna Large Print is an imprint of Library Magna Books Ltd.

Printed and bound in Great Britain by
T.J. (International) Ltd., Cornwall, PL28 8RW

CONTENTS

Or were I in the wildest waste,
Sae black and bare, sae black and bare,
The desert were a paradise,
If thou wert there, if thou wert there.

Robert Burns

Prologue

A shot rang out, rising above even the grind of the engines. One of the trucks slewed sideways, its windscreen shattered, its driver slumped over the wheel. The man seated beside him hastily pulled on the brake. The column promptly followed a well-ordered drill, the armoured cars forming square round the supply trucks, the men presenting their rifles and manning their machine-guns, while sweat dribbled down their faces.

When the column halted, the dust and sand raised by the vehicles' wheels continued to rise into the air for some minutes, a plume visible for miles, even in the glare of the afternoon sun. But presumably, Edio Rometti thought, even without the dust the Italian presence would be known for miles, simply by the growl of the engines cutting across this total silence that was the Cyrenaican desert.

Which was why someone, or several someones, had been waiting for them. But he had known they had to be there. There had been only the one shot, and a man was dead, or dying. Edio Rometti got down from the lead truck, stamped his boots on the ground; behind him, his men were doing the same, like him, keeping the trucks between them and the dunes from whence the shot had come. They wore the khaki uniforms, complete with puttees, high-crowned khaki pith helmets and the white equipment of the Cacciatori d'Africa.

Edio pushed his helmet back on his head, raised his goggles, and took his binoculars from the case hanging from his belt beside his revolver. He was a handsome man, young for a colonel, with a little pencil moustache. Not tall, his shoulders were broad, well delineated by his tight-fitting tunic.

He was also experienced in desert campaigning, which did not mean he enjoyed the desert. There were many places he would rather be; right now, if he had his choice of anywhere in the world, it would be enjoying a coffee at one of the street bars off the Via Veneto, with pretty girls to ogle and a peaceful afternoon in front of him. It would be cool.

It was never going to be cool where he now was, some 750 kilometres south of Benghazi. The desert stretched interminably on every side, brown and yellow, even white in places. It undulated; in any one of the many dips and hollows there could be a Bedouin army, waiting. Save that there was no such thing as a Bedouin army, for which he supposed he should be thankful.

Now the column had gone just about as far as trucks and armoured cars could go. They had left the oasis of Tazirbu at dawn, and driven another fifty kilometres; the headman in the oasis had told him the Senussi band had passed through only two days previously. But the Senussi were riding camels, and in front of him now was the Ramlat Rabyanah, soft sand which was no good for his vehicles.

He was in any event at the extreme limit of his petrol range; the trucks now carried only sufficient to get him back to civilisation. But perhaps the shot meant that he had caught up with the Senussi at last.

Edio Rometti had mixed feelings about that. Professional pride, and now a desire to avenge the man who had been hit, clashed with an understanding that he was the intruder here. Born in 1900, he was thirty years old in this summer of 1930. He had been eleven when the Italian Army had conquered Libya, driving out the Turkish overlords who had ruled this vast country for so many centuries. Young boys do not usually question what their seniors are doing, at least while they are doing it successfully. Edio had stood on the pavement and cheered as loudly as anyone when the armies had come marching home.

11

He had known then that he would be a soldier. He had achieved that ambition, without ever considering that he might find himself out here in the desert hunting what was officially described as a band of brigands, but who he well knew were simply patriots trying to defend what was their country against the colonialist invaders.

It was not even a situation that could be laid at Mussolini's door. The conquest of Libya had been officially completed when the Duce was just a schoolmaster struggling to be an editor. But the Duce, with his dreams of a revival of Imperial Rome and, more realistically, his determination to challenge France for control of the Mediterranean littoral, was not going to give up any earlier African conquests – he was even dreaming of new ones. Edio knew he was not alone in holding an equivocal attitude towards the Duce. As a professional soldier, he had been caught up in events. He had been an eighteen-year-old lieutenant, newly commissioned, and had never fired a shot in anger before arriving at the front, the day before the Germans and Austrians had launched the attack which had become the Battle of Caporetto, the greatest Italian disaster of the First World War. His memory of the battle was of ashen-faced men throwing down their rifles and running away as hard as they could. That memory should have been obliterated by the total victory gained at Vittorio Veneto only months later, a triumph that had effectively driven Austria out of the War. But for Edio, the memory remained. Vittorio Veneto had been gained with British and American help, most noticeably in the air. Caporetto had been an entirely Italian disaster.

Edio Rometti had sought a resurgence of the national spirit as much as anyone. The idea of Fascism repelled him. But if it was necessary to restore the country's greatness, then he would go along with it, as long as was necessary. No one could argue that Mussolini and his henchmen, however reprehensible some of their methods, had made Italy at last a country to be respected. But like their colonial mentors, the British and the French, being respected meant policing vast areas of the globe, seized just because they were there – it was impossible to discover what claiming to own huge areas of empty desert added to the national exchequer – at a constant drain in money and lives.

But the man who had fired that shot must be hunted down, and those who might be supporting him.

Captain Castelfiardo saluted. 'Driver Siccorio is dead, Colonel.' Edio nodded, and continued to sweep the desert in front of him. He saw nothing. No doubt the assassins were already withdrawing towards where their camels would be waiting, and they would make off south, towards the border of French Equatorial Africa. Except that the headman in Tazirbu had told him that five Bedouin, and one European, had passed through his village with only two camels; he had with difficulty prevented them from commandeering some of his own people's animals, and would not have succeeded had not the Italian pursuit been so close. Six men, and two camels, and they had come across a dead camel only two hours before. The animal had simply been ridden to death in the Senussi's haste to escape.

Six men, and one camel! And one of the men was the European Edio so badly wanted to capture. It was still a hundred kilometres to the frontier of French Equatorial Africa. His orders, while requiring him to seek and destroy the band that had attacked the outpost further north, did not authorise him to cross the French frontier. Mussolini might dream and even make plans, but as yet he had no wish to confront, militarily, what was reputedly the finest army in Europe.

'We cannot go into the sand sea, my Colonel,' Castelfiardo pointed out.

'Equally we cannot allow one of our people

to be murdered and do nothing about it,' Edio said. 'The column will remain here, and make camp. I wish twenty men. They will carry food and water for four days.'

'You are going to pursue those men on foot?'

'For two days, yes. They will not expect it. That shot was a last act of defiance, because they feel sure that we have reached the end of our power to follow them. Also, it was intended to halt our pursuit, because those people are now on foot themselves.'

'With respect, Colonel, twenty men ... you do not know how many Senussi there are.'

'The report from the village said not more than six.'

'If they have linked up—'

'In the sand sea? That is hardly possible, Captain. I am going to get those men. They have less resources than us, little food and water. Always consider the other man's difficulties, Captain, rather than your own. If we do encounter a larger party, I will retreat, to you, here, and if they follow, we will wipe them out. You will be in command until I return. And be prepared to fight.'

'Yes, Colonel,' Castelfiardo said, looking very unhappy.

Edio grinned, and slapped him on the shoulder. 'Do not worry. I shall come back to you. With a prisoner. Or a prisoner's head.'

'They have stopped, and formed a laager,' Clayton Andrews said, handing Yusuf his binoculars. 'Maybe you did the trick.'

Yusuf ben Hashim grinned, his white teeth gleaming through his full black beard. 'Without their vehicles, they are nothing. They know this.'

'It sure looks like it. But we'd better make ourselves scarce.' Clayton Andrews took his glasses back, restored them to his case, and slid down the slope from which he had fired the fatal shot – at Yusuf's command. He regarded it as a futile act of defiance, as well as an act of murder – not to mention the waste of a precious bullet: there weren't many left.

The Senussi were very happy to have the American with them, to make use of his expertise and especially his marksmanship, but they insisted he fight this war their way. He couldn't argue with their reasoning, or he wouldn't be here at all. Sometimes he wondered why he was. Certainly his parents, those so respectable middle-class paragons of right-wing Connecticut society, would have been aghast had they known where their son was at this moment, and what he was doing.

Mom and Dad had actually been quite happy at his notion of taking off to see the world. They had not believed that their son could remotely be a Communist, but they had had to accept that he had come out of college with some very left-wing, liberal ideas – and those did not go down very well in Connecticut society, where the support for President Coolidge had never wavered, and had now willingly been transferred to President Hoover. Better let the lad see the world, they had reasoned, and come back a better man, able to move into Dad's stockbrokerage firm and make something of himself. They had had no idea that Clay's idea of seeing the world had been to take part in a desert war, simply because it was the only way he could actively oppose Fascism.

Besides, he liked the Senussi. As he liked the desert. There was a cleanliness here that was lacking in urban America. He even felt that the Senussi liked him. It had taken time. Clay Andrews was a little man, only five foot six inches tall. He was powerfully built, but that was not readily apparent when he was fully dressed. He was clean-shaven with somewhat crushed features, quite different to the tall, bearded, big-featured Bedouins. Besides, this was a private war. The Senussi, which was what the Italians called them – the correct name was Sanusiyah – were fundamentalists. The sect had been founded by Sidi Muhammad ibn Ali as-Sanusi al-Mujahiri al-Hasani al-

17

Indrisi, a hundred years before, basically to oppose the corrupt and cruel Ottoman rule. Sidi Muhammad had died in 1859, but by then the sect was widespread, not only in Cyrenaica, but throughout the Sahara.

The Turks had treated the Senussi with contempt, as they treated all Bedouin with contempt; they had so much insurgency in their declining empire that a massacre here or there hardly raised their blood pressure. The Senussi, for their part, had watched the Italian takeover with optimistic anticipation. Anything had to be better than the Turks. They had only slowly realised that to be ruled by Italians was actually worse than being ruled by the Turks, if only because the Italians, while certainly less cruel, were a good deal more efficient at things like collecting taxes and bringing those they considered criminals to justice. The revolt had not started in earnest until after the First World War, but it had gathered pace over the past few years. It was not a war Clay supposed the Arabs could ever win: Italy was a modern power, with military resources far outstripping those of any desert tribesmen. But it was the sort of cause he had always wanted to support. And besides, although he had no time for Communism, he hated Fascism more.

Even in the beginning, the Senussi had been quite happy to have an American recruit, especially one who was prepared to obey their laws, neither drank alcohol nor smoked, and appeared to accept that women not only had no place in society, but were inviolate. They had only come to value him when they had discovered that he had one talent above all others: Clay Andrews was a crack shot, who had represented the United States in the 1924 Olympics. Now he had proved his value once again.

Their remaining camel waited at the foot of the slope, held by one of the tribesmen. The party that had carried out the raid had split up once it had become clear they were going to be seriously pursued. It had been Yusuf's business, with this small remnant, to lead the Italians deep into the bottom half of the country they claimed, until their pursuers literally ran out of gas. Of course, where the going was passable, trucks could travel faster than camels, and the Italians had managed to come very close; hence the loss of their other animals. But they were at last in a sand sea, and surely the trucks would have to stop.

Which made that last act of criminal defiance the more foolhardy. Especially as it had served no purpose. The Italians might not be able to come on, but they were hardly going to disappear immediately. And meanwhile, Yusuf's group were down to this one camel, and very little food and water. 'What do we do now?' Clay asked.

'We wait.'

'We cannot last more than another twenty-four hours,' Clay said.

'In twenty-four hours the Italians will have withdrawn,' Yusuf asserted. 'Then we can return to Tazirbu, and obtain food, and water, and camels.'

'They were not very co-operative the last time,' Clay pointed out.

'Because we had no time to impose ourselves upon them. The Italians were too close. Once the Italians have gone, then we will dictate to that sheikh. Those are not fighting men. There will be no trouble. Have you not yet learned, Clay, that in the desert it is patience that always wins the day?'

'Patience and determination,' Clay said, and looked back at the dune they had just abandoned, and the sudden row of topees that had appeared there, plodding forward.

Yusuf saw them too, and swore under his breath. 'They would enter the sand sea, on foot?' asked one of his men, morale wavering.

'Are we not in the sand sea, fool?' Yusuf asked. 'On foot! Take cover.'

Five of the men huddled behind the next rise. The herder took the camel further back; without the animal they were in even more serious trouble. Clay levelled his binoculars. 'Twenty men,' he said, 'and an officer. From their equipment, they are ready for a march of several days.'

'Bah,' Yusuf said. 'They do not know the desert as we know the desert. We shall pick them off, one by one. Now, we will fire into them, and they will lie down to return fire, and we will withdraw. Believe me, my friends, they will not keep up that game for very long. Load.'

'I have no bullets left,' said one of the Arabs.

Yusuf glanced at him, then at Clay. 'Give him some of yours.'

Clay checked his bandolier. 'I have four bullets left.'

'I have two,' said the other Arab.

'I have none,' said the remaining man.

Yusuf checked his own bandolier. 'I have three.' He knew the herder had none.

'Nine bullets, even if every one hits a target,' Clay said. 'There are twenty-one men out there.'

'We have our swords.'

'They have their bayonets.'

Yusuf glared at the Italians, steadily approaching, rifles at the ready, expecting to be shot at. Men who were both brave, and determined, and disciplined, as he knew from experience. 'We must get away,' said one of the Arabs.

'We cannot get away,' Yusuf said. 'Not all

21

of us. Those men are equipped and rationed for several days. They are already too close.'

'Then what must we do?' asked the other Arab.

'Looks like surrender,' Clay said, practically. He was not at all sure what that would involve. They had killed at least one Italian soldier. *He* had done that. As the Italians did not recognise that the Senussi were fighting a war, that made him guilty of murder. But surely not until after a trial, when all sorts of factors, not least American pressure, could be brought to bear.

'Surrender,' Yusuf muttered. 'They will hang us.'

'I've been thinking about that,' Clay said. 'A trial—'

'Bah! You think it will be a big thing? They will try us by drumhead court martial and hang us, or shoot us, on the spot. No, no, if we are to die, it must be for a worthwhile purpose. Why are we lost? It is because we have run out of bullets. Because our rifles are old and out of date. Because we have no proper weapons with which to fight a war.' That seemed a statement of the obvious. 'So you must get away,' Yusuf said.

'Me?'

'You must leave here. You will take all our food and water, and the camel. Achmed will guide you to safety.'

'I can't abandon you,' Clay protested. 'I

was the one who shot that driver.'

'The Italians do not know that, nor will they find out. You will get away, and you will go to England, and you will obtain arms. Listen. In the first instance, go to Sheikh Hafsun ibn Abdullah al-Fadl. He is far to the west, in Tamanrasset. That is in the Hoggar Mountains. French territory. Achmed will guide you. Sheikh Hafsun is a very wealthy man, and is a supporter. He will give you money. Then you will go to England. When I was a young man, several years ago, I fought in Afghanistan, against the forces of Amanullah Khan. We lost that war, but I learned a great deal. I learned of a man called Martingell. An English knight. But a man who deals in arms. I even saw him once; he was in Afghanistan, delivering arms to Amaruddin Khan, the rebel leader for whom I was fighting. This man, I was told, will deliver arms, in quantity and quality, modern weapons with their ammunition, to anyone in the world who can pay his price. Go to this man, Clay, and tell him what we need. Then you will save our cause.'

'You're talking about months, maybe years, before I can do this,' Clay argued.

'In months, in years, the Senussi will still be here, fighting the Italians,' Yusuf promised him. 'But you will do this more quickly than that.'

23

PART ONE

The Money

It takes a lot of money to die comfortably.
Samuel Butler

The Proposal

Sophie Elligan laughed as she chased her golden retrievers through the heather. On a cool autumnal afternoon the Chiltern Hills were a good place to be. Anywhere was a good place to be, to Sophie, even with the world apparently collapsing about the ears of every financier in Europe, as it had already done in the States. Germany, being the most heavily in debt, was the hardest hit; Momma and Poppa were in dire straits. But this was England!

Even with her marriage on the verge of collapse? It was not something she was prepared to accept. She blamed Richard's moods over the past few months on the financial situation, as well as the broken leg he had sustained on his last business venture. That no doubt also accounted for his heavy drinking. But it did not account for the way he had cut her out of the partnership they had shared so successfully, or the way he seldom smiled at her any more.

Sophie was just thirty. She was a tall woman; her figure was good, and she had small, exquisitely piquant features. In thick

27

skirt and heavy jumper, thick stockings and brown brogues, she looked every inch a member of the English 'county' set to which Richard belonged by right of birth and his erstwhile commission in the Guards. Very few people knew of his other life. Or hers.

Only in her hair, which, in defiance of current fashion, she wore long and at the moment loose, an auburn cloud drifting past her shoulders, had she broken the mould. But she had been breaking the mould all of her life. Sometimes disastrously. She was not going to change now, no matter how sour life had become. She could still laugh at it. That was terribly important.

She paused, because she had run out of breath; the dogs, barking eagerly, continued their rampage for a few moments longer, then stopped to look back and discover what had happened to their mistress. They were actually on the way home from their walk, and the house was in sight, on the far side of the lane. And down the road there was at that moment approaching a car, a Morris Eight, bumping over the uneven surface; Elligan House was a long way from any main road.

She wondered who it could be; their only usual visitor was Dr Plummer from Bristol, come to look at Richard's leg, and she did not expect him today. Drawing deep breaths she descended the shallow slope and crossed the road, the dogs now bounding behind her. She walked into the semi-enclosed yard of the old farm building just as the driver of the car was getting out.

Ned Carew, Richard's old batman and now right-hand man, who doubled as gardener and chauffeur when there was no business to be done, emerged from the shed behind the house to see who the visitor was. Ned was a big, solid young man, with normally friendly features that could on occasion look uncommonly fierce. As now. He did not take to strangers. But he was relaxing as he saw his mistress approaching. He worshipped her. But then, Sophie thought contentedly, so did so many men. She enjoyed it, even if Ned's eyes, so deep and penetrating, were occasionally disturbing.

She gave him a wave to inform him that she was now in control, and approached the car. 'Good morning.' She spoke English with only the faintest of accents. 'May I help you?'

The young man raised his cap. He was actually some inches shorter than herself, but was quite good-looking beneath a very heavy suntan. 'Would you be Mrs Elligan?'

And he was, judging by his accent, an American. Sophie was intrigued, even if she felt an immediate quickening of her heartbeat; strangers calling at Elligan House always did that to her. 'I am she.'

'I'm actually looking for your husband.'

'Who isn't available right this minute,' Sophie said, trying to evaluate him. Well dressed, certainly, in a conventional manner. And he had been severely exposed to the sun, some time quite recently, she estimated. 'Perhaps I can help you, Mr...?'

'Andrews, ma'am. Clayton Andrews.'

'Of?'

He grinned. 'I suppose you could say, Hartford, Connecticut.'

'How exciting. I have never been to the United States.'

'Well, it's not exactly the place to be right now. All gloom and doom.'

'If you're speaking financially, it's not all that bright over here. Won't you come in?'

'That's very kind of you.'

She led him into the comfortably furnished lounge; Ned Carew watched them disappear with smouldering eyes. The dogs crowded past them to lie on the hearth rug in front of the roaring fire.

'They don't bother you, I hope?'

'Nope. I love dogs. We have them at home.'

'I normally have a glass of champagne when I return from my walk,' Sophie said. 'Will you join me?'

'Thank you very much.'

She herself opened the ice box and took out the bottle.

'Allow me.' He removed the cork, expertly; their shoulders touched. Then Sophie reached into the cupboard for the glasses, and he poured.

'Here's to ... well, a happy meeting.'

'Snap.' She gestured him to a chair, sat on the settee. 'What did you wish to speak with my husband about?'

'It's a business matter.'

'My husband has only one real business, nowadays, Mr Andrews. And if it is that you wish to discuss, then you may as well do it with me. In case you don't know, my maiden name is von Beinhardt, and I am the daughter of Claus von Beinhardt, of the Hamburg arms company of that name.'

Clay's eyes widened.

'My husband acts as my father's agent,' Sophie went on. 'Because he is experienced in the field. He learned his craft when working with Sir James Martingell.' She paused.

'It was actually Sir James I came to England to see,' Clay said. 'But I'm told he is dead.'

'Sadly, yes.'

'Did you know him?'

'I saw him die, Mr Andrews.'

'Oh!' Once again Clay was taken aback. 'When I inquired after him, I was actually given Major Elligan's name, as a possible contact–'

'There you have it.'

'You mean, you actually saw Martingell die? I was told–'

'That he was killed in an engagement with Afghan tribesmen, four years ago. Yes, Mr Andrews.'

'And you were there?'

'We were part of a delivery team,' Sophie said.

He gaped at her, clearly trying to envisage this elegant, so well-groomed, pretty woman being involved in a gun battle in the wilds of Afghanistan. Sophie enjoyed shocking people. 'I have travelled quite extensively, in the arms trade,' she said. 'With my husband, of course.'

'Of course. Will he be interested in dealing with me?'

'That depends upon how and with what you wish to deal, Mr Andrews.' She could see no point in telling this man that Richard was in bed upstairs, and could not possibly undertake any arms deliveries for at least four months, according to Dr Plummer.

Clay felt in his inside breast pocket and took out a manila envelope. 'I have here a list of what my principals require.'

Sophie slit the envelope with her thumb, unfolded the several sheets of paper inside, read quickly and with great concentration.

Then she raised her head. 'This is an enormous order. For the Senussi?'

'Have you heard of them?'

'Enough.'

'I hope you don't suppose that Mussolini has any right to their country?'

'I don't suppose Mussolini has any right to anything, Mr Andrews. But–'

'I understand Sir James Martingell supplied arms to the Somalis for their fight against the then Italian Government,' Clay said.

'So he did, Mr Andrews. But that was some years ago, before the War. And he gave it up when he discovered just how barbarous the Somalis could be. I was going to say that the difficulties of getting any large supply of arms to the Sahara would be immense. We obviously couldn't go in through the coast held by the Italians, and I don't think the French would be very happy were we to attempt entry through Algeria or Morocco. They also have their problems with rebellious tribesmen.'

'We would organise the delivery. If you feel your husband would be interested . . .'

Sophie's brain was racing. The profit on such a shipment would be very large. Sufficient to tide them over – her parents as well – until the markets settled down and regained their strength. But with Richard unable to make the delivery . . . Suddenly she was excited. But she mustn't show it. She tapped the sheets of paper. 'You have the necessary financing?'

'I do.'

Sophie got up, went to the bookcase, and took out a large atlas. This she spread on the table. Clay stood at her shoulder, inhaling her scent. He found her a most attractive woman – at least partly because of her past – despite the obvious fact that she was hostile to his approach.

Sophie found the appropriate page, studied north-west Africa for several seconds. 'I suppose it could be done,' she said. 'But it would still be an immense undertaking. We would have to charter a ship. Will your funds rise to it?'

'They are not unlimited,' Clay said. 'I would require an estimate.'

'Yes. Well, leave these papers with me, and I will put them to my husband.'

'Do you think he will deal?'

Sophie raised her head. 'Frankly, Mr Andrews, I would say not.'

They gazed at each other. Perhaps the most attractive thing about her, he thought, was her cool arrogance. Based on a very real confidence. If she had indeed delivered an arms shipment to Afghan rebels, a delivery which had undoubtedly not gone according to plan or James Martingell would still be alive, then she had adventured on a scale probably greater than himself. Now, in her own home, surrounded by her dogs and her self-created ambience, she was totally dismissive. Of even the large amount of money she was being offered. He was not a man to be slapped down. 'Perhaps I should go to Hamburg,' he suggested. 'And speak with your father.'

'If that is what you wish to do, certainly. But my father accepts commissions as and when my husband and I recommend them.'

'Well, then, there doesn't seem that much more to say, Mrs Elligan. You did say you would put your husband in the picture?'

'I did. And I will.'

'Then I'll leave you my card. I'll be at that London address for at least the next week.'

Sophie took the card and glanced at it, then placed it on the silver tray by the door. Clay went to the door then checked. 'I think you should know, Mrs Elligan, that some very brave and devoted men are dying, every day, in this little war.'

'I am sure they are, Mr Andrews. Are you speaking of Senussi, or Italians?'

'I'm afraid I was rather rude,' Sophie confessed. 'But you did say always to begin negotiations with a negative approach.'

She was sitting on the bed beside her husband, a dog's head on her lap. Richard Elligan was a tall, handsome man, of slim

35

build and slightly aquiline features; his years in the Army, which had begun with his being badly wounded at the Somme, had left their mark in a certain stiffness of both manner and body, but, only a few years older than his wife, he was as fit as any man his age. Save that he was at the moment incapable of leaving his bed, his right leg encased in plaster from the thigh to the ankle.

He was, Sophie knew, still passionately in love with her, or at least her body, in his sober and less introspective moments. But he had always been a little afraid of her, firstly in the manner she had courted him rather than the other, correct way – at least in his eyes – and then in the way she had insisted on accompanying him on that last great adventure with James Martingell. Even more had she frightened him by her ability to ride and shoot – to kill where necessary – and take risks and suffer hardships as well as any man. He knew that Sophie, whatever the odds, physical or psychological, would never let him down. He was not so sure she felt the same way about him. Whether she was actually as in love with him, physically or emotionally, as he would have liked, and required in a wife, was another matter; her cool personality was very difficult to penetrate.

'Did I do the right thing?' she asked.

'Absolutely. The Senussi. Africa. Africa is where the original Martingell fortune, in both money and reputation, was made, you know.'

'I do know, Richard. Aunt Cecile died out there, remember, helping James. And if I didn't know, Mr Andrews reminded me.' She got up, went to the dressing table, and poured them each a whisky with a splash of soda. She returned to the bed, gave him his glass, and again sat beside him. 'I didn't tell him anything about you. What do you think?'

'I think it is too difficult. Quite apart from me.'

Sophie had brought the atlas upstairs and laid it on the table. Now she went to it and flicked the pages. 'I don't think it would actually be difficult at all, if we can make a landing somewhere in Rio del Oro or French West Africa. Supposing this man Andrews can organise it as he says he can, and his people will meet us.'

'Can the Senussi enter French territory?'

'They can go wherever they please, in that vast desert.'

'But if the French catch up with them, or us—'

'We'll have to make sure they don't.'

Richard drained his glass, and gave her hand a little squeeze. 'There is something about this idea that makes me ... well—'

'Not nervous? Not you, Richard. Anyway, you won't be involved.'

His head came up. 'Just what are you suggesting?'

She gave a little smile. 'I have never seen the desert. The North African desert.'

'It killed your aunt,' he reminded her. 'What you are suggesting is absurd. Quite apart from, well...' He held up the glass.

Sophie refilled it. 'What don't you like about the idea? I mean, the general idea.'

He shrugged. 'I suppose ... selling guns to Muslim tribesmen to kill Christian Italians.'

'It's a point of view, if a slightly racist one. Your Christian Italians are killing every Muslim tribesman they suspect of being Senussi. I think we should go for it.' She returned to sit beside him. 'I think we have to go for it. We need the money.' Richard's eyebrows arched. 'I had a letter from Mama this morning,' Sophie went on. 'It would appear that the economic situation is more serious than we first supposed. The Americans, having gone bust, are calling in their overseas loans. These are big figures, which most European governments simply cannot meet. So it looks as if we are in for a prolonged money drought.'

She watched his expression. This was a situation which even she found difficult to grasp. She had never taken much interest in the financial side of the business. She knew, just after the end of the War, that Germany had been in a serious state; she could remember the gigantic inflation of only seven years ago. That had affected her family less than most, because Claus von Beinhardt, her father, had always invested overseas, principally Britain, and they had remained quite wealthy people. But what she had seen around her had been distressing, and as part of the peace terms included the shutting down of all major German arms manufacturing firms, the future had been grim. Claus von Beinhardt had not shut down, of course; he had merely gone underground until he could find buyers for his *matériel* – and an agent to handle the transactions for him. That had been James Martingell, put in a similar position by the British. Martingell had always skated very close to the law in his dealings before the War. The story was that he had only avoided a lengthy gaol sentence by agreeing to sell all his production to the British Government at the start of the War; he had fulfilled that obligation faithfully and well, which had earned him his knighthood, but also the boot as soon as hostilities ended.

Thus the two old collaborators, who had parted so bitterly twenty-odd years earlier, had again been in harness. It had been a venture that had cost Martingell his life, and brought Sophie herself into the centre of this so sinister but so exciting and so profitable business. And since then there had been ample funds ... 'I wish you'd tell me the truth,' she said. 'About how heavily *we* are involved.'

Richard sighed. 'I'm afraid both your father and I have invested fairly strongly in American stocks. Those are now lost, it seems. But if our English and German investments are also going down the drain, we are going to need every penny we can lay hands on.' He squeezed her hand. 'I'm sorry. Maybe I should have kept you more informed. But I didn't want to bother you.'

She squeezed back. 'I'm not bothered. But I see your point. I'll go into town tomorrow and finalise the deal.' She winked. 'And collect the money.'

'You?'

'I'm the one he's been negotiating with.'

Richard gazed at her for several seconds. 'This Andrews. Give me your impression.'

Sophie made a moue. 'He seemed very capable. Very dedicated. But also very nice. Attractive.'

That was not what Richard had expected her to say. But if he knew her capabilities, and trusted her, he was also well aware of her insatiable lust for excitement and adventure. 'We'll talk about it,' he said.

Richard watched his wife prepare for bed. He enjoyed doing this, because she remained a quite beautiful woman, at least in his eyes. She brushed her magnificent hair, a red-gold wonderland. He was so happy that she had resisted fashion and kept it long. And not even the constraints of fashion could diminish her splendid breasts, only matched by the powerful muscles in her thighs, the curve of her buttocks.

He wondered if she was considering having an affair ... with this itinerant American, who had clearly impressed her? He wondered if he should be angry, even outraged, at the idea of that. And found that he was not. Sophie knew, of course, that he had been in love, as he had supposed, with Martingell's daughter before he had ever met her. That was history. She did not know that he had once had a brief affair with Martingell's wife. Poor Lady Anne, her death sentence commuted, but still locked up for life for shooting her own son; she had been very fortunate to escape the hangman.

What a tangled life that woman had led. But then, he supposed, he had led a hardly less tangled life. When he closed his eyes he could still hear the shouts of the Pathan tribesmen attacking his position, the screams of his own men being cut to pieces by the Pathan women ... all history, when he could lie here and contemplate this work of art who belonged to him ... or did she? She held up her nightdress, and he shook his head.

She folded the garment over the back of a chair, crawled on to the bed beside him, waited for him to stroke her as she knew he liked doing, and as she enjoyed, slowly lowered herself on to him as he cupped her breasts, slid a hand down his stomach and groin to find him. 'You're excited,' she remarked.

'So are you.' He kissed her. 'It's your baby,' he said. 'You finalise it. Then we'll see about organising the delivery.'

The Agents

Sophie Elligan regarded London as her favourite city. She had spent some time there as an art student a few years previously, and it was there that she had first met Richard. She knew the West End well, and plunged unhesitatingly into the maze of slightly seedy streets that arced away from Charing Cross Station; Trafalgar Square was only a few hundred yards away to one side, as was the Embankment and the river to the other. Here there were several hotels, of a sort, most as seedy as the street itself. She attracted glances from the passers-by, not only because of her looks, but also because of her clothes, which were in the height of fashion. She wore a mustard yellow woollen suit with a pleated skirt and green collar, cuffs and belt; her shoes and gloves were black, her stockings flesh-coloured. Her hat was a green cloche, her stole black mink. Her handbag swung slightly as she confidently approached the address Clayton Andrews had given her.

The receptionist was old and grubby; he typified the hotel itself. He blinked at her from behind rimless glasses. 'Gentlemen

43

don't receive ladies in their rooms,' he remarked.

'Then will you ask Mr Andrews to come down,' Sophie said, patiently.

He had been considering her. 'You're foreign,' he observed.

Sophie knew that however hard she tried to perfect her English, there always remained an accent. 'Yes,' she said. 'I am foreign. So is Mr Andrews, right?'

'Well, you see,' he pointed out, 'I can't go up and leave the desk unattended.'

Sophie refrained from stamping her foot; obviously it was too much to expect a dump like this to have a phone in the bedrooms. 'Well, then...' She opened her handbag, took out a five-pound note, neatly folded, and slid it across the counter. 'Why don't you just blink.'

He regarded the note for a moment, then unfolded it to make sure it was what it pretended to be. Sophie smiled at him, crossed the lobby, and climbed the stairs. 'Number Five,' he remarked, perhaps to himself. Clearly, if she and the gentleman were both foreign, he was not concerned with their moral welfare.

Sophie was only slightly out of breath when she reached the upper floor, looked along the corridor. A maid who looked every bit as grubby as the desk clerk regarded her with astonishment. Sophie gave her a bright smile and located Number Five. She knocked, and waited. And was surprised when the door opened; Andrews had apparently been shaving, and there was foam everywhere. 'Holy smoke!' he remarked.

Sophie raised her eyebrows. 'I'd expected your husband,' he explained, wiping his face with a towel.

'I told you, we're business partners,' she said. 'And you began your negotiations with me.'

'Ah. Yes.' He glanced furtively past her at the open-mouthed maid. 'Can you come in?'

'I'm here,' she pointed out, and stepped past him as he held the door wide.

He closed the door, leaned against it. 'They don't really approve of women in men's rooms.'

'I have gathered that. But I bought my way in.'

'Say, did you do that? Well—'

'But I don't know for how long,' she said, nose wrinkling as she looked at the unmade bed, the grimy window, inhaled the slightly acrid smell. There was a chair and a table, and she sat at this.

'You took me by surprise,' he explained, hastily pulling on a shirt.

'We are prepared to fill your requirements, Mr Andrews,' she said. 'On our usual terms, as regards payment. That is, half down and half on completion of the delivery. We will need a landing place, which you will specify. We will provide the ship. You will arrange for us to be met, when we land, by our customers, so that we may complete the transaction. Is this understood?'

He seemed taken aback by her brisk efficiency. Then he went to his suitcase and took out a map of North Africa. This he spread on the table in front of her. 'You will need to sail south of the Canary Islands. I assume we are speaking of a steamer?'

'It will be a steamer.'

'Good. You will pass between Fuerteventura and Cap Juby. You will bear in mind that this is a very dangerous coast, with a big swell.'

'That means big surf,' she pointed out.

'Yes. It will not be practical for you to land the cargo on an open beach. You will make the port of Boujdour. That is in Spanish Morocco, what is known as Rio del Oro. Boujdour is a small place, with few facilities.' He grinned. 'Or Customs officers.'

'But there are some?'

He nodded. 'My people will neutralise the port. At least long enough for you to land the goods and leave again.'

'And you?'

'Does that bother you?'

'Let's say I'm interested.'

46

'I shall be there to meet you. But once the guns are ashore, it will be necessary to move very fast. Into the desert. The Spanish authorities will certainly become interested very quickly. But from Boujdour to the border of French Morocco is only a hundred and fifty miles.'

'What sort of transport will you have?'

'Hopefully, there will be motor transport. There is a track.'

'And when you reach the border?'

'There will be no problems at the border. Once across, we will make for the Hoggar plateau.'

Sophie studied the map. 'It looks kind of a long way.'

'Twelve hundred miles.'

'Motor transport the whole way?'

'We shall try to arrange this. If not, it will have to be by camel.'

'What are the roads like?'

He grinned. 'There are no roads. There are tracks, which are known to the Bedouin.'

'So what sort of time scale are we talking about?'

'If we can provide motor transport the whole way, a fortnight.'

'And if you cannot? You told me the matter was urgent,' Sophie reminded him.

'It is. But that we get the weapons we need is more important than the time. We are fighting a war for our independence. We have been fighting for years. We are prepared to go on fighting for years. Until we win. Your guns will enable us to do that.'

He certainly meant what he said, she realised. She almost caught some of his fervour. But it was her business to dot all the i's and cross all the t's.

'What happens if you are arrested by the French?'

'We must try not to be. The French can be far more severe than even the Italians.'

'Sounds interesting. I'll wish you luck, Well, Mr Andrews, if you'll let me have that down payment, I can set the ball rolling.'

He was still standing by the table, and thus at her shoulder. 'As we are partners in business, perhaps you could call me Clay.'

She tilted back her head to look at him. Here he comes, she thought, and wondered how far he would go. And then wondered how long it might have been since he had had a white woman?

'We're not in business, yet, Mr Andrews,' she said. 'Not until the money is paid.'

'You're quite the businesswoman,' he remarked. But he went to his suitcase, took out a chequebook, and leaned over the table to write the cheque. 'One hundred and twenty-five thousand pounds sterling,' he said.

The cheque was drawn on a London

48

clearing bank, and bore only his signature. 'You mean you're spending your own money?' she asked.

'Chance would be a fine thing.'

'But it's in your name. You're telling me these Arabs have trusted you with a hundred and twenty-five thousand pounds of *their* money?'

'That's right.'

'They must indeed have a great respect for you. Very well.' She folded the cheque and put it in her handbag, 'I shall now go to our bank and deposit this cheque. I'm afraid the transaction cannot begin until it has cleared.'

'How long will that take?'

'Two or three days. Will you be remaining here?' Once again she looked around her.

'I shall,' he said. 'You don't approve.'

She shrugged. 'I can't help wondering why, with so much cash at your disposal, you're not staying at the Savoy. It's just up the road.'

'It's not my cash,' he pointed out.

'Of course.' She pulled on her gloves, went to the door.

'Will I see you again?'

She supposed she had put him off by her coolness. 'Would you like to?'

'I would like that very much. Shall we make a date, for three days' time?'

She shook her head. 'I shall not be here.

As I do not expect the cheque to bounce, you see, I shall go to Germany anyway and make arrangements for the shipment to be prepared. I shall return in a week. We could meet then, if you are still here.'

'I shall be here,' he promised.

'And if the cheque has cleared.'

'It will have.'

'Very well then. A week today. But...' another glance around the room, 'not here.'

'At your home?'

'Definitely not. I shall be at the Savoy. Join me there for lunch, a week today, and I will be able to confirm our arrangement and give you dates. Is that satisfactory?'

'Very. I'll look forward to our meeting. And if the cheque has bounced?'

'Then you will have a wasted wait, and a wasted visit to the Savoy, because I shall not be there.'

'Of course.' He hurried across the room as she was about to open the door, and held her hand. 'I had not suspected that arms dealing could be such a pleasurable business.'

His fingers were tight, his head inclining towards her. 'Let us both hope the cheque doesn't bounce, Mr Andrews,' she said, freeing her hand and opening the door in the same movement.

Clay stood at the window to look down at

the street, watch her leave the building and walk briskly in the direction of Charing Cross Station. What an attractive woman. Perhaps the more so because she had been so unexpected.

He had been celibate for some three years. The Senussi women were as carefully guarded as the Crown Jewels; he did not know what they thought of that, but presumably as they had been brought up to their unrelenting purdah if they ever had thoughts of men, other than their husbands, those were immediately rejected as unclean. Being something of a cynic, for all his romantic vision of everything that was good in the world opposing Fascism, he could not help but wonder if they did not occasionally, or even often, have thoughts of each other – but that was not necessarily a crime in Arab eyes. Any more than it was a crime for men to wish to couple. He had received more than one invitation himself. That he had refused had been at least in part, he understood, because of his white Anglo-Saxon Protestant upbringing. In New England, the word Protestant was interchangeable with Puritan. But it had also partly been because while he valued the Senussi and their cause, valued their courage and determination, he did not wish to become one of them. He was an American, and in the course of time he intended to return home, and take up his life, and move on to prosperity, marriage and children. He did not think he would be able to fulfil such a role had he submitted to the caresses of a man like Yusuf.

Discipline, there was the key to a successful life. Which was not to say he did not want, sometimes with an almost animal intensity. Especially when he had found himself back in civilisation, surrounded by sweet smells, rustling skirts, absorbing femininity. Yet here again he had preserved that iron discipline. He was in England to fulfil a mission, not his desires. And for so long had he preserved that discipline, he had never doubted it would carry him back to Africa.

He had never supposed his mission would involve him with a woman so compelling as Sophie Elligan. So ... there had almost been a suggestion that she found him as attractive as he had found her. But she was married. Back to his Connecticut Puritanism. Yet it seemed they were going to be meeting again, and more than once ... if she really intended to deliver the guns herself. And in Boujdour the meeting would be on his terms. He found that a most exciting thought.

'Good heavens!' Claus von Beinhardt finished scanning the order; it was several pages long. 'To fight against the Italians, you say?'

'Your father-in-law, and my aunt, sold guns to the Somalis to fight against the Italians,' Sophie remarked.

'And it turned out badly.'

'Because Martingell made off with the money. This time the money will remain in the hands of a Beinhardt.'

'Now, that for a start is ridiculous, Sophie. How can a young woman like yourself traipse off into the Sahara with a quarter of a million pounds worth of arms and ammunition?'

'All you have to do, Papa, is supply the merchandise and the ship to take me to this place Boujdour. I know you have both. Once there I shall deliver the goods and be given the balance of the money.'

'By a bunch of Arabs. What happens when one of them decides to rape you?'

'I shall blow his brains out,' Sophie said. 'Although perhaps I will aim lower down.'

They gazed at each other across the huge mahogany desk, one of the few articles of furniture Claus had managed to rescue when the original Beinhardt mansion outside Bonn had been sold, and which rather over-filled the now small office on the Hamburg waterfront. He supposed Sophie could hardly recall those opulent days; she had been hardly a teenager when they had been swept away by the War. But she seemed to have every intention of recreating them, if she could.

Claus understood that he did not know his daughter as well as he could, and perhaps, should. Her beauty always surprised him. He himself, somewhat small and hunched, with narrow features to go with his narrow shoulders, had clearly played little role in the genetic side of her appearance. Her mother Clementine, large and broad and jolly, had no doubt been responsible for Sophie's height and figure. But not even a loving husband could describe Clementine as beautiful even in her youth. Sophie was a throwback to her Aunt Cecile, who had dominated the family and indeed the House of Beinhardt, until she had made the mistake of falling in love with that rascal Martingell, and going off adventuring with him – and dying, at an obscenely early age. Now Sophie proposed to do the same.

But she had at least adventured before, with her also English husband, and survived – he had never been sure exactly what and how much. Sophie could see his concern. 'In any event,' she said, 'I shall be protected by the American.'

Claus von Beinhardt snorted. Like most of his countrymen, he did not like Americans. Had it not been for their quite unreasonable entry into the War, Germany might have won, or at least been able to obtain a satisfactory peace. How different things would have been. 'And you suppose you can trust *him?*'

'As a matter of fact, I do.' Sophie smiled. 'Supposing his cheque doesn't bounce.'

'Ha! And may I ask what Richard thinks of the idea?'

'Richard doesn't know of it yet. Of the delivery schedule, at any rate. He believes everything is waiting on the cheque. As indeed it is.'

'And when he finds out?'

'I will take care of that.'

'Ha! Well, the idea is unthinkable.'

'Papa...' Sophie leaned across the desk. 'Are you saying we do not need the money? Richard has told me that you, and we, are very nearly bankrupt. I know you have enough guns in your warehouse to start a war, but we cannot eat guns, can we? We can only eat what the guns sell for. Now we have a sale, which will put us back on our feet. We have no choice.'

Claus again stared at her for several seconds. Then he got up and walked to the window to look out at the river, and the ships and barges on it. 'Does your American friend know the situation?'

'No, he does not. Nor should he. He is the one who is desperate. I think we should keep it that way.'

Claus turned back to face her. 'You must have adequate protection. As Richard is unable to go, I will accompany you.'

'You, Papa?' Sophie did not know whether to be amused or aghast. Her father was not and had never been an adventurer. And he was sixty years old. 'You're too old.'

'James Martingell was several years older than I when he delivered those guns to Shensi.'

'And he died doing it.'

'He was killed, Sophie. He didn't die of old age.'

'He damn near did,' Sophie said. 'Now you are the one who is being absurd, Papa. Richard will arrange protection for me.'

Claus gave another of his snorts. But he was happy to have been talked out of it; he knew his limitations. 'Are we going to tell your mother about this?'

'I don't think that would at all be a good idea,' Sophie said.

Sophie took a suite at the Savoy for the night. They couldn't afford it, if the cheque had bounced. But the cheque hadn't bounced. She arrived in time for lunch, waited in the lounge off the Riverside Restaurant. She was pleasurably excited, the more so because she was by no means certain how the meeting was going to turn out, how she wanted it to turn out.

Richard had been a dear, had asked no questions, made no suggestions. But he was on her father's side, that she simply had to have an adequate back-up, and was telephoning around his old Army pals to see if he could discover one. But the real issue was whether he trusted her sexually. And whether she trusted herself.

Because it was all happening. She had been to their bank before the Savoy, and the money was nestling in their account. She had never doubted that. And there he was, coming up the steps from the lobby, somewhat diffidently. But he was wearing a good suit, and was acceptable even in these exalted surroundings. 'Mr Andrews.' She smiled at him as one of the under-managers brought him to where she was sitting. 'A glass of champagne?'

'Great.' She signalled the waiter, and sat down.

Clay did also. 'All well?'

'All is perfect, Mr Andrews. Clay.' She smiled at him.

'Great,' he said again, took his glass from the offered tray, sipped. 'Sophie.'

'I have already wired Hamburg,' Sophie said. 'Now things can be set rolling.'

'When will you sail?'

'One week from today.'

'Say, that's better than I hoped. And when will you be at Boujdour?'

'Weather permitting, a week after we sail.'

'Then I had better make tracks.'

'Where to, precisely?'

'We have agents in Spain. I will contact them. Then I will get down to Africa as fast as I can.' He grinned. 'As a tourist heading for Marrakesh. Our agents will have alerted our people in the desert. We'll be waiting for you.'

They smiled at each other over lunch.

'This is the first time I have done business with a beautiful woman,' Clay confided.

'You say the sweetest things,' Sophie replied.

'May I ask you a question?'

'Of course. I don't have to answer it.'

'I got the impression that it was your husband who was the gunrun– I beg your pardon. Who did the business. But I haven't even been allowed to meet the guy.'

'Is that the question? My husband is otherwise engaged.'

'You mean he's out of the country?'

'I mean he's otherwise engaged.'

'Leaving you footloose and fancy free.'

'Leaving me to run my half of the business, Clay,' she said. 'Which at this moment happens to be you.'

'I like that.'

'And the Senussi,' she added.

'Touché. You know...' His hand crept

58

across the table, his fingers touched hers. But he didn't say anything more.

'Tell me,' she suggested.

'I can't do that.'

'You mean you would like to go to bed with me.'

His head jerked, his cheeks scarlet. 'You know that?'

'Of course.'

'And you're not mad?'

'Why should I be mad? Can there be a greater compliment?'

He scratched his head. 'I sure have never met a woman like you before.'

'You mean you have never met a female gunrunner before. That's reasonable.'

'You mean you would ... shit!' He gulped. 'I beg your pardon.'

'Be my guest. What is so horrendous about me?'

'You're just out of this world. You're married, you're rich, you're powerful, I guess—'

'And you?'

'I'm just a mixed-up freedom fighter.'

'A fugitive from the once-affluent society,' Sophie observed.

'Yeah,' he said. 'Well, I guess I'd better be going.'

'When are you leaving England?'

'I'm on the night train and ferry, Dover-Calais. I'll be in Spain day after tomorrow.'

Sophie looked at her watch. 'The train

doesn't leave until six. It seems to me that now we're in business together we should get to know each other better in more salubrious surroundings.'

He gulped, and looked left and right. 'Like ... here?'

'Well, not in this dining room. But if we leave discreetly and go up to my suite, I don't think we'll have any trouble.'

He looked positively furtive as he followed her from the dining room and to the lifts. She found him fascinating, not so much as a human being but because she found it difficult to envisage him as a character from *The Desert Song*. They arrived on the seventh floor, where the floor waiter hovered. Sophie beckoned him. 'Mr Andrews and I have some very important business to discuss,' she said. 'We do not wish to be disturbed.' She slipped two five-pound notes into his hand.

'Of course, madame.'

She led Clay along the corridor and unlocked her door. 'Do you settle every situation with money?' he asked.

'It's the quickest and best. Ladies are not supposed to entertain gentlemen in their rooms. Certainly not in the Savoy.'

'And that chap can be trusted to warn off the detective?'

'Yes. He will also fetch us a drink, if you'd like one.'

'I think I need to be sober.'

'I think you're right.' Sophie sat on the sofa, patted the space beside her. 'Tell me how many men have you killed?'

'Hell ... I have no idea.'

'Really?'

'Well, one shoots at people, and sometimes they disappear. You never really get to know whether they're dead or not. You ever killed anyone?'

'Three. And I know they were dead.'

'Shit.'

'Now I've put you off completely.'

'I'm curious,' he confessed. 'You have the money, the goods...'

She kissed him, lightly, on the lips. 'I am about to entrust my life and my fortune to you. Don't you think I have a need to discover if you're up to it?'

He gazed at her, and she took off her hat and allowed her hair, hitherto pinned up, to escape down onto her shoulders. 'You mean,' he said, 'that if I once have you, I am not ever going to let anything happen to you. Has it occurred to you that I may not want to let you go, either?'

'Let's cross that bridge when we come to it. The most important thing in either of our lives right now is the guns and their safe delivery. We both need to be absolutely certain about that. So we need to be absolutely certain of each other.'

61

'And your husband?'

'My husband is a very certain man,' Sophie said, and kissed him again.

His hand strayed to the bodice of her dress, and she clasped it before moving it to her lap. 'Let's talk about the delivery,' she said.

Clay couldn't be sure whether he was walking on earth or in the sky as he left the Savoy. Sophie Elligan, he thought. A woman who made up her own rules for life, and practised them, too. He had almost thought she was going to have sex with him, there and then. Now he realised she had never intended that. But she had virtually promised ... what? Simply that all things might be possible, once the delivery had been made.

Her way, she supposed, of making sure of his allegiance. But again, once they were in Boujdour ... yet her confidence was unsettling.

He wondered what sort of relationship she had with her husband? But that was pointless thinking. He was clearly never going to be allowed to meet Major Elligan, and after this afternoon he did not wish to. Only Sophie mattered. She had said the guns were the most important things in their lives. But he would argue with that.

It had been so long since he had been with

a woman he had felt like a virgin. And he had never been with a woman possessing such velvet skin, such flowing hair... The scent of her, the feel of her, the presence of her, still filled his mind.

She had achieved her objective. He had fallen in love! Of all the absurdities, when it was his business to deal with her and then to return and fight with Yusuf and the Senussi, engage in a war to the death with the Italians. This was no time to fall in love.

But he could dream a little, that she might agree to stay out with him, and fight with him ... and die with him? That magnificent body lying in a pool of blood, its beauty disappeared? He gave himself a little shake. He had walked up the pavement to Trafalgar Square, where he could take the Underground to Waterloo. It was just past four, so he had some time to spare.

He paused for a moment to gaze at Nelson's column, a monument to Britain's erstwhile greatness, he supposed, and a car pulled in beside him. Clay paid no attention to it, only reacted when the door opened virtually in his face. 'What the fuck—'

Hands grasped his lapels and he was jerked inside, only then realising that the rear of the car was curtained. And that it contained four men: the driver, one in the front seat, and two in the back, the two who had manhandled him into a sitting position between them. The car was driving round the square at some speed. He had been snatched in broad daylight. But this was London, not Chicago! 'What the hell do you think you are doing?' he demanded, having got his breath back.

'We wish to talk with you,' one of the men said.

As he had already surmised, his kidnappers were Italian. 'So talk,' he snapped. 'Then let me out. I have a train to catch.'

'Back to Africa, eh?' asked the other man.

'Is that any business of yours?' Clay demanded. He was determined not to reveal any fear of them, but the whole business was very sinister.

'Yes, it is our business,' said the first man. 'You are an agent for the Senussi. You have been buying guns in England, from the so-beautiful Mrs Elligan.'

'You lay a finger on her–'

'Oh, but we are going to do just that. However, right now there is you. Do you realise we could kill you?'

'You wouldn't get away with it. Not in London.'

'Do not fool yourself, Signor Andrews. No one will give a damn if your body is found in a ditch.'

'So what's stopping you?' Clay demanded, beginning to pant.

'We think it would be a better idea for you

to return to the desert, to your friends, and tell them that we know everything they are doing, everything they are planning. Tell them that their money, collected with such diligence and such patience, has all gone to naught. Because there will be no guns. Tell them these things, Signor Andrews. Tell them that their cause is hopeless.'

'You think they'll stop fighting you? Never!'

'We think they will be discouraged, Signor Andrews. We think they will be so discouraged they may even kill you for having failed them. That is their business. But without that money they must realise that they cannot buy guns, and without guns they must also know that they cannot fight our army. I think they may realise that their resistance is over, that Il Duce has conquered them, as he always said he would.'

The car was slowing. Clay had no idea where they were, but he presumed they had a plan. 'You can't stop the arms shipment,' he panted. 'It has already begun.'

'No, no,' the first man said. 'It is being conducted by Mrs Elligan. When we have finished with you, it shall be our pleasant duty to persuade Mrs Elligan to abandon it. We are looking forward to that.'

'You bastards!' Clay shouted, and struck at his first tormentor. But the man behind him grasped his arms and the punch didn't land. The man facing him hit him, however, several times in the stomach. The pain was intense, and he doubled over, gasping and retching, to be struck another blow on the back of the head. His face went down and encountered the man's knee coming up. The blow sent him to the edge of consciousness, and he was only dimly aware that his arms had been pulled back again and his wrists bound behind his back. Then his ankles were similarly bound, and the rope passed back up to his wrists, to leave him hog-tied. An evil-smelling rag was then thrust into his mouth and secured there with another length of rope. Christ, he thought, if only I could get these bastards at the end of my gun. But his gun was in the left luggage at Waterloo.

The car stopped, and the door was opened. Both men in the back got out, carrying Clay between them. They stood at the side of the road, and rolled him down a shallow parapet. His body struck various objects and he received several more bruises. Then he came to rest, on his side, staring at an earth bank. 'Don't miss your train,' recommended the man standing above him. Then the car doors slammed, and the engine roared.

By twisting his head Clay could see

66

buildings above him which were all in darkness, and he reckoned he was on a deserted site, almost certainly still in London, because they had not driven far enough. He still didn't know where he was.

But he had to get free to warn Sophie that she was in grave danger. The thought of what those thugs might do to her if they got hold of her made his blood run cold. Desperately he worked his wrists together, but could make no impression on the ropes; he had already lost all feeling in his hands. He felt that his mouth was a better bet – the cord holding the rag in place wasn't so tight.

He wriggled to and fro until his face came up against a stone projecting from the embankment, firmly held in place. Slowly he got his cheek against it and slid over it until it wedged in the cord. Then he began straining and pushing. Soon enough it slipped out of the cord and slashed into his cheek. He tasted blood, but kept at it, and at last the cord slipped. Then he still had the problem of getting rid of the gag, which could only be done with his tongue, all the while terribly aware that it was growing dark and that he had almost certainly missed his train. But it was Sophie he was worried about. He worked his jaws, threw back his head. 'Help!' he shouted. 'Is anyone there? Help!'

He waited, and heard nothing. He tried

again to free his wrists, without success. Now he had lost all feeling in his legs as well. He shouted again, and again. He was hoarse when a voice said, ''Ullo, 'ullo. What's all this then.'

'Help me,' Clay gasped.

A few moments later he was free, if still hardly able to move because of the cramp in his limbs. 'Somebody tied you up,' the constable remarked.

Clay rubbed his hands together, while he tried to think. He would have preferred not to have been rescued by the police, but as he was rescued... 'I must get to a phone,' he said,

'You'll come down to the station,' the policeman said. 'Can you walk, or shall I send for a vehicle?'

Clay tried to get up, staggered for several seconds, but found he could stay on his feet. 'It's not far,' the policeman said, encouragingly.

'A phone—'

'There's one at the station.'

Clay supposed that was probably his best bet. But ... he looked at his watch. It was a quarter to seven; he had lain in that ditch for two hours. 'You need a drink,' the policeman said. 'There'll be one at the station.'

'A phone,' Clay said to the duty sergeant.

'Let me use your phone.'

'After you've told us just what happened, young fellow,' the sergeant said.

'Here, have a cuppa,' the constable said, presenting Clay with a cup of tea. 'I think he's a Yank,' he told the sergeant who looked disapproving. Like most British policemen, he associated Americans with Chicago, especially when they were found bound in a ditch, and Chicago-style crime was something London could do without.

Clay drank some tea; he was very thirsty. His brain was racing. To tell the truth about what had happened would involve him in a very long session with the British police, which at the end of it could mean his being deported – back to the States. But he had to get a warning to Sophie. 'Yes,' he said. 'I am an American. I am visiting England, and was set upon by these thugs. Now if you'll let me–'

'What thugs?' the sergeant asked.

'How should I know? Please, will you–'

'Do you have any identification, sir?'

'Yes. Here. Take it all.' Clay emptied his pockets of passport and wallet. 'Just let me use your phone. It's most urgent.'

The sergeant opened the passport, checked the photograph with Clay's face. 'You say you didn't know these men?'

'I never saw them before in my life,' Clay said, truthfully. 'The phone–'

'This wallet has money in it,' the sergeant pointed out. 'You weren't robbed. So what were these characters after?'

Clay had been formulating a story. However far-fetched, all he needed was for it to be believed long enough to get Sophie off the hook. 'They were after Mrs Elligan. I was with her at the Savoy, and they thought we were together when they snatched me.'

'Who is Mrs Elligan?'

'She's a friend. A very wealthy woman. I think they meant to snatch her for ransom. That's why I have to use the phone. To call her and warn her.'

The sergeant regarded him for several seconds, obviously not believing a word of it. Then it occurred to him that he had nothing to lose by allowing the phone call, and he might even learn something. He picked up the telephone. 'What number?'

'The Savoy Hotel.'

The sergeant waggled his eyebrows. 'Get me the Savoy Hotel, dearie,' he told the switchboard operator. A few seconds later he handed the receiver to Clay, pushing the speaker across the desk.

'Savoy?' Clay said. 'Let me speak with Mrs Elligan, please.'

'Mrs Elligan has left the hotel, sir,' the clerk said.

'Left? But ... she was staying the night.'

'She was booked in for the night, certainly,

70

sir. But she changed her mind.'

'My God! When did she leave?'

'Mrs Elligan checked out at half-past five, sir.'

'Where did she go?'

'I'm afraid I do not know that, sir.'

'But she took a taxi, right?'

'I do not know, sir.'

'You can find out, can't you?' Clay realised he was shouting, and hastily lowered his voice.

'If you will hold the line, sir, I will ask the doorman,' the clerk said.

'Your lady left, sir?' asked the sergeant.

'Yes. Listen, she is in grave danger.'

'From the people who kidnapped you, sir?'

'Yes. Listen–'

'But if the hotel didn't know she was leaving,' the sergeant said, 'how could these would-be kidnappers know?'

'They'll have been watching the place.'

'While kidnapping you, sir? We're talking about quite a gang, are we?'

'Yes. Listen–'

'I have spoken with the doorman, sir,' the clerk said. 'Mrs Elligan did take a taxi. To Paddington Station.'

'Thank you,' he said, and hung up. 'Supposing she caught a train, say at six o'clock, what time should she have arrived in ... Bristol? Cheltenham?'

'The journey should take about two hours, sir, depending on the train she caught. But we don't know which one, do we?'

Clay bit his lip. In any event, there was no way she was going to reach her home much before nine, and it was now only just past seven. She was out there, perhaps perfectly safe, or perhaps already in the hands of the Italian agents. His shoulders sagged. 'What are we going to do?' he asked.

The sergeant smiled benignly. 'I think you should have another cup of tea, Mr...' he looked at the passport, 'Andrews. And then you can tell us, in as much detail as you can remember, just what happened to you this evening. We'll need you to describe the men, as well. After all, sir, we do wish to find these people, don't we?'

When Clay had left, Sophie had a long, deep, hot bath. She needed that, to calm herself down, and relax, and understand just what she had done, what she was doing. She had no conscience about flirting with that young man. Almost seducing him, as she could so easily have done. Her only quibble with the afternoon was that she might not have done well enough. Aunt Cecile would probably have gone the whole way.

As for the morality of it... Her entire life had been based on what she had been told of her famous aunt, the woman she apparently so closely resembled – well, faded family photos confirmed that, even if they could not depict Aunt Cecile's colouring. Aunt Cecile had been the elder sister, and there had been no sons. Thus she had been accepted from a very early age as the heiress to the Beinhardt Arms Company – and the Beinhardt fortune.

Cecile had lived on a commensurate scale for all of her short life, sleeping where she chose, choosing men as she desired them. She had chosen the famous gunrunner James Martingell to be, not only her partner in the business, but her husband. She had insisted upon accompanying him to East Africa to sell guns to the Mad Mullah, as he had been called, and had died of malaria. But she had died as she had lived, adventuring and *doing*. How Sophie wished she could have known her.

Mama, the younger sister, had never been management material. Thus she had been married off as quickly as possible to someone who was. The only condition had been that Papa should take the name Beinhardt, and he had been perfectly willing to do that. But already the collapse of the international arms business had been evident, as the world had plunged into war, and peripherals and private concerns, whether buying or selling, had been sucked into the general conflict. Since then it had been a case of picking up the pieces. As Mama and Papa had never had a son either, the ultimate responsibility had been hers, as she had accepted from an early age. But Germany's defeat, and the embargo placed by the victorious Allies on the manufacture and sale of arms, had seemed to end her career before it had even begun. She recalled being with her father, as a teenage girl, in London in 1919 when Claus had tried to interest James Martingell in renewing their old partnership, and been turned down flat.

When, so strangely, she had made the acquaintance of Richard, a man who had begun as Martingell's enemy but had become his friend and partner, it had not been with any thought of gunrunning in mind. Her abortive art career had come to an end – she simply did not have the talent – and here was a handsome, virile and, above all, exciting man, who lived an exciting life. She had made all the running, because he had so appealed to her. That he had provided her with more excitement, more danger, more understanding of what living and dying were all about had been a bonus. She still lived in her dreams, the shouts, the shrieks, the flying bullets, the smells and the scents, the cold, the exhaustion, the sheer ambience of that Afghanistan adventure, when she had

74

proved herself as good as any man. That thanks to that adventure she had been able to set the House of Beinhardt back on its feet had been the ultimate reward.

She and Richard had appreciated each other, in the sense that they found each other's bodies attractive, each other's company stimulating, and they both wanted the same things from life and were prepared to work shoulder to shoulder to achieve their ambitions. Was that love? Sophie didn't know. They had been comfortable, together, and they had always trusted each other – to do the right thing by the business. Because the business came first.

She had been very angry when he had refused to let her accompany his last delivery. She did not see how anywhere in the world could be more dangerous than the border between China, Russia and Afghanistan, and she had survived that. Had his refusal been love for her?

She had not been able to resist a feeling of satisfaction when he had come home with his leg so badly broken it had necessitated nearly a year in bed. She grieved for his pain, but it might not have happened had she been there. Perhaps he knew that, which had created the rift between them. Now she had been given the opportunity once again to resurrect the fortunes of the House, despite what might be happening in the business world. But if she was going to do that, she was going to do it her way. On that she was determined.

She dressed herself, repacked her valise, and went downstairs. 'I've changed my mind about staying the night,' she told the clerk.

'Oh. Ah–' He looked embarrassed.

'Of course I shall pay for the room,' she told him, and wrote a cheque.

'There is nothing unsatisfactory, I hope, Mrs Elligan?' asked the under-manager.

'Nothing at all. I just need to get home sooner than I had anticipated.'

'May we look forward to the pleasure of your company again?'

'Of course.' She picked up her valise and went outside.

'Taxi, madam?' The major-domo stood to attention.

'Yes, please. Paddington Station.'

A taxi was summoned, and she sat in the back while being whisked away; she would be home by about eight, she reckoned. Having enjoyed a complete triumph. The taxi swung down a side street to avoid the worst of the traffic, and had to pull to the left as a large car forced its way past them. 'Bloody hell,' the taxi driver remarked as the two fenders touched with a scraping of metal, before the taxi was forced onto the pavement.

A woman passer-by screamed, but before Sophie could get her thoughts together – she had been happily day-dreaming – the back doors on either side were wrenched open, and she found herself staring at two men even as she realised that a third had coshed the driver so that he slumped across the wheel. Sophie swung her valise and hit one of the men across the head. But he had hold of her wrists and was pulling her out of the car, while the man behind her was pushing, his hands digging into her buttocks. She opened her mouth to scream and was struck in the stomach. She gasped and was bundled into the back seat of the limousine, landing on her hands and knees against the rear seat; the vehicle immediately drove away.

Dimly she heard people shouting. She tried to push herself up, and was forced down again by a hand on the back of her neck, so that her arms gave way and she found her face against a man's shoes. 'Stay down,' a voice commanded.

She panted, felt the car swing round several corners, and then suddenly halt. Hands gripped her shoulders and pulled her up, as the door was opened and she was thrust out into the evening air. But only for a second. Another car was waiting by the kerb and she was bundled into this. She saw that this street was empty and realised immediately that the first car must have been stolen. At least now she was allowed to sit on the back seat, but she didn't think her position had improved. The car had curtains, which were drawn in the back, and there were now four men, two in the front and two in the back. She had got her breath back. 'Just what are you trying to do?' she asked, as coldly and as calmly as she could.

'Shut up,' said the man on her right.

The non-driver in the front had her valise which he had opened to examine the contents. Most of these he threw on the floor, but the priced arms list he waved at his companions. 'A quarter of a million pounds' worth,' he said excitedly.

'That is a lot of guns, Mrs Elligan,' said the man beside her.

'I have no idea what you are talking about,' Sophie said.

'Was not this order given you by a certain Mr Andrews, an American? A deal in guns, to be supplied by your father, Claus Beinhardt, to the Senussi in North Africa,' the man said.

'That is complete nonsense,' Sophie said. 'Where are you taking me?'

'Some place quiet,' the man said. 'Where we can have a talk, eh? Soften you up.'

Sophie turned her head to look at the man on her left, and had her arms seized from behind and twisted so that she could not stop herself turning right round to face the other man. 'You touch me...' she warned.

He grinned, dug his fingers into the neck of her blouse, and pulled. The material ripped and she gasped. Then he did the same to her petticoat and that split too, leaving her breasts exposed. 'Carlo likes playing with women,' said the man holding her arms. 'He likes hurting women. Do you like being hurt, Mrs Elligan?'

Sophie kicked as hard as she could, but the angle was wrong and Carlo easily caught her leg, to her consternation carrying it over his head and on to the other side, so that he was between her knees. Carlo held her thighs and drove his hands upwards into her knickers, feeling beneath the material. Sophie screamed. She had not intended to, but no one had ever treated her like this before.

'You listen,' the man spoke into her ear. 'We do not wish this arms delivery to go ahead. We wish you to go home and forget all about it. You have the first payment. Keep it and spend it. See, we make it possible for you to have a great profit. But no arms must go to Africa. You understand what I am saying?'

'I'll see you damned,' Sophie gasped.

'You know,' the man said, 'we could kill you now. It could never be traced to us, because we leave the country tonight. But we do not want to kill a beautiful lady like you. We do not even wish to scratch your face so that you are no longer beautiful. What we want you to do is abandon this arms shipment, and then tell anybody else who might be interested in such activity what will happen to them if they attempt to take your place. You understand this?'

'Fuck off,' Sophie snapped.

'As you wish. It is time for her to have a little drink,' he said.

The car stopped, the two men in the front got out and pulled her out into the night. The man who had assaulted her also got out and while his companions held her arms, forced her to her knees, then knelt in front of her, grasping her jaw between powerful fingers so that her mouth was held open.

Sophie gasped and tried to free herself, but the grip on her arms was too powerful. Now the fourth man uncorked a bottle and held it to her lips. She inhaled the smell of the castor oil and made another desperate effort to get free, without success.

No, she thought. No, no, no. This cannot be happening. All her adventuring in the past had been with Richard at her shoulder, and a gun at her waist. Both had provided total protection. While with men like Clay Andrews, she had been in charge. Now...

The castor oil filled her mouth. She tried to spit it out but the man hit her in the stomach so that she involuntarily swallowed. Instantly her mouth was filled again, and again, and again, as the procedure was repeated. Then she began to vomit. The men released her and she fell on her face.

'You have brought this on yourself,' the man with the bottle told her. 'But you will recover. Maybe you will even feel better for it, eh? So, go home and spend the money and forget about the arms. Next time we shall not be so gentle.'

The Trap

It was some time before Sophie could bring herself to move. She felt sick, and filthy, and degraded. She continued to vomit for several minutes, crouching on her hands and knees, only slowly realising that she had lost her shoes; they must have come off in the car. But more than anything else she felt a sense of outrage, of consuming anger, not merely at what had been done to her, but at the concept that those bastards could suppose they could frighten her off. She wanted to destroy them. She wanted the Senussi to kill every Italian in North Africa. She was going to help them to do that.

Now she was feeling cold, as well as bruised and battered and still desperately ill. It was quite dark. She pushed herself up and crawled up the embankment, stood there for a few minutes while she tried to get her bearings. She couldn't see any lights or houses, and she was not standing on a main road. On the eastern horizon there was a dull glow in the darkness. London. But it was several miles away.

Then she saw lights coming towards her. Instinctively she ducked back down into the parapet, then realised she had to get home. She stood up and waved her arms and the car slowed, drove past her, then stopped and backed up. 'Good God!' said the man behind the wheel.

'She's not wearing shoes,' said a woman's voice.

'Please,' Sophie said. 'Please help me.'

'She's *foreign*,' remarked the woman, as if that explained everything.

'I am as British as you are,' Sophie snapped. 'Will you help me?'

'Well ... to do what?' the man asked, carefully looking her up and down. He had a moustache and wore a cap and was in his forties, Sophie estimated. She couldn't see his companion clearly.

'Do you know where we are?'

'Well ... don't you?'

'Listen,' Sophie said. 'I have been assaulted and beaten. I am freezing. All I want to do is get home.'

'You smell,' the woman said.

'I've been sick.'

'Have you been drinking?'

'I have not been drinking,' Sophie said. 'I need help. May I get in?'

'Well ... I suppose so,' the man said. 'Assaulted? Were you ... ah...'

Sophie got into the back seat, shivering. 'I have not been raped. I was made to drink castor oil.'

'Good lord,' the woman said. 'You need to go to the police.'

Sophie realised that was probably the only way she was going to get real help – and there was no necessity for the police to discover what had really happened. 'Yes,' she said. 'Can you take me to them?'

'There's a station in Ascot,' the man said.

'I think we need to recapitulate,' the inspector said. He was embarrassed, because while Sophie had been allowed to take a much-needed hot shower, she had refused to put on her vomit-stained clothes again. She had been found a dressing gown to wear and a pair of woolly socks for her feet. After several cups of tea she still felt icy cold. She had also been examined by a doctor which had been nearly as unpleasant as the assault itself. He had gone off muttering, but had been able to confirm her insistence that the assault had not been sexual.

Now her presence was proving a disruptive element in the station, with constables trying to find every excuse to walk past the door of the interview room in order to catch a glimpse of the rather gorgeous red-haired woman in such deshabille.

'Please do,' Sophie said. 'I would like to get home.'

'Home being?' He was decidedly suspicious, as she had shown no desire and made no request to inform anyone of what had happened. But there was no way she could contact Richard except in person, or he'd go spare and try to get out of bed and do himself an injury.

'My home is in Gloucestershire.'

'Ah. You live alone?'

'No. But my husband is ill. I wish to return to him.'

'But not to telephone him to tell him you are all right?'

'No,' Sophie said. 'He does not know anything has happened to me. He thinks I am away for the night. I do not wish to upset him.'

'I see. Now, these men who attacked you, you cannot describe them.'

'They were men,' Sophie said.

'Who rammed your taxi and abducted you.' The inspector had been in contact with the Metropolitan Police. 'Simply to ... ah, beat you up, and feed you castor oil?'

'They took my handbag, and my money.'

'I see. But you did not recognise any of them as people you might have met, or even known.'

'I had never met any of them,' Sophie said. 'Look, all I want to do is go home. Can't I go home?'

'A serious crime has been committed, Mrs Elligan.'

'Suppose I prefer not to bring charges?'

'Well–' He looked scandalised.

'I can do that, can't I?'

'You can, but I am afraid it would be very foolish of you. Don't you wish these men to be caught and punished for what they did?'

'Not if it is entirely going to disrupt my life,' Sophie said.

He gazed at her for several seconds. Then he said, 'Tell me about this American, who was trying to find you. He was also abducted and beaten up, and left in a ditch.'

Sophie frowned at him. 'Clay?'

'That is his name, I believe. Clayton Andrews.'

'Is he all right?'

'I believe so, apart from some bruises. His principal problem appears to be anxiety. I'm sure you'll appreciate, Mrs Elligan, that when two people who know each other, and who in fact lunched together, are both separately abducted and beaten within the space of a couple of hours, that there has to be a link. We need to find that link.'

Sophie was thinking furiously. 'Has Mr Andrews preferred charges?'

'Now that is another odd thing. He has not preferred charges. His sole concern is you.'

'Then he will be relieved to learn that I am all right.'

'But you are not all right, Mrs Elligan.'

'I think I am. May I go home, now?'

'Don't you think you should contact Mr Andrews, and reassure him?'

'I'll do that when I get home. If he contacts you, tell him I am all right and that nothing has changed.'

'Meaning what?'

'That is my business.'

Another long stare. 'You know, I could have you charged with wasting police time.'

'Inspector, you have been wasting *my* time. Okay, I was abducted and beaten and then released. I flagged a car down and asked for help. They brought me here. Now I wish to go home. I will have to ask for your help to do that. My clothes are filthy and I have no money. But whatever you lend me will be repaid.'

'And you still refuse to bring charges against the men who assaulted you?'

'I would prefer not to. It's over. I want to forget it, just as rapidly as I can.'

'Well,' the inspector said, and the telephone at his elbow jangled. He picked up the receiver. 'Yes? Not a lot. Yes. That's all right by me. I just want to see the back of her.' He hung up. 'You're in luck, Mrs Elligan. We have located someone who is driving down to Cheltenham tonight, and is willing to give you a lift. So it won't cost you anything.'

'Thank you. Is it possible for me to obtain

some clean clothes?'

'I'm afraid not, at this hour and such short notice. I am sure the gentleman will not mind.'

The gentleman turned out to be hardly older than herself, a heavy-set man, somewhat hard-featured, but impeccably dressed and with a public school accent. 'Walter Pemberton,' he said, shaking her hand. 'My friends call me Wally. Can you walk?'

'Sophie Elligan. Why shouldn't I be able to walk?' Sophie asked.

'Well, you've no shoes—'

'It's not raining, is it. I'm sorry if I'm a bit snappish, Mr Pemberton, but I'm very tired—'

'And you've had a hard time.' He escorted her into the forecourt, and she picked her way carefully towards his car, watched by several interested policemen.

'I do apologise for the stink,' she said.

'Not at all.' He opened the door for her, and she slid into the warm interior of a surprisingly large car. She couldn't make up her mind how to take his remark – presumably the police had informed him of the situation – so she decided to ignore it.

'It's very good of you to drive me home,' she said. 'It's a very long way.'

'Sixty miles? Not really. And I was going to Cheltenham anyway.'

'That was very lucky for me,' Sophie said.

'I would say you deserve some luck,' he remarked, started the engine and drove out of the yard. 'It'll take a couple of hours, so just sit back and relax.'

Sophie rested her head on the back of the seat, closed her eyes. If her body ached, it seemed, in every bone and every muscle, not to mention more intimate places than those, her brain was surprisingly clear, her only real worry whether Clay might have been more seriously hurt than the police had suggested. More importantly that he might have been sufficiently frightened to wish to call the whole thing off. She didn't think he was the sort of man who would be easily frightened but she still needed to get in touch with him as quickly as possible, and she didn't know how that could be done.

'Would you like a drink?' Pemberton asked.

Sophie opened her eyes.

'There's a flask in the glove compartment. And it's seven-fifteen. Good aperitif hour, don't you think?'

Actually she did feel like a drink, even if she had no idea what alcohol would do to her empty stomach. She sat up, opened the glove compartment, took out the flask, unscrewed the cap and filled it, then held it out. 'Oh, not for me while I'm driving,' he said.

She raised her eyebrows. She had put him down as a rugby-playing layabout who would not give much thought to safety on the road. She drained the cap herself, felt the brandy tracing its way down her chest, and a few seconds later felt considerably better. 'Aches and pains, eh?' he asked. He was obviously dying to talk about it.

'A few,' she said. 'In and out.'

'Bastards,' he said. 'The police will get them, you know. They always do.'

'If they're still around,' she said without thinking.

'Oh, they'll be caught,' he said again, and glanced at her. 'Unless they've left the country.'

She frowned. Just how much had the police told him? They really had no business to have told him anything.

'Yes,' she agreed.

They drove in silence for some minutes as they passed through Reading. 'May I ask you a question?' Pemberton ventured.

'Depends what it's about.'

'Oh, not about *that*. I mean, well ... not my business, what?'

'Yes,' she agreed.

'I was going to ask you if your husband's name is Richard.'

'Why, yes, so it is.' Sophie was surprised. 'Do you know him?'

'I think I may. I used to know a Richard

Elligan at school.'

'Rather a long time ago,' Sophie said. 'And ... may I ask *you* a question?'

'Anything you like.'

'How old are you?'

'Me? I'm thirty-three, sad to say.'

'Richard is forty.'

'Oh, quite. He wouldn't remember me. I was just a kid when he was a sixth-former. Rugby, wasn't it?'

'Yes,' Sophie said thoughtfully, trying to work out whether one actually went to an English public school for seven years; she'd have thought it was more like five on average. But he had the right school ... She supposed the reason she was suddenly suspicious of him was that she was suddenly suspicious of all men. Yet she realised with some surprise that she was not afraid of being alone with him in his car. The unease was caused by the coincidence that he should have been available to the police to drive her home, that he should be claiming to know Richard when it was highly unlikely that he could have done so ...

'Richard went into the Army, didn't he?' Pemberton asked. 'Irish Guards. Wounded on the Somme and all that.'

'You know a lot about him.' She gave a little smile. 'Almost as much as I know myself.'

'Old boy's network, don't you know. But

he left the Army a few years back, didn't he? Lost track of him. So what's he doing now? If I'm not prying.'

You are prying, Sophie thought. But he was doing her a favour and the question was easily parried. 'He's retired,' she said. 'He left the Army when his father died and he came into an inheritance.' Which was perfectly true, even if the inheritance had hardly been sufficient to live on.

'Lucky for some,' Pemberton remarked.

'We manage,' Sophie said.

'Do you travel a lot?' Pemberton asked.

That was definitely it. She didn't know who this man was, but she could now be quite sure that his happening to be at the police station and offering to drive her home had not been a happy coincidence. 'We holiday when we can,' she said. 'Mr Pemberton, would you mind if we didn't talk any more? I'm so very tired.'

'Of course. Bad of me to keep you awake.'

She actually did doze off, having resolved to keep awake. His voice seemed to come from a long way away. 'Home, Mrs Elligan.'

'Oh!' She sat up. 'However did you find it?'

'The police gave me directions.' He pulled into the yard, braked.

Sophie tried to remember if she had told the police exactly where she lived, and decided she hadn't. But presumably they had ways of finding these things out. She got out. Both Ellen and Ned were standing in the doorway; they had never looked so reassuring. 'I can't tell you how grateful I am, Mr Pemberton,' she said. 'Will you come in and have a drink? Or are you still bothered about driving?' She was hoping he'd refuse.

He looked at his watch. 'Half-past eight. I think I could manage one, thank you. Not so far to go now, eh?'

'Oh. Well, then... Ellen! Ned!' She went up the steps.

'We have been so worried, madam,' Ellen said.

'About me? I wasn't due back tonight.'

'All these telephone calls ... the master is very upset.'

'Then I'd better go right up. Ned, will you mix Mr Pemberton a drink.' She smiled at him. 'I'll be down in a moment.'

'Husband not well?' Pemberton asked innocently.

'Right this minute, no,' Sophie said, and went upstairs.

'Sophie!' Richard was sitting up in bed and, as Ellen had indicated, was looking distinctly agitated. 'What in the name of God has been going on?'

'Not so loud.' Sophie closed the door.

'That fellow Andrews has been on the phone, and the police. They said you were in grave danger ... what happened to your clothes?'

Sophie was taking them off in exchange for a housecoat of her own; she desperately felt like another bath, a really hot one, but that would have to wait until she had got rid of Pemberton. 'Listen,' she said, and quickly outlined the events of the evening, leaving out only her bedroom tête-à-tête with Clay.

'Christ!' he said. 'Those swine. When I–'

'Forget them,' she said. 'I'm a big girl, remember? Which is not to say I don't hope the Senussi wipe the floor with them.'

'You think they were Italian agents?'

'I have no doubt of it.'

'But ... the Senussi? You're not going ahead with the shipment?'

'You're damned right I am. You spoke with Clay. Did he suggest anything about pulling out?'

'He was simply worried about you.'

'Then I am going to Hamburg the day after tomorrow to join the ship. Can you manage?'

'Of course I can, my darling. But I don't think I can let you go ahead. The danger–'

'Bugger the danger,' Sophie said. 'Meanwhile, we have a problem closer to home.' She told him her suspicions about Pemberton.

94

'So what do you reckon?' Richard asked when she was finished.

'Do you remember him?'

'No, but I wouldn't if he was seven years younger than me. That's a long time in one's teens.'

'But could he possibly have been at school with you?'

'I don't think so. Entry is normally at thirteen. You think he's a fake?'

'I think someone in the British Government has a suspicion that we may be running guns to Africa, or intending to do so, and Pemberton has been detached to keep an eye on things and see what he can find out. Which is all the more reason for me to disappear as quickly as possible. They can't touch you while you're lying in bed with a broken leg, and they can't touch me once I'm in Germany. Right?'

'It's so damned dangerous,' he grumbled. 'Christ, if I wasn't lying here...' He looked up. 'Do you trust this fellow Andrews?'

'Yes,' she said, and knew she was flushing. 'Shouldn't I?'

'I have no idea. I've never met the fellow. But he was certainly anxious about you.'

'Well, if he calls back, tell him it's all systems go. Now let me go deal with Pemberton.'

She bent over the bed to kiss him and he caught her hand.

'Are you all right?' he asked. 'I mean, really?'

'I'm all right,' she said. 'Really.'

'All well?' Pemberton asked, doing a double take at her brocade housegown, and obviously wondering just what, if anything, she might be wearing underneath. He was drinking a whisky and soda provided by Ned who had remained in the drawing room, perhaps to make sure the stranger did not make off with the family silver.

'Oh, quite,' Sophie said. 'My husband asks me to thank you again for your help.'

'Chap does what he can,' Pemberton said. 'Did he remember me?'

'Vaguely,' Sophie lied.

'Well...' Pemberton finished his drink. 'I'd better be getting along.'

'Or your wife will be worried?'

'I'm not married, don't you know. What are you going to do?'

Sophie raised her eyebrows.

'I mean ... well ... the police said you weren't going to prefer charges.'

'That is correct.'

'I'd have thought you would wish the men to be picked up?'

'Not really. It's over and done with.'

'If I may say so, Mrs Elligan, that is a very unusual attitude. Remarkable. Well ... would you have any objection if I called again, in a few days? Just to see you're all right.'

Sophie smiled. 'Why, Mr Pemberton, what a charming idea. Please call again, in a few days.'

She slept surprisingly well, but then she was exhausted. Next morning she was packing when the phone rang. 'It's Mr Andrews,' Ellen said. 'That American.'

'Oh, thank God!' Sophie ran downstairs to the phone. 'Clay! Are you all right?'

'I'm all right. But you–'

'I'm fine. Where are you calling from?'

'I'm in Paris. I catch a train in half an hour. But Sophie, those men–'

'Were Fascist agents trying to frighten us off. Listen, I'm leaving for Hamburg tomorrow and we'll be at sea the next day. With the goods.'

'You mean you're going ahead?'

'Of course I'm going ahead.'

'Sophie ... what did they do to you?'

'They knocked me about a bit, and made me drink castor oil,' she said. 'They thought I was a poor helpless little woman who would surrender.'

'And you're not,' he said admiringly. 'Sophie, I love you. I adore you.'

'I'll see you in Morocco,' she said.

I love you. I adore you! It was a long time since Richard had said such things to her.

That was the trouble with marriage, Sophie thought. It becomes commonplace. Had Richard *ever* said such things to her?

Morocco! Total adventure. And Clay! And perhaps at the end of it those Fascist thugs!

'I've been thinking,' Richard said, when she sat with him to have lunch. 'I simply cannot allow you to go charging off all on your own.'

'Now, Dickie,' she said. 'I am going to be perfectly safe. Clay will be waiting for me when I land. And I couldn't possibly take Elsie on such an expedition; she'd have the heebee-jeebies.'

'Of course you couldn't take Elsie. But we don't know that Andrews will be waiting – and with these Italian thugs roaming all over the place. Ned has agreed to go with you.'

'Ned?' She was astonished.

'He is the best possible man for the job. He's a better, and quicker, shot than anyone I know, including myself. He knows the business, what to expect and what may need to be done. And he'll do it. He's utterly ruthless when pointed in the right direction. And he worships you.'

'Yes,' Sophie said thoughtfully. 'You don't think that's a risk?'

'Ned?' Richard smiled. 'He worships me even more. You remember Mbote, Martingell's shadow? Mbote would have died for Martingell.'

'Mbote *did* die for Martingell,' Sophie pointed out. 'I don't want anyone dying for me.'

'But you'll take Ned.'

Had Richard given her a bodyguard, or a chaperon? She could believe that Ned was utterly ruthless when pointed in the right direction – and the direction had been chosen by Richard! Aimed at Clay?

Sophie went downstairs. Ned was polishing the car.

'Do you like sea voyages?' she asked.

'Best possible way to holiday, madam.'

'This isn't going to be a holiday, Ned.'

'Life is what you make of it, madam.'

'There's a profound thought. Ned, I just want to get one thing absolutely straight between us.'

'Of course, madam.'

'On this delivery, I am the boss. I give the orders and you carry them out. Right?'

For just a second a shadow passed across his normally cheerful face. Then he gave one of his grins. 'Absolutely, madam.'

The cry of the muezzin awoke Edio Rometti, as it always did. There were times when he wondered why, as they were so determined to civilise and Europeanise Libya, his superiors did not abolish the Muslim religion. Especially now that the

99

Senussi seemed to have gone out of business. He stretched and stroked Lalia's thigh. The good things in life included waking up every morning and having Lalia's thigh to stroke. Now she smiled as she woke up and rolled into his arms. Thick black hair clouded his face; he could feel more thick black hair clouding his groin as well. Heavy breasts moved against his chest. She was a delight.

Edio thought that if he were not an officer and a gentleman, he would marry Lalia. Sadly, he was an officer and a gentleman, and Italian officers and gentlemen did not marry half-caste women, even if, she claimed, the male half was Italian. To do that would not only make a vast dent in his career prospects – it would probably kill his mother. And things were going well. He sat up, lit two cigarettes, gave the woman one. His last mission had been a total success and he had received a commendation for the way in which he had handled it. That thug Yusuf had disappeared, deserting his men. Optimists presumed he had died in the sand sea; his companions, when captured, had said this was what had happened. Edio had not believed them. He was pretty sure that Yusuf had escaped across the frontier into French Equatorial. But that was irrelevant. His organisation had been destroyed. Including the

American. The prisoners had also claimed Andrews had died in the sand and the heat. Edio supposed this was more likely; an Arab could survive where an American could not. But that too was irrelevant.

Lalia was pouring a bath. One of the refinements Italian civilisation had brought to Benghazi was running water, and Lalia, having enjoyed this pleasure in the primitive surroundings of her youth, adored bathing. Especially with him. Edio crossed the bedroom to the bathroom, quietly, and squeezed her naked bottom as she leaned over the tub. She gave a little squeal of pleasure and turned into his arms.

The phone rang. Edio cursed under his breath. Here was another innovation of civilisation, one he could well do without at moments like this. He picked up both phone and receiver. 'Rometti.'

'General Garzanti wishes to see you, Colonel.'

'When?'

'Now, Colonel.'

'It is six-thirty in the morning,' Edio protested.

'The matter is urgent.'

Edio hung up. 'Damn and blast and shit,' he commented.

Eduardo Garzanti was a mountain of a man. He perspired constantly. Edio wasn't surprised at that; he was surprised that the commanding general had survived so long in Cyrenaica.

He was also laconic. 'Your friends are back in business,' he remarked as Edio saluted. 'Sit down.'

Edio slowly sank into a chair before the desk. 'My friends?'

'The Senussi you are supposed to have destroyed six months ago.'

'That is not possible, with respect, General.'

Garzanti picked up the sheet of paper on his desk. 'You reported the man Andrews as being missing, probably killed.'

'That is correct, General.'

'A week ago he was in London, buying guns. He appears to have had at his disposal a very large sum of money.'

'Andrews, in London?' Edio could not believe his ears.

'He is dealing with a German arms firm, Beinhardt and Company, through their London agent, a man called Elligan. This Elligan was once an associate of the famous James Martingell. It appears that our secret service has a big file on this Martingell. Before the Great War he ran guns to the Somalis for use against our troops in East Africa. Even then he was agent for this Beinhardt and Company. Now he is dead, but it seems that his erstwhile associate has taken over his position. This Elligan is married to the daughter of the current Beinhardt. It is a family affair.' He allowed himself a brief smile.

'And Yusuf?' Edio asked.

'Another man you reported as missing believed killed,' Garzanti remarked. 'Well, perhaps he is. We have no information regarding him. But Andrews is certainly still working for the Senussi, and for something fairly important, as they gave him a hundred and twenty-five thousand English pounds to spend. Now, the moment our agents learned of his whereabouts they attempted to stop this transaction.'

Edio frowned. 'They did not kill him?' He was a fighting soldier, and while quite prepared to shoot any Senussi who came within range of his gun while actually bearing arms, did not believe in murder.

'No, they did not. It was felt that might upset the English police – we have no doubt that they, or their Special Branch, certainly, are well aware of Andrews', and Elligan's, business – and Il Duce is anxious to remain on good terms with Great Britain, at least for the time being. An attempt was made to warn Andrews off, and equally to warn these Elligans off.'

'You mean they beat Andrews and Elligan up,' Edio said, disparagingly.

'That seemed appropriate. Only it seems

that Elligan is ill in bed, so they had to deal with his wife instead.'

'They beat up a woman?' Now Edio was aghast.

'That also seemed appropriate. It was assumed that these gangsters would get the message that we know all about their activities, and that they have no hope of success. The intention was that Andrews would return to North Africa and tell the Senussi chieftains that he had failed in his mission, or better yet, that he would merely drop the whole thing and return to the United States. Either way it would be a disaster for the Senussi. They are desert tribesmen. There is no way that they can replace a hundred and twenty-five thousand pounds just like that.'

'So which of those two options did Andrews take?' Edio asked. 'I should have thought that for him to return to the Senussi and admit his failure would have been highly dangerous. For him.'

'We do not know which option he has taken, or will take,' Garzanti said. 'Andrews has disappeared. After his, ah, meeting with our agents, he took the boat train to Dover, crossed to Calais and took the train to Paris. We had agents looking out for him in Paris, but he eluded them and no trace has been found of him since.'

'That is poor work,' Edio remarked.

'I agree with you. However, we would seem now to be able to estimate his intentions. Our agents in Cherbourg were alerted, as well as Le Havre. No sign of him has been seen there.'

'If they missed him once they could miss him again,' Edio pointed out.

'Indeed. However, our people believe he *is* returning to Africa.'

'Then he is a fool. No doubt the Senussi will bury him up to his neck in sand, remove his eyelids and let the flies and the ants and the buzzards get on with it,' Edio suggested.

'Andrews is returning to Africa,' Garzanti said, 'because, four days ago, the SS *Bremerhaven* sailed from Hamburg. This ship is under charter to the firm of Beinhardt and Company, and amongst her passengers, her only passengers in fact, were Mrs Elligan and an English servant.'

Edio stared at him with his mouth open. 'You mean—'

'That this woman has determined to ignore our warning, and is shipping the guns anyway.'

'Do we know there are guns on board?'

'The manifest says farming implements. We have seen such manifests before.'

Edio scratched his head. 'Whoever set out to intimidate this Mrs Elligan cannot have done a very good job.'

'Perhaps. Or perhaps she is a far more

dangerous woman than we supposed.'

'So, do we know the destination of these farm implements?'

'Boujdour, on the Spanish Moroccan coast.'

'And have we alerted the Spanish authorities to wait for the ship and impound its cargo?'

'No, we have not done that, Colonel.'

'Well, then, the French. If the guns are landed, they will have to be taken into French Morocco before they can reach the Senussi.'

'We have not alerted the French either. For two reasons. One is that we do not wish the French to become involved in our affairs. As I am sure you know, there is every possibility that our two countries may be at war in the not too distant future, as they seem determined to block our every expansive move in the Mediterranean, and they will not surrender Corsica, which is rightfully Italian. At this time, there is a strong possibility that the Spanish may back the French.'

Edio did some more scratching. He knew little of and cared less for the Duce's political ambitions. He was only aware that they were highly risky.

'The second reason is that we wish to end this rebellion once and for all,' Garzanti went on. 'If we alert either the Spanish or

106

the French, and the cargo is confiscated, we shall then be embarked upon a long lawsuit the outcome of which will be unclear. The goods may even be returned to Beinhardt, to be shipped again at a more convenient moment, for them. No, no, Colonel. If those guns are on their way, we want them to continue on their way, until we can deal with them thoroughly. And both the shippers and the recipients. Now, once the guns have been landed at Boujdour, they will be transported as rapidly as possible to the Senussi in the east. Our information is that those chieftains who would still oppose us are gathered in the Hoggar region. From the Hoggar plateau, it is, as you know, only a matter of two hundred and fifty kilometres to the Libyan border.'

'That is true,' Edio agreed. 'But the guns will have been divided up amongst the tribesmen long before that they reach Libya.'

'Our agents in Tamanrasset suggest that they will be delivered en bloc to the Senussi leaders. The actual delivery still has to be paid for, and it is highly unlikely that the House of Beinhardt will let the guns out of their possession until that payment has been made. The caravan must be seized at the very moment of this delivery to the Senussi. That way we will not only get the guns, we will get the Senussi as well.'

Edio got up and went to the huge map on the wall of the general's office, studied it. 'The problem is that we do not know where the delivery will take place.'

'We will know. We have sent a very reliable agent to Boujdour. He will be there by the time Mrs Elligan and her goods get there. He will then track the caravan. There is no risk of any handover being made until the true desert has been reached. As I have said, our agents consider that there will not be a handover before the Hoggar. In any event, the progress of the caravan will be monitored, and you will be kept informed of its progress by radio.'

'Me?' Edio asked.

'Of course you, Colonel. Are you not our most famous desert warrior? And this is also a business you left unfinished. You are now being given the opportunity to complete the job. You will command a task force. However many men you consider necessary.'

Edio continued to study the map, while he tried to take in the situation. 'If I stationed myself at Ghat,' he said, prodding the little town on the Libyan border. 'I will be, as you say, within two hundred and fifty kilometres of the Hoggar. But there is no good road. Even with tracked vehicles I will still be a good eight hours away. If I am informed of the delivery as it begins to take place, the Senussi will have received the guns and disappeared long before I can get to them.'

'That is very true. So Ghat will not be satisfactory.' Slowly Edio turned to face him. 'It is our opinion that you should take up a position *west* of the Hoggar,' Garzanti continued. 'So that you will be able to intercept the caravan the very moment it makes contact with the Senussi.'

'With respect, General, you are asking me to lead my people into French territory.'

'Weren't you going to have to do that anyway?'

'I was considering a raid, in and out in not more than twenty-four hours once we knew the position of the caravan and the time of the delivery. You are suggesting that I take up a position, inside French territory, for several days,'

'I do not see the difference, Rometti.'

'The difference, General, is that while we could represent a raid to seize the guns as a hot pursuit of known enemy tribesmen, which would probably cause an international row, but one that could be smoothed over, we cannot represent establishing a post on French territory as anything else than an infringement of French sovereignty. Some people would call it an act of war.'

'You are being pessimistic. That is about the most desolate area in all the world. On that map are marked all the French forts and outposts. You will see that they are widely scattered. All you have to do is avoid such places, seize an isolated oasis and wait for the signal from our agents. The odds on the French finding you are more than a hundred to one.'

'But if they do?'

Garzanti leaned back in his chair. 'If you are discovered, by say a patrol, or even a larger body, it will be necessary to destroy them. If this is impossible, and you are forced to surrender, the Italian Government will of course disown you as a madman trying to start a war on his own, and leave you to whatever fate the French may decide. I am told that Devil's Island is very unpleasant at this time of the year. Or any time of the year. I recommend that you are not caught.'

Edio gazed at him. 'So,' Garzanti said, 'as I have indicated, you have carte blanche as to who and how many and how equipped your people shall be. I will only say that there is no time to waste. We estimate that the *Bremerhaven* will be in Boujdour in no more than a week, and the guns will be in the Sahara very shortly after that.'

Edio saluted. 'Oh, by the way,' Garzanti added, 'carry out this mission successfully, Rometti, and you will have a brigade. I give you my word.'

A brigade, Edio thought contemptuously, as he opened the door to his apartment. 'What was so urgent?' Lalia inquired.

Having bathed, she had returned to bed, as was her habit. Edio thought that a naked Lalia sitting up in bed was about the most enjoyable sight a man could have, certainly after an unenjoyable half-hour with a commanding general. 'I am to take a trip,' he said, closing the door behind him, and taking off his belt as he approached the bed.

'Oh, no,' Lalia said. 'For how long?'

'I do not know. Probably a fortnight.' Or possibly forever, Edio thought. He was being sent to his death, or to life imprisonment. Even if he caught up with these gunrunners and their Senussi friends, destroyed them and captured the guns, if that had to take place *west* of the Hoggar his chances of accomplishing it without the French finding out about it in sufficient time to cut off his retreat were remote. And Garzanti knew that.

'You will leave me all alone for a fortnight?' Lalia asked, fingering one of her nipples, as she knew he liked to see.

All alone, Edio thought. If he thought Lalia the most adorable of women, he also knew she was the most insatiable. The moment he was safely out of sight she would have a parade of men in here. And if he was required to die, why should he not at least enjoy his last few days on earth? 'I will not leave you,' he said. 'If you will be lonely, how would you like to accompany me for a holiday in the desert?'

Lalia giggled excitedly.

The Delivery

'That has got to be the most desolate piece of coastline I ever saw,' Ned remarked, peering through binoculars at the continuous surf about four miles away to the east; the surf pounded on a yellow sand beach behind which there appeared to be nothing but more yellow sand for as far as the eye could see. 'You say there's a harbour someplace, madam?' He was unfailingly polite, unfailingly servile. Sophie had anticipated perhaps having to slap him down once they were out at sea. She wondered if she was disappointed that this had not been necessary. They spent most of each day in each other's company, or certainly within sight of each other, and he had never once attempted to cross the bounds of propriety.

'He adores you,' Richard had said, 'but he adores me more.' Richard was a shrewd judge of character.

'There is a harbour, Ned,' she assured him, and went up to the bridge to stand beside Captain Pfuhl.

She was excited and, although she would not admit as much even to herself, apprehensive. They had passed inside the Canaries the previous night, and were now very close. To what? To completing her first delivery? No, that was only just beginning. To being arrested by the Spanish? That was certainly a possibility, although Clay had assured her it would not happen. Well, then, to seeing Clay again? The thought made her heart pound. But with Ned around she would have to keep her emotions under control.

'There!' The captain pointed and Sophie saw a break in the surf. 'It is not a true harbour, Frau Elligan. But it is a sheltered roadstead, most of the year. There is even a dock, alongside which we may lie ... if they give us permission.'

He levelled his telescope, while Sophie used her glasses. 'They are flying flags.'

The captain nodded, satisfied. 'Entry is permitted. If you will excuse me, Frau Elligan.'

Sophie got the message that he needed to concentrate and went back down the ladder. 'Almost there, Ned. We'd better prepare.'

She went to her cabin, checked her make-up, confined her hair in a snood, added her sun helmet which she strapped beneath her chin, letting the thin gauze veil droop down over her face to give some protection from the sun, pulled on her gloves and returned on deck to watch the freighter turning into a rather frightening entrance because of the huge rollers pounding the sand to either side.

Now she could see houses, the yellow and red flag of Spain floating in the gentle breeze, and quite a few people ... some of them she observed with a pitter-patter of her heart, wearing the romantic uniforms of the Spanish Foreign Legion. But there were also some people wearing Arab dress, actually on the dock, and with them ... Clay Andrews!

The *Bremerhaven* nosed alongside, the warps were thrown and made fast, and the gangway run out. The Spanish Customs officer came on board to be greeted by Captain Pfuhl, and then introduced to Sophie. 'Senora Elligan!' He spoke German, and bent over her glove. 'Jaime Estoril at your service. You wish to land a cargo?'

'Farm implements.' Sophie gave him the manifesto.

'Ah!' He looked down the pages. 'For the Bedouin of the Hoggar. This is a big venture.' Sophie could only wait. 'But Señor Andrews has explained it to me. American generosity, eh? And at such a time. I am sure the Arabs will be grateful. When do you commence unloading?'

Sophie looked at the captain; it was his cue. 'I wish to be unloaded and out of here

115

as quickly as possible, señor,' Pfuhl said. 'There is little protection if the weather comes from the west.'

'Of course. The men are standing by.' He smiled at Sophie. 'So is Mr Andrews.'

Minutes later she was in his arms, briefly, as she had to hold him off. 'Not here,' she whispered.

'My dearest girl. Are you all right? Those men–'

'Are history,' she told him. 'You remember Ned Carew?"

'Of course.' Clay obviously didn't, but he shook hands anyway. 'Good to see you again. And my thanks for escorting Mrs Elligan. She's in safe hands now.'

'My instructions are to see madam safely back to England,' Ned said.

Clay raised his eyebrows. 'Richard worries about me,' Sophie explained. 'Ned, I think we could all do with a drink.' She escorted Clay into the saloon. 'Now tell me, does that Spaniard really believe we are unloading farm implements for use in the Hoggar?'

'It's not as unlikely as you think. There is water in the Hoggar and cultivation. They could do with some farm implements.' He grinned. 'No, he doesn't believe that. He has been well paid. And given a guarantee that the guns are not for use against either his own people or the French. And, you see, both the Spanish and the French are very happy to watch the Italians being discomfited; they have been providing some finance to the Senussi throughout this war.'

'All the world is one vast intrigue, eh?'

'It always has been.' He picked up her hand. 'Are you sure you're all right?'

'I told you, a few Fascist thugs are not going to bother me.'

'Then when can we ... well–'

'Business first,' Sophie assured him, but gave him a reassuring smile as Ned served her whisky.

But the time was fast coming when she would have to make up her mind whether or not she wanted ... if only she knew what she wanted!

The unloading took the rest of the day. The goods had to be handled carefully as even the bribed Spaniard would have had to take action had any of the crates been dropped and had spilled out a pile of rifles. But by nightfall the camel caravan had been loaded.

Sophie, accompanied always by Ned, took the opportunity to explore the little town, watched by one or two rather sallow Spanish women, hot in their European clothes – as was Sophie herself – and also by the various Bedouin men, women and children, and inspected by their dogs as she wandered past the little houses, painted in pale shades of pink and blue mingled with yellow and white. Overlooking the town was the minaret, and she could hear all the time the roar of the surf. A road led north from the town, along the coast, but there was little sign of any civilisation to the south. No sooner were they ashore than she became acutely aware of the insects buzzing all around her.

'Behind God's back,' Ned commented.

'I reckon on putting back out to sea at first light tomorrow, Frau Elligan,' Pfuhl said. 'This is no coast on which to be caught out.'

Sophie nodded, and went in search of Clay. 'Are you satisfied?'

'Very. This is all we wanted.'

'Well, I'm sorry to say I can't hang around. So, if you'll make the final payment now ... perhaps you'll have dinner with me on board the steamer? I promise you Ned will not be around.'

Which still left her options open.

'I'm sorry. The final payment is to be made upon delivery of the guns to my Senussi employers.'

'What did you say?'

'Simply that, while I may be satisfied as to quality and quantity, they wish to see for themselves. And to have the weapons, to be sure.'

Sophie glared at him, all thoughts of an

affair suddenly vanished. 'You mentioned nothing of this in England. You said payment would be made on delivery.'

'That I did.'

'I had assumed it was to you, here.'

'I'm sorry I did not make myself clear. I meant to the Senussi.'

'Which is where?'

He waved his hand. 'In the desert.'

'I see. And when do I get my money?'

'The moment they are satisfied, they will pay the money, and I will send you a certified cheque.'

'Do you take me for a fool, Mr Andrews?' Her desire was entirely submerged beneath her anger. And yet...

Clay raised his eyebrows. 'I thought you trusted me.'

'I did. And I seem to have been mistaken. Suppose I were to have those guns reloaded, now, and taken back to Germany?'

Clay raised his eyebrows. 'I do not think you can do that. You have been paid for them.'

'Half.'

'That is generally regarded as completing a contract.'

'Suppose I were to tell the Spanish exactly what are in those crates?'

'That would indeed be a mistake. The Spanish here are in our pay.'

'I seem to have formed entirely the wrong

impression about you,' Sophie remarked, making the decision that had been lurking at the back of her mind ever since their first meeting. It would be enormously risky, and it would drive Richard wild ... but it would be an adventure, her adventure, in a place she had always wanted to adventure ... and did she not have Ned to take care of her? 'You think you hold all the cards. Very well. You say payment is to be made on delivery of the guns to your friends. It will be paid to me.'

He stared at her, mouth open. 'You intend to come into the desert yourself?'

'That has now become my intention, Mr Andrews,' she said coldly. 'You will have to give me an hour to pack and dress myself properly. Oh, and to write out a message for Captain Pfuhl to convey to both my husband and my father, explaining exactly what I am doing, and tell them that unless they hear from me that I am fit and well and have been paid within two weeks, they are to tell the whole world what has happened. That will include informing the Italian Government. And incidentally, if you, or any of your thugs, attempts to lay a finger on me, I shall shoot him, or you, dead.'

'Ah.' Actually, he was looking delighted at the thought of her company. 'I'm afraid it will be longer than two weeks.'

'Another of your tricks?'

'Believe me, Sophie, I would never do anything to harm or deceive you. But it is a long journey, from here to the Hoggar, by camel. Which is where the delivery is to take place.'

'Camels?' Sophie inquired. 'You spoke of motor transport.'

'Couldn't be done, I'm afraid,' Clay said. 'It has simply proved impossible to obtain tracked transport. We shall have to go by camel. Actually, camels are far more reliable.'

'They are also slower.'

'I'm afraid they are. We'll get there. But we are talking in terms of six weeks, at the least.'

She gazed at him for several seconds; six weeks, in the desert, with Clay ... and Ned, to be sure. 'Very well,' she said. 'I will say seven weeks, to make allowances for delays. But not an hour longer.'

Captain Pfuhl was aghast. 'You cannot go into the desert with a bunch of Arabs, Frau Elligan.'

'I have Ned, Captain. And I will be perfectly safe if you deliver those messages. These people will, as soon as they can raise the money, need more guns. They dare not antagonise their source of supply.'

The captain scratched his head.

Ned was no less aghast. 'You sure you

know what you're doing, madam?' he asked.

'I am going to collect the money that is owed to us, Ned. And you are going to help me.'

Ned's turn to scratch his head. 'The desert can be a tough place,' he commented.

The desert! It beckoned her like a beacon on a dark night. 'You realise it's going to be an uncomfortable trip,' Clay said that evening. 'No baths for a couple of hundred miles. My recommendation is that you have a good soak before the ship leaves.'

She took him at his word; Captain Pfuhl was not casting off until dawn in any event. She washed and perfumed every inch of herself, then washed her hair and tied it up in a bandanna beneath her helmet, from which her veil dropped to protect her complexion, and then handed over her bags to be loaded on a camel. Ned was already dressed and waiting, also wearing a sun helmet, armed with both rifle and revolver, and looking very aggressive.

'Please don't shoot anyone,' Sophie requested.

'Only in your defence, madam.'

'Have you ever ridden a camel?' Clay asked, escorting her to the head of the waiting caravan.

'As a matter of fact I have, once or twice. In Persia.' He seemed both surprised and relieved. Ned also had a nodding acquaintance with the beasts, so they mounted and followed Clay and his Arab guide out of the town. Behind them trailed the fifty-odd camels, each with a driver; most of these were on foot, but there were a dozen mounted who ranged to and fro, both to keep the caravan in line and to act as guards. 'Are these Senussi?' Sophie asked.

'Indeed. My friends.' She was glad he had said that because she found the way the Arabs looked at her, their gazes seeming to slide all over her body, somewhat off-putting. 'It's because you're not veiled,' Clay explained.

'I am veiled,' she protested.

'That little square of gauze? They can see your face through it.'

'Would you like me to wear a yashmak?'

He shrugged. 'Only if you want to. They will have to get used to the idea that you are different. I think that is a good idea.'

It had not occurred to Sophie that she might find herself the only woman in the company of more than fifty men, of whom only two were of her own race and culture. But as the Arabs were unfailingly polite she soon got used to the idea and began thoroughly to enjoy herself. Of course the desert, as promised by Clay, was an intensely uncomfortable place, as was riding a camel for several hours a day. The sand got everywhere, combining with the sweat that turned her body into a sticky mess. The heat was sometimes so intense it was difficult to breathe, although Clay did most of his travelling by night and the caravan always rested, shading itself as best it could, during the hottest hours of the day.

She was continually thirsty for they were carrying their own water and it had to be rationed; there was none for washing, and if this did not seem to bother the Bedouin, it left Sophie feeling most uncomfortable, mentally as well as physically. But over it all there was the romance. For all the discomfort the desert was everything she had expected it to be, and the sight of the moon streaming across the endless dunes and wadis as they plodded to the east made up for everything.

Together with the presence of Clay. She hadn't really been able to decide – she hadn't wanted to – what had aroused her interest in him in England. Save that he was living an intensely romantic life – and a dangerous one, in which she had become involved. Then, when she had felt he had double-crossed her, she had been intensely angry. But here in the desert he rose to his full stature. The Arabs obviously worshipped him and carried out his least command without hesitation. He rode a camel as though born on the back of one.

He knew all the right things to do whenever there was the slightest problem. When he told her the reason the Arabs believed in him was because he was a crack shot, she believed that too.

Had she come here to have an affair with him? To live out her own fantasies, as Richard had managed to live out so many of his? That would be a betrayal of all the pair of them stood for. Yet the temptation was enormous and she was grateful that getting together was not possible, certainly at the beginning of the journey. This was because they never had any privacy and also because of the ever-present Ned. But in any event, in her state of continuing filth she had no desire to let any man too close to her, let alone to remove any of her clothing. But the intimacy, both mental and physical, was there, as they shared a small tent during the heat of the day, more often than not too exhausted to do more than sleep, but often she would awake to his touch, as he ran a finger softly up her sleeve and across her neck, removing a layer of sand and dust and sweat.

If she was still determined to make him wait, both for the money and because of the way he had deceived her, England seemed a very long way away.

The whole safari seemed very easy. Too

easy. The quick acceptance by the Spanish of their story, the ease with which they had loaded up and walked out of Boujdour, the desert itself ... but it wasn't *that* easy. On the third day, by which time they were well into French territory, Clay leaned across to touch her arm and point. It was early in the morning and they had been on the move most of the night. Her eyes were drooping shut and she wanted only to get into her tent and sleep. But she jerked upright to look in the indicated direction and saw a camel and rider standing on a ridge perhaps half a mile away to the north.

It was a brief glimpse because as soon as the watcher realised that he had been seen he disappeared. 'Another caravan?' she asked.

'No. He, or others, have been there throughout our journey, watching us.'

'Oh, Jesus. Watching us for whom?'

'That I cannot say. He looks like a goum.'

'A goum?'

'An Arab soldier in French pay,' Clay said. 'That would not be unreasonable as the French Government have got to be interested in where we are going and who we are meeting. And that would not be any cause for concern. But on the other hand, he could be an Italian scout.'

'But we're in French territory.'

'It's a big desert. And you may be sure that

to the French, should they come across him, he will just be another Bedouin.'

'What are we going to do? Can't we, well ... get rid of him?'

He grinned. 'Who's a bloodthirsty girl, then?'

'I didn't mean kill him. But surely we could frighten him off.'

'That wouldn't be a good idea for two reasons. One is that he is unlikely to be alone. I would estimate there are perhaps half-a-dozen of them. If we go charging up there they will just scatter and regroup. We have neither the men nor the time to do anything about it. The second reason is that if they *are* French scouts, and we start shooting at them, we might bring the Foreign Legion down on us, and that we can do without.'

'So what *are* we going to do? Supposing they are Italian agents with a wireless?'

'The Italians cannot do anything about us as long as we are in French territory,' Clay assured her. 'Anyway, we may be able to lose those fellows when we get to our first oasis. That'll be in about three days' time. We'll be just about out of water by then and so probably will they. But we'll have the water.'

'Do you think they'll attack us?'

'We're too many. I think they'll be forced to swing off before then and reach another oasis. By the time they come back to pick up our trail, we'll be well ahead.'

'It all sounds too easy. When you say oasis, will there be enough water for me to have a bath?'

He grinned. 'I should think we can manage that.'

It was something to look forward to. But now she had a sense of urgency, turning to look up at the next ridge every few minutes. The watchers were no longer to be seen. Clay had no doubt they were still there, keeping out of sight. He also had a radio, mounted with its batteries on the back of a camel, with which he could keep in touch with his friends, wherever they were.

And then, at last, the oasis. Palm trees, houses, a minaret, friendly greetings ... and a bubbling spring that was used to irrigate a small area of fields outside the little village. Clay was warmly greeted by the headman who apparently knew him. To him, with great ceremony, Clay presented two rifles and a hundred rounds of ammunition; the rest of the villagers fired their own weapons – ancient muskets, some of them muzzle-loaders – into the air in glee.

'Those weapons,' Clay told Sophie, 'are handed down from father to son, generation after generation. They are more valuable to these people than your most priceless family heirloom in England.'

Sophie was more interested in the promised bath, which took a good deal of effort. An earthenware tub was produced in which she could sit as long as she left her legs outside. This was laboriously filled by a line of Arabs equipped with small buckets. Then she was left alone in the interior room of the headman's house, or so she supposed. But she had barely removed her clothing and lowered her bottom into the tub, shivering slightly as the water was surprisingly cold, than she discovered she was being peered at through the door by several children. 'Oh, come in if you wish,' she said, not wanting to make a fuss.

They sidled in, grinning and whispering, watched her soap – she carried her own – with great interest, which increased when she had to stand up to wash her legs. But it was her hair that attracted them most, as she washed it in turn and it lay in a wet red stain on her shoulders and back – they seemed disappointed that the hair on her pubes was so much lighter in colour. 'Would you believe this is the first time I have ever bathed to an audience?' Sophie asked.

They giggled, and clapped their hands; one of the girls asked a question. 'You'll have to say that again,' Sophie suggested.

'She wishes to touch your hair,' Clay said.

Sophie's head jerked; he was standing in the doorway. For a moment she did things with her hands, then realised she could not really hide. 'How long have you been there?'

'Not long. I came to make sure these kids weren't troubling you.'

'Well, they're not,' Sophie said. 'Of course you may touch my hair,' she told the children, and bowed her head so that it flopped past her face. 'Thank you, Clay, for your consideration.'

He remained standing in the doorway. 'I had an idea you and I might have something going,' he said.

'I never mix business with pleasure.' She picked up her towel.

'And when the business is over?'

'We can reconsider the matter.'

He gave a little bow and withdrew. Ned was waiting when Sophie went outside. 'Just say the word and I'll dot that fellow,' he promised. Sophie blew him a kiss.

They dined with the headman and his leading citizens. This was an all-male occasion, but Sophie was allowed to sit in, Clay having explained that she was a great woman in England, not to be excluded. And besides, she owned the guns, thus far. The Arabs were impressed; their women, who were serving the food, less so.

Sophie remembered Afghanistan and dug her fingers into the mutton stew with as much enthusiasm as anyone, aware always of the eyes watching her; the story of her bath had been circulated round the village. The headman laughed as he spoke with Clay, watching Sophie all the time. 'I assume the joke is at my expense,' she said.

'I wouldn't say it is a joke. He asks if, when the guns have been delivered and you are a free agent, you would consider returning here and becoming his wife.'

'One of them, I suppose.'

'Of course. But he would honour you above all others.'

'You will have to tell him that I think it's a lovely idea, but I happen to be already married.'

'I don't think I will tell him that,' Clay said. 'We don't want to disappoint his hopes. I'll tell him you'll take the matter under consideration.'

They remained a full day in the oasis, resting and filling their waterskins. Ned followed Clay's example and shaved, much to the amusement of the Bedouin, while Sophie had another bath as there was no guarantee of another for several days. 'How far is it to the Hoggar from here?' she asked.

'Another six weeks.'

'Jesus! And six weeks back again?'

'Once the guns have been delivered, you and Ned become just travellers in the desert. You can then go north and make for

131

Algiers. There is actually a road when you reach Ghardaia.'

'Will you be coming with us?'

'I'm afraid not. My business is to stay and fight with the Senussi.'

'Six weeks,' she muttered. 'But there will be other oases?'

'Of course.'

Six weeks! Actually, time soon ceased to have meaning. Sophie didn't know whether they were following a given track or a compass course. They went on their way most of each night, then paused for rest and food and sleep as soon as the sun began to grow hot; they lived off dates as soon as the mutton they had secured at each oasis was consumed; they drank water that had a taste all of its own, from the skins in which it was carried; and remained perfectly healthy, even if both Sophie and Ned lost weight.

'Do you know what I'd give for a whisky and soda?' he asked her one day.

'Snap,' she agreed. 'But think of the good it's doing us.'

They passed their time in learning to speak Arabic, after a fashion, and in learning too the ways of the desert, which was neither all sand nor as completely arid as it appeared on the surface. Vast areas were hard, stony soil, through which wadis, or long-dried river beds, cut like knife wounds in the soil. But apparently the wadis were not always as long dried as they appeared. Occasionally they would find little patches of small, brightly coloured flowers. 'That means there's water under there,' Clay explained. 'A subterranean stream, probably not more than a few feet down.'

The Arabs dug and soon water was bubbling up for them to refill their skins. It was dirty water, but that did not seem to bother them. By now dirt and sweat, sand and flies, were no longer relevant. Neither was privacy. Sophie squatted when she had to like any of the men and paid little attention to them, while she was no longer as interesting to them as she had been in the beginning.

She continued to protect her face with her veils which fairly rapidly disintegrated, but that was her only concession to the civilisation to which she presumed she would one day return; she no longer felt even that was guaranteed. Especially when they had to endure a sandstorm. Both Clay and the Arabs saw it coming, with the darkening sky and the rising wind. They took instant action, arranging the camels in a close laager, unloading the crates of guns and ammunition and piling them in the middle of the circle, erecting tent walls in the direction of the wind, and then huddling down in the centre. 'Will it be very bad?' Sophie asked.

'They usually are,' Clay said.

'For how long?'

'How long is a piece of string? Maybe a few hours, maybe more than a day. Maybe...' He shrugged.

Ned sat beside her, as protective as ever. 'Have you ever been in a sandstorm, Ned?' she asked.

'No, madam, I haven't. They say you should experience everything once.' It was a point of view, she supposed.

The sky continued to darken and the wind continued to rise. It had reached about gale force, already carrying with it a cloud of stinging sand, before the real sandcloud arrived. Then for several hours time ceased to have even less meaning than normal. Sophie sat with her knees drawn up, sharing a kind of canvas hood with both Clay and Ned, heads close together. They had a single small waterskin and a handful of dates to sustain themselves. Speech was impossible because of the noise, while the flying sand penetrated everywhere, so that even the dates became coated.

Yet amazingly they and the caravan survived. When the wind finally ceased some twelve hours later, it took them some time to dig themselves out of their private dune; they found all the others doing the same thing, the camels stamping and snorting ... and the desert completely changed – where there had been a rough track was now a soft sand sea and where there had been dunes was now flat sand. 'This should have done our trackers,' Clay said, with some satisfaction.

Slowly, wearily, every bone in her body aching, Sophie mounted her camel. Clay squeezed her arm. 'We're nearly there,' he promised her. 'Another fortnight.'

The motor column bumped to a halt and Edio Rometti got down to use his binoculars to watch his Bedouin scouts coming back to him; they were riding camels. It was first light and still quite chill, although the sun was already a molten threat on the eastern horizon. 'How much farther, Edio?' Lalia inquired, leaning out of the window. They had been driving all night and she was distinctly ruffled. 'I would so like a bath.'

'And you shall have one. Soon,' Edio promised her. 'Well?' he inquired, as the scouts came up to him.

'The oasis is three miles away, effendi.'

'Do they know we are here?'

'They will know if we approach any closer in the vehicles.'

'How many people?'

'Perhaps a hundred, effendi. That is men

and women and children.'

Edio nodded, and summoned Captain Castelfiardo; he had brought along all of his experienced desert fighters that he could find. He had, in fact, prepared this expedition most carefully, always bearing in mind that it was his career at stake. He had under his command a hundred Italian soldiers, and fifty Bedouin on whose loyalty he could count. They had assembled at Ghat to await news from their agents in the French Sahara, and when they had been advised that the arms caravan was within a hundred miles of the Hoggar, moving more slowly now as the ground began to rise, he had given the signal. They had left Ghat and the border at dusk the previous evening and, driving all night across the foothills of the Ajjer, passing north of the 6000 foot high Mount Adrar Edekel, had reached their present position, some 125 miles north-east of Tamanrasset.

Now he needed the shelter of the nearby oasis to rest and prepare his men, obtain water and overhaul his vehicles. And satisfy Lalia. 'We will approach the village on foot, Captain,' he said. 'Spread out your men to either side. I will take the Bedouin in the centre. Our objective is to occupy the oasis, with as few casualties as possible. Amongst them, or us. Understood?'

'Shall I take the machine-guns, Colonel?'

'No. I said, I do not wish casualties, if it can be avoided.'

Castelfiardo saluted and hurried off. Edio returned to his command truck, checking the chambers in his revolver. 'There is going to be a battle?' Lalia's voice was high. 'You did not say there would be a battle!'

'There will not be a battle, my pet,' Edio said. 'We are simply going to take the oasis. And then, you shall have your bath.' She gave one of her giggles.

Having her along had actually been less of a pleasure than he had supposed it might be. He had not known a woman could complain so much. Lalia had spent the last week complaining about the heat and the flies, the food and the water, the hardness of their bed and, on occasion, the lack of their bed. She had also complained about the way the men had looked at her. Edio wondered what would happen to her if by any chance he were to be killed, or even badly wounded. Castelfiardo, he knew, did not like her. But then, Castelfiardo did not like any women.

He signalled his Arabs and they fell in behind him. They were armed with modern rifles and they had sworn hatred to the Senussi. But this village did not contain Senussi, so far as he knew. 'We are not here to kill without reason,' he told them. 'All we

137

need do is frighten them into surrender.'

They grinned and the guides waved them forward. Edio had left twenty Italians on guard at the column and he gave them a last look back as he topped the first rise. Lalia had got out of the command truck and was leaning against it, while the breeze ruffled her dress and fluttered it away from her legs. She would insist on wearing a dress, cut in the latest fashion well above the knee. And she did not believe in underwear!

He waved his men forward and they marched over the undulating sand, the column now lost to view. To his right he could see the helmets and rifles of his two wings, also advancing, keeping their places relative to the centre. It was just seven in the morning and the sun was already high in the sky, starting to burn with all its usual intensity. The guides signalled and then waited for him to reach them. He lay beside them and focused his binoculars on the village.

It was the usual cluster of pale-painted houses, arranged in a couple of narrow streets, all leading to the minaret in the centre. The spring was to one side and there were cultivated fields beyond. Once you had seen one oasis you had seen them all, Edio reflected. But the place was big enough to conceal his trucks, at least for the day or two that was all he needed. Of course the tracks would remain, but they were only visible to an aircraft, supposing such a thing was to be found in this part of the desert, or to anyone who actually crossed his path. That would be very bad luck, were it to happen.

He had his corporal wave the flag to indicate that the wings should advance, then fell to studying the oasis again. People were emerging from their houses. Some women were heading to the fields accompanied by several children. Their menfolk were gathered in groups to drink coffee. He could make out the muezzin climbing down from his tower having done his work for the next few hours. There were flags waving to left and right – his two wings were in position. And just in time for one of the women had seen the waving flags. He watched her waving her arms in turn and no doubt screaming as she gathered her child in her arms and ran back towards the village. She might not have recognised the flag, but the risk of a band of marauding Touaregs was always present.

Edio stood up, drawing his sword and waving it. His men gave a great 'Ooorah' and ran down the slope, several of them firing their rifles as they did so. Out in front as he was, he realised he was in as great a danger at this moment as even at Caporetto, from his own people. It was not something to be considered. He ran down the slope, his sword in his right hand, drawing his revolver with his left. Now all the women were screaming and running to and fro, those who had elected to stay out of the village brought up short by the bayonets of the flank forces, now also running in as hard as they could. Others sought the shelter of their houses, while their menfolk dashed inside to emerge with their matchlocks, hastily priming the ancient mechanisms. 'Halt!'

The Bedouin soldiers checked their advance, as did the Italians on either wing. 'We mean you no harm,' Edio shouted, speaking French. 'We wish merely to live with you for a few days. Throw down your weapons, and no harm will befall you.'

He stopped, staring at the village. The women and the children had nearly all disappeared by now, but several of the men were still visible and a dog was barking. 'Advance!' Edio raised his sword and the three lines moved forward. Then a shot rang out, and another and another. One of the Arabs gave a grunt and fell on his face. Edio himself felt a sudden pain in his right arm, and dropped his sword. 'Take cover,' he bawled. 'Take–'

He fell to his knees, blood streaming down his arm, as his men gave a tremendous roar and ran forward, shooting as they did so. The two wings also charged, having seen their comrades, and more important their commanding officer, fall. 'No!' Edio tried to shout. 'Wait–!'

The morning exploded into terrified sound, punctuated by the cracks of the rifles. Thank God he had not brought up the machine-guns, Edio thought, as the morning rotated about him.

He listened to the sound of engines; the trucks had driven to the sound of the firing. He tried to sit up and found Lalia kneeling beside him. 'My darling!' she screamed. 'You are hurt. My darling–'

Dr Guarda was on his other side and an orderly was at his head. 'Let us get this tunic off,' the doctor said.

'Listen,' Edio said. 'The men. They must stop–'

'It will soon be done,' Guarda said reassuringly, cutting away at the blood-stained tunic.

'Oh, Edio,' Lalia was moaning and weeping. 'Oh, Edio. You said you would not be hurt.'

'My people?' Edio said.

'One is dead,' Dr Guarda told him. 'Two are wounded, but not severely. Neither...' he peered at the bloody gash in Edio's upper arm, 'are you. Providing it does not infect. Iodine.' The orderly produced the bottle.

'You cannot put iodine in such a wound,' Lalia shouted.

'It is the best. The pain will be severe,' he warned, and carefully applied the brown liquid. Edio gave a little moan as the pain bit. But he had to believe it was doing more harm to any germs that might be around than to him. And it only lasted a few minutes by which time Guarda had bound the arm up and was arranging a sling.

'Oh, Edio,' Lalia said. 'You are a hero. A wounded hero.'

Or a mass murderer, Edio thought. 'Help me up.' The doctor and the orderly got him to his feet. 'Give me my sword.' Lalia gave him his sword; he held it in his left hand. 'You stay here,' he told her.

'But ... my place is with you.'

'You will be with me. When I have sorted out the village.' He took a step forward and swayed as the sand seemed to be moving up and down. 'Brandy,' he said.

Guarda held the flask to his lips, he took a deep drink and felt better. 'You should go to bed,' the doctor recommended.

'I will. When I have arranged a bed.'

He walked down the slope, staring at the oasis. There was only the occasional shot now and only the occasional scream, too. The village looked almost exactly as it had done when he had first seen it just a short while before. Save for the Italian and Arab soldiery, prowling from house to house behind their bloodstained bayonets, and the piles of white cloth that were scattered to and fro. And the smell of death that was rising into the morning air.

Castelfiardo waited before the first of the houses. 'You are wounded, Colonel?'

'A scratch,' Edio said. 'What has happened?'

Castelfiardo stood to attention. 'It is my duty to report that all resistance has ceased, Colonel. I am informed that you have lost one man with three wounded, including yourself. I have five wounded, none seriously. That is the total of our casualties.'

'And the inhabitants?'

'My men are making the tally now.'

The line of white-clad corpses was growing.

'At the moment the count is thirty-four men dead, plus sixteen women and eleven children.'

'Dead?' Edio snapped. 'All dead?'

'My men were incensed when they saw you fall, Colonel.'

'Women and children?'

'It was difficult to tell in the houses who were armed and who were not, Colonel. These people are fanatics.'

At defending their homes, Edio thought. Would I not also be a fanatic? He went forward, Castelfiardo anxiously at his side. 'No one has escaped the village, Colonel. Most of the women and children were shot trying to do that.'

'Where are the rest?'

Castelfiardo pointed to the little square that fronted the spring. The water was discoloured as it flowed towards the fields, but would, no doubt, regain its proper colour. Edio gazed at the thirty-odd women and children, huddled together, some lacking yashmaks in their terror, faces contorted with fear and anger. 'What are we to do with these people?' Castelfiardo asked.

'They are our prisoners.'

'And when we go away again, Colonel?'

'They will no doubt seek help.'

'And tell the world what happened here.'

'I hope you are not suggesting that we kill them in cold blood, Captain.'

'It would be best.'

'I am not into murder,' Edio told him. 'I did not wish any casualties at all.'

'They fired on us, Colonel.'

'After we had already fired on them,' Edio pointed out. 'As for telling the world, do you not suppose our own people are going to do that? I want those women and children kept under guard. And Captain – if there is the slightest hint of rape I will have the guilty party, or parties, shot.'

Castelfiardo stood to attention. 'Yes, Colonel. The woman Lucarto is waiting. Shall I find you accommodation?'

The two men stared at each other. Castelfiardo could hardly have made a more direct accusation: Edio had his woman, the rest were forbidden to touch. Edio reminded himself that he was the commanding officer. 'Yes, Castelfiardo,' he said. 'Find us accommodation.'

A huge pit was dug outside the oasis and the dead bodies thrown in. Even so, as the task could not be completed before noon, the smell hung on the still air. The women and children watched with smouldering eyes as their goats were slaughtered to provide food for the conquerors.

By now Edio had been overcome with weakness caused by the pain and the loss of blood, and had to lie down in what had apparently been the headman's hut. Lalia sat beside him. 'I hope we are not going to stay here long,' she complained. 'It stinks. You never told me there was going to be fighting and killing.'

'I did not wish there to be,' Edio muttered. 'What is happening outside?'

Lalia went to the small window. 'They are camouflaging the trucks.'

'Good,' Edio said. 'That is good. That is–'

There was a knock on the door. Lalia opened it and Castelfiardo stood to attention. 'We have received two radio messages, Colonel.' Edio sat up. 'The first is that the arms caravan is now just two hundred kilometres west of the Hoggar. I have marked it on the map. That places them a hundred and fifty kilometres south of us here.'

'And the second?'

Castelfiardo's face was eager. 'Is from our people in the Hoggar itself ... a group of Senussi warriors and sheikhs have left Tamanrasset to ride to the west.'

'When did they leave?'

'At dawn this morning. My estimate is that the two groups will meet at dawn tomorrow.'

'And we are a hundred and fifty kilometres away. Prepare to move out, Captain, as soon as we have replenished our water.'

'And you, Colonel?'

'What about me? Lalia, my spare uniform.'

'You are not capable of commanding, sir,' Castelfiardo said.

'He is right,' Lalia said.

'Do you think I am going to remain here?'

'I think you must, sir,' Castelfiardo said. 'Otherwise you will risk your life. A fever ... no, no, I will command. I know what to do.' Edio chewed his lip. What Castelfiardo was saying made sense, and were it any other subordinate he would have agreed without hesitation. But Castelfiardo ... a man who had no compunction about killing. Who actually enjoyed it. 'And I think it is urgent, sir,' Castelfiardo said. 'The report from the Hoggar also said there is rain about.'

Edio raised his head, frowning. He knew that although it seldom rained in the desert, when it did it was likely to do so with considerable force. 'I am not that ill, Captain,' he said. 'I will accompany you. But you will have to be in tactical command. Now listen to me very carefully. Your orders are to seize and destroy that caravan. Nothing more than that.'

'They will resist,' Castelfiardo said.

'I understand that. But there must be no indiscriminate killing.'

'The Senussi?' Castelfiardo's tone was contemptuous.

'I was thinking of the people with the caravan. Our information is that they may include Europeans.'

'Who deserve only to be hanged,' Castelfiardo said. 'You must allow me the discretion to act as I consider necessary, Colonel. I cannot go into battle with my hands tied behind my back.'

Edio sighed. But again he knew the captain was right. God damn and blast that unlucky musket shot, he thought. 'Just remember that I shall be there, Captain. Watching you.'

Lying in the back of the command truck,

Edio listened to the roar of the engines as they moved out. He was in considerable pain and the jolting added to his discomfort, but he had refused the sedatives Dr Guarda had offered. 'I am glad we are not going to have to fight in the next battle,' Lalia said, rather as if she were discussing a coming cocktail party. 'Oh, Edio, I am so worried for you.'

'Worry for the people in the caravan,' Edio said.

'So now, you see,' Clay said, spreading the map in front of Sophie and Ned. 'We will rendezvous at dawn tomorrow morning.'

Sophie stared at the seemingly endless spaces in front of them. 'How will they find us?'

'They will follow this track, in this direction.'

The caravan was just waking up, the drivers kneeling towards Mecca for their morning prayers. Ned was busy making breakfast. But today the sky looked different: immediately above it was blue enough, but to the east there were great banks of cloud. Clay was studying the cloud formation too, frowning.

'Are we going to have another sandstorm?' she asked.

He shook his head. 'Those are rain clouds.'

'Rain? In the desert? Oh, boy! Water! I thought it never rained here.'

'Oh, it does. Perhaps not more than once a year. But it can be very severe.'

She grinned as she accepted a cup of coffee from Ned. 'Worse than the sandstorm?'

'Yes,' he said, tersely. 'Prepare to move out,' he shouted at his drivers.

Instantly all was bustle. As she did every morning, Sophie looked up at the ridges to the north. She saw nothing, but Ned stood beside her. 'He was there, earlier.'

'Well, he's been there just about every day for the past six weeks,' she commented.

'Fair gives one the creeps,' Ned said.

Sophie brushed her hair, a not very satisfactory exercise as it sadly needed washing. But if it was going to rain . . . 'We're just about there, Ned. This time tomorrow, we'll have completed the delivery and be on our way home.'

'I'm looking forward to that. Will the American gentleman be accompanying us?'

She glanced at him. 'He may, for the beginning of the journey. But as soon as he's sure we're safe, I imagine he'll want to rejoin his friends.'

Ned made no comment, but his expression said a great deal.

They mounted their camels and the rest of

the beasts were dragged into line, complaining as always. The outriders took up their positions and the caravan resumed its journey. 'Will there be baths in the Hoggar?' Sophie asked, riding beside Clay.

'There will be. Tamanrasset is a sizeable town. That's why we have to hand over the guns before we get there; there's a French garrison.'

'And we're just exploring the desert, right?'

'Looking at the mountains.'

'What mountains?'

He pointed and by squinting she could just make out the blue peaks, far in the distance. 'The bigger one is Mount Tabat,' Clay said. 'That's over nine thousand feet. The slightly smaller one is Assekrem. That's well over eight thousand.'

'Would you believe that I had no idea there were mountains down here?'

'Well, you learn something every day.' But he was looking to his left, at the outrider who was signalling. 'I'll have to go see what's bothering him. You stay here.'

The caravan continued on its way while Clay cantered his camel over the rising ground to the left to where the scout waited. Sophie watched him go and then saw him making his camel sit as he levelled his binoculars. He came back in some haste. 'Dust, rising to the north-east,' he said.

'Are those your friends?'

'I was expecting them from the south-east. I've told Haroun to investigate. Anyway, dust ... that would have to be a lot of camels, travelling fast, or...' He scratched his chin.

'Or what?' Sophie's heart was giving that little pitter-pat she knew so well.

'Or it's caused by motor vehicles. It would be damned bad luck to encounter a French patrol at this moment, having got so far.'

Sophie considered. 'I don't see how it can be a French patrol.'

He glanced at her. 'Why not?'

'Well ... you say there is a garrison in Tamanrasset.'

'Yes.'

'So that is where such a column would be going.'

'Yes.'

'In which case the garrison will be expecting it.'

'I would say so.'

'But we are in constant contact with your agents in Tamanrasset, who seem to know everything that is going on. Surely they would know that the garrison was expecting either a relief column or reinforcements, and would have warned us about it.'

Clay stroked his chin again. 'That's very logical thinking,'

'And you don't think women are capable of that.'

151

'I think you're a bloody marvel. But if it's not French—'

'Shouldn't we do something about it?'

'There's nothing we can do about it. Yusuf and his people have already left the Hoggar to come to us.'

'Can't we raise them by radio?'

'Probably. But they have to have these guns. So we have to chance our arm. We'll be together by dawn.' He looked up at the ever darkening sky. 'Hopefully.'

They stopped for lunch. 'We'll carry on immediately,' Clay told his drivers. 'No point in waiting for that.'

They didn't argue; they were all looking apprehensively at the sky. Ned as usual sat beside Sophie. 'I don't like the look of things, madam,' he said.

'What in particular?'

'Anything. I don't like the look of the weather. And why hasn't that Haroun chap come back?'

The same thought had occurred to Clay. Once the meal was finished and the noonday prayers completed, he got the caravan moving again, and then rode up to the high ground on the left. This time Sophie went with him. They topped the rise and he surveyed the desert through his glasses. 'Not a damned thing.'

Sophie took the glasses and looked in turn. 'Then where is he?'

'God alone knows. His camel could have stumbled in a hole and broken a leg–'

'Do camels do that?'

'Not as a rule. Anyway, that dust has gone. Could have been a local sandstorm.' He wheeled his camel.

'Aren't you going to find Haroun?'

'My ... our business is delivering those guns.'

'You can't just abandon him,' Sophie protested.

'He'll find us. Or we'll find him, after the guns have been delivered.' He rode down the slope.

Sophie hesitated, biting her lip. The thought of being abandoned in this empty, waterless wilderness... Despite the heat she gave a little shiver. 'Come on,' Clay called.

He was essentially a man of action, of decision. He reminded her of Richard. But Richard would never have abandoned one of his people. It had been Richard, when given the opportunity to escape the Afghan tribesmen with her, who had chosen to ride back, guns blazing, in an attempt to rescue Martingell. She had willingly followed him. But there was nothing she could do now. To ride off by herself after Haroun would accomplish nothing because she still did not know enough about the desert.

She urged her camel after Clay's. 'Look,' he said as she caught him up. 'This is a tough business. I thought you knew that.'

'Tough, yes. I know that. But it doesn't have to be a callous one.'

He glanced at her. 'Sometimes it is necessary to be callous. We're not only dealing in guns, Sophie. We're dealing in lives as well. So many lives that one can't be that important.'

'Haroun was your friend.'

'He knew the score. I hope he still does.' He increased his speed to a trot, leaving her behind.

For the rest of the day Sophie rode beside Ned, who could tell she was in a bad mood and kept quiet. That night they as usual camped in a laager while the clouds built overhead. This meant that the usual savage drop in temperature did not take place and Sophie awoke just before midnight, feeling oppressively hot. There was not a star to be seen and the night was the darkest she could remember. She wriggled out of her sleeping bag and pulled on her boots – like everyone else she slept fully dressed – then left her tent and wandered out to where the camels were hobbled, grunting and spitting. The four sentries let her pass them, deducing that she needed privacy.

She stood about fifty yards away from the camp, listening. But there was no sound out there. Yet somehow she felt that she and the caravan were not alone. It had to be some kind of sixth sense, she knew, because none of the others, experienced desert travellers, seemed aware of it. Or perhaps it was the spirit of Haroun, crying out for succour.

She heard a sound behind her and turned. Ned stood there. 'You all right, Mrs Elligan?'

'Yes. Just restless. Must be the weather.'

'It's oppressive,' he agreed. 'I would say it is certainly going to rain tomorrow.' His breath rushed in the darkness as he grinned. 'It'll make a change.'

'Yes,' she said. 'You ever been afraid, Ned?'

'Everyone has to have been afraid, some time,' he said. 'What are *you* afraid of? Now.' She hadn't revealed any fear before.

'I wish I knew. Maybe it's just because we're so nearly there.'

'Makes sense. Come back to bed.' He held out his hand, then hastily withdrew it.

Ned Carew, she thought. Who adored her. More than ever after the two months they had spent in such intimate surroundings. She wondered if Ned would have abandoned Haroun?

Haroun had not returned at dawn. But another scout came hurrying back, shouting the news. 'Yusuf is close by,' Clay said. 'Well, we don't have to move today. We just wait for him here.'

Sophie scraped sand and dust from her face and hair, looked up at the sky. The clouds seemed lower yet. She was actually looking forward to the storm. She thought she'd stand out in it, even strip off and let the water just swamp her. She thought that would be the most wonderful feeling in the world. But it was necessary to prepare herself to meet the famous Yusuf. He arrived mid-morning, with some twenty other Bedouins riding camels, and leading a good many more; most of these were laden with supplies and some were obviously remounts.

Yusuf embraced Clay and greeted him in Arabic. Sophie and Ned stood together some distance away, but soon Clay was leading his friend towards them. They were still speaking Arabic, too fast for her to understand, but Sophie didn't need the language to know that Yusuf found her attractive, which Clay now confirmed. 'He says you are like a goddess,' he said. 'And that is not only because you have brought the guns.'

'Well,' she said. 'All he has to do now is pay me.'

'Of course.' Clay translated and Yusuf grinned.

'The money waits for you in the Hoggar,' he said.

Sophie bristled. 'But I am supposed to

hand over the guns now. That wasn't the agreement.'

'The agreement was that you would trust me,' Clay said.

'Well...' Sophie flushed. That was before you abandoned Haroun, she thought. But she couldn't say it. 'I do. But these guys–'

'Are as honest as I am,' he assured her. 'Would you really expect Yusuf to bring a hundred and twenty-five thousand pounds in gold out here into the desert without being certain of the goods?'

'You mean he doesn't trust *you*?'

Clay decided to ignore that question. 'It is only another hundred kilometres and you shall have your money,' he assured her.

'And meanwhile he goes off with the guns.'

'You can hardly expect him to take them into Tamanrasset under the eyes of the French garrison.'

Sophie bit her lip and glanced at Ned. His face remained expressionless although his eyes gleamed and his fingers played over the trigger of his rifle. 'Trust me, Sophie,' Clay said. 'As you have trusted me so far.'

'I can hardly do otherwise,' she muttered. 'As these are all your people.'

'They are all servants of a great cause,' he said. 'As are you.' He waved his arm and the Arabs shouted their agreement.

As they did so, the machine-guns began to chatter.

PART TWO

The Desert

And they are gone: aye, ages long ago
These lovers fled away into the storm.
                                John Keats

Rain

For a moment Sophie had no idea what was happening as Ned threw both arms round her and hurled her to the ground, retaining his grip as he rolled over and over into the shelter of the nearest gully. Her hat and her veil came off and she gasped, initially angry at his treatment of her. But all the time she could hear the deadly rattle of the machine-guns, and now too she could hear the screams of men and horses and camels as the bullets tore into them.

Ned rolled off her and she tried to sit up. He seized her sleeve and jerked her down again. 'Keep out of sight!'

But she had to see and, more cautiously this time, looked over the lip of the gully. The Bedouin caravan had dissolved. Men and animals were sprawled on the sand, bleeding and screaming. Others were gathered in small groups, firing their rifles at the ridge about a mile distant which had suddenly become lined with riflemen and machine-guns. The men up there were impossible to distinguish as they wore Arab robes over their uniforms. But she did not doubt they were the people who had caused

161

that cloud of dust.

Meanwhile other men were trying to unload the camels, to break open the boxes and get at their own machine-guns. But they would not have the time. Of Clay and Yusuf there was no sign; perhaps they were already dead. And still the bullets thudded into the helpless caravan. 'We have to get out of here,' Ned said.

Sophie shook her head. She wanted to stay and fight. Even if Clay had proved less of a romantic hero than she had supposed, she still wanted to help him overcome those terrible figures on the ridge. 'They're all getting away, madam,' Ned said.

Sophie looked over her shoulder. Camels and horses and men were streaming across the desert, being picked off by the rifles on the ridge. There was almost no resistance now. 'Come *on*,' Ned urged. 'Keep down.'

Sophie crawled out of the gully, but, hampered by her skirt, immediately fell down again. Now she could hear the shouts and cheers of their destroyers who were coming down from the ridge, firing their rifles at anything that moved; the machine-guns had done their work and ceased firing. Even as Sophie pushed herself up again there was a spurt of sand close by. Someone was firing at *her*, and shouting at her too. 'Ned!' she gasped.

'I think we'll have to surrender,' he said

and rose to his knees, his arms in the air. Sophie hesitated just a moment then followed his example.

They looked at a scene of utter devastation – dead and wounded camels, horses, men, shattered boxes of rifles and bullets spilling onto the sand. 'We can't be the only prisoners,' she muttered.

In fact they weren't, but they were the only ones that interested their captors. The surviving Arabs who had not managed to get away were simply herded together at gunpoint and made to squat in a group, always under the guns of several of the Italian soldiers as Sophie now recognised them to be, as they discarded their jibbahs and burnouses to reveal their uniforms. But most of the soldiers crowded round the two Caucasians, using the opportunity to pull at Sophie's clothing and prod her in various places, mostly her buttocks.

I must not scream, she told herself. Even if she knew what these people were capable of. I must not scream. Ned attempted to defend her and was struck in the stomach with a rifle butt that had him on his knees, coughing and spitting, while one of the soldiers plucked the revolver from its holster on his belt. 'Stop that!' Sophie shouted and received a slap on the backside that made her gasp with mingled pain and outrage.

Now the chatter became interspersed with grins and she realised they were asking each other if she too might not be armed. Two men promptly gripped her arms and a third attempted to push up her skirt. When he realised it was divided, he made a comment and fumbled at her belt. I must not scream, she told herself again, resisting the temptation to kick him as she remembered what had happened the last time she had attempted that.

A voice broke into the babble, loud and crisp. The men reluctantly released her, so suddenly she sat down with a bump, from which undignified position she looked up at an officer. She did not like his appearance, with his little moustache and his jutting jaw, but surely he had to be a gentleman. He was speaking to her but in Italian. She shook her head. 'No comprendo.'

He switched to French, and this she could understand, just. 'Parlez-vous Anglais?'

He peered at her frowning. 'Yes,' he said. 'I understand English. You are English?'

It would have taken too long to explain exactly what she was, so she nodded. 'Yes, I am English. Do you have a doctor?' For Ned was still gasping for breath.

'I am looking for an American,' Castelfiardo said.

Sophie ignored him as she put her arm round Ned's shoulders. 'Easy,' she whispered. 'Easy. Are you in pain?'

Ned shook his head. 'When I get my breath back–'

'You, woman, I am speaking to you,' Castelfiardo said. 'Where is the American? Is this man American?'

'This man is my servant,' Sophie said, ideas forming in her mind.

'He is not American?'

'No, he is not American.' With a great effort, Sophie helped Ned to his feet.

'Then where is the American?'

'I do not know,' Sophie said. 'He left.'

'Ha. You are responsible for these weapons?'

'I am not,' Sophie said. 'My servant and I are travelling in Africa, and we joined this caravan. We did not know they were carrying guns.'

Castelfiardo peered at her. 'You expect me to believe that?'

'Yes, I do.'

'You take me for a fool,' he said, and looked left and right.

The sergeant standing at his shoulder made a remark and the captain grinned, and demurred. Then he gave a series of orders and turned back to Sophie. 'If you not tell me the truth, it will go very hard with you.'

Sophie drew a deep breath. 'I have told you the truth.'

Castelfiardo reached out and drew his

finger down her cheek, then let it continue down her shirt front to her waist. Sophie needed an effort to remain breathing slowly and deeply. 'You are a beautiful woman,' Castelfiardo said. 'Perhaps I give you to my men, eh?'

Sophie gathered her saliva and spat at him. He wiped his face. 'Or perhaps I take you for myself. The spoils of war, eh?'

'Touch me, and I'll have you hanged,' Sophie said.

Castelfiardo raised his eyebrows. 'So, you are a powerful woman, eh? I like powerful women.' He pointed. 'Go over there.'

Sophie turned her head and saw that the Italian soldiers had re-erected one of the tents. 'I will not,' she said.

'Then you will be carried.'

Sophie bit her lip and glanced at Ned, who was clearly on the verge of an explosion. 'Don't be stupid,' she muttered. 'He won't hurt me.'

'But, madam, he's going to–'

'I know what he's going to do, Ned,' she said. 'But he holds all the trumps at the moment. Be patient.' Ned chewed his lip in impotent anger as she walked away from him, past the grinning soldiers, and into the tent. It was actually her tent; it had collapsed rather than been shot to pieces, and her blanket was still there.

She heard Castelfiardo behind her and a

moment later the tent flap fell into place. 'Now, you see, we are alone,' he told her.

She waited, standing with her back to him. Don't anticipate, she told herself. He is just a man with a lust. 'So tell me, the American. He bought the guns from you, eh?'

'I told you,' Sophie said. 'He invited me to join his caravan to visit the Hoggar. I did not know what he was carrying.'

'And I have told you that I do not believe you. Is that your bag?'

It lay where she had left it. 'Yes.'

'Pick it up and give it to me.'

She obeyed, and he riffled through it, found her passport. 'Sophie Elligan,' he said. 'We will find out all about you, Mrs Elligan. And then you will be tried, condemned and hanged. Do you have any idea what it is like to be hanged? Here in Africa it is done in public, with the crowd jeering, and waiting for you to reveal yourself with your kicks. Do you know this?'

Sophie gazed at him. 'If that is how it is done.'

Castelfiardo grinned. 'Perhaps you do not believe me. You will see. But first, you will be good to me, eh?' Another grin. 'Then I may be able to help you.'

Sophie contemplated spitting again, but then reckoned that might earn her a beating; he was clearly very aroused. She unbuttoned her blouse. 'Not that,' he said.

'The skirt. It is your ass I want, woman. Your ass. Drop the skirt and bend over.'

Sophie drew another deep breath, unbuckled her belt, and let the skirt fall about her ankles. Instantly he seized her shoulders, turned her round, and bent her over, one hand on the nape of her neck, the other dragging down her drawers. A moment later she felt him brush her flesh – and heard a loud ahem from beyond the flap. Castelfiardo shouted in Italian and there was a reply from a voice belonging to the sergeant.

Castelfiardo uttered several unmistakeable oaths, then released her neck. Sophie fell to her hands and knees. 'Dress yourself,' Castelfiardo commanded, pulling up his own pants. He had certainly been on the verge.

Hastily she pulled up her drawers and skirt, buckled her belt. Castelfiardo had already stamped outside and she followed as far as the flap to see what had happened. The trucks were rolling down the slope towards her, the machine-guns remounted on the vehicles. They pulled to a halt in a cloud of dust, and she watched a tall, handsome man step down; he wore uniform and his right arm was in a sling. From his insignia he was clearly senior to Castelfiardo; from his face and expression *he* was most clearly a gentleman. She gave a great gasp of relief, followed by another as she watched a young woman also getting out of the truck; she was clearly of mixed blood, but pretty and vivacious; incongruously, she wore a dress.

Behind her was another man who also had a moustache, together with a little pointed beard; although he wore a uniform, there was no insignia, and Sophie guessed he was the unit's doctor. Castelfiardo stood to attention, making his report. The colonel listened with an expressionless face, but he glanced right and left at the death by which they were surrounded.

The woman was also looking around her, her nose wrinkling in distaste. Now she came up to Sophie, looking her up and down, and speaking in Italian; presumably she could tell at a glance that Sophie's clothes were not as they should be. '*No comprendo,*' she tried again.

Lalia turned to Edio for support. Castelfiardo had given him Sophie's passport and this he now opened to compare the photographs, standing immediately in front of her. 'You are Mrs Sophie Elligan,' he said in perfect English.

'Yes,' Sophie said.

'Your husband is Major Richard Elligan, late of the Welsh Guards.'

'My husband retired from the Army some years ago,' Sophie said.

'And took up gun-running.'

'I know nothing about that.'

'But we know all about you, Mrs Elligan. Gun-running is an offence that carries the death penalty here in Africa.'

'We happen to be in French Africa, Captain.'

He gave a quick smile. 'But we will soon be in Italian Africa, Mrs Elligan. You need to remember this. Where is Mr Andrews?'

'I do not know.'

'Will you deny that he was with your party? My dear Mrs Elligan, we have had you under surveillance since you landed at Boujdour. And when we captured your man ... what was his name, Haroun? ... yesterday, he told us all about you.'

Sophie refused to let herself panic. 'Mr Andrews was with the caravan, yes. But if he is not amongst the dead he must have got away. I was taking shelter, with my servant, who was beaten by your people.'

'They were all very excited,' Edio agreed.

'And that man tried to rape me,' Sophie said. 'He would have, had you not arrived.'

'He says he was searching you for concealed weapons.'

'He is lying.'

Edio considered her for a few seconds, then nodded. 'It will go in my report. Now–'

The doctor was speaking, quickly and urgently. Edio looked up at the sky; the clouds were very low. The two men engaged in an argument, then Edio turned back to her. 'It seems we are going to have a rain storm. This will be severe, but should not last very long. I will tell my men to take down your tent and we will all shelter in the trucks. That is best.'

'You realise this track is actually a wadi,' Sophie said.

'Do you know so much about the desert?'

'I know what I have been told. That it would not be a good place to be caught by the rain.'

'Who told you this?'

'Clay Andrews. He has spent a lot of the past couple of years in the desert.'

'I know that,' Edio said, somewhat grimly. 'Therefore I accept he is probably right.' He gave more orders. The Italians stopped burying the dead and assembled, getting into their trucks, which they drove back up to the ridge and parked in a sort of laager. 'Just in case those Senussi come back for their weapons,' Edio said. He peered at Ned who had been placed in the command truck and was in the back with Dr Guarda; Edio and Lalia and Sophie were all in the front. Castelfiardo had his own truck. 'That man is your servant, I am told.'

'That is correct.'

'You travel alone in the desert with a single man servant?'

'I'm emancipated,' she told him.

Another consideration, then the rain began.

The first drops hit the canvas roof of the truck with a snapping sound, almost immediately lost in a blinding flash of lightning, accompanied instantaneously by a huge peal of thunder. Lalia screamed and started bouncing up and down; Edio had to put his arms round her to quieten her. 'She does not like the lightning,' he explained to Sophie.

'I can't say I cared much for that one myself,' she confessed. 'Where did it hit?'

'It went into the sand,' Edio said, re-assuringly.

Then there was another flash and an almost instantaneous peal of thunder, and another, and now the rain was pounding so hard it was necessary to shout. Sophie looked back at Ned and he gave her the thumbs-up sign. He seemed to have recovered. She supposed it would be quite possible for the two of them to take over this truck, certainly as the Italians didn't seem to be considering that possibility, but she didn't see that doing them a lot of good, surrounded as they were by all the others. 'What are you doing in French territory?' she shouted into Edio's ear.

He grinned. 'Looking for you.'

'Do the French know this?' He shook his

head. 'But when they find out–'

'By the time they find out,' Edio said, 'we will be across the border in Libya. We shall leave as soon as the rain stops.'

'What about the guns?'

He pointed, and she tried to peer through the windscreen; the rain was now falling so hard it was almost a solid sheet, but she could see down into the wadi which was already several inches deep in water. 'The guns will all be sucked into the sand,' Edio said. 'You were right about it being safer up here.'

But hardly more comfortable, she thought, as water was now getting in round the edge of the canvas roof. Lalia was again chattering anxiously and Edio gave her a kiss. 'What happens to us when we get to Libya?' Sophie asked.

'Ah, that is a serious matter,' Edio said. 'You will be tried for gun-running.'

'You just said that carries the death penalty?'

'It does. But I do not think a pretty lady like you who is also a foreigner will be executed. A term in prison, perhaps–'

'Is that good?'

'No,' he said. 'But it is better than being dead. What is that?'

A face had appeared at the window, a soldier almost lost in the teeming rain. Edio bellowed at him in Italian and the soldier bellowed back. Then he bellowed at Lalia who made a face but raised herself up so that he could slide underneath her. 'What is the problem?' Sophie shouted.

'There is some subsidence,' Edio told her. 'One of the trucks is in trouble. I shall not be long.'

He moved Lalia off his lap and she sat next to Sophie with a thump. Then he opened the door and got out, his uniform immediately darkened by the rain. He banged the door and Lalia broke into another torrent of comment and complaint. Dr Guarda's head appeared behind them, talking to her. 'Don't you speak any English?' Sophie bawled.

'A little, signora.'

'What are you saying?'

'This is bad, signora. Very bad.'

'Why?'

'Feel.'

She frowned at him, then realised that the truck was moving. 'Shit!'

'This ridge is collapsing,' Guarda said.

'What are we going to do?'

There was a very definite movement beneath them and Ned appeared beside the doctor. 'I think we should get out, madam.'

'Into this rain?'

Lalia began to scream in a continuous high-pitched sound.

'Well, madam—'

'It is going!' Guarda shouted and left them to make for the back of the truck.

Sophie discovered that the vehicle was at an angle; she had slid down against the door and Lalia had slid down on top of her, still screaming. And the truck was still moving, sideways, as the water-logged sand crumbled away.

Desperately Sophie scrabbled at the handle and the door fell open. She fell out of the truck, landing on her hands and knees. Lalia fell on top of her, legs kicking and still screaming. Ned jumped beside them and picked them each up by an arm and a leg to throw them from beneath the truck, which now turned right over and then sank into the sand to be half submerged. There was no sign of Dr Guarda.

'Edio!' Lalia was shrieking. 'Edio!' But she could no longer make much noise as her mouth was full of water.

To her horror, Sophie discovered that she had sunk up to her ankles in the suddenly liquid sand, while the rain was beating on her head and shoulders with a force that left her half senseless. Ned pulled her to her feet, put his mouth against her ear. 'Over there!' he shouted. 'We must get off the ridge.'

'We can't leave her,' Sophie said. 'She'll drown in the sand.'

Ned grunted, but pulled Lalia up. She

struck at him and he slapped her face, cutting her lip. She stared at him in consternation, presumably never having been so treated before. But when he grasped her wrist to pull her along, she no longer resisted.

Sophie was already climbing through the dissolving sand. Vaguely she was aware of other trucks and men, shouting and fighting to keep their vehicles upright. No one paid any attention to her.

They fought their way out of the laager and reached the far side of the ridge. This too was crumbling away, but the area beyond was flat, and if there was water everywhere, it was not very deep. 'Just keep going!' Ned shouted, still dragging Lalia.

Sophie stumbled on, falling to her knees with great splashes, stumbling up again. She had no idea of the direction they were taking, was only afraid of falling into another water-filled wadi. Then she found herself on an outcrop of rock, from which the sand had been washed away. It was a small mesa, perhaps twenty yards across. The rain hissed down but it was all running off. She knelt, feeling the huge drops pounding on her back and her head, listening to the rumble of the thunder, careless now of the lightning plunging into the sand all about her. She was only half aware that Ned and Lalia had joined her.

Ned crouched between the two women, his arms round each of them, hugging them as reassuringly as he could.

Sophie had no idea how long they crouched on the slab of rock, buffeted and pounded by the rain and the wind, senses dulled by the unending thunder. It was Ned who first realised that the storm was passing over. The thunder rumbled in the distance, the rain slackened to a drizzle, the clouds were higher and less black, and there was even a patch of blue sky away to the east. Slowly he straightened, every muscle cramped. Sophie did likewise, staring at him in consternation. He had lost his hat and his shirt was torn; it was also plastered to his skin. His trousers were torn too, up one leg, and water was running out of his boots.

She looked at Lalia, who still knelt, head down. Her dress had all but disintegrated and she did not appear to be wearing any underclothes. Her hair was a matted mess. Then she realised that she could hardly look any different and looked down at herself. Her shirt was torn, and also doing its best to be a second skin. Water was running out of her boots and her skirt made waterlogged noises every time she moved. She was both chilled to the bone and desperately uncomfortable.

She looked at what had once been the ridge. It had dissolved almost to the level of the plain around it. Out of it were sticking pieces of trucks and men. But there were people moving up there, shouting, calling for help and being answered. 'We must get off this rock,' Ned said.

Sophie peered over the side. There was still water everywhere, and now the first wisps of steam were rising as the heat began coming through the clouds. 'Can we get up there?' she asked.

'We must stay down here,' he said. 'But out of sight.'

She frowned. 'You mean–'

'Listen, madam. Those men are going to get something going, and leave. If they find us, we will have to leave with them, to stand trial in Libya. We must stay here and hide until they have gone.'

'And then? We have no food, no weapons...' She forced a smile. 'I suppose we're not short of water, at the moment. But we can't possibly survive.'

'Andrews and those Arabs will come back for us,' Ned said. 'Or if not for us, for such of the guns as they can find. They have to. It is *their* only hope of survival.'

Sophie chewed her lip. What he was saying made sense. But the thought of deliberately staying out here in the desert, with the nearest oasis probably a hundred miles away ... Lalia suddenly realised the storm was over, reared back on her haunches, and opened her mouth. But before she could scream Ned had thrown both arms round her waist, the pair of them rolled across the mesa and fell off the edge with a huge splash.

Sophie slid behind them, also went off the edge, and realised the drop was only some four feet to a pool of water, in which the pair of them were wrestling. Lalia's skirt had ridden up to her thighs and she was attempting to knee Ned in the groin, while he had one hand over her mouth and the other round her waist. 'Gag!' he gasped. 'Christ, she has sharp teeth, Gag, madam.'

Sophie looked down at herself, then at the woman. But Lalia had to be considered an enemy. She knelt beside her, caught the flailing legs, dug her fingers into the sodden skirt, and pulled as hard as she could; most of it came away, whereupon Lalia actually stopped kicking, taken entirely by surprise. Sophie exerted all her strength, tore the dress into strips and moved up to the girl's head. Ned saw she was ready and released Lalia's mouth, sliding his hands down to grasp her neck. Lalia made a gurgling sound and Sophie passed the length of dress round her head and over her mouth, securing it behind her head.

Lalia's gurgling grew louder and she pulled an arm free to strike at Sophie's face, but Ned released her neck to grasp her arms and twist them behind her back. 'She's a right tiger cub,' He panted. 'You got any more of that dress, madam?'

Sophie tore some more of the skirt into strips, and between them they bound Lalia's wrists behind her. By now she had ducked her face several times in the water and was panting and spitting. They rolled her on her back and propped her against the mesa. Both found themselves staring at her, for she was naked from the waist down. Then they both hurriedly looked away and found themselves looking at each other. Ned's cheeks were pink. He held up his hand to show the blood. 'Near bit me to the bone.'

'Keep it clean,' Sophie said. 'She probably has rabies.'

Once again they looked at the girl. Lalia's eyes were flashing, her breasts heaving against what was left of her dress, and she kept trying to cross her legs, unsuccessfully. 'We'll have to find her something to wear,' Ned suggested.

'Yes,' Sophie replied, without thinking. And then did think. Why should we? as she remembered her treatment in the car. 'You don't have to look at her, but you have my permission to do so if it makes you feel good.' Ned gulped.

Sophie listened to the shouts. But there was no way they could be tracked to this rock; the Italians would have to suppose they had drowned in the sand sea – at this moment the literal sand sea. They huddled against the rock. Gradually Lalia's struggles subsided as she grew weary. They drank some water and she stared at them with huge eyes. 'Listen,' Sophie said. 'We'll let you have a drink, if you promise not to shout. Savvy?'

'I think she understands you, madam,' Ned said. 'But we'll just make sure.'

He knelt beside Lalia and held her neck in his hands while Sophie released the gag. Lalia flopped forward and drank, greedily. Then Sophie replaced the gag. By now the sun was high and the desert was shrouded in mist as it sucked up the moisture. They could not see fifty yards, but they could still hear noises from the ridge. Someone was shouting 'Lalia!' Lalia stirred, and Sophie wagged her finger.

Then they heard the roar of an engine. One of the trucks at least had been restarted. Soon there was another, then another. Then the noise began to fade. Cautiously, Ned peered round the side of the rock. 'Four of them,' he said. 'Moving out. To the east.'

'Going back to Libya as fast as they can, I imagine,' Sophie said. 'They've done what they came for.'

'And suffered a bit.'

'So have we,' she reminded him.

'We'd better stay put for a while,' Ned

said. 'Just in case they come back.' Sophie nodded and leaned against the rock. She felt absolutely drained of energy or even willpower. This was partly from the physical battering she had undergone, she knew. But the emotional and psychological battering had been no less severe. She had thought it all a great adventure, considered herself a reincarnation of Aunt Cecile. Now it had all collapsed. The Senussi would not get their guns, she would not get her money – very possibly she would never see Clay again – and she now had to remember that while Aunt Cecile might have adventured in the biggest possible way, she had also died on her last adventure.

Now the sun was really hot, and the mist was burning off. Ned touched her arm and they moved round the rock to gain some shelter. He picked up Lalia and carried her round, then looked at Sophie. 'I think we can take her gag off now,' Sophie said. 'But leave her wrists bound.'

Ned took off the gag and Lalia spat at him. He reacted instinctively, raising his hand and then lowering it again. 'I suppose she has reason,' he said and sat beside Sophie again. 'You hungry, madam?'

'I could eat a horse.'

'Well ... there could be one lying around.'

'Cooked?'

'I think it's worth seeing what we can find.'

She nodded and looked at Lalia. Who spoke vigorously in Italian. 'I have an idea she's cursing us,' Ned said. 'What shall we do with her?'

'Does she excite you?'

'Well, madam...' He flushed. 'She has a good body. And having to look at it all the time...' He grinned. 'Just as well I'm too damned hungry and tired to think of sex.'

'Just as well,' Sophie agreed. 'Leave her here. If she wants to run off into the desert in the nude with her hands tied behind her back, that's up to her.' She pushed herself up and followed Ned up the now very gentle hill. Behind them Lalia began shouting, and these, Sophie felt, were definitely swear words.

Slowly they picked their way up to where the laager had been. Here there were three trucks half buried in the sand. But no bodies, Sophie was glad to see; the Italians had taken their dead with them – those they could find. Ned was wrestling with the door of one of the trucks and finally succeeded in prising it open. 'For God's sake be careful,' Sophie begged.

He winked at her and climbed into the vehicle, re-emerging a few minutes later waving a haversack. 'There's a couple of tins of beef in here.'

'Holy Hallalujah! How do we get them open?'

'*Voilà!*' He showed her the bayonet he had also found, and very rapidly opened the first tin.

Lalia emerged, staggering up the hill, still shouting. They untied her hands and shared the meal, eating with their fingers. 'I don't think anything has ever tasted so good,' Sophie said.

There was still enough water lying around to give them a drink, but it was fast disappearing. 'I don't suppose you could get that truck working?' Sophie asked.

Ned shook his head. 'The engine is buried in sand. We'd need a team of mechanics, and then another team of horses to drag it out.' He looked down the hill. 'We should look down there, madam.'

Sophie stood beside him and shuddered. Even at a distance and after the flood she was sure she could see the death and destruction that lay in the wadi; the Italians hadn't bothered with the Arab dead. Or with their prisoners, who had entirely disappeared – there was no indication whether they had drowned or had managed to make their escape. 'I'll go,' Ned said. 'Shall I tie up the young lady again?'

Sophie and Lalia gazed at each other. 'No,' Sophie said. 'Leave me the bayonet. And see if you can find her something to wear.'

Ned grinned, emptied the haversack of the

184

remaining tin of meat and some personal belongings of the soldier to whom it had belonged and set off down the hill. He had also managed to find a water bottle, presently empty. Whatever would she have done without him? Sophie wondered. Lalia made to get up, but Sophie shook her head. 'Just sit there,' she commanded. Lalia considered for a moment, looking at the bayonet, then sat down. 'Good girl,' Sophie said.

Whatever were they going to do with her? Or was it academic? Ned felt sure Clay and Yusuf would come back. But why should they, on the evidence of their behaviour thus far? Clay had already demonstrated his ruthless pragmatism. Now he had to presume that both she and the guns were as lost as Haroun had been. In which case the three of them were going to die a pretty miserable death of heat and thirst, right here. Lalia gave her an anxious smile. Perhaps the same thoughts had been running through her mind.

Ned trudged back up the hill carrying the haversack, which bulged. 'Anything?' Sophie asked.

'Some food, and I managed to collect a little water.' He sat down. 'There's one hell of a mess down there. Dead bodies, dead camels, but I reckon quite a few of those rifles have survived. I found one crate virtually untouched. And quite a few lying around. I didn't bring one because it would have to be taken apart and cleaned and greased, and I don't have the facility to do that, but it can certainly be done. And here...' He delved into the haversack and brought out the remnants of a jibbah. 'Try this for size.' He held it out and Lalia hesitated, then took it, wrinkling her nose.

'Where did you get that?' Sophie asked.

'I took it off a dead body,' Ned said.

'Oh, Ned!'

'What she doesn't know can't hurt her, madam. And she's at least decent.' For Lalia had dropped the garment over her shoulders and smoothed it down her hips.

'What do you reckon she was doing with the Italians, anyway?' Sophie asked. 'Is she an Arab?'

'Half-caste I would say.'

'Then you think she was a prisoner?'

'No, madam. Not in view of her anxiety to get back to them. I reckon she was somebody's girlfriend. Most likely that colonel's. He seemed quite a decent bloke. Thirsty?'

'Oh, yes. But ... shouldn't we ration it?'

'Don't seem all that much point. If your friends come back in the next twenty-four hours, we won't need it. If they don't, well...'

Sophie held the canteen to her lips, took a

quick gulp. She didn't feel like eating, although Lalia dug into the second tin of corned beef with enthusiasm. 'English iron rations,' Ned mused. 'They get everywhere.'

Sophie had closed her eyes against the glare. Now she opened them again. 'Ned, I'm sorry.'

'What for?'

'I really didn't bring you out here to die.'

'I didn't have that in mind, either, madam. We'll survive.'

She sighed, and closed her eyes again.

'But if we don't, madam,' Ned said. 'I'd like you to know that there's no one I'd rather go out with. I mean...' he flushed, 'I don't want you to die, but ... shit, I'm not making a very good job of this.'

She squeezed his hand. 'You're doing fine.'

He licked his lips. 'What I meant was, madam ... I think you're the most wonderful woman I have ever known.'

'Thank you, Ned. You're pretty good yourself.'

'I mean, I don't want you to think I'm in any way disloyal to the major. But ... shit, I'm talking too much.'

'It's a time for talking, Ned. For saying what you really think, what you really feel about life.'

He turned to face her; their faces were only a few inches apart. For several seconds they gazed at each other. Then he said, 'I love you, madam. I adore you. I have loved you for years. Oh, madam–'

She held his hand against her breast. 'I think I love you too, Ned.'

'If we get out of this–'

'I think we shouldn't make plans until we do get out of this. But if we were able to have a good meal, and a bottle of wine, and a hot bath ... oh, how I want a hot bath.'

'Yeah,' Ned said.

Sharing it, she wondered? But that was a crazy idea. Yet the fingers on her breast were moving, very gently, sliding across the material, seeking a nipple, and finding. What am I doing, she thought. Dying! So why not ... but he couldn't possibly want sex with her, a bedraggled, filthy mess. Yet she had told him to say whatever he really wanted to. So what did *she* really want to say? That this great big inarticulate hulk had come to mean so much to her she would commit adultery with him?

That would be a joint betrayal of the man they both loved. That was far more important than her amatory thoughts about Clay Andrews. But if they were going to die, in any event... 'Hey,' Ned said. 'Where are you going?'

Lalia had got up. Now she curled her lip and made a remark in Italian. 'I think she wants to be alone for a moment,' Sophie said.

'Oh.' He looked embarrassed as usual, as Lalia wandered round one of the half-submerged vehicles. 'Do you ... ah ...'

'As a matter of fact, no,' Sophie said. 'I am utterly dehydrated. Well–'

He kissed her mouth. For a moment she was too surprised to react, then she parted her lips and allowed his tongue inside. Now suddenly his hand had gained in urgency, was pulling her shirt open – she only had two buttons left anyway – while she in turn found her hand sliding over the front of his trousers. It had been so long, for both of them, looking at each other, sharing everything, and now, perhaps about to share death... 'Oh, Ned,' she whispered, when he released her to breathe.

'Madam,' he said. 'Please forgive me.'

'Forgive you?'

Lalia was coming back quickly, waving her arms. Ned scrambled up, shaded his eyes. 'Not the Italians?' Sophie begged.

'Somebody,' Ned said. 'If it's not the Italians–'

Sophie also stood up, peered into the shimmering desert haze. Camels. A lot of camels. 'Holy Hallejuah!' she shouted. 'They've come back.'

The Harem

Sophie made to wave her arms and Ned caught them. They looked at each other. 'We must let them know we're here,' Sophie said.

'Say you forgive me,'

'There's nothing to forgive. I wanted it as badly as you. But I forgive us both.'

'And now?'

'It's our secret, Ned. I can't offer you more than that, right now.'

'And the girl?'

Sophie bit her lip. 'She doesn't understand English. We'll work it out. Trust me, Ned. I won't betray you.'

'I never supposed you would, madam. I just wanted us both to be sure what we are doing.' She kissed him lightly. 'Yes,' she said. 'I'm sure.' As if, she thought, she could ever be sure of anything in her life again.

They waved their arms, and the camel riders waved back. Half an hour later she was in Clay's arms, being hugged and kissed, while Ned stood by with smouldering eyes. 'My God!' Clay said. 'We had no idea that you had survived. That you could survive. But–' He looked around him at the

190

remains of the Italian expedition.

Sophie told him what had happened while the Arabs inspected Lalia. She folded her arms and tossed her head at them, but she was actually afraid. Sophie also explained how they had picked her up. 'The Bedouin will have her,' Clay said.

'No,' Sophie said. 'Please, Clay. She's suffered a great deal.'

'We have all suffered a great deal,' Clay said. 'And she is an enemy. It is thanks to her boyfriend, or boyfriends, that we have lost our guns.'

'They are not all lost, Mr Andrews,' Ned said.

Clay glanced at him, then nodded. 'We must save what we can.' The Arabs were already rooting around in the debris of their encampment. 'If you really wish to save this girl, you must take her as your servant,' Clay said.

'Why, yes,' Sophie said. 'That would be a good idea. I don't suppose you speak any English?' she asked Lalia.

'I speak Arabic,' Lalia said, getting the gist of the conversation.

'Oh! Great!' She glanced at Ned, whose face was a study. 'Well, then, as of now you are my servant. Do you understand?'

'I understand,' Lalia said. 'You beat me.'

'Ah ... no. I am not going to beat you, Lalia. Unless you misbehave. Behave, and I will try to see that you reach your home. You do have a home?'

'My home is Benghazi.'

'Right. Then we shall try to make sure you get back there. But first, we must find you something decent to wear. Ned?'

Ned nodded and led them down the slope to the wadi. 'If I am good,' Lalia said, 'will you take me to your home?'

'That might be a little difficult. But I will see what can be done,' Sophie promised.

Yusuf and his men had uncovered quite a few dead bodies, already unpleasant as the heat grew. 'Where are the Italians?' Yusuf asked.

'Those of them that survived the storm drove away,' Sophie told him. 'They went east.'

'I would like to cut out their hearts,' Yusuf growled, gazing speculatively at Lalia, who moved closer to Sophie for protection. 'We were betrayed. Who did this?' Now he was looking at Sophie.

'Don't be ridiculous, Yusuf,' Clay said. 'She was nearly killed herself.'

Yusuf snorted. 'Now we have no guns.'

'There are a few. And some boxes of ammunition. And I would say we'll find some more by following the wadi.'

'This will take much time,' Yusuf said. 'What will happen when the Italians come back?'

'I don't think they're coming back,' Sophie said. 'They were breaking the law, in any event, by being here at all.'

Another snort, but Yusuf went off to oversee his men's search, and also to send a party further down the wadi in the hopes of finding some more weapons. 'What exactly is the situation now?' Sophie asked, as they ate their midday meal, cooked on an open fire, but protected somewhat from the sun by a canvas lean-to.

'It is simply a matter of collecting as much as we can,' Clay said.

'And Ned and I?'

'Yes. Well–'

'I should point out that I kept my side of the bargain,' Sophie said, 'and delivered the weapons. It is not my fault that the Italians knew we were coming and laid a trap for us, nor is it my fault that we had that rain storm.'

'Oh, quite,' Clay agreed. 'We shall have to talk about it with Yusuf and the sheikhs when we get to Tamanrasset.'

'When I hope you will remind them that they owe me a hundred and twenty-five thousand pounds.'

'Yes. I shall do my best, of course.'

'Your best?' she cried.

They were speaking English, but he still cast anxious glances at the men around them.

'You must be patient,' he said. 'As you say, you've done your bit. Now you can sit back and relax. And when we get to the Hoggar–'

'When we get to the Hoggar,' she said. 'When will that be?'

'A few days,' he assured her. 'I thought we had something going, guns or no guns.'

'And money or no money,' she remarked. 'I'm afraid I am a businesswoman, Clay. I said we might get together, might, when this deal is completed. In my book, that means when the final payment has been made.'

'Ah,' he said sadly.

Yusuf sent messengers to the Hoggar to call up more men to search for the guns; he also needed additional provisions. The radio had been lost in the storm. 'I don't think we are accomplishing anything here,' Sophie said. 'I would like to go on ahead.'

She could tell that Clay was deeply upset at the way their relationship was developing, but suddenly he no longer mattered. So, what was she going to do? This whole thing had turned out very badly. When she thought of the number of lives that had been lost ... presumably that was no concern of hers, as these people imagined they were fighting a war. But Clay had more or less said that he doubted she would be paid in full.

And then there was Ned! In human terms

he was a plus. But what on earth was she to do about him? Easy to say that she could very well fall in love with him as she had never loved anyone before. Not even Richard in the early days of their marriage. But abandoning Richard was not an option, even supposing Ned would accept it. Besides, their backgrounds were so very different, socially, economically, even politically and historically. Richard had actually fought against the Germans in the War, but that apart, he had been her social equal and had been the sort of man to forgive and forget. Was Ned?

She only knew that she wanted to get out of the desert, to clean clothes and daily baths and an absence of sand everywhere and all the time. Then she thought she would be able to think straight. But she couldn't leave without the money!

At least the Hoggar promised some relief.

'We cannot spare you an escort,' Clay said. 'One man as a guide.'

'If you will give us a rifle each, and a revolver as well,' Sophie said, 'We will take care of ourselves.'

He nodded. 'I don't blame you for wanting a change of scenery. All right. The guide's name will be Sufad. He will take you into Tamanrasset, to a safe house belonging to a Senussi sheikh. You understand this must be done as clandestinely as possible, as we do not wish the French to become overly interested in our affairs.'

'I understand.'

'Sheikh Hafsun ibn Abdullah al-Fadl already knows of you,' Clay went on. 'But I will give you a letter to him. You will be his guest until we return. Again I must ask you, and your servants,' he glanced at Ned and Lalia, 'to keep as low a profile as possible. If the French authorities discovered there was an Englishwoman, or even more, a German woman, in their midst, they would want to ask questions.'

Sophie nodded. 'Well, then ... you'll be able to enjoy a little luxury until I get back to you. It shouldn't take long.'

He gazed at her so wistfully that she stroked his chin. 'You understand I need time to, well ... get over this catastrophe.'

'I do understand that, Sophie. That is why I think a good rest in pleasant, safe sur-roundings will do you the world of good.'

'Then come soon,' she said.

They left that evening, meaning to ride through the night and rest and shelter from the sun during the heat of the day. 'Do you still trust these people, madam?' Ned asked.

He had entirely reverted to being her faithful servant, and she did not know how to change that – or if she wanted to. Lalia was just happy to be away from the Bedouin. 'I think we have to, for the time being,' Sophie said. 'I believe Mr Andrews is trustworthy.'

Ned snorted almost as loudly as Yusuf.

Next day they saw the mountains rising above them, seeming much higher now they were closer. 'Ahaggar,' their guide said, using the more correct name, 'rises in places three thousand metres.'

'We don't have to go up that high, do we?' Sophie asked, remembering the mountains of the Hindu Kush and the Himalayas – after traversing them she had not supposed she would ever be warm again.

'No, no, lady. Tamanrasset is on the south side of the mountains. Not very high.'

Tamanrasset Oasis was actually on the road from Algiers to Kano in Nigeria, and was a busy place, as was the road. It was also a much larger place than Sophie had expected, dominated by the square fort from which drooped the tricolour of France; the first thing she observed was that there were soldiers everywhere; the town was walled and they had to pass through a high gate, guarded by a patrol of Foreign Legionnaires; they stopped outside the town while Sophie took off her skirt and boots and wrapped herself in a haik, leaving her feet bare – that they were white feet was not very important as she could have been a Berber. The two women wore their yashmaks and kept their haiks close, to entirely conceal their hair, while Ned held his burnous across his face. But Fusad was apparently known to the French, and they passed through without difficulty to find themselves in a town of close-packed houses, narrow streets and towering minarets. Once in the kasbah they had to walk, leading their animals, the streets were so crowded. Small boys ran beside them, donkeys brayed as they blocked their paths, camels grunted and seemed to pass the time of day with their own animals, veiled women leaned out of windows to shout and scream at those opposite, apparently merely exchanging gossip, men stroked their beards and peered at the newcomers, and the sun beat down out of a cloudless sky, seeming to draw every possible odour – mostly unpleasant – from the packed mass below.

Sophie's bare feet ached and she stepped in several loads of animal dung. But eventually Fusad paused before a very large and high wooden door set in an equally high wall, and struck this several times with his stick. The door was opened by an Arab. 'These are they who are expected,' Fusad said, somewhat biblically.

The Arab stepped aside and they led their camels into a larger courtyard, surrounded by buildings, so as to be utterly private from the streets or houses around it. Behind them was the high wall, on the inside of which there were stables. To their right was what Sophie guessed was the kitchen by the various smells emanating from it – and these were mostly pleasant. To their right were what she estimated to be barracks for al-Fadl's retainers. Straight ahead of them was the main building, two storeys high; the upper floor was fronted by a trellis-work wall, behind which she could see people moving – the harem. She was reminded of Sheikh Ranatullah's house in Jellalabad, and could only hope her visit here would have a happier outcome than on that occasion.

Certainly they were greeted warmly enough by the sheikh himself, a tall and distinguished-looking man with a long white beard, who bowed as Sophie offered him her hand. She was taken aback by the richness of the room in which she found herself, in such total contrast to the odorous and dusty street outside. Her feet were sinking into deep pile carpet, while her eyes were caught by the burnished brass ornaments which stood on tables against the walls – she presumed it was brass – and by the huge pile of very richly stuffed pillows and rugs heaped in the far corner. As there were no chairs, she had to presume that was where the sheikh would normally sit. 'The famous Mrs Elligan,' he said in good English. 'My house is at your disposal, great lady. As am I.'

'You are so kind,' Sophie said.

'And these are your servants?' Hafsun ibn Abdullah al-Fadl clapped his hands and some of his servants hurried forward. 'Your manservant will be cared for,' the sheikh said, and indicated that Ned should accompany one of the waiting men.

Ned looked at Sophie and she gave him a reassuring smile. 'These people are our friends, Ned,' she said. 'I will send for you as soon as it is possible.'

Two veiled women were waiting for herself and Lalia. 'I am sure you will wish to wash the desert dust from your bodies,' al-Fadl said, 'and change your clothes. Then it will be my pleasure to invite you to eat with me.' He glanced at Lalia but did not indicate if the invitation would be extended to her.

'It will be my pleasure to accept,' Sophie assured him, and followed the women out of a door at the back of the room and up a flight of stairs. She did not think she had ever been in a proper harem before; Ranatullah's had not been very elaborate, and in any event his women had been entirely hostile. Here all were smiles as they were escorted through a door that had to be unlocked by a male guard – Sophie could not help but wonder if he was a eunuch as he lacked a beard – and found themselves in surroundings no less luxurious than on the lower floor, the carpets and cushions being of a similar soft and rich style, while there were a dozen women waiting for them; in the privacy of the harem these did not wear the yashmak – although all wore haiks and undershirts and were totally concealed from the neck down – and they were of all ages from a young teenager, Sophie estimated, to a woman of over forty, who now came forward to greet them.

'I am Hadija,' she announced. 'I am wife to the sheikh.' Sophie wasn't sure she shouldn't curtsy; the woman had an almost regal air. Instead she bowed and Lalia did likewise. 'Your bath is being prepared,' Hadija said. 'You will take coffee?'

'Thank you.'

Sophie was escorted to the cushions and invited to sit. Hadija sat beside her. The other women and girls crowded round to peer at her, especially her hair. Lalia was left standing on the far side of the room. 'My servant,' Sophie said.

Hadija clapped her hands and Lalia was given a cup of coffee. They were also offered a plate of various sweetmeats, which were, literally, very sweet, and did something to offset the almost bitter taste of the extremely strong coffee, even if they were covered in the small flies that swarmed everywhere. The liquid was in fact so strong that Sophie felt almost light-headed as it traced its way down her chest. 'You have crossed the desert,' Hadija remarked, 'bringing weapons to our people.'

'That was what I set out to do,' Sophie agreed. 'But we got caught in a rain storm.'

'Ah. Yes,' Hadija said. 'We experienced such a storm here only a few days ago.'

'The same storm,' Sophie said. 'And I'm afraid it washed away some of the guns.' She didn't see any point in adding to the gloomy situation by telling her hostess about the Italian attack.

'But that is not good,' Hadija said. 'That is very bad. Were you not paid for the guns?'

'Yes, I was,' Sophie said. 'And I delivered them, all but. No one suggested to me that we could be wiped out by rain in the Sahara.'

'It is very bad,' Hadija said again. 'Your bath is ready.' Apparently it had to be done in the presence of the entire harem. Sophie was stripped of her clothing, of which she was glad to see the back, and then immersed in a large tub. When she beckoned Lalia forward to join her, Hadija shook her head. 'She can use the water afterwards,' she said.

Sophie waggled her eyebrows but Lalia seemed content to wait. The water was sweet smelling and she had to submit to being massaged by various women, who did not seem to mind getting their garments wet, fascinated as they were by the whiteness of Sophie's skin, the freckles which had appeared everywhere and, most of all, her hair.

She had experienced this too in Anatullah's harem, so she was not particularly embarrassed by it all, although she did try to protect her private parts from the questing fingers – she could do nothing about her breasts, which were more thoroughly massaged than ever by a man. Here again the Arab women were fascinated by their size. It was all great fun and even sexually stimulating, until Sophie, turning her head right and left, realised she was being watched.

The inner wall of the harem was hung with drapes, brilliant with various multi-coloured designs; it was in glancing at one of these drapes that she saw something move and realised that the drape had a small hole which a moment before had been filled with an eye. She wanted to cry out in anger, but decided against it. She was in these people's power and had to accept whatever they wished, or whatever were their habits.

But who had it been? Al-Fadl himself? Surely he could enter the harem whenever he wished. The eunuch? That was certainly possible, but did eunuchs like looking at naked women? Some other member of the household she had not yet met? The possibilities were endless and needed to be forgotten.

Sophie was lifted from the bath and wrapped in soft towels, then drenched in perfume while her hair was brushed and dried, continuing to arouse enormous interest from the Arab women. When at last she was allowed to dress she felt quite exhausted; they had ridden all night to reach the oasis and it was now the middle of the day. The clothes were simple enough – an inner sort of shirt that reached her thighs, then the haik, then the yashmak, while on her head was set a little jewelled felt cap, round and brimless. She decided against asking to put on her knickers and skirt, which were filthy and had been thrown contemptuously in a corner.

This done, the ladies all knelt for their midday prayers, leaving Sophie and Lalia standing alone, gazing at each other. Lalia looked longingly at the water and Sophie nodded. The half-caste girl immediately stripped off and sank into the tub with a sigh of pleasure.

This aroused Hadija who had finished her prayers. 'I did not give her permission to bathe,' she said angrily.

'I did,' Sophie said.

The two women gazed at each other, while

Lalia splashed happily. 'She should be whipped,' Hadija said at last. 'Now listen, Mrs Elligan, the sheikh wishes you to eat with him. You understand this is a great honour.'

'I do.'

'He does not usually eat with women,' Hadija said, plainly put out. Sophie wondered if she had ever had the pleasure. 'You are to go to him, now.'

Sophie nodded and gathered the skirt of her haik. They had not given her shoes to wear, but the carpeted floor was soft and soothing on her bare feet. 'Madame,' Lalia begged.

Sophie turned. The bath had been surrounded by women and Lalia looked somewhat at bay. 'My maid is not to be harmed,' Sophie warned.

Hadija bowed.

'I have been to Algiers,' al-Fadl confided ingenuously. 'And there I observed that Frenchwomen do not wear the yashmak. Is this true of all European women?'

'Yes,' Sophie said, suddenly becoming breathless. Had he really been the one looking at her in her bath?

She had been escorted downstairs to the large reception chamber by one of the women who had whispered in al-Fadl's ear before leaving again. Sophie had no idea what she had been telling him. Now she and the sheikh were alone, save for a female servant. Once again she was drinking coffee when all she wanted was a square meal and a bed. 'But you are wearing a yashmak,' al-Fadl pointed out gently.

'It was given to me by your women.'

'I would have you take it off. I wish to look upon your face ... as it is not forbidden by your laws.'

Sophie untied the yashmak and laid it on the cushion beside her; she and the sheikh were seated, or rather, she supposed, ensconced, in the pile of cushions against the wall, the sheikh leaning on his elbow while she sat straight, her legs folded beneath her haik. 'You are a very beautiful woman,' al-Fadl commented.

'You are very kind,' Sophie said.

'And such hair ... do many European woman have such hair?'

'Some.'

'When I was in Algiers, I observed that French women revealed their legs by the shortness of their skirts. Some wore skirts above the knee. This is indecent, is it not?'

'Oh, indeed,' Sophie agreed.

'When you are in your home, do you wear skirts above the knee?'

'I am not French,' Sophie pointed out.

'Ah.' He clapped his hands and four more servants entered bearing a large bowl, which was placed in front of him. Sophie knew enough about Arab habits by now to understand both that she would be required to eat with her fingers – which did not bother her in the least she was so hungry – and that she was also required to wait until the sheikh had eaten his fill, which was galling.

But to her surprise, he gestured her to dip her fingers at the same time as he did. Their hands touched as they each secured a piece of meat, and then chewed, slowly and thoughtfully. She could only hope that Ned and Lalia were also being fed.

'Tell me what happened in the desert,' al-Fadl said.

Sophie related the events of the past week, again omitting her brief captivity by the Italians. 'Do you think any of the guns will be recovered?' al-Fadl asked.

'Oh, yes. Quite a few had been recovered before I left,' Sophie said.

'But not all.'

'Well, no. Some were undoubtedly lost.'

'How many?'

Sophie sighed. 'I would say about half.'

'That is a serious matter.'

'I know.'

'Can these missing guns be replaced?'

'I would think so.'

'By you?'

'By my father, yes. May I ask you a question?'

'Of course.'

'Are you Senussi?'

Al-Fadl held up his hand and a servant hurried forward with a napkin to dry his fingers. 'I support them.'

'I see. These replacement guns would have to be paid for.'

'Have they not already been paid for?'

'I brought the entire original order with me, Sheikh al-Fadl. It is not my fault that they were washed away in a desert storm.'

'And the Italians?'

'I knew nothing of them.'

Al-Fadl resumed eating. 'It is still a serious matter. You have been paid a great amount of money for these guns.'

'I have received half of what is promised. I am awaiting payment of the rest.'

They gazed at each other as they ate, and the penny suddenly dropped. 'You financed the shipment!'

'I have said, I support the Senussi.'

'Then you owe me one hundred and twenty-five thousand pounds.'

'And you owe me several thousand rifles and machine-guns and ammunition.'

'I see,' Sophie said, as coldly as she could. 'You refuse to honour your debt.'

'You have not honoured your obligations.' He held up a finger as she would have spoken. 'The weather is the work of Allah. Men learn to accept the whims of Allah.

Women also.'

Sophie swallowed a last piece of meat. 'I am very disappointed, Sheikh. I had supposed you were an honourable man. But if that is your attitude, then the sooner I return to England the better. I will need to discuss the situation with my father.'

'What is there to discuss?' al-Fadl asked. 'When Andrews and Yusuf return here, we will make up a list of everything that is missing, and you will send to your father for these missing items.'

'I am not so sure he will agree to this.'

'But of course he will agree, Mrs Elligan. I am sure your husband will persuade him. Will he not be anxious once again to look on your face? Your so beautiful face. And touch that so beautiful hair?'

Once again the penny dropped. 'You mean to keep me as a hostage?'

'I would like to entertain you, as my guest, for a while,' al-Fadl said. 'Is that thought not pleasing to you?'

Sophie raised her head. 'No, it is not pleasing to me, Sheikh. That is kidnapping.'

'You are my guest,' al Fadl said again. 'This pleases me. Merely to look upon you pleases me.' Again he raised his hand and again the napkin was brought forward. One was brought for Sophie as well and she gathered that the meal was at an end. The pot was carried away and they were alone save for the one servant who stood respectfully at the far side of the room out of earshot. 'When Andrews and Yusuf return here,' al-Fadl said, 'you will write to your husband and explain the situation, and inform him that you will remain in Tamanrasset awaiting the arrival of the replacement guns and ammunition. You understand this?'

'Yes,' Sophie said. 'And if I refuse?'

Al-Fadl gazed at her for several seconds. 'Then you may well have to spend the rest of your life here.'

'You would not dare!' Sophie snapped. 'The French—'

'The French know nothing of what happens inside my harem,' al-Fadl said. 'Nor do they wish to. An Arab's home is private to him alone. If you are going to stay here, I will take you into my harem. I cannot marry you as I have four wives already, and you are also married. I would make you my concubine. I would like that very much. I may do that anyway.'

'Adultery is a terrible crime in Islam,' Sophie gasped.

'Not when it is committed with a gaiour,' al-Fadl pointed out. 'The rape of a gaiour is considered almost as a necessity, once in a lifetime, for a true believer.' He stood up. 'But life in a harem is not necessarily all pleasure. Discipline is strict. I maintain a very strict rule in my harem. Come with me.'

Sophie stood up, with some difficulty; her legs were cramped from being folded beneath her, and in addition were feeling quite weak. Had Clay suspected this might happen? Had he known? The bastard.

The door was opened for them by two menservants, which ended any idea that she might somehow attack the sheikh and make a run for it. But she couldn't do that in any event as it would mean abandoning Ned and Lalia. So she walked behind him, followed all the time by the two men servants as they climbed the stairs to the harem. Am I going to be raped? she wondered. By this decrepit old man? Well, then, should she go down fighting, or just submit, and wait. Wait for what? If she could no longer count on Clay...

The harem doors were being opened for the sheikh. Here the men servants halted, but Sophie followed him inside, to pause in consternation. The women were all waiting, fully dressed, lined up behind a wooden frame consisting of four uprights connected by parallel beams. In the centre of this frame, on her back, lay Lalia. She was naked but her body was unmarked, at least recently. On the other hand her cheeks were flushed and her eyes swollen, as her hair was wild. Her arms were suspended above her head from the nearest crossbar. This should have enabled her to sit up, save that her feet were also secured, only they had been carried upwards and passed through two holes let into the other crossbar, so that she was quite helpless. The whole contraption and Lalia's position made Sophie think of pictures she had seen of medieval stocks, only tilted onto its back. She ran forward. 'What have you done to her?'

'Madame!' Lalia wailed. 'Madame!'

Al-Fadl stood at her shoulder. 'Nothing has been done to her yet. But she is about to be punished for having dared to bathe without permission.'

'I gave her permission,' Sophie snapped.

'You had no right to do that,' al-Fadl pointed out. 'But I feel it is right that you should witness her punishment, both because she is your servant and because, if you enter my harem, you will become subject to such punishments yourself. Commence,' he told Hadijah. 'Twenty strokes.'

Hadija produced a thin cane from underneath her haik, and swished it once or twice. Lalia screamed.

Sophie made to run forward and had her arm seized by the sheikh. 'Stand still,' he commanded. 'Or you will suffer it yourself.'

Hadija struck Lalia across the soles of her bare feet. Lalia screamed even louder. 'You have heard of this, I am sure,' al-Fadl said.

212

'It is called the bastinado.'

Sophie panted, as Hadija fell into a rhythm. Lalia screamed again and again, while the soles of her feet turned red and seemed visibly to swell. 'It is very painful,' al-Fadl confided, 'but is a very useful method of punishment because, you see, it leaves all of the victim's female attributes untouched and unharmed. All that will happen is that her feet will swell and she will not be able to walk for a week or so. That is from twenty strokes. For serious mis-demeanours, the punishment can be as much as a hundred strokes. Then she might not walk for a month. She has fainted,' he pointed out, as Lalia stopped screaming.

One of the women ran forward with a wet cloth with which she bathed Lalia's face. Lalia woke up and promptly began to scream again while Hadija resumed beating her. Sophie could hardly breathe and she was dripping sweat.

But at last the twentieth stroke was delivered. Hadija handed the cane to one of the other women and herself released Lalia from the frame. Lalia rolled and writhed, and had to be held down by several of the women while Hadija applied an ointment to her feet. 'Reflect upon what you have seen,' al-Fadl said, and left the harem.

Reflect, Sophie thought. Reflect. She sat in

a cushion with Lalia's head on her lap. The half-caste girl continued to moan and writhe, only half awake; Hadijah had given her a sedative drink. Remarkably, although none of them had dared protest against the savage beating, the women now seemed entirely sympathetic, and were as anxious to care for Lalia as Sophie herself. 'Our master is not a hard man,' Hadija insisted. 'But he will be obeyed.'

Sophie merely glanced at her. And who, she wondered, told him of Lalia's 'misdemeanour' in the first place? It was more than ever clear that she had to get out of the sheikh's house. And then? Go to the French for help? And be arrested for gunrunning? She needed to talk with Ned. 'I wish to speak with my servant,' she told Hadija the next morning, having spent an uncomfortable night as Lalia had continued to moan and groan and twist and turn, while every so often she would touch something with her by now grotesquely swollen feet and wake up with a shriek of agony.

Hadija nodded. 'She will be able to speak, soon enough.'

'I meant, my man servant.'

Hadija frowned. 'That is not possible. You are forbidden to leave the harem and he may not enter here.'

'I do not belong in a harem,' Sophie said

angrily. 'It is not our way in Europe. My servant is necessary to me.'

'If you persist in this madness, you will suffer the bastinado yourself,' Hadija warned.

Sophie dropped the subject; she did not even know if Ned was all right. Dearest Ned! She had thought him her biggest problem only a few days ago. A problem she had been looking forward to solving, or not solving, as the mood took her. Now ... what a catastrophe this adventure had turned out to be.

So, should she not surrender and write to Richard as al-Fadl wanted, and then resolve herself to wait here for six months until the new guns arrived? If they ever did, lacking the funds to pay for them. And if al-Fadl truly meant to let her go. Once he had the guns, there was no need for him to do so.

She had got herself into the most terrible mess. But the next day Clay and Yusuf arrived in Tamanrasset.

The Escape

To Sophie's relief she was allowed out of the harem to talk with Clay; indeed, she was summoned to do so. Equally to her relief, al-Fadl was not present, although she had to suppose he was, as always, watching and listening from an adjoining room. 'Sophie!' Clay held both her hands, but oddly, on this occasion, did not draw her forward for a hug and a kiss. 'You're looking much better. Nothing like a bit of R and R, eh?'

She sank onto the cushions, still holding his hands, so that she drew him down with her. 'You know the situation?' she spoke in a whisper.

'I have been told it, yes.'

'The sheikh will not pay me the balance of the money, because he says not enough of the guns have been recovered. How many have you recovered?'

'I would say about two-thirds.'

'So he owes me another eighty thousand pounds.'

'Ah ... technically, perhaps. The sheikh does not see it that way.'

'Just what do you mean by that?'

'The deal was for a quarter of a million.

216

Now, you have only delivered two-thirds of the merchandise. Two-thirds of a quarter of a million is just over a hundred and sixty-thousand. You have received a hundred and twenty-five thousand. So the most that is still owed to you is forty-five thousand.'

'That is outrageous!' Sophie snapped, forgetting to whisper. 'It's robbery. That wasn't the agreement at all.'

'I think you should accept it. Because the sheikh feels that actually, as you have let him down, he need not pay you *anything* more. The point is that of the guns recovered most are in a terrible condition after being immersed in water and sunk in the sand. Nor are we sure any of the ammunition is still usable.'

'Just whose side are you on?'

'The sheikh is by way of being my employer.'

'Do you realise he wants to take me into his harem?'

'I know he would like to. You are a very beautiful woman.'

Sophie glared at him. 'And you would let him do that?'

'I don't think there is anything I can do about it. If you were to accept the forty-five thousand as full and final payment, I might be able to persuade him to let you go.'

'I thought you had something going for me yourself.'

'I do. But I have learned one has to separate the possible from the impossible and go for that.'

'And I am impossible for you, is that it?'

'If the sheikh wants you, then you are, I'm sorry to say. Believe me, Sophie, I did not want it to turn out this way. But you determined to come on this delivery, and—'

'He is your employer. Well, you can tell your employer that if he lays a finger on me I will have him charged with rape.'

'If he decides to lay a finger on you, Sophie, the outside world will never know of it, or you, again.'

Sophie refused to admit to fear. 'Do you think you can frighten me, Clay Andrews? My husband and my father know where I have gone. Richard will soon be back on his feet again and he will come looking for me. And I can tell you that you and your Arab friends will find yourselves looking down the barrel of a gun. Don't forget that Richard Elligan once took on nearly the whole Afghan nation and won.' She paused for breath and to collect her thoughts before her exaggerations went quite over the top.

Clay was regarding her with a quizzical expression. 'I think he may be too late for you,' he said quietly. 'I wish you to think about the present, rather than an optimistic future. You have another forty-eight hours, I would say. Al-Fadl wants you, but he would rather you came to him willingly. If you would be willing to accept the forty-five thousand on offer, I think I can persuade him to let you go rather than risk any international crisis. If you are stubborn, well, he will have you anyway, and there will not be another cent. Think very seriously about these things.' He got up, bowed to her and left the room.

Sophie was seething, with a mixture of anger and apprehension. The thought of just surrendering to that white-bearded old thug ... it was the humiliation of the surrender rather than any anticipated fear or disgust of what he would want to do to her and with her. The thought of being conned out of her money was equally humiliating.

But losing her temper was going to accomplish nothing. She had to think, and plan, and do. She was Sophie Elligan. She had elected to come on this journey because she had been sure she could cope. She had watched Richard at work, and even more, she had watched Richard's mentor, Sir James Martingell, at work. She had felt she was as good as they as she had shared their triumphs and disasters and emerged triumphant. Now it was necessary to prove just how good she was. Just how determined. And just how ruthless.

The door opened and the sheikh came in.

Sophie did not rise, and he seated himself beside her. 'I trust you had a satisfactory conversation with Mr Andrews,' he said.

'He put me in the picture,' Sophie said.

'That is good. I felt that you would understand things better, coming from a man of your own race, your own religion. But a man dedicated to the cause of the Senussi. As am I.'

'He made me understand these things,' Sophie said. 'He also told me how wealthy you are,' she lied. 'Is this true?'

'I have a modest portion,' al-Fadl agreed.

'Supposing I accepted your offer? How would I be paid? You are not going to give me a cheque drawn on some French bank, I hope.'

Al-Fadl smiled. 'I do not keep my money in banks, Mrs Elligan. I like to be able to look at it.'

'You mean you keep it here? You must need a lot of people to guard it.'

'Why should this be so? I am al-Fadl. The whole world knows this. And the whole world knows that if anyone attempted to rob me, my people would hunt him down, even to the ends of the earth.'

'And when they found him?' Or her, Sophie thought, suddenly breathless.

'They would cut off his hands and his feet, his genitalia and his tongue, and leave him lying in the street,' al-Fadl said. 'This is well known as the punishment for theft.'

'All of that?' She was genuinely aghast.

'In the case of ordinary theft, merely the hand is cut off. But in the case of someone like myself ... so you see, I am as safe here with my half-dozen servants as if I were in the fort surrounded by French Foreign Legionnaires.'

'I understand,' Sophie said. 'And if the thief were a woman? One of your wives or concubines, perhaps?'

'We do not mutilate women,' he explained. Sophie gave a stifled sigh of relief. 'But a wife, or a concubine, who betrays her master, and not necessarily by stealing, must still be punished, perhaps even more severely than a man. She is placed in a stout sack, along with a dog, a cat, and a rat, and suspended from one of the beams in the yard until all movement within the sack has ceased.'

Sophie clasped both hands to her neck. 'It is quite amusing to watch,' al-Fadl said. 'Because in the beginning there is a great deal of movement and a great deal of noise, too. And then the blood starts to penetrate the sack, and one wagers, whose blood is that? Very amusing. But why are we discussing such a subject? Do you know, I have only ever had to execute one of my women.' He stroked his beard, thoughtfully. 'She betrayed my bed. Yet the fact that I did what is necessary has kept all the others in line. So you see, you would be safe here too.'

'I understand,' she said again. And at least, she thought, I need have no conscience about shooting this murdering bastard, if I have to – and am given the opportunity. 'But if I accept your money, will you let me go?'

Al-Fadl gazed at her for several seconds, then he stretched out his hand to pick up some strands of her hair and allow them to trickle through his fingers as if they too were gold. 'I do not think I can do that now, Mrs Elligan – Sophie – now that I have looked upon you. I think all my life I have dreamed of someone so beautiful, so fair, without even knowing of what I was dreaming. Now that you are here, I must have you. I will have you. But...' he held up his finger as she would have spoken, 'I will deal fairly with you. Come to me of your own free will, and I will send the forty-five thousand pounds that is still owed to your husband, or your father, whichever you prefer.' He chuckled. 'Is that not a fair price?'

Sophie swallowed. 'I am sure. But Mr Andrews said that I had forty-eight hours to consider and make up my mind.'

Al-Fadl stroked his beard. 'Do you require that?'

'It is a great step you are asking me to take, my lord,' Sophie said. 'Yes, I require that.'

'Very well. You have forty-eight hours. You see, I wish to be fair to you in every way. Forty-eight hours beginning now.' He smiled. 'In that time, I shall take not one of my women to my bed, so that I may be filled with vigour when you are brought to me. On Saturday morning. It is our day of rest. But we shall not rest, you and I.'

She wondered how old he was, when he had the romantic concepts of a schoolboy. And he had to be destroyed. That was better. That was Martingell thinking for her. 'May I ask a question?'

'You may ask anything you wish.'

'What is to become of my servant?'

'She may remain here with you.'

'I meant, my male servant.'

'My women do not have male servants.' Another smile. 'Unless you wish him to be castrated.'

'I wish him sent home.' Al-Fadl shrugged. 'I wish him to take the money to my husband.'

Now the sheikh raised his eyebrows. 'You would trust him with so much money?'

'He is an old family retainer,' Sophie said. 'He is absolutely trustworthy. But ... I will have to speak with him first.'

'My women do not speak with men, except me.'

'I am not yet your woman, sheikh. I need to speak with him, to instruct him, and to tell him what to say to my husband. If I am to stay here with you of my own free will.'

'Then you have decided?'

'I need two days to be absolutely sure.'

'You are a stubborn woman. I shall have to beat you.'

'When you are my master, you may do so. After I have spoken with my servant.'

'I do not think I can allow this.'

'What is troubling you? We will meet here, if you wish, and your people may be present.'

Al-Fadl stroked his beard, then nodded. 'You may speak with him.'

Ned knelt before her. Two of al-Fadl's servants stood by the door. But they did not understand English. 'Are you all right?' Sophie whispered.

'I am fine, madam. These fellows are good company, if a little uncouth. But you ... we heard Lalia screaming.'

Sophie nodded. 'Listen.' She outlined the situation.

Ned gave a low whistle. 'What are you going to do?'

'You,' Sophie said, 'are going to get me out of here.'

He frowned at her.

'Can't you do it?' she asked. 'There are only six man servants, right? And a couple of eunuchs, and a dozen women. Can you get hold of some weapons?'

'I should think so, madam. But–'

'But what?'

'Madam, if we are going to break out of here, it will be necessary to kill all of these people. Certainly the sheikh.'

'I understand this. If it will relieve your mind, the sheikh boasts of being a murderer.'

Ned gazed at her as if realising that he had never properly evaluated her before. 'It is what my husband would do were he here,' Sophie said.

'I am sure of it, madam. But once we have done that, we shall be wanted people. If they were to catch up with us–'

'We should be tortured to death,' Sophie said.

'You are prepared to risk this?'

'Yes. Are you?'

He did not answer that directly. 'Where should we go? The fortress and claim the protection of the French?'

'I don't think that would work,' Sophie said. 'Firstly, from the point of view of the French, if we go to them after shooting our way out of here, we would be troublemakers and probably murderers and therefore locked up. Secondly, they would very rapidly be informed that we are gunrunners, which is another reason for us to be locked up, for a very long time. And thirdly, once we *were* locked up, we'd be sitting ducks for any Arab out to avenge al-Fadl.'

Ned licked his lips. 'Then–'

'We must go east to Egypt.'

Ned was aghast. 'Madam, that is more than a thousand miles. And mainly across Italian territory.'

'Across territory claimed by Italy on the map. There aren't many Italians in it.'

Ned scratched his head. 'If you don't think it can be done, Ned,' Sophie said, 'then we will abandon the idea. I have to tell you that the sheikh has agreed to let you return to England with the money he still considers he owes us. So, there is no necessity for you to risk your life.'

'And you will remain here?'

'That is the deal.' Sophie's mouth twisted. 'I am to enter his harem.'

'I could not permit that.'

Sophie's heart pounded. For a moment she had doubted ... but could she really ask him to take such a risk? 'You must be sure, Ned. The odds on our survival are about a hundred to one, I would say.'

Ned smiled at her. 'We'll survive, madam. But I must say one thing.'

'Of course.'

'Before we left England you told me that you were the boss in this expedition and that I must do whatever you required me to do, without question.'

'Yes, I did. But I withdraw that stipulation now. If you help me it must be because you want to.'

'I will help you, madam. But on one condition.—

'Name it.'

'That I am now in command, that you will do whatever I tell you to do, without question. Only that way can I save your life.'

Sophie gazed at him. 'Of course,' she agreed. 'I accept that condition.'

'Very well,' he said. 'Now listen carefully. Saturday is the Muslims' day of prayer. It actually commences on Friday night. That is when we shall make our move. Do nothing, say nothing, until I tell you. Do you understand this?'

'Yes,' Sophie said. She was not required to attend al-Fadl's bed until Saturday morning.

She dared not of course confide in Lalia, could only hope and pray that the girl's feet would be usable by Friday night. To this end she became very jolly hockey sticks and insisted Lalia stop moping and weeping and endeavour to get about, which she could do well enough – having spent most of her life barefoot, her soles were as tough as leather.

But she remained bitter which was all to the good. 'I hate this place and these people, signora,' she said. 'But they say we are going to stay here.'

'Be patient,' Sophie told her.

Equally there was no chance of contacting, or even seeing, Ned during the intervening thirty-six hours. She had to trust him to be doing whatever was necessary. She dared not let herself think of the risk. The fate al-Fadl had promised her was unthinkable enough. But Ned, mutilated beyond belief ... it could not happen.

But she could not change her mind and stop what was happening now, as she could not speak with him. So she thrust herself into the life of the harem, playing games with the inmates, smiling indulgently at their conversations which were concerned entirely with sexual matters, both in dis-cussing the probable sizes and capabilities of various men they had seen – but never their lord and master – and indulging in lesbian fantasies and caresses amongst themselves.

Sophie was herself an object of great attraction to them, and not only because of her colouring and statuesque beauty – she had lived in the outside world and known other men. They wanted to learn as much about her adventures as possible. While intending to have her for themselves as soon as it could happen.

'Our lord must have you first,' Hadija

explained. 'And then we shall see. But I expect you will be an odalisque.'

'Which is?'

'The favoured one who will be summoned to his bed time and again, until you are pregnant.'

'Will that not make you jealous?' Sophie asked.

Hadija smiled. 'It will not make *me* jealous. I am too old to go to my lord's bed. He likes them young. Younger than you, indeed, as a rule. It is because you are so different that he wishes you. But you will make the others jealous, yes. Do not be afraid. I will protect you. And you will grant me your favour.'

'Ah,' Sophie said. 'Yes, of course.' She wondered what it would be like to have sex with Hadija and had a suspicion it would be infinitely preferable to having sex with al-Fadl.

Friday seemed the longest day of Sophie's life. She determinedly made herself act as normal as she could, but she could not help standing by the trellissed windows to look at the sun; they had taken away her watch and there was a complete absence of clocks in the harem, even in the entire palace, so far as she had observed. The women prayed when the muezzin called the noonday hour, then ate their midday meal with the usual chaff and laughter, and then settled down for their siestas, from which they were awakened with startling suddenness by the doors being thrown open to admit the sheikh.

Everyone hastily got up and bowed or knelt, hands together. Sophie had got the drill by now and did likewise, as did Lalia. And then realised she was looking at al-Fadl's feet, as he was standing immediately before her. 'Well, woman?' he demanded. She raised her head; he had not been so peremptory before. 'You have had sufficient time,' he said.

'It was to be tomorrow, my lord,' she protested.

'This is some game you are playing,' he said. 'My people tell me that your servant is preparing to depart, therefore you have made your decision. You made it yesterday.'

Sophie's heart was pounding, and there seemed lead balls in her stomach. 'You said tomorrow, my lord,' she insisted stubbornly.

'Ha! You have had sufficient time,' he repeated. 'Are you unclean?' He looked at Hadija. 'Is she unclean?'

'No, my lord,' Hadija said.

'Well then, perfume her and bring her to my bed. This evening, after prayers.' Sophie gasped.

'Do you wish her shaved, my lord?' Hadija asked.

'No,' Sophie cried.

Al-Fadl considered her for a few moments. Then he said, 'Not this time. It will be a new experience. Afterwards, perhaps.' He turned and left the harem.

'Well, then,' Hadija said. 'This is the moment of your glory.'

'To be raped by that obscene old man?' Sophie shouted.

'Hush, woman. If I were to tell our lord what you have said, you would be bastinaoed, and on your buttocks rather than your feet. Then you would know what pain is like. Now let us attend to you.'

Sophie panted, but there was nothing she could do, save betray their plans. If only there was some way of letting Ned know. As far as he was aware, she would be in the harem when he came looking for her. If she were in the sheikh's bed...

The women were fussing excitedly. A bath was prepared and Sophie was dunked in the heated water. They soaped her with their usual enthusiasm, even Lalia getting into the act, then dried her and perfumed her while Hadija dressed her hair. Then she was dressed in a single silk garment, rather like a nightgown, and her yashmak tied in place. 'There,' Hadija said. 'Now you will please our lord.'

Sophie wanted to tear the yashmak off and stamp on it. But she had to keep her nerve, play her part. To do anything else would be to betray Ned.

Hadija herself escorted her along the corridors, all in the upper floor of the house, until they reached the sheikh's private quarters. The way led over a verandah from which they could look down at the court-yard. That was empty but Sophie saw that the sun had only just set. Ned would be preparing his move.

A eunuch stood outside the sheikh's door. 'My lord expects us,' Hadijah said.

The eunuch bowed and opened the door. They stepped through into a little lobby, at the far end of which was an archway decorated with quotations in Arabic. Beyond the archway there was an enormous divan and on this al-Fadl was lounging, but sitting up as the women entered. He also wore only a single garment, and Sophie needed only a quick glance to realise that however old he was, he was both virile and excited. Her stomach rolled. Hadija bowed. 'The lady Sophie, my lord.'

Al-Fadl stood up and came towards her, stretching out his hand. 'You grow more beautiful every time I look on you,' he said.

'You flatter me, my lord,' Sophie said.

He held her hand and drew her to him. Hadija bowed again and withdrew. A moment later the doors closed. Al-Fadl held Sophie against him. He was stronger than she would have thought possible and so eager. His hands roamed over her shoulder blades then down to hold her buttocks, then back up again to hold her neck and drive his fingers into her hair while he released the yashmak.

To her relief he made no attempt to kiss her, but now his hands came round in front to cup her breasts. 'Remove the robe,' he said.

Sophie licked her lips but still she could only obey until and unless Ned made his move. Besides, she had to find out where he kept his wealth. She stepped back, lifted the robe over her head, and dropped it on the floor. 'Such beauty,' al-Fadl said, and leaned forward to stroke her pubes.

'Will you not indulge me, my lord?' Sophie asked.

'This is what I am about to do.'

'No, no, my lord. You are about to indulge yourself.'

He frowned. 'Then what is it you wish of me?'

'I wish to know if you are really the wealthiest man in North Africa. When I know this, I can come to you, willingly and unafraid.'

He regarded her for several seconds, then gestured at a chest in the corner of the room. 'There, you see.'

'A chest?'

'It is filled with coins and precious stones.'

'May I look?'

He led her across the room, turned the key, and threw up the lid. Sophie gasped at the tangled mess of glowing richness in front of her. She thought of the book, *The Count of Monte Cristo*. 'Well?' al-Fadl asked. 'Are you satisfied?'

'I am satisfied, my lord.'

He closed the lid and turned the key. 'Now I shall satisfy myself.'

Again he lowered his head to nuzzle her pubes, while his hands went round her buttocks and seeped between. Stand still, she told herself. Stand still and suffer. Until ... and at that moment there was the sound of a shot, followed by several more.

Al-Fadl jerked upright. He was still very close, and Sophie brought up her knee with all the force she could manage. It thudded into his groin and he bent forward again, gasping in pain. Sophie knew she had to finish the job, reminding herself that this man had himself executed one of his wives in the most horrible possible fashion. And found it amusing! She clasped her hands together and brought them down on the nape of his neck. He went straight on down, his face thudding into the tiled floor. Sophie looked around the room. In the far corner there was a washstand with a china ewer and basin. She ran to this, picked up the ewer, emptied the water on the floor and went back to the sheikh.

He was just stirring and Sophie hit him as hard as she could. The ewer cracked and then split, but al-Fadl went down again with another thud and this time lay absolutely still, surrounded by a growing pool of blood seeping from his shattered skull. Sophie stood above him, panting. Was he dead? She had killed before in that desperate gun battle in the mountains of Afghanistan, but that had been at a distance; she had not been within touching distance of the men she had shot down. Nor had she been naked.

She picked up her robe, ran to the door and it burst open to admit Ned. He carried two rifles and two revolvers were tucked into his belt. She looked past him and saw the eunuch sprawled across the doorway.

He looked at her, biting his lip. He had never actually seen her naked before. 'Is he dead?'

'I don't know.'

Ned entered the room and stood above the sheikh. Then he levelled one of his rifles and squeezed the trigger. Al-Fadl's back seemed to split open. Ned looked up. 'You know it had to be.'

'Yes,' she said. 'The women—'

'We'll deal with them now. Will you get dressed?'

Sophie dropped the gown over her head, ran down the corridor behind him. 'The men–'

'Are all dead.'

She gasped. Richard had told her that Ned was utterly ruthless when pointed in the right direction, but this man was far more deadly than she had ever imagined.

They reached the entrance to the harem, from which there was a high-pitched babble of sound. The eunuch on the door stared at them, then reached for the bellrope to summon assistance. There wasn't any to summon but Ned shot him anyway. 'Ned! You're not going to kill the women?'

'You mean just leave them there, locked in? Is there no other entrance?'

Sophie shook her head. 'But we must get Lalia.'

'It's a risk.'

'If we leave her they'll tear her apart.'

He hesitated, and she almost thought he was going to remind her of her promise to do as he wished without question. Then he threw the doors open. 'You'd better speak to them.'

The women stared at the big man with the gun; none of them had actually seen Ned before. Then someone screamed and the shriek was taken up by the others.

Hadija stepped forward. 'What is this madness?'

'I am leaving,' Sophie said. 'Lalia, come here.'

Lalia hurried forward. 'Oh, signora!'

'Collect my things,' Sophie said.

Lalia scurried around, collecting the European garments as well as some spare haiks and Sophie's topee.

'You will die,' Hadija hissed at them. The other women had all retreated against the far wall.

'Listen to me,' Sophie said. 'We are going to lock you in here. Any attempt to break out and you will be shot. Understand this.'

Hadija bared her teeth. Lalia hurried through the doorway, the clothes clutched in her arms.

'Let's go,' Ned said. 'But first, a little life insurance.' He pointed at Hadija. 'You will come with us.' Hadija opened her mouth to scream and he stepped against her, wrapping his hand round her throat. 'If I squeeze,' he said, 'you'll not see tomorrow.'

Hadija panted but made no effort to resist him. 'Remember,' Ned told the other women, 'one sound from in here, and Hadija gets it. Then I come back for you.'

They backed through the doorway, and Sophie closed the doors and locked them, then she and Lalia moved various articles of furniture against them. 'Will they not break through the trellis work?' Sophie asked.

'Not until they have had time to think,'

237

Ned said. 'And then they'll still have to get down to the ground. By then we will be far away.'

'With her?'

He grinned. 'She's our pass-key. All set?'

'We must get the money,' Sophie said.

'Where is that?'

She led them back to al-Fadl's apartment. Hadija gave a little moan at the sight of the sheikh's body. Sophie opened the chest. Lalia gave a little shriek and even Ned's eyes widened. 'Saddlebags,' he said. 'She's in your care.' He handed Sophie a revolver and a long-bladed knife, presumably taken from one of the guards. 'You'll do what you have to do?'

'Yes,' Sophie said.

He hurried off. Lalia was now staring at the dead body of the sheikh. 'Oh, signora,' she said again.

'It was necessary,' Sophie explained.

'You will die,' Hadija hissed. 'I will watch you die. I will smile when you die.'

'Don't hold your breath,' Sophie warned her. Hadija glanced at the door. 'Make a move,' Sophie said, 'and I'll let Lalia have you.' Hadija licked her lips. But Lalia also licked her lips.

Ned was back in a few minutes carrying four double saddlebags. They filled each of these with coins and precious stones. 'How much, do you reckon?' Ned asked.

'Enough,' Sophie said and smiled at him. 'Now they'll want us for robbery as well as murder and kidnapping.'

'So let's get out of here. But we'll take a little more insurance.' He knelt beside al-Fadl's body, pulled the huge ring from his forefinger. 'I imagine that's pretty well known in this neighbourhood.'

They hurried downstairs. There were two dead bodies lying in the downstairs room and another in the courtyard. 'The others are in the quarters,' Ned said.

'Don't you think people in the street heard the shots?'

'Maybe. But they don't do too much investigating of other people's business around here. Especially of what goes on inside al-Fadl's house.' He led the women into the stables, and they saddled and harnessed six camels. Four of these were for riding; the other two were laden with the money and as much food and water as they could carry, taken from the sheikh's kitchens.

Ned gave Sophie one of the rifles and a bandolier, as well as a revolver. While he was arranging things, Sophie changed into her western clothes and felt a lot better. 'Will you not give me a gun?' Lalia asked. She had had nothing to change into.

'Later, perhaps. Now, then, ladies, this is it,' Ned said. They were all wrapped in haiks

239

and burnouses, the women wearing yash-maks. 'Now listen very carefully, Hadija,' Ned said. 'You and I are going to walk together, and you are going to make the right replies to any question asked of you, or I am going to push this knife clear through you. Use the ring and you can have it when we are safely away. Savvy?'

Hadija inhaled deeply. They walked the camels to the gate and he opened it. Sophie didn't know what to expect, but the street was deserted; most of the inhabitants of the district were at prayer. Ned closed the gates; there was no way of locking them from the outside, but they were trusting in the likelihood that no one would visit the sheikh until well into the morrow.

Sophie wondered where Clay was. She also wondered what his reaction would be to the news of what had happened. Would he come after them? Someone would, that was certain.

'Nice and slow,' Ned said. It was now utterly dark, with only the occasional lantern hanging on a street corner. And still they saw few people. Those they did greeted them courteously, if somewhat uncertainly; a white man, and what appeared to be three Arab women leading six camels through the streets towards the outer gates would certainly be an object of curiosity.

There were four sleepy Foreign Legionnaires on the gates. 'Do your stuff,' Ned whispered in Hadija's ear.

'I am Hadija, principal wife of Sheikh Hafsun ibn Abdullah al-Fadl,' Hadija said. 'I am on a visit to my father's village. Here is al-Fadl's ring.'

The Legionnaire corporal peered at the ring and they were allowed through. Then they were descending the sides of the hill towards the desert. 'Good girl,' Ned said.

'I will sing when you are executed,' Hadija said.

'I'll be listening,' he promised.

'How much time have we got?' Sophie asked.

'I would say about twelve hours,' Ned said. 'It all depends on how soon those women get their act together.'

'And then? They will track us easily enough.'

'We agreed it would be dangerous, madam. It is not over yet.'

She squeezed his hand. 'I know. I am just happy to be with you.'

'You let me go now?' Hadija asked, when they were some distance away from the town.

'No chance. You're coming with us for a while.'

'You mean to kill me.'

'Actually, I don't. We will let you go as

soon as it is safe.'

They broke all the rules by keeping moving throughout the day, with just an hour's break for lunch. They scrutinised the desert behind them as the mountains began to fade, but saw nothing.

By dusk they were exhausted and slept in turns for several hours – one staying awake to watch Hadija, who seemed to have accepted her situation although she was sulkily brooding over it – before resuming their journey at midnight, not speaking, nodding in the saddle, but driven by the knowledge that if they could put fifty-odd miles between themselves and the first pursuit they stood a chance.

'I reckon we're in Italian territory,' Ned said twenty-four hours later. And still there was no one behind them.

'Well, then,' Sophie said encouragingly, 'there are only nine hundred miles to go.'

As usual, personal considerations had become submerged beneath the sweat and the sand and the exhaustion. Nine hundred miles at perhaps twenty miles a day meant well over a month. Within five days they had run out of water and were forced to dig for it, which they did successfully enough. And three days later they saw palm trees.

They dismounted from their camels and left Lalia in charge of both the animals and

Hadija. They had no doubt of her loyalty; quite apart from her hatred of the Arab woman they were her only hope of regaining civilisation. Sophie and Ned crawled forward, their rifles slung, their revolvers in their belts, until they reached a vantage point from which they could look down on the tiny patch of green.

It was late afternoon and the heat was beginning to leave the sun. There was the usual cultivated patch just outside the village and here some women were at work. But the village itself was very small, hardly a dozen houses, and there was no minaret. 'They have camels,' Ned said. 'Ours are pretty tired. It would be a fair swap.'

'Will they go for it, you reckon?'

'Probably not.' He glanced at her.

Sophie swallowed. She had known what had to be done in al-Fadl's house, and it had been easy to convince herself that al-Fadl deserved to be executed in any event, as well as his servants, who would have partaken in the murder of the woman and whatever other murders he might have commanded over the years. But these were innocent women and children, and perhaps men as well.

Ned saw her concern. 'We won't kill if we don't have to. You never know, they may be willing to trade.' He grinned. 'It's not as if we're short of a bob or two.'

'They mustn't know that.'

He nodded and they returned to the camels and the two women. Ned opened one of the saddlebags and took out various coins and jewels which he stowed in his pockets. Then they all mounted and walked their camels over the dune and down the slope towards the village. They were spotted immediately and there was a great deal of running to and fro. But they kept their rifles slung and moved with slow and apparent confidence.

By the time they were within a hundred yards of the houses the men had gathered to meet them. Sophie counted eighteen, all armed, although with pretty ancient rifles; even so, the odds were tremendous. She glanced at Ned, but his face was calm and as resolute as ever.

They approached to within twenty yards of the waiting men, then he held up his hand and brought his camel to its knees, stepping down with great dignity. The three women followed his example. Lalia, as instructed, stood immediately behind Hadija, knife in hand.

'I am Edward Carew,' Ned announced in his best Arabic. 'I am travelling on a mission for Sheikh Hafsun ibn Abdullah al-Fadl. You know of Sheikh al-Fadl?'

The man who was presumably head of the village – his beard was grey and there was gold thread running through his burnous bowed. 'We know of the sheikh.'

'We seek food and water,' Ned said, 'and camels.'

'You wish our camels?' the headman asked, while there was a rustle of anxiety from behind him.

'We will buy them and exchange our own. These are good beasts. They need only rest.'

'Al-Fadl is far away in the Hoggar,' the headman remarked. Sophie could not determine whether it was a warning or an inquiry.

'You know of Yusuf ben Hasim?' Ned asked.

'We know of Yusuf,' the headman said.

'He is close behind us,' Ned said. Which was probably not a lie, Sophie thought.

'And he too is on a mission?' the headman asked.

'His mission is to make war upon the Italians,' Ned said. 'We have brought Sheikh Yusuf many guns, modern rifles...' He tapped his own. 'Now he is ready to make jihad. But we must get to Egypt first.'

'You have no escort?' the headman asked mildly.

'Do we need an escort?' Ned said contemptuously. 'We have these.' Again he tapped his rifle and then the revolver in his belt. 'And we have gold coins with which to pay for your camels. Leaving ours in part

245

exchange,' he said again.

The headman considered this for several seconds. Then he said, 'Show me these coins.'

Ned dug into his pocket and pulled out several of the coins. The headman came forward, took one and examined it. There could be no doubt that it was genuine. Then he looked past Ned and Sophie at the camels, and Lalia and Hadija ... and the saddlebags. He was no fool. 'We will trade,' he said. 'You will eat with my people?'

'We are in great haste,' Ned said. 'But we will buy food from you, as well as the camels.'

'You refuse to eat with me?' the sheikh asked, as mildly as ever.

'It will be a great pleasure to eat with you, Sheikh,' Ned said. 'Let your people bring the food to us, here.'

The sheikh stroked his beard, and now he was looking at Sophie. 'You fear treachery,' he remarked.

'A man travelling alone in the desert must watch his back at all times, Sheikh.'

'A man and three women,' the sheikh observed. 'One of whom dresses as a man and carries arms. This is not as it is written. Can this woman use her arms?'

'This woman is a world-famous traveller,' Ned said, and decided it was time to impose a little will. 'And yes, she can use her arms.'

He looked left and right, picked out a spit over the fire, from which was suspended a cooking pot. 'Is there food in that pot?'

'There is food,' the sheikh said.

'Tell your women to take out the food and replace the pot.'

The sheikh raised his eyebrows, but shouted the commands. Two of the women removed the pot, emptied the half-cooked lamb into another pot and replaced the first. 'Sophie,' Ned invited.

Sophie pushed her topee back on her head, allowing her hair to come flooding onto her shoulders – she had discarded both haik and burnous – and unslung her rifle, taking deep breaths to calm her nerves. It was actually quite a large target; she had fired at and hit much smaller objects in the past. And some of those shots had been in defence of her life. But this was the first time she had been called upon to perform to an audience. The Arab men were nudging each other, grinning and whispering. Women did not figure in their life except as sexual objects, mothers and cooks.

Sophie levelled the rifle and squeezed the trigger. The pot exploded into a hundred pieces. The women screamed, the men clapped their hands. Sophie lowered the gun, still breathing deeply.

'By Allah,' the sheikh said. 'She is a woman in a thousand. Will you sell her to me? I will give you all our camels for this one.'

'She is not for sale,' Ned said. 'You asked for a demonstration of her power and she has given you this. Now let us eat and complete our business.'

The sheikh looked at Lalia and Hadija. 'And those? Can they shoot as well?'

'Of course,' Ned said.

For the time being, at least, they had gained the ascendency. Food was served and the sheikh and one of his men sat with them. This was as Ned insisted, but the Arabs were not disposed to argue; none of them had ever sat down to a meal with three women before. They were curious, however, and Ned had to have the sheikh command them to retire when they would have come too close.

Hadija seethed throughout the meal, desperate to tell the sheikh who she, and they, really were; but she was seated next to Ned, and she had a wholesome fear of both his strength and his resolve; she had seen the bodies of both her husband and his guards. The Arab women replenished the water skins, and the camels were brought forward. When they left the oasis towards dusk, they were freshly mounted and physically at ease.

'That was too easy,' Sophie said.

248

'Too easy,' Ned agreed.

They walked their camels into the darkness, Ned as usual picking out the stars to guide them in a generally easterly direction. 'You think they will follow?' Sophie asked.

'I would imagine so. Certainly when Yusuf reaches them.' He grinned at her. 'We'll soon have every sheikh in the Sahara lusting after you, madam.'

They gazed at each other both remembering that morning on the rain-soaked desert. I love you, he had said. I adore you. I have always adored you. Clay had used those very words. But Clay had turned out to have feet of clay. Perhaps that was being unfair. Perhaps he regarded this holy war in which he had become involved as being superior to any personal considerations. In which case he was still a man to respect. But not to love.

She wondered if he would accompany Yusuf in the pursuit ... and what he would do if they caught up with them?

Meanwhile, Ned. An electric spark had passed between them, born of intimacy over a long period, cemented by having killed, virtually shoulder to shoulder. That had happened between Richard and herself as well, but how long ago...

The first fingers of dawn crept out of the

desert in front of them. Lalia had already nodded off several times and jerked herself back into wakefulness just before falling from her seat. 'Do we stop now?' she asked, plaintively.

'Soon,' Ned told her.

They rode on into the morning, until the sun was well up and the heat began to penetrate. Then Ned found them a dune beneath which they could camp, at least until noon. While the women prepared breakfast, he climbed up the sand hill and peered to the west. 'Nothing there,' he said, sliding back down to join them.

'Perhaps they're not coming after us,' Sophie said.

'We have killed an Arab chieftain,' Ned said. 'Their vengeance will follow us to the end of the world.'

He had been speaking English, and Lalia was in any event nodding off and was now fast asleep and Hadija sat wrapped in her haik, staring at them. But she spoke no English. Sophie suppressed a shiver. 'I have heard how the Mad Mullah's vengeance pursued James Martingell,' she said. 'Even to the extent of kidnapping his wife and child.' She glanced at him. 'We will have to stand shoulder to shoulder, always, Ned.'

'And the major?'

Sophie bit her lip. 'I do not know.'

'Do you love him, madam?'

Sophie turned her hands outwards. 'I admired him. I still do. But–'

'Does he love you?'

She shrugged. 'Again, I do not know. He loves possession of my body.'

'Any man would wish that, madam.'

She looked up, and they stared at each other. 'Then call me Sophie,' she said.

The Survivors

'What are we going to do?' Ned asked.

'Survive,' Sophie told him. She could see no further ahead than that, at this moment. Nor did she want to. The future was a huge imponderable, both immediately and distantly. It had to be reached, step by step, stage by stage. Thus only the present mattered, so long as they kept moving forward.

Right this minute she did not even want to do that. She had never imagined that she, Sophie von Beinhardt Elligan, would ever lie naked upon the desert sand in the arms of a naked man, not having had a bath for several days, lacking make-up and with even her hair unbrushed for that time ... and be utterly happy. If that so imponderable future held even one surprise as gratifying as this one, it would be worth reaching.

The only concession to convention they had allowed had been to remove themselves some distance away from the still sleeping Lalia; Hadija, much to her disgust, had been bound hand and foot to keep her out of mischief, and left beside the tethered camels. But now that Ned was spent and she sated, the future had to be both considered and repelled. Because she had never supposed that she would ever cheat on her husband, either. However much she enjoyed flirting, however much she had enjoyed *considering* sex with Clay Andrews, she had never intended it to happen.

As for Ned ... she stroked his cheek with her finger. It was quite a while since he had shaved, and with his growth of beard and his big, bold features, he looked like an Arab himself. Then why not be an Arab? she asked herself. Both of us. We are wealthy beyond our wildest dreams, we love each other, and we are at this moment utterly free. We could live this life forever.

He grinned at her, took her fingers into his mouth to give them a quick suck. He was so gentle. So big, so strong and so gentle. But so ruthlessly violent, too, when he had to be. It was a combination she admired and wanted in her man. 'Better move round the other side of the dune,' he said, standing up to gather his clothes. As he did so, a shot rang out.

Ned spun round and fell to the sand.

'Ned!' Sophie screamed. But there was only a little blood and a moment later he raised his head.

'Shit!' Relieved, Sophie rolled over just in time, for another shot rang out and sand puffed where she had been lying. But in rolling over she had come into contact with her rifle, which she now aimed and fired at the dune from whence the shooting seemed to have come.

Ned also returned fire while gathering up their clothes. The shooting had by now awakened Lalia, who went into one of her monumental screaming fits. Hadija was also shouting in some dialect of her own. 'Round the dune,' Ned bellowed at Lalia, running to unhobble the camels.

Sophie meanwhile emptied her rifle at the dune and grabbed another clip of cartridges from her haversack. Oddly, there had been no more shots from the rise. 'Do you think we got him?' she gasped, still watching the sandhill, while Lalia's screams subsided and Ned led the camels round the hillock. He had left the outraged and still yelling Hadija on the ground. Now Sophie joined them.

'Could be,' he said. 'You'd better get dressed.' Lalia was staring at both of them, just realising what they must have been doing.

'Are you hurt bad?'

'Just a scratch,' he assured her. 'I went down by reflex action.'

'Thank God for that.' Sophie used one of her shirts to bind up the gash in his arm, then pulled on her clothes, strapped her topee under her chin, and felt a good deal better. Ned also dressed and climbed up the dune the better to see.

'One man,' he said. 'Riding off as fast as he can.'

'A bandit?' Sophie asked.

'I don't think so. He was sent to find us and chanced his arm. His main body can't be too far behind.' He chewed his lip. The idea of making a forced march in the mid-day heat was not appealing, but they were in an indefensible position if there were sufficient pursuers to outflank them. 'We have to go.'

They released Hadija, who went into her usual 'I shall watch you die' routine, mounted and set off again, but the false suggestion of security they had briefly enjoyed had quite gone. Now they constantly looked over their shoulders, only too aware that their tracks would be simple to follow, and that they would have to stop and rest at some time. The sun beat down on them with relentless force. Oh to have another rainstorm, Sophie thought – and she had never supposed she would ever wish that again, as long as she lived.

Ned kept searching for something to help them, as they left the patch of sandy desert and started moving over stony ground, but it was dusk before he located a steep-sided wadi some distance to their left. He led them to this and they hobbled the camels in the shelter of the high sides which rose some eight feet above the dry river bed. 'Here we stand,' he told them.

Lalia gaped at him and Hadija cursed him. 'Can we?' Sophie asked.

'I don't know,' Ned said, unpacking the various bundles. 'We have four rifles and two revolvers. We have about seventy rifle cartridges left, and thirty revolver. All depends on how big a force is behind us. But if, as I suspect, there aren't more than a score of them, we have the firepower to deal with them.' Sophie licked her lips. 'What you need to bear in mind,' Ned said, 'is that we must shoot to kill, and we must not waste any of the cartridges. No aimless banging away. Right?'

'Right,' Sophie said. 'Are we going to give her one?' Lalia continued to look from one to the other, trying to understand what they were saying.

'I don't think there is any point,' Ned said. 'She'd just waste our bullets. Sophie...' he touched the revolver in her belt, 'you must be very sure about this. If I get hit too badly to continue, you must shoot me. I will do the same to you. And if we are clearly beaten, you must shoot yourself. Under no circumstances must you let yourself be taken alive.'

Sophie nodded. 'I love you,' she said. 'If we die, we die together.'

The night drifted slowly by. They slept in

turns, huddled beneath their blankets, for it became very cold; even Hadija, once again tied up, subsided. The only sound was the stamping and grunting of the camels, until just before dawn a wind sprang up and whistled across the desert. Sophie supposed it was the longest night of her life, and there had been some pretty hairy nights in Afghanistan and China.

She awoke with a start as Ned touched her arm, and she realised it was just before dawn. He gave her some dates to eat. Lalia was also awake; they could hear her teeth chattering, but that might have been the cold. Hadija was silent, but they fed her as well, and gave her water to drink.

Sophie drank some water and watched Ned climbing up the side of the wadi. She realised that he had made them each an embrasure, and even a firing step, cut out of the hardpacked dry earth with his knife. 'Nothing yet,' he said.

'How long do we wait?'

'All today. If there is a pursuing party to which that fellow belonged, they can't be more than twenty-four hours behind us. If they haven't turned up by tonight, then we'll assume he was on his own.'

She stood on the little ledge beside him, her rifle resting in the earth embrasure. The other two rifles were upright beside them, together with the bandoliers of cartridges.

Lalia remained in the bottom of the wadi, close to the camels and the saddlebags containing the coins and jewels. Over a hundred thousand pounds worth, Sophie thought. The future of the House of Beinhardt, and the house of Elligan, waiting on the next few hours. 'There,' Ned said.

Sophie's head jerked. She squinted into the morning and saw the line of camels topping the last rise behind them. 'Fourteen,' Ned said, with some satisfaction.

'Who do you think they are?' Sophie asked. 'From that village, or from Tamanrasset?'

'I would say Tamanrasset, after a stop at the village,' Ned said. 'Not that I can recognise any of them beneath their burnous.'

'What do we do?'

Ned continued to study the camels, which had now stopped to let one of their riders dismount and inspect the ground. 'They have our trail,' he said. 'So they will come directly to us. Now, Sophie, we must drop as many as we can in the first volley. Are you ready?'

'I am ready.'

'Take numbers two, four, six, eight, if you can,' Ned said.

Sophie levelled her rifle, watched the tracker remount, and the column turn towards the wadi, as indicated by the tracks. 'Now,' Ned said, and squeezed his trigger.

Sophie fired as well. Number two threw up his arms and tumbled from his camel. Number four also fell, but she wasn't sure if she had hit him or if he had jumped down. Number six she was sure she had hit. Number eight was already dismounted and taking cover. The wadi reverberated with the sounds of the shots, and Lalia commenced to wail.

Sophie sent another shot towards the pursuers, but by now they were all dismounted and behind the hill. Then her trigger clicked and Ned pressed a fresh clip of cartridges into her hand. She peered across the little valley between the wadi and the hillock. Three men lay on the ground, not moving. The rest had gained cover by retreating to the hillock, but she was sure a couple of them had also been hit. The camels ranged to and fro, bellowing and kicking.

Lalia was making a moaning sound, while Hadija might have been growling. 'Not so good,' Ned muttered.

'They can't get at us,' Sophie said. 'Can they?'

'They can pin us down and send back for reinforcements.'

'That could take days. We could escape tonight.'

'And go how far? If they were to catch us in the open desert...' He chewed his lip. 'We have to carry the fight to them.'

'How?'

He was still examining the ground. 'Can you hold here?'

'For a little while, I should think.'

He nodded. 'Just a little while. I am going to go up the wadi. It bends towards the hillock just over there. If I can get there I can enfilade their position. Don't worry, I'll have them, and you, in my sights all the time, and if they try to charge you I'll bring them down.' He grinned at her. 'So will you, right?'

'Right,' Sophie said. 'Ned ... take care.'

He winked, but before he could move there came a shout. 'Sophie! Sophie, are you there?'

'Bloody Andrews,' Ned muttered. 'At least we know who to aim at.'

Sophie said nothing. After all that intimacy, a death in the desert, for one or the other. Maybe both.

'Sophie!' Clay shouted. 'This is madness. You are going to be killed. Listen to me. Surrender, and I believe I can save your life.'

'Keep him talking,' Ned said, and crawled away from her.

'Sophie!'

'How do you propose to do that, Clay?' she called.

'If you surrender to me, I will hand you over to the French authorities. You will be charged with murder, but I believe you can present a case for self-defence.'

'And then what?' Sophie called.

'You will be sent to prison.'

'For how long?'

'I don't know. It'll be some years. But it is better than being dead.'

'I think I'll take my chances here,' Sophie said.

Ned was now out of sight, having rounded the bend in the wadi. And now the sun was high behind her, the heat bouncing on her back and her head; she had taken off her topee so as to present less of a target. There were a few minutes' silence, then suddenly a shot rang out. Earth spurted from the lip of the wadi and the shot was immediately followed by several more. Sophie kept her head down; they had nothing to shoot at, unless and until they stood up to see if she had been hit.

Minutes passed and she cautiously raised her head again. Presumably red hair stood out against the desert colours, for immediately there were several more shots to send her down again, face pressed into the earth. 'Aaiaiai,' Lalia howled.

Hadija was also shouting, but Sophie couldn't make out what she was saying.

The sounds of the shots drifted away. Most of the pursuing camels had by now also withdrawn behind the ridge, while their own camels continued to snort and stamp, agitated by the shooting.

'Sophie!' Clay called. She didn't reply, but cautiously eased her head up again to look. 'Are you hit, Sophie?'

He was standing up, with two other men. Sophie took a deep breath, and her fingers curled round her trigger. 'It is a trap!' Hadija shouted.

Sophie half turned and Ned fired before she could. One of the Arabs collapsed, and Clay and the other one promptly disappeared. But their companions immediately returned fire, and to her horror Sophie heard a shout of pain from Ned followed by a clatter. Oh, my God! she thought; he's been hit. Again!

If I am killed, he had said, you must shoot yourself. But he need not have been killed, merely wounded. Ned, bleeding to death only a few yards away.

She had to go to him. She gazed at Hadija, tempted to shoot her there and then, pulled down her rifle; the movement was rewarded with another flurry of shots, this time directed at her. She ducked against the side of the wadi as bullets flailed around her, and to her consternation saw that one of their camels had been hit. It went down with a huge roaring, and its companions began rearing and snapping even more. Lalia was now screaming at the top of her lungs.

Sophie decided Ned was more important than executing Hadija, made to move along the wadi to his aid, and heard shouts. She swung back again, bringing up her rifle, and saw the Arabs – there were several of them – running across the dip at her. She threw herself back at the embrasure and emptied her magazine, but she was in too much of a hurry to aim properly and only one fell. Then the others were upon her, leaping down into the wadi, swinging their rifles. They had obviously been told to take her alive.

But she couldn't permit that. She threw her rifle at the nearest man, drew her revolver and had it struck from her grasp. She panted and tried to turn, but was held round the waist by another of the men. A third grasped her legs and swung them from the ground, then they all dropped her. She went down with a crash on her back and stared up at them, utterly winded. One of them placed his booted foot on her chest, lightly, but with the threat of squeezing all the breath from her lungs were he to exert pressure.

Wasn't that the best thing, to end it all as quickly as possible? Sophie tried to sit up and to her surprise the man moved his foot. She looked left and right. There were six men standing around her; two more had seized Lalia, who had stopped screaming and was panting in terror. Another shot the wounded camel.

And standing above them, on the edge of the wadi, was Clay, his burnous thrown back. 'Silly girl,' he said. 'I do not know if I can help you, now. Bind them,' he told his people. 'And go finish the Englishman.'

'Cut me free,' Hadija shouted.

Clay nodded to another of his men, then towards Sophie. She was dragged to her feet, her hands pulled behind her back and her wrists bound together. The same was done to Lalia who was now weeping.

The men used their opportunity to squeeze their breasts and their buttocks, and pull Sophie's hair which was now entirely loose. She refused to say a word or utter a protest. If Ned was dead, or about to be killed, then she had nothing more to live for anyway.

They chattered amongst each other as Clay slid down the side of the wadi to stand before her. She could not entirely catch the gist of what they were saying, but Clay interpreted. 'My men are saying that as you are going to be executed anyway, I should give you to them now. They are very angry about their comrades who you have killed.'

Sophie merely stared at him. Hadija had joined them, shouting at them and waving her arms. 'And she wants you all to herself,' Clay said. 'Should she not have you, as you murdered her husband?'

Still Sophie refused to speak. 'Or perhaps I should take you myself,' he said. 'I've been looking forward to that for a very long time. You're quite a little prick-tease, aren't you.'

Still she stared at him. Again the Arabs chattered at him and this time he nodded. 'I have told them they can have the Italian woman,' he said. 'She is only a Benghazi whore, anyway.'

The Arabs surrounded Lalia and commenced stripping her. Lalia gave a couple of her shrieks, then subsided into giggles as she realised what they were after. 'Do you wish to watch?' Clay asked.

He was clearly very angry with her, but Sophie could also tell that he remained deeply in love with her, and that he was innately too much of a gentleman either to assault her or abuse her. 'No,' she said.

'The gold,' Hadija said, coming up to them. 'It is in the saddlebags. It is my gold.'

'It is your husband's gold,' Clay told her. 'It is up to the elders to decide who it belongs to.'

'The elders,' she sneered.

'We will take it, and you, back to Tamanrasset,' Clay said.

'And her?'

'Her too. But first she will come with me.' He swept Sophie from the ground and climbed up the side of the wadi, then set her on her feet again.

The two men he had sent along the wadi came back, and this time Sophie could understand them. 'The infidel is not there, effendi.'

'Not there?'

'There is blood and a rifle. But the man is not there.'

'That is impossible. Watch her.'

Clay ran along the side of the wadi for some thirty yards, then checked. The Arabs were indeed watching Sophie, appreciatively, while their companions took turns at raping Lalia. Not that they were encountering any resistance. Ned! He hadn't been killed. But...

Clay came back. 'He's left a very clear trail. He's crawled away up the wadi. But he's hit. There's blood everywhere. You!' he bawled at two of the Arabs who had already satisfied themselves on Lalia. 'Go find that infidel. Kill him.'

'No,' Sophie said. Clay turned his head. 'Please,' Sophie said.

'Is he your lover?'

Sophie tossed her head. 'No,' she lied. 'But he has been a most faithful servant. Whatever he has done is because I have told him to. Let him go.'

'Tell me why I should do this?'

'If you do...' she took a deep breath, 'I will give you what you want.'

'Freely and willingly?'

'Freely and willingly.'

He considered her for several seconds, then nodded. 'I will accept that, Sophie.' He spoke to his people who had now finished with Lalia. Lalia lay on the ground in a state of naked exhaustion; her back was scarred by the sand and the stones into which it had been ground, but then so were her face and knees. Hadija squatted beside the camels and the money. The Arabs started digging graves for their dead.

Sophie knelt beside Lalia. 'I am sorry,' she said in her limited Arabic.

'They did not take *you*,' Lalia hissed.

'That is coming later,' Sophie said.

Clay had been investigating the camels and the saddlebags. 'Are you really going to return that money to the sheikh?' Sophie asked. 'Or to her?'

He glanced at her. 'The sheikh has no use for it, where you put him. As for Hadija, she will have to put in a claim. And this would buy an awful lot of guns.'

'That is owed to my father in payment for the guns you already have,' Sophie said.

'Now, don't start that again,' Clay said. 'We shall see.'

More orders and the Arabs brought their own camels forward.

'We shall camp here for tonight,' Clay said.

The camp was pitched in the shelter of the wadi. Tents were erected, food was cooked. Lalia was allowed to dress. Clay took the heavy saddlebags from the camels and placed them inside the tent he intended to share with Sophie. Hadija protested, but he told her it was for all of their safety. 'You do not trust your own men?' Sophie asked innocently.

'I doubt there is a man in the world can be trusted with a hundred thousand pounds in gold,' Clay said, realistically. He was in no hurry to get his hands on her. Well, she supposed there was no reason for him to hurry as it was going to happen anyway. But she continued to suspect that while he wanted her, desperately, he needed to work himself up to it, as even if she submitted wholly as part of their bargain, it would still be at least psychological rape.

Then what of her? With Ned gone, she wanted only to curl up and weep herself to death. There was no ounce of fight left in her system, mind or body. Yet she would go through the motions and fulfil her part of the bargain. Because she had always suspected this situation was going to arise, and now at least she need feel no guilt? Or because she still had a yen for this man? Her enemy. Who was going to take her back to at least a long prison sentence, even if he saved her from the guillotine.

The Arabs lit a fire and ate some dates washed down with water; there was nothing else. And all the while he stared at her, while his men chattered noisily, and slapped Lalia on the shoulder, and told her they would have her again that night. This did not seem to be unduly worrying for the half-caste girl.

By the time the meal had ended it was dark; there was no moon but in the clear sky the stars twinkled. 'It'll be a cold night,' Clay said and stood up.

Sophie got up also. The Arabs shouted encouragingly at their leader and Clay stood aside to allow Sophie to walk before him to enter the tent. Once inside, she sank to her knees as there was not a lot of headroom. Clay knelt beside her. 'Would you believe that I feel like a bride?' she asked.

'And I feel like a groom. We've covered a lot of mileage, time and distance, to come to this.'

'I'm afraid it's a few days since I had a bath,' she said.

'It's a few *years* since I have had a woman,' he pointed out. 'And over the past few months I only ever wanted it to be you.'

'Ah,' she said. 'Well...' She unbuttoned her shirt.

'Are you in a hurry?' he asked.

Sophie checked, gazing at him. It was dark in the tent, the only light the reflected glow of the fire. 'I got the impression you might be.'

He held her shoulders and gently laid her on her back, then lay beside her, on his elbow, slowly lowering his mouth to hers. 'Would you believe that I would like it to be romantic?' he asked.

'I promised to be whatever you wish,' she said. 'But you know—'

'I know. You have just lost an old and valued friend, and you face a bleak future. I would help you if I could, Sophie. But my life is dedicated to helping the Senussi gain their independence. If I were to let you go, I would be no more use to them, and I would have betrayed a sacred trust. Why did you have to kill the sheikh?'

'He was trying to rape me.'

'And you are a woman who reacts violently to mistreatment. But I am about to rape you.'

'We made a deal,' she said.

'Yes,' he said, thoughtfully. Slowly, almost reluctantly, he released the rest of her buttons and pulled her shirt apart. She had long given up wearing any underclothes in the desert heat, save for a pair of drawers. Gently he circled her nipples with his forefinger. 'You are so utterly beautiful,' he said. 'One is almost afraid to touch you, in case you splinter into a thousand pieces. But in reality, you're as tough as old nails, aren't you?'

'You would have to ask the sheikh that,' she said, with a lightness she did not feel.

'Or Ned Carew?' Suddenly his hand slid up to her neck. He could, after all, feel passion and jealousy.

'Or Ned Carew,' she said, as coolly as she could. He kissed her again, his hand still on her neck. And now there was real passion. His hand slipped down to caress her breasts, and then further, to fumble at her belt. Sophie let him get on with it; his bringing up the subject of Ned had quite ended her interest in what was happening.

There was an unearthly scream ringing through the night. Clay rolled off Sophie and sat up as the night became filled with explosions. Then another scream, this time from Lalia ... but it was not a scream of terror, rather of defiant exultation. 'That bitch!' Clay scrambled to his feet, reaching for his revolver holster and drawing the gun.

Sophie threw both arms round his legs and brought him down in a rugby tackle. He struck the ground heavily and the revolver flew away. Sophie scrabbled after it and reached it, rolling on her back to aim it at him. He had regained his knees and now he glared at her, while outside the tent the sound of shooting ended, leaving only the shouts of Lalia and the cries of dead or dying men. Then the flap of the tent was lifted and Ned stood there.

Sophie gasped in consternation, for Ned was shirtless and his left arm was bound up in a bloody rag. But he carried both a rifle in his right hand and a revolver thrust into his belt, and the rifle was pointing at Clay. 'No!' Sophie shouted.

Ned hesitated. 'Ned,' she said. 'Oh, Ned. Are you all right?'

'I'm alive,' Ned said. 'What has this bastard done to you?'

'Nothing,' Sophie said, thrusting the revolver into her own belt to refasten her shirt. 'Those Arabs–'

'I took them by surprise,' Ned said. 'And Lalia helped.'

'You go outside,' Sophie told Clay.

It was his turn to hesitate, looking from her to Ned and back again. But he knew that it was the two of them who had destroyed Sheikh al-Fadl's household; he could not doubt their ruthlessness. Slowly he got up. Ned stepped aside, still keeping him covered, and he went outside. Sophie followed. 'Oh, Ned,' she said. 'Are you really all right?'

'Yes,' he said, and put his arm round her to give her a squeeze.

Sophie looked at a scene of utter devastation. One of the Arabs had had his throat cut, another had been knifed in the back and was also dead. Four had been shot at close range and were sprawled about the wadi in the obscenity of death. Hadija was also dead, knifed in the chest. 'She beat me,' Lalia said simply.

Sophie swallowed. 'The others ran off,' Ned said. 'But I don't think they'll be back for a while. As for this one–'

'Leave him,' Sophie said.

'To come after us again? Besides, after what he was doing to you–'

'He was doing nothing to me, Ned. If we take the camels, he will have to walk back to that oasis. We will leave him sufficient food and water to do that. But it will take him a couple of days and then he will have to find his way back to Tamanrasset, which will take him even longer. By the time he can mount another pursuit, we will be out of his reach.'

Ned hesitated. Clearly his instincts were to complete the job and he had never liked Clay, in any event.

'Please, Ned,' Sophie said. 'He wanted to help me.'

'Let's move out,' Ned said.

'You are condemning me to death,' Clay said.

'I don't think so,' Sophie said. 'You know the desert, and how to survive in the desert. And I am sure you will find your remaining friends, or they will find you. There is sufficient food here for you all to survive until you can regain the oasis. After that, well ... that is up to you.'

'While you will have triumphed again. As you always triumph, do you not, Sophie?'

'I must try to do so,' she pointed out. 'Well...' She held out her hand. 'As you said in the tent, we followed quite a winding path to get here. I will wish you good fortune.'

He squeezed her fingers. 'I have an idea we will meet again.'

'I would hope not,' Sophie said. 'If you have any ideas about coming after me in England, forget it. I think Ned would shoot you on sight. I might even do that myself.'

'Now, tell me what really happened out there in the desert, Colonel.' General Garzanti leaned back in his chair, while Edio stood to attention in front of the desk; his right arm was still in a sling.

'It is exactly as in my report, General,' he said. 'We destroyed the Arab caravan, and the guns, but were then overtaken by that rain storm. It was the storm caused our casualties; four men drowned. And...' he sighed, 'one woman.'

'And two trucks lost, as well as one machine-gun,' Garzanti observed. 'And that business in Tamanrasset?'

'I know nothing of that, sir.'

'The French are sure you had something to do with the sheikh's death,' Garzanti pointed out. 'They are also, of course, making political representations about your being inside French Sahara at all.'

'Yes, sir,' Edio said. 'That was bound to happen.'

'But you carried out your mission,' Garzanti said. 'I am sorry about the woman. It was unwise of you to have her with you, in any event.'

'May I ask what happens now, sir?'

'Oh, we are not going to throw you to the wolves, Rometti. But I think it would be best for you to leave Libya for a while. You are being transferred to Somaliland.'

Edio's mouth fell open, and was snapped shut again. 'Eritrea?'

'That is the northern half of the colony. But you will go to Somaliland proper.'

'But, with respect, General, that is–'

'Behind God's back?' Garzanti smiled. 'It is not the most salubrious place on earth. And very hot. I am told it is even hotter than the desert. However, it is one of our colonies, and it must be garrisoned.'

'You promised me promotion, General, if my mission was successfully carried out.'

'The success, or failure, of your mission is presently being evaluated, Colonel. You will be informed of that evaluation in due course.'

'And meanwhile, Somalia,' Edio said. 'I feel I must register a protest, General. You are sending me virtually to a prison, with no prospect of promotion.'

Garzanti tapped his nose. 'You are a confounded pessimist, Rometti. I am sending you to a theatre where there will be every opportunity for advancement within a very few years.' Edio frowned. 'I am sure you know what happened to General Baratieri's army, in Ethiopia, in 1896,' Garzanti said.

Edio's frown deepened. 'General Baratieri's army was defeated at Adowa in 1896 by the Ethiopians. There was a massacre.'

'That is true. We have never forgotten that, Rometti. What we have lacked are leaders strong-willed enough to avenge that defeat. Well, now we have as leader a man with the strongest will in the world. It is just a matter of time. And when we seek that revenge, Rometti, you will be there, commanding a brigade against those savages. It will be your greatest opportunity for glory.'

Edio's forehead cleared. 'Yes, General. Thank you for telling me this.'

'Very good. You will hand over your command in the meantime to Captain Castelfiardo, and leave immediately.'

Edio saluted and turned to the door, then checked, and turned back again. 'And the Senussi?'

'Ah, the Senussi. Well, we shall have to wait and see. But if you really did destroy that arms shipment, I doubt we shall have many more problems with them.'

The sheikhs sat around the fire and drank coffee. 'That woman is a fiend,' Yusuf said. 'And now she has got away.'

'We do not know that,' said the man sitting beside him. 'She could have perished in the desert. Together with her servant.'

'She has not perished in the desert,' Clay said.

'You know this?' asked another of the sheikhs.

'I am very sure of it,' Clay said. 'But there is nothing to be done about her now. It is what we do next against the Italians that is important.'

'There is nothing we can do against the Italians,' Yusuf said sadly. 'Without guns, we can do nothing. The old men are saying that we must seek peace.'

'Peace?' asked the man beside him. 'With the Italians? Why can we not buy more guns?'

'Because Sheikh al-Fadl is dead,' Yusuf said. 'And his money has been stolen.'

'Sheikh al-Fadl is not the only supporter we have,' someone suggested.

'He was the only one wealthy enough to buy guns for us,' Yusuf said. 'It is over, my friends. We have been defeated.' He snorted. 'By a woman!'

'We will track her down,' someone said. 'And we will avenge the sheikh. And our cause.' He looked at Clay. 'You will do this thing.'

'Ah ... no,' Clay said.

'You will not help us avenge the sheikh?'

'The sheikh was attempting to violate Mrs Elligan,' Clay said. Beards were pulled. Was this not a man's, certainly a sheikh's, prerogative? 'In addition, Mrs Elligan had my life in her hands, and she gave it to me,' Clay went on. 'If you wish to go on fighting, I will stay and fight with you. If you can raise the money to buy more guns, I will attempt to negotiate for you. But I will not commit murder for you.'

The Arabs muttered and Clay got up and left them to it. Yusuf followed him. 'I have said, we must make peace, because we no longer have the means to make war,' he said. 'I believe it will be possible for us to negotiate a reasonable peace, which will allow us to resume our lives, as long as we accept the Italians as masters. That is a bitter pill for us to swallow, but if that is how it is written, that is how it shall be.'

Clay nodded. 'I understand. And I know just how bitter you must feel.'

'It is my duty,' Yusuf said, 'to hunt that woman down, if it takes for the rest of my life, and destroy her. It is my duty to hear her scream for the death of my uncle.'

Clay swallowed. 'I understand this. You must forgive my refusal to take part in it.'

278

'I understand that this is not your way, Clay. But it is the way of my people. What will you do now?'

Clay considered for a moment. 'I think I will go home,' he said.

'To America? You will stop fighting?'

Clay shrugged. 'I can't fight if there is no war, can I? But ... maybe there'll be another war, soon enough.' He grinned. 'I'll keep my eyes open.'

'There is a gentleman to see you, sir,' Elsie said, presenting the silver tray with the card on it. Richard Elligan looked up from the book he was reading. His leg was now all but mended and on Dr Plummer's recommendation he was taking long walks every morning to strengthen the recently knitted bones, but after the months in bed it was still an exhausting business and he had just returned from a hike to sit down with a glass of sherry.

He took the card from Elsie's tray; she was doing her best to fill in for Ned Carew as both maid and butler. 'Walter Pemberton. Now, I have heard that name before. Show him in, Elsie.'

Elsie hurried to the door of the study and opened it to admit Pemberton.

'Richard Elligan? We've never actually met. But I helped your good lady when she had a spot of bother a few months ago.'

Richard stood up and shook hands. 'Of course. I remember. I never had the opportunity to thank you. She said you were at school with me.'

'Well...' Pemberton flushed, 'I may have been mistaken.'

'One often is. Sherry?'

'Thank you.' Pemberton waited while the drink was poured, sipped. 'Your wife not here?'

Richard gestured him to a chair. 'Now, I think you know that she is not, Mr Pemberton.'

'One tries to keep informed,' Pemberton agreed. 'May I ask when last you heard from your wife?'

'I last heard from her four months ago, Mr Pemberton. She was taking an ocean cruise, and since then has been out of touch.'

'What you mean is, sir, that you last heard from her on board the steamer *Bremerhaven*, probably from the port of Boujdour, in Spanish Morocco.'

Richard gazed at him. 'And since then, nothing,' Pemberton went on. 'As I imagine her message informed you that she was going off into the desert... Four months. Are you not worried?'

'You seem to know a hell of a lot about our affairs, Mr Pemberton.'

'As I said, sir, one tries to keep informed. *Are* you worried, sir?'

'Of course I'm worried,' Richard snapped. 'On the other hand, Sophie is very capable of taking care of herself and her message informed me that she would be out of touch for at least two months.'

'But not four,' Pemberton pointed out.

'If you have something to say, Mr Pemberton, I suggest you get on and say it.'

'Well, sir, far be it from me to be the bearer of bad news, but–'

Richard frowned. 'Just what do you know of her?'

'We try to keep in touch with events that may be of interest to us, sir. There have been some very odd events in the southern Sahara recently. Firstly, there is a report that an Italian force was actually in the French Sahara, west of the Hoggar. That has caused quite a furore in Franco-Italian diplomatic circles.'

'How does that affect my wife?' Richard asked, continuing to pretend ignorance.

'Well, sir, the rumour is that the Italians were after a shipment of guns being delivered to the Senussi, for use against the Italians. Our information is that the caravan transporting the guns was wiped out...' Richard sat up straight. 'The destruction was completed by a rainstorm. As you probably know, sir, while it is very unusual for there to be heavy rain in the desert, when there is the results can be devastating.'

'I know that,' Richard muttered.

'Of course, we have no positive information as to who was accompanying the caravan. But there is talk that there were Europeans involved and that one of them was a woman.'

He stared at Richard and Richard stared back. 'You say the caravan was completely wiped out?' Richard asked.

'That is our understanding,' Pemberton said.

'Just who are you, anyway?'

'Ah, didn't I say? My card.'

It merely read, Foreign Office.

'I really am sorry to be the bearer of such dismal news, Mr Elligan.'

'Look,' Richard said. 'Get out.'

Richard poured himself a whisky and soda, and sipped it while he stared at the wall. Sophie, dead? He found that difficult to credit. Sophie had always seemed indestructible. But the most indestructible of women could not be expected to take on the Italian Army and a desert rain storm with any hope of success. Sophie, he thought. Gone. And with her, a hundred and twenty-five thousand pounds, the money that had been going to put them back on their feet, financially.

Was that an unworthy thought compared with her death? And he had not given a thought to Ned who would have died at her side.

He had felt from the beginning that this venture would turn out badly. But she had been so determined, so excited at the prospect of an adventure where she would be the principal ... He wondered if Andrews had gone as well. And if they had had an affair in the desert before catastrophe struck?

He had been furious when he had received the letter from Captain Pfuhl. She had just taken off, on her own, with Ned, to be sure of the money? Or to be with Andrews? Something else he had suspected from the beginning. Well, she had got more than she had bargained for. Was that any way to think of his wife?

But he found himself thinking more of the money.

He did not feel like facing the Beinhardts, so instead, when three more months had passed with no word, he wrote to Claus, telling him what Pemberton had told him. As nearly a year had past since Sophie had set off from Boujdour, there was no reason to suppose Pemberton had not been right. Surely she would have contacted him by now had she been alive. Predictably, their reply was bitter. They had been against Sophie taking such a risk from the beginning, Claus von Beinhardt insisted. He laid the blame for the entire tragedy on Richard and considered their partnership at an end.

It was all very well for him, Richard thought; he had the original hundred and twenty-five thousand pounds. A good part of that would be needed to pay for the actual armaments, but as much of the goods had been out of stock he would still make a profit. The real profit was buried in the Sahara, with Sophie.

While for him ... Richard now was as fit as ever in his life, his leg entirely mended although it gave him twinges when it rained. Yet he was not going to starve; his inheritance remained sufficient for him to live a very quiet life. But what was he going to do with that life? He was an arms dealer without any supply. He was also a man without a woman.

'You don't reckon the mistress will be coming back?' Elsie asked.

'No, I don't.'

'Or Ned?'

'Or Ned. It's just you and me, Elsie.'

Elsie giggled. But there was no prospect there. Apart from the giggle, Elsie was overweight and unattractive. However, he did need a woman. Yet Sophie, if considered dead by the Foreign Office, would not be officially dead until her body was produced ... or seven years had elapsed.

He walked the dogs over the open land behind the house. Even they, however fond of him, were really Sophie's. He came home, poured himself a sherry, settled down with the newspaper, flicked the pages, and paused in consternation.

Hearing Today, said the headline. *The appeal against the conviction of Lady Anne Martingell for the murder of her son will be reopened today, in the light of fresh evidence obtained by her solicitors. Lady Martingell, the widow of the famous gunrunner James Martingell, was found guilty of the murder of her son Winston at Bristol Crown Court six years ago, and was sentenced to life imprisonment. She always maintained that she had shot Winston Pennyfeather in self-defence, and the case against her rested on the evidence given by the third party present, Lady Martingell's maid Claudette d'Mettre. Now it would appear that Mademoiselle d'Mettre has, on her deathbed, retracted her evidence, and there is some hope that Lady Martingell may be released after four years of false imprisonment. The appeal will be heard at the Central Criminal Court, London.*

Richard stood up. Anne Martingell. Anne would be ... around fifty, he supposed. Ten years his senior. Yet he could still remember that tumultuous afternoon they had spent together in the Savoy Hotel, an afternoon more stimulating than any even he had ever known. An afternoon that had coloured his entire life!

He strode into the pantry.

'Elsie,' he said. 'I am going up to London.'

PART THREE

The Revenge

I will most horribly revenge.
William Shakespeare

The Return

Having knocked on the door, Sophie found herself drawing deep breaths as she waited. There had been times over the past four years when she had doubted she would ever stand here again – there had been times when she had doubted she would ever wish to stand here again. But it was time to pick up the threads of her civilised life again. Supposing she could.

She was beginning to doubt it was possible, at least here in Germany, the new Germany, the Germany of 1934, so entirely different to that of 1930. Had she not seen some of it with her own eyes, she would not have believed it possible that a nation could have changed so much, so rapidly, from a continuous, insecure semi-hysteria to a disciplined and fervent belief in itself – but a discipline and a belief that was created, she was sure, by fear. The door opened, and a maid stood there, very prim in a black dress over which she wore a starched white pinafore, with a matching cap. 'Is Count von Beinhardt in?' Sophie asked.

'The Count is at his office, Fraulein.'

Now, how did she guess I am not married?

289

Sophie wondered. She had never seen the woman before.

'Well, then is the Countess in?' she persisted patiently. The maid looked her up and down. She would not be sure of what she was seeing, Sophie knew. A tall, strongly built woman, with auburn hair worn long, although presently pinned up, with a fair complexion heavily freckled, with strong, handsome features – there would be something familiar about those. And with eyes it was difficult for the maid to meet. There were eyes that had looked on too much catastrophe, but at the same time sufficient triumphs as well to make them glow like emeralds. 'Who shall I say is calling, Fraulein?'

'Tell her Sophie.'

The maid caught her breath. She would have heard the missing daughter spoken of. Now she held the door wide. 'Will you not come in?'

'Thank you.' Sophie stepped past her into that so well-remembered drawing room.

The maid hurried to an interior doorway guarded by a curtain, while Sophie drew off her gloves and looked around her. Most of the furniture she recognised. But she would never have expected to see a large framed photograph of Chancellor Hitler over the mantelpiece. 'Sophie?'

Sophie turned at the almost whispered

name. For all her adventures of the past four years, she supposed she could not have changed as much as her mother. Always plump, Clementine von Beinhardt had ballooned into a grotesque caricature of a woman. Now she charged forward like a tank. 'Sophie! My God! We thought you were dead. We knew you were dead. You had to be dead! Richard told us you were dead. Oh, Sophie!'

Sophie allowed herself to be embraced and hugged her mother in return. 'But as you see, Mama, I am not dead.'

'But–' Clementine held her away, to look at her face, then at her clothes, the very latest Paris fashions, from her elegant cloth coat with its huge fur collar, to her printed georgette dress, now revealed as she threw the coat open, to her neat hat and her black suede shoes and handbag. 'Where have you *been?* Four years! You went off into the desert and I did not know. When Claus told me I nearly had a seizure. Oh, Sophie–'

Sophie held her hands and guided her to the settee before she had another seizure. 'I have been adventuring. I am sorry I have been unable to get in touch with you before. It was just not possible.' She simply had not wanted to, until she and Ned had sorted out their affairs and determined exactly what they wished to do with the rest of their lives.

'But...' Clementine was panting. 'You have

to tell me everything.'

'I will tell you everything,' Sophie said. 'But when Papa gets home.'

Claus was no less astonished than his wife when he arrived home to find Sophie in their midst. 'My dear girl,' he cried, embracing her again and again. 'My dear, dear girl.'

Then they listened, far into the night, while Sophie told them as much of her adventures over the past four years as she felt they were entitled to know. 'But ... four years?' Clementine asked.

'Well, there was a lot to do. First we had to escape all those people who were after us. Principally the Senussi and the French. The French could not of course pursue us into Italian territory, but they kept making representations to the Italian Government in Benghazi to find us and have us arrested.'

'For running guns,' Claus said thoughtfully. 'But ... you were not running guns to any enemies of the French.'

'That is true,' Sophie admitted. 'But it was necessary for us to escape from Tamanrasset, and I am afraid a few people got killed.'

'Oh, Sophie!' Clementine exclaimed. Even if she knew all about the Afghanistan adventure, she refused to admit even to herself that she had a daughter who had killed someone, much less someones.

'It was necessary, Mama. Anyway, we did eventually get to Egypt, but then it was necessary to keep a very low profile.'

'Don't tell me the British were after you as well?' Claus inquired.

'I don't think they were. As far as the French were aware, we were Germans. And the Italians were keeping a low profile because of their invasion of French territory; their pretence was that we did not exist and had never existed. But you see, we had to get rid of the money.'

'Money? You mean you obtained the final payment?'

'Of course,' Sophie said. 'But it was in coins and jewels. We had to be very careful.'

'So what did you do?'

'Well, we sold the jewels, piece by piece. To do this and not arouse too much interest in who we were and where we had come from, it was necessary to move about Egypt, even down into the Sudan and as far as Abyssinia.'

'You have been to Abyssinia?'

'Oh, yes,' Sophie said. 'I'm afraid we did get cheated over the jewels, almost universally, but we simply had to have cash. And anyway, there was so much–'

'How much?' her father asked.

'Then when we had the cash,' Sophie went on, ignoring the question, 'we had to deposit it in various banks. As it was all in different currencies, this took us some time. But we managed it. Some is in Khartoum, some is in Cairo, some is in Alexandria, some is in Malta, and some we actually brought into France and it is on deposit there.'

'How much did you get?' Claus asked again.

'We will discuss that,' Sophie said.

'But you say it is all in various bank accounts, held by you?'

'In the joint names of me and my partner, yes.'

'Ah. Yes, you keep saying we. Who is this partner?'

'The man who helped me to escape from the Arabs. He is no one you have ever met.'

'You are speaking of the American, Andrews?'

'No,' Sophie said. 'I am not speaking of the American.'

'Then who?'

'As I said, it is no one you have ever met.'

'But you have given him power over our money.'

'That is something we have to discuss,' Sophie said. 'I have, if you like, given him power over me.' She gazed from face to face defiantly.

'Oh, Sophie!' Clementine wailed. 'But what of Richard?'

'I intend to go to see Richard when I leave here,' Sophie said, 'and explain the situation to him. I am sorry about this, but that is how it has worked out. Do you know how he is?'

'I have not spoken to Richard for more than two years,' Claus said. 'Nor do I ever wish to speak with him again. Our business relationship is terminated.'

It was Sophie's turn to say, 'But–'

'It was when he wrote to us to inform us that he had learned you were dead,' Clementine said. 'Oh, the wretch.'

'The whole catastrophe was his fault in the first place, allowing you to go off like that on your own,' Claus grumbled.

'Now, Papa,' Sophie said severely, 'you know it was my idea to do that.' Even if she had realised that her marriage was over, she remained very fond of Richard.

'He was your husband,' Claus said. 'He had the power to stop you, if he wished.'

'Oh, really,' Sophie commented. 'This is not 1900, you know, Papa.'

'It is still a husband's duty, and his business, to control his wife,' Claus said. 'That is how it is in the new Germany.'

Sophie looked at her mother. Who flushed. 'It is the will of our Leader, Adolf Hitler,' she explained.

'Just who is this character, anyway?' Sophie inquired.

'He is our Chancellor. He is making Germany great again,' Claus said.

'I see,' Sophie said. 'By disciplining women.'

'By disciplining the whole country,' Claus declared. 'I hope you have not come back to be a troublemaker, Sophie. The Nazis know how to deal with troublemakers.'

'I came back to see my parents,' Sophie said. 'I am not a German citizen any more. I have no intention of staying to worship at the shrine of this new god. I am leaving tomorrow.' She smiled at them. 'I hope you will not object to giving me a bed for the night?'

'The money,' Claus said at breakfast. 'You said there was a great deal of money.'

'There is some money,' Sophie said cautiously. 'I can let you have the twenty-five thousand that is outstanding.'

'Twenty-five? What is outstanding is a *hundred* and twenty-five thousand.'

'I'm afraid not,' Sophie said. 'I told you that the caravan was wiped out by a rain storm. All the guns were lost. Some were recovered, but it was a small number, and most of them were ruined by immersion in sand and water. The Senussi refused to pay the full balance and after much discussion we settled on twenty-five thousand.'

Her father glared at her. 'I could have you

296

arrested,' he said. 'I am a member of the Party. I am a personal friend of our gauleiter. I can have you sent to a camp.'

Sophie's gaze remained cool. 'I do not think that would be a very good idea, Papa,' she said. 'If you did that you would not even get the twenty-five thousand pounds, and my partner, who is beyond your reach, would make such a publicity stink that no one would ever buy your guns again.'

Claus's mouth opened and shut in frustrated anger. 'I will be leaving Germany today,' Sophie said. 'And when I reach my destination, I will send you a cheque for the money.'

'Oh, Sophie,' Clementine said. 'Won't you stay a little while? After four years—'

'I had expected a better welcome,' Sophie said.

'You mustn't let your father upset you,' Clementine said, when they were alone as Sophie packed her overnight bag. 'He is in a very upset state.'

'I should have thought he'd be pleased to get some money, even if not all of it,' Sophie said.

'Oh, he is. He will be. It is not so much the money. He is now manufacturing guns for the Reich.'

'The Reich?'

'That is what we are now called. The Third

Reich. The Third Empire.'

'Where is this empire?'

'It will happen, in the east. Herr Hitler says so.'

'Mama,' Sophie said severely. 'The age of creating empires, marching armies, is past. This Herr Hitler appears to have a screw loose.'

'Sssh,' Clementine begged. 'If Freda were to hear–'

Sophie was astonished. 'You are afraid of your own maid?'

'She is a party member,' Clementine explained. 'If she were to go to the police–'

'They would lock me up on the say so of a servant, for suggesting that Herr Hitler is a nutcase?'

'Sssh,' Clementine implored again. 'To criticise the Fuehrer is a criminal offence.'

'Then the sooner I am out of Germany the better,' Sophie said and kissed her mother. 'I'm sorry things have turned out the way they have. I will try to keep in touch in future.'

'Sophie...' Clementine caught her hands. 'Will you not stay? Germany is your home. Things will get better. And I would so like to have you with me. I get so afraid–'

'I am sorry, Mama. Germany is not my home, now. And I do not think it will ever be again. I am sorry you are afraid. As you say, perhaps things will get better.'

She had wired Ned from the station in Germany and he met her at the Gare du Lyons. 'That was a quick trip. How did it go?'

Sophie made a face. 'Worse than I had expected. One should never go home.'

He held her close. Even after four years of the most complete intimacy, he still loved to feel her against him. As she knew and enjoyed. He was in love. Well, so was she, she supposed. If she was capable of love. It could only ever be Ned, now. 'Did your father accept your offer?'

'Not exactly. But it is the only one he is going to get.'

He escorted her to a taxi, gave the name of their hotel. 'I have a pile of brochures waiting for you,' he said.

'Where?'

'Spain, Portugal.' He grinned. 'Italy.'

'And France?'

'Oh, indeed.'

'Well, Italy is obviously impossible. And Spain ... I do not like the news coming out of Spain. Anyway, a decision will have to wait until I come back from England.'

'This time I must come with you.'

She shook her head. 'Definitely not.'

'I cannot let you face him alone.'

'Do not be melodramatic. Richard is very civilised.'

'When he chooses to be. I have seen him behaving in a very uncivilised fashion. So have you.'

Sophie kissed him. 'I am neither an Afghan nor a Turk nor an Arab. Richard knows that I can behave in an uncivilised fashion as well.'

Once again, a doorstep, and a maid she had never seen before. Behind her, the taxi driver opened his newspaper; he had been told he might have a longish wait.

'Mr Elligan is out, madam. But Lady Martingell is at home. Who shall I say is calling?'

Sophie was trying to get her thoughts in order. Lady Martingell? That had to be the famous Anne! Here, with Richard? But two could play at the shocking game. 'You may say that Mrs Elligan has come home. And as it is my home, I shall come in.'

She pushed the door wider, sending the maid with it, and entered the hall. 'Mrs—' The maid was gasping. 'But ... you're dead!'

'You will shortly find out that I am very much alive,' Sophie told her, taking off her coat and gloves and handing them to her, before entering the drawing room. This was empty, but she heard steps on the stairs and returned to the doorway.

'Harriet?' a woman asked. 'What is the matter with you?' Then she looked at the doorway and Sophie. 'And who may you be?'

'You'll be Anne Martingell,' Sophie said. 'We met ... oh, fifteen years ago.'

The woman was in her middle fifties, she estimated, handsome rather than pretty, with a slender body; her reddish-brown hair, so like her own, Sophie realised, was streaked with grey, but she stood very erect, even if some of her confidence was ebbing, and she was realising who this had to be. Slowly she came down the stairs. 'So we did. You were just a girl. We were told you were dead. Richard was told you were dead by the Foreign Office.'

'Whose information is not often accurate,' Sophie said. 'May I ask where are my dogs?'

'Ah.' Anne Martingell reached the hall floor. 'I'm afraid we had them put down.'

'Put down?'

'Well, they were rather old, and ... I'm afraid they did not take to me.'

'I see,' Sophie said grimly. 'And did you also have Elsie put down?'

'Elsie gave notice,' Anne said. The two women gazed at each other. 'Richard and I have known each other a very long time,' Anne said, somewhat defensively. 'I think he knew me before he knew you.'

'And in a biblical sense,' Sophie agreed.

Anne's mouth twisted. 'He thought you were dead. When my case came up for review, following that wretched girl Claudette's withdrawal of her original evidence against me, Richard was there. When I was acquitted, he invited me down here.' She gave a little shrug. 'I had nowhere else to go.'

'I can see that. I think we could both do with a drink.' Sophie returned into the drawing room, opened the ice box, and took out a bottle of champagne. At least that hadn't changed.

Anne followed her. 'May I ask what are your intentions?'

Sophie removed the cork with a gentle plop, poured two glasses. 'You mean, do I intend to move back in? May I ask what is your situation?'

Anne licked her lips as she took the glass. 'Richard and I–'

'Are very old friends, you said.'

'Yes. We are very comfortable. But ... when he brought me here, he supposed you were dead.'

'Oh, quite. And you had nowhere else to go.' Sophie drank champagne and sat down.

Anne sat also. 'I really don't know what to say. I mean, I suppose the decision has to be Richard's.'

'Between you and me? I would have supposed the decision was mine.'

Anne's eyebrows arched. 'Our situations are strangely similar,' Sophie remarked.

'Here we are, two women, immaculately dressed, being immaculately polite, both with backgrounds of violence and sudden death. I imagine we would both say that, when we have killed, it has always been in defence of our husbands or lovers...'

Her turn to arch her eyebrows.

'I think you know too much about me, Mrs Elligan,' Anne said. 'I shot my husband to save Martingell's life, that is correct. I shot my son to save my own life. That is a terrible admission to have to make.'

'Yes,' Sophie said. 'Perhaps I am fortunate in not having a son. Believe me, I bear no grudge against you for having taken advantage of Richard's offer. Nor do I hold any grudge against Richard for making the offer, supposing as he did that I was dead. In many ways what has happened has made things easier for me. I did not come here to resume my position as Richard's wife. I think our marriage was ending even before I went to North Africa. However, we were business partners, and he is entitled to a share in the profits of our last venture.'

'You mean there are profits?'

'Indeed.' Sophie opened her handbag. 'Here is a cheque for twenty-five thousand pounds, made out to Richard Elligan. I hope he will accept it, and then our relationship can end on a happy note.'

Anne took the cheque, gazed at it. 'This is

very generous of you.'

'Not at all. It is business.'

'Where are you staying? You can, of course–' She hesitated, flushing.

'Stay here? I don't think that would be a good idea. Are any of my clothes still here?'

'Well–' Anne's flush deepened.

'Absolutely. I doubt they'd fit me now, anyway. I hope you gave them to a good cause.' Sophie finished her drink and stood up. 'My taxi is waiting.'

'Where can Richard get in touch with you?'

'I don't think that would be a good idea, either.'

'But ... he may want to.'

'I'm sorry. I still don't think it would be a good idea. Does he mean to marry you?'

'I ... we haven't discussed it.'

'Because you were both assuming it could not happen until after seven years. Well, if he does wish to marry you, Lady Martingell, tell him to put an advertisement in *The Times*. It should read, *Assistance please, Sophie*. It will have to be run for a week, I'm afraid, as I do not get the paper every day. However, if I see such an advertisement, I will provide him with the material for a divorce. Is that satisfactory?'

'Again, I feel you are being more than generous. I feel so wretched–'

'Please don't. I have enjoyed meeting you

after all these years.'

'There's just one thing...' Anne followed her to the door. 'Richard has told me that when you went off you took with you his most faithful servant, a man called Carew. I know he'd like to know what happened to Carew.'

'Ned Carew is alive and well and living in France,' Sophie told her and left her to make of that what she could.

'Would you believe it?' Sophie asked. 'The woman must be at least fifteen years older than him.'

'But they are old comrades in arms,' Ned said. 'They can share their ghosts together.'

'As can we,' she reminded him.

They sat in deck chairs on the portico of the house they had bought in the south of France; they had calculated that after four years the mysterious Europeans who had caused such havoc in Tamanrasset and then disappeared into the desert had been written off by the French authorities. Even after paying out fifty thousand pounds to their erstwhile partners they were still very wealthy people, and their tastes were not extravagant. At the moment. They had adventured for too long and too hard to wish to play very hard now. They just wanted to lie back and enjoy comfort and each other.

She found it remarkable, and delightful, the way in which they had settled into domesticity after that wild four-year-long adventure. She found it incredible that two such basically civilised human beings should ever have stood shoulder to shoulder, killing people. She wondered, with secret glee, what the kind people in the shops they used, in the bars and restaurants they patronised, and more than any of those, the gendarmes who were unfailingly polite to the wealthy Englishman named Smith and his assumed wife – Sophie still wore her wedding ring – who had come to settle in their little community on the shores of the Mediterranean, would say if they had an inkling who they really were.

But no less astonishing and delightful was the other side of Ned's personality and character that she had unearthed. She knew that she had been restlessly uncertain in her marriage to Richard, however much she had pretended at happiness. She had pursued him because of the aura of romance with which he had been surrounded, and she had enjoyed every minute of their adventuring together, however dangerously tragic some of their circumstances. But when he had intimated that for her, at least, the adventuring was done, her restlessness had grown. She knew that Clay Andrews, with his equally powerful aura of international intrigue and adventure, had strongly attracted her. She knew she had been attempting to compose herself, mentally and physically, to have an affair with the American before she had been overtaken by events. But she would have been overtaken by Ned, she supposed, even had there been no events. It had not been something that she had expected to happen. Ned had always been there, virtually unnoticed, simply for that reason. It had been pleasant to know that he adored her, and would be faithful to her, but that essential difference of background, of both class and up-bringing, not to mention experience and nationality, had made a meaningful relation-ship impossible. Or so it had seemed.

Even when *they* had been adventuring in the desert, and in Egypt and Abyssinia, with their lives entirely dependent on each other's courage and faithfulness – and she had been gloriously happy – she had refused to contemplate the future, because it had seemed so uncertain in personal terms. Yet she had marched straight at that future. Easy to say that was her way of dealing with life. But breaking with Ned had never been an option. And in return had come the slowly growing appreciation that he was not just a servant, as he had begun life, but was sufficiently well-educated to wish to know more, and sufficiently well-endowed intellectually to understand and enjoy what he was learning.

She had fallen in love, for the first time in her life. And the last, she was determined. If only she could become a mother for him. But there was yet time. She was only in her mid-thirties. Another year of total domestic bliss ...

During which they could watch the world go by. Haphazardly, to be sure, and often disturbingly. Sophie could not help but be concerned at events in Germany, at Hitler's murder of his erstwhile storm trooper associates, at the way Germany was being mobilised to carry out the will of just one man ... and where that will would carry them no one knew.

Equally both she and Ned were interested in events in Africa. Even while they had been plodding towards safety the Senussi had finally capitulated to the might of Italy. They had lacked the weapons to continue the war. Sophie refused to accept that the catastrophe had been her fault; it had been up to Clay Andrews and his friends to allow for both the Italians and the rain storm. But at least Cyrenaica, and all Libya, now appeared to be pacified; Mussolini's African Empire had been consolidated. Now it appeared that he was thinking of expanding in other directions. It was at Christmas in this same year of 1934, the first Christmas

Sophie and Ned had been able to celebrate in Europe since 1929, that Italian troops exchanged fire with Abyssinian troops at the oasis of Wal-Wal.

It was a confused event, with the Abyssinians, who were supposed to be escorting an Anglo-Abyssinian commission charged by the League of Nations with defining the border between Abyssinia and Italian Somaliland, claiming that the Italians had opened fire without warning, and the Italians claiming that they had merely been replying to fire from the Abyssinians. The point at issue was that the Italians had no business to have occupied Wal-Wal oasis at all, as it was well within territory generally recognised as Abyssinian.

'Just like they did at the Hoggar,' Ned remarked. 'Leopards never change their spots.'

'I imagine the League of Nations will have them chased out,' Sophie said. 'Shall we lunch in town?'

It all seemed so far away now.

'Letters for you, General,' said the orderly.

Edio held out his hand for the envelopes. At least one would be from his mother who he had not seen for a year, since his last home leave just before Christmas 1933. And he was not going to see her this Christmas either. He recognised her handwriting immediately, put the letter aside to be read at his leisure. The other two envelopes were somewhat different. One was official, the other was in a handwriting he did not recognise, and was postmarked Benghazi.

Frowning, he sipped some of the thick black coffee which had been placed at his elbow by his orderly, and slit the official envelope first. It was from General Garzanti, of all people.

My dear Edio, Garzanti had written – what cheek – *I hope you are enjoying life in Somalia...* Edio looked out of his tent flap at the endless brown earth of the desert. Somehow this desert was far more desolate and uninviting than even the Sahara – as well as being twice as hot ... *especially now that events are moving in our favour. I anticipate hearing great things of you in the coming months. However, I am writing to offer you some information that has come my way from our secret services. This information is that Clayton Andrews has returned to Africa. I do not know if you are aware of it, but one of the terms in our agreement with the Senussi in 1932 was that Andrews would be handed over to us. However, it was claimed by the Arabs that he had already left the country and returned to the States.*

This was actually true, as we ascertained. Andrews returned to his home state of Connecticut, and entered his father's

*stockbroking firm in New York. But now he
appears to be on his travels again. Knowing his
reputation and his interests, we must presume he
is acting, or preparing to act, as an agent for the
Abyssinian Government in the procurement of
arms. We cannot of course do anything about
him while he is in Addis Ababa. But should he
endeavour to bring guns into the country it will
have to be through either British, French or
Italian controlled territory. I mention these
things because I am sure that you would like to
lay hands on this scoundrel as much as our
secret service. For the time being, I will wish you
success in whatever lies ahead.*

Edio snorted as he put down the letter. Of
course he would like to lay hands on
Clayton Andrews. But he did not suppose
he was going to. As for what 'lay ahead', as
far as he was concerned things had, as
usual, got out of hand. He thanked the Lord
it hadn't been any of his troops involved at
Wal-Wal, although he had difficulty in
maintaining his position east of the border,
when no one knew for sure where the
border was. But that the Italians had fired
first no one could dispute who had actually
been there, however the Duce's government
might be trying to fudge the matter diplo-
matically. Now the wrath of the entire
League of Nations would be brought down
on the Italian Army – and its commanders.

Edio had now spent four whole years in

this pesthole. And again he had not been able to fathom why he was there at all, except as a punishment for having fouled up in the Sahara. As for why the Italians were there at all ... they were there, he had deduced, because this was one of the few parts of Africa not already gobbled up by the French or the British, and because Somaliland was a part of Africa nobody really wanted. The British and the French maintained small colonies on the Horn of Africa, but after their long and bloody war with the Somalis themselves, against the so-called 'Mad Mullah', they had not sought to expand their holdings. So Mussolini, rather like a jackal, Edio thought in strict privacy, had grabbed what was left – Eritrea north of the Anglo-French holdings, and Somaliland proper south of them. Which was where he was now.

But as Garzanti had suggested when handing out the appointment, there was also a more sinister reason for the Italian occupation of Eritrea and Somaliland. Mussolini was out to avenge the catastrophe of Adowa in 1896. But of course the stage had to be properly set and for four years Edio had done nothing but swelter in the sun, drill his brigade and watch the growing sicklist. The only pleasures offered the Italian troops was a weekend in Mogadishu, from which they had invariably returned

suffering from the clap as well as monumental hangovers. Maintaining discipline
was growing increasingly difficult. As for
dreams of glory on the battlefield...

He slit the second envelope, which was
addressed simply, Brigadier-General Edio
Rometti, Italian Army Headquarters,
Mogadishu, glanced at the letter, frowned,
and then bent his head over the somewhat
crabbed handwriting. *My dearest, darling
Edio. Did you give me up for dead? I cannot
blame you. Oh, the adventures I have had, the
scenes I have witnessed. The time my life has
been in danger. But I kept myself alive by
thinking always of you.*

Edio turned the sheet over to look at the
signature. Lalia? But Lalia had died in the
rain storm, drowned with that German
woman and her English servant. *Now I have
returned to Benghazi, to find that you have
been sent far away. Edio, my darling man, let me
come to you. Send for me. I will love you as you
have never been loved before. I adore you. I am
your own truly loving woman. I dream of you.*

Write soon. Lalia.

Edio laid down the letter. Could it be a
hoax? But why should anyone wish to
pretend to be Lalia after all of these years?
That didn't make sense. And she still loved
him. Well, he still loved her. He had wept
bitterly when he had realised she had gone,
disappeared in the rain and the sodden

sand. Four years!

But ... if she had survived, had Sophie Elligan and that huge brute of an Englishman also survived? Perhaps the French had been right after all and they had been responsible for that shake-up in Tamanrasset. What a tangled world it was.

But to have Lalia, loving, lovely, always-anxious Lalia, back at his side, might even make Somaliland a pleasant place. He reached out for a sheet of his headed notepaper, dipped his pen; this was not something that could be handled by a secretary. And looked up in annoyance as the opening was darkened by that secretary.

'A wireless message, General. General Graziani is on his way, and will be here this evening.'

General Graziani was supreme Italian commander in East Africa. He was a relatively young man, and as a strong supporter of the regime carried a great deal of prestige. Edio had only met him once when he had been commander-in-chief in Libya, and had been impressed. His very presence indicated that there were great things afoot, although they had taken a long time to develop. Edio had all his available men on parade for the general's arrival. He could have wished they had both been smarter and more numerous. But the general seemed pleased enough. 'A fine body of men, Rometti,' he said, as they sipped an aperitif before dinner. 'Is there a very long sick list?'

'I am afraid so, your excellency.'

'What is your effective strength?'

'Approximately four hundred men fit for duty in each regiment, your excellency. Twelve hundred in all.'

'You must try to do better. Weed out the malingerers, General. Send those who are really sick down to Mogadishu. You will receive draft reinforcements as soon as is practical. These men you will train and accustom to desert and mountain warfare as thoroughly as you can. This summer you will break this camp and advance to the north-west.'

Edio swallowed. 'To the north-west, your highness? That will be into Abyssinia.'

'Not immediately. But yes, this will be your ultimate destination. It has been decided to make this incident at Wal-Wal a *casus belli*.'

'You mean we are declaring war on Abyssinia?'

'I doubt that will be necessary, General. When it happens, this will be a police action and you will be carrying out a punitive expedition. When you receive the order to advance, you will follow the course of the River Shebelle. There is even a road and the

315

river will provide your people with water. You will advance to the town of Dildug. That is fifty kilometres within Abyssinia. Once there you will fortify yourself and await reinforcements and further orders.'

Edio licked his lips. 'And if my advance is opposed?'

'You will brush aside any enemy force encountered, General.'

'I imagine there will be quite a few.'

'You will have two thousand men, you will have modern artillery and machine-guns, and you are an experienced desert fighter. This country is not very different to the Sahara. You will also receive close air support.'

Edio raised his eyebrows. He had never fought in conjunction with the air force. 'A squadron of bombers has been ordered out and will be here by the time you cross the border. It will attack any enemy positions which could prove troublesome.' Graziani gave a grim smile. 'Most of the Abyssinians have never seen aircraft before, much less been bombed. It will cause a great of panic.'

'And probably some civilian deaths.'

'It would be a grave mistake to treat any Abyssinians, regardless of age or sex, as a civilian, General. Once you cross the border, you will have every man's hand against you. And every woman's too. Be sure your men understand this.'

'Yes, sir. And what of the rest of the world? Will we not have them against us too?'

'The rest of the world is irrelevant, General. Only one nation matters, apart from Italy. That nation is France.'

'It is France I am thinking of, your excellency. They are certain to oppose us. They always have.'

'Times change, General. The French have discovered a more frightening apparition in Europe even than Il Duce. They are alarmed by the moves that Herr Hitler and his new German regime have made against Austria. That is why Monsieur Laval has recently been in Rome for talks with Il Duce. The French wish our support should it be necessary to stop Hitler. This we are perfectly willing to give, but there must be a quid pro quo, eh? Thus Monsieur Laval has agreed that we should be allowed to, shall I say, rectify certain frontier anomalies that exist in Africa. This is one of them.'

'A few square miles of Abyssinian desert?'

Graziani grinned. 'As you have said, the Abyssinians will certainly resist our advance into their territory. One thing will lead to another. Our aim is Addis Ababa and the entire country.'

'But ... the world will accept this, your excellency? I am thinking of the League of Nations.'

'The League of Nations will certainly not

accept it. But the League also has a record of accepting *faits accomplis*. That is why haste is of the essence. Before the League wakes up to what is happening, before the French realise they have been tricked, we must be in Addis Ababa. Believe me, they may shout and scream and rave, but there is no way they are going to go to war to drive us back out again.'

Edio swallowed again. This was international chicanery on a vast scale. He rather wished the general had not been so frank. 'So I say to you again, General,' Graziani said. 'You must carry out your orders with absolute efficiency, absolute ruthlessness. You must seize Dildug within a week and you must be prepared to resume your march the moment you are brought up to strength. This is a war our nation must and will win.'

'Yes, sir,' Edio said sombrely.

'You need have no doubts,' Graziani said. 'We are throwing our entire military might into this contest. Il Duce has even authorised the use of poison gas to destroy enemy positions. That is something else the Abyssinians have never encountered.'

'But ... poison gas? That is barbaric!' Edio cried.

'General, the people you are about to fight are barbarians.'

'Yes, sir. How soon will this advance be ordered?'

'As soon as the hot weather ends.' Graziani gave another of his grins. 'We do not wish your people to have sunstroke, eh? But our aim is to be in Addis Ababa by Christmas.'

'It certainly looks as if the Eyeties mean trouble in Abyssinia,' Ned said, studying his newspaper. 'They are pouring men and munitions into Somaliland as if there was no tomorrow.'

'I thought Italy was just about broke?' Sophie pruned her roses with great concentration.

'Countries can always find money to go to war,' Ned observed. 'The question is, what is the League going to do about it?'

'Is it any interest to us, my darling?'

She put down her shears and sat beside him, and he said, 'Probably not. But this is.'

Sophie raised her head.

'Here's that advert,' he said.

Sophie took the paper. To the words: *Assistance please: Sophie,* had been added, *can we meet?* 'What do you reckon?' Ned asked.

'I think I'll have to go along with him. I did promise.' She kissed him. 'And if we get a divorce, you and I could get married.'

'It's not exactly as you wanted,' Ned pointed out. 'There was no talk of a meeting.'

'What are you suggesting?'

'I really don't know. But you put up that code as a means of him being able to reach you without giving away our location. Now he wants to meet–'

'I don't think there's a problem.'

'Not even if he and this Lady Martingell have fallen out?'

'Not even then. I'm not going back to him, Ned. You know that.'

He hugged her. 'So where will you meet?'

'Neutral ground, I think. Not in France, because that may give him ideas on where to look for us. Not in England, because that's his territory. Belgium. We'll meet in Ostend.'

Ned wanted to go with her, but she refused. She didn't want him either embarrassed or losing his temper. 'I'll be back in three days,' she said. 'One up, one there, and one back.'

They drove across the border into Spain, went as far down as Barcelona, and sent a wire from there with the instructions, arranging the meeting for the following week. 'Spain, Belgium, he'll be totally confused,' Ned said.

'That's what I intend him to be.'

But she was pleasurably anticipatory as the train chugged north; she had to change at Paris. This was doing something at last. Was she again feeling restless? She supposed it was part of her nature. But on one thing she was totally determined: wherever next she adventured, if the occasion ever arose, it would be with Ned.

She arrived in Ostend in the September dusk, took a taxi to the hotel where she had booked a room and where she had summoned Richard to meet her. She had a bath and was just putting on her underwear when there was a knock on the door. She pulled on a dressing gown, went to the door. 'You're a few hours early,' she said as she opened it ... and gazed at Clay Andrews!

The Business

Sophie instinctively made to close the door but checked when he asked, 'May I come in?' He was so polite. She studied him. His face had aged certainly, but retained its boyish charm. If his complexion had suffered from his years in the desert, she supposed the same could be said for hers. He was, as the last time they had met in civilised circumstances, very well dressed.

Sophie stepped back as he entered the room and closed the door. 'It's been a long time,' he said.

'I had supposed forever,' Sophie said. She continued to back away from him, reached her dressing table, and slid her hand into the drawer to find the revolver without which she never travelled.

'Still as gun happy as ever,' he remarked, making no attempt to stop her.

'Just in case you reckon we have some unfinished business,' she said. 'But ... *Richard* sent you?'

'In a manner of speaking, yes.' He looked left and right. 'Is your large lover here as well?'

'No. But I do assure you that I am perfectly capable, and perfectly willing, of taking care of myself.'

'Don't I know it. May I sit down?'

She gestured at the one chair in the room, herself sat on the bed. 'I asked you a question.'

'And I said, in a manner of speaking. I have just paid a visit to your husband. I'm sorry, but I was quite unaware of your domestic difficulties. I had a contract to offer him and you. But he told me that you had separated and that he did not know where you were. But he could get in touch with you. So ... here I am.'

'A contract?' She couldn't believe her ears. 'The Senussi war is over.'

'When one war ends, another begins. Do you know Abyssinia?'

'As a matter of fact, I do.'

'Well, then, as you almost certainly also know, Mussolini intends to invade it in the not too distant future.'

'It seems likely. And you are now working for the Abyssinians. You do choose the oddest friends. From what I saw of them, and have read of them, they are even more savage than the Senussi.'

'They are about to take on the forces of Fascism,' Clay said.

'You sound like a political statement.'

'And you, I know, have no time for causes, good or bad.'

'That's right, Clay.'

'But you have always had a head for business. Your husband told me that he is now entirely retired from the armament business, owing mainly to the fact that he has fallen out with his source of supply, your father. I assume you know this?'

'Yes.'

'I considered going direct to your father, but Richard considered it might be a better idea to come to you instead. Wherever you were.'

'You are asking me to supply weapons to you? After what happened the last time? Do you suppose I need my head examined?'

'The last time was a colossal series of bad luck,' Clay said. 'Surely you understand that?'

'You set out to trick and deceive me from the beginning,' Sophie said coldly.

'I did not. I had to go along with my employers. You know that.'

'Even to the extent of incarcerating me in that thug's harem.'

'I'm sorry.' He smiled at her anxiously. 'But you emerged triumphant, as always.' He felt in his inside breast pocket, took out one of those manila envelopes she knew so well. 'Haile Selassie will defend his country against the Italians when they make their move. He will defend it with the bodies of his people because they don't have much else. He has perhaps ninety thousand men under arms, but these arms are mostly matchlock rifles. He has a few machine-guns, pre-Great War vintage. He has an air force of twelve rather old machines. Mussolini has something more than a million men under arms. He has guns and modern machine-guns. He has a modern air force. There is even a report that he has authorised the use of poison gas–'

'That's impossible,' Sophie declared. 'No civilised nation would ever again use gas.'

'If one wants to win badly enough, all things become possible,' Clay pointed out.

'And what do you want from me? Do you suppose I can conjure up an air force? Or perhaps a battleship to lie off Mogadishu and frighten the Italians?'

'What you can conjure up, Sophie, are modern rifles and machine-guns, and perhaps even a howitzer or two. It may not be sufficient, but it will be a start, and it will have to do, for a start.' He leaned forward. 'When this war begins, Abyssinia will have the sympathy of the world. But not a lot more than that. Politics is a dirty business. The French want to be friends with the Italians because they're becoming afraid of Germany. The British will probably go along with the French. Whether they do or not, neither Britain nor France are going to sell any weaponry to Haile Selassie for fear of upsetting Musso. My people won't give any licences either.'

'And you think the Nazis will?'

'Hitler and Mussolini aren't exactly on speaking terms since Musso blocked Hitler's attempt to move into Austria last year. I think the Nazis might not be against helping to give Musso a bloody nose in Africa.'

'So you're back to arming savages.'

'I'm back to fighting Fascism.'

'You wouldn't call Nazism a form of Fascism?'

'One thing at a time,' Clay said. 'Britain and France can stamp on Hitler any time they want. Okay, so they want Italy on their side when they do and I think that's a grave mistake. But Mussolini's Fascism is the one that needs opposing, right now.' He paused for breath. 'Will you help me?'

He had laid the envelope on the table. Sophie reached across and slit it open, took out the sheets inside. Once again she was astonished at the size and scope of the weaponry required. Clay was watching her expression. 'The price tag is half a million,' he said. 'And this is on the up and up.'

The adrenalin was pumping through her arteries. 'How, on the up and up?'

'Half on signature. Quarter on satisfactory inspection of the goods. Quarter on final delivery.'

'Delivery where?'

'You'll land the goods at the north end of Kenya. We can't bring you in any closer because the Horn of Africa is well watched by the Italians. But there's an island off the coast of Kenya – Patta. There's nobody there, just bush. Just north of Patta our pilot will meet you; he will be in a fishing dhow flying the Union Jack upside down. He will bring you in on the inside of Patta and our people will meet you. I will also be there. The goods will be inspected there and the second payment made. They will then be transported north. There are roads of a sort and there will be wheeled transport. This time I guarantee it. It's approximately four hundred miles to the Abyssinian border. Then another couple of hundred to a town called Gidole. That's where the delivery will take place and the final payment made.'

Sophie flicked the pages of the requirement list again. 'I don't think you know that my father and I are also estranged,' she said.

'Oh, come now.'

'Fact,' she said. 'He required a somewhat larger share of the, shall I say, final payment made by Sheikh al-Fadl before his untimely death, than I was prepared to make.'

'I see. You have a remarkable gall, Sophie, in ever accusing me of cheating.'

'In this modern world, it is every man, or woman, for himself. Or herself. So you see, if I am to go back to my father with this proposition it will require eating a large portion of humble pie.'

'And that you're not prepared to do.'

'I'm a businesswoman, Clay. I will do anything to further my business interests, if I regard the reward as satisfactory.'

'I would have thought half a million pounds was ample reward for anyone.'

'I am not going to see much of that half million,' Sophie pointed out. 'I don't think Papa will let me get away with anything more than a small share. Maybe fifty thousand.'

'So?' He was frowning.

'As I am the one you are relying upon to organise and make the delivery, I require an additional fee of fifty thousand pounds, to be paid to me personally.'

'Are you joking?'

'Half now, before I begin to set things in motion, and half when I deliver the goods.'

He gazed at her for several seconds. 'Are you sure you don't have an advanced case of hubris?'

'I am simply placing a proper valuation upon my worth,' Sophie said.

He got up and came towards her. She left the revolver lying on her lap, but with her finger round the trigger. He sat on the bed beside her. 'You are quite the most amazing woman I have ever met. Do you know I fell in love with you the first time I saw you?'

'So you said at the time,' Sophie said very softly. 'But–'

'Oh, yes, things got in the way.' He placed his hand on the nape of her neck, drifted his fingers up into her hair. 'That doesn't mean I ever stopped loving you. Or will ever stop loving you.'

'Even after that sheikh had had a go at me?' Her knees were weak. This man had always had that effect on her.

'Even after,' he said, bringing her face forward so that he could kiss her on the lips. The last time he had done that, she remembered, had been in the desert.

She parted her lips for him, while her brain raced, and she determinedly got hold of her emotions. I am not going to cheat on Ned, she told herself. No matter how much I wish to have sex with this man. But kissing can be considered part of our business transaction. His hand was on her breast, gently caressing the soft mound, then moving across to open the dressing gown. Sophie brought up the gun. He pulled his head back. 'Would you really?'

'I might.'

'And it's become a habit.' He released her. 'What did Lady Caroline Lamb say on meeting Byron? That he was mad, bad, and dangerous to know? I think that sums you up very adequately.'

'But like Lady Caroline,' Sophie pointed

out, 'you keep coming back for more.'

He shrugged. 'I'm a sucker. Do we have a deal?'

'I can't say. I will have to go to Hamburg and check with Papa.'

'Shall I come with you?'

She considered him. He is desperate to have sex with me, she thought. Perhaps at this moment that is more important to him than the guns for his friends. And how the nearness of him had the adrenalin flowing.

'No,' she said. 'I have arrangements to make. Meet me here, in this hotel, in one week.'

He hesitated, then nodded. 'You're the boss lady. Tell me, when this transaction is completed, if all goes according to plan–'

'Ask me again when the transaction is completed,' Sophie told him.

'Holy shitting cows,' Ned commented, when he read the proposed manifest. 'These fellows are really preparing to fight a war.'

'It won't be of their making,' Sophie pointed out.

'You reckon? Suppose we pump this amount of armament into Abyssinia, and Musso doesn't after all invade? You reckon the Abyssinians are just going to sit on these guns and not use them?'

'I really don't think that's our concern,' Sophie said. 'But you don't like the idea.'

She hoped he was not going to pull a Richard on her.

'Oh, I think it's a brilliant idea,' Ned said. 'Although I had supposed we were retired.'

'One last killing,' she said. 'With a minimum figure of a hundred thousand for us. Doesn't that sound good?'

'It sounds tremendous. The one thing I don't like is taking the guns in through British territory.'

'They won't know a thing,' Sophie assured him. 'But there is one aspect of the situation we need to consider. Clay Andrews would dearly like to get his hands on me.'

'I got that impression in the Sahara. But you saw him off.'

'In a manner of speaking. What I am saying is, we can't afford to antagonise him, at least until the guns have been delivered and the final payment made.'

'What you are saying is that if he tries to get into your sleeping bag I mustn't object? Forget it.'

Sophie kissed him. 'I imagine he'll find that difficult, as I am assuming you will already be in my sleeping bag. But let him flirt if it'll keep him happy.'

What am I doing? she asked herself, as the train rumbled north once again. I should not be touching this with a barge pole. We do not really need the money and it will be dangerous. Ned had suggested they stood a strong chance of offending the British Government – if she genuinely believed they would not know about the shipment until after it had been made, they were still certain to find out about it sooner or later – and she was chancing her arm with Clay.

Simply because she sometimes wished, in her midnight hours, that Ned had not made his return from the dead quite so soon? Another hour ... you are a libidinous bitch, Sophie Elligan, she told herself. Just think of the money.

'Why, Pemberton,' Richard Elligan said. 'Good of you to call. But I suppose it isn't, really. You've not met Lady Martingell.'

Walter Pemberton gave a little bow. 'I know the name.'

'I imagine you do,' Anne said, sitting down and gesturing Pemberton to a chair.

'Drink?' Richard asked.

'Perhaps later,' Pemberton said.

'Ah. So this *is* business.'

'I'm afraid so. A week ago you had a visit from Mr Clayton Andrews.'

Richard sat down also, beside his wife. 'Tell me, Pemberton, am I under surveillance?'

Pemberton gave a little cough. 'It is necessary to keep our eye on things, sir.'

'I see. Well, yes, Mr Andrews did come to

call. He was once a friend of my wife's, before our separation, and he happened to be in England–'

'Mr Elligan, please,' Pemberton protested. 'May we be adult about this? Clay Andrews is a well-known agent provocateur operating in Africa. His business is aiding and abetting all those native Africans who may be inclined to resist European rule.'

'Dangerous fellow,' Anne murmured.

Pemberton shot her a glance. 'Andrews' business, when he comes to England, is usually to purchase arms for whatever cause he happens to be currently supporting. I am sure you remember that it was he involved Mrs Elligan in that unpleasantness a few years ago.'

'Yes,' Richard said. 'You were nosing around then, too.'

'That shipment of arms nearly caused a diplomatic rift between France and Italy,' Pemberton said. 'Now we have Andrews, who we strongly suspect is in the business of buying some more arms, paying a visit to a well-known arms dealer. I think you should tell me just who he is working for this time and what exactly he wants.'

'I think you should know, Pemberton, as I am sure you do, that I am entirely retired from the arms business.'

'Mr Andrews does not seem to be aware of that.'

'True. But I put him right.'

'Is that so. Where did you send him?'

'I told him to find someone else to do business with.'

Pemberton felt in his pocket and took out a notebook. 'One week ago, Mr Andrews was in Ostend, where he met up with Mrs Elligan.' He raised his eyes.

'There's a coincidence,' Richard agreed.

'Oh, really, Mr Elligan. We happen to know that Mrs Elligan, together with a companion of hers...' another glance at the notebook, 'Mr Edward Carew, returned to Europe last year, after a considerable stay in the Middle East. We know that Mrs Elligan was in charge of the shipment of guns to the Senussi that caused so much trouble five years ago. Since her return to Europe, while we know she visited both her father in Hamburg and you here, we have lost track of her, and her dossier has been closed. But not destroyed, Mr Elligan. Fortunately. Now here she is again, meeting with her old comrade-in-arms, most clandestinely. Are you saying you did not know of this?'

'Ah...' Richard was realising that he could get himself into deep waters by perjuring himself. 'Very well, Mr Pemberton. I put Andrews in touch with my wife. It is her father who supplies the guns.'

'Then you know where your wife is living in Belgium?'

'I don't think she is living in Belgium. I have a contact for her in the newspapers. I used this and put her in touch with Andrews.'

'I see. And would it be your estimation that she will do business?'

'I should think that is quite likely.'

'With whom, do you imagine?'

'I'm afraid I have no idea.'

'Would it interest you to know that our agents in Addis Ababa reported seeing Mr Andrews in that city earlier this year?'

'Addis Ababa? Good Lord.'

'Indeed. So let us assume that Andrews is buying arms from the Beinhardt Company for shipment to Abyssinia. How do you suppose he will hope to get them there? Down through Egypt and the Sudan? That would be quite impossible. We would have him before he got to Cairo. Through the Sahara? I should have thought both he and Mrs Elligan had seen enough of the Sahara to last them a lifetime. They are wanted there, anyway, by both the Italians and the French. Through Somaliland itself? That is ridiculous. Up the Congo? That would take them years. So that leaves Kenya. British territory.'

'Don't you want to help the Abyssinians, Mr Pemberton?' Anne asked innocently.

'What I, or the British Government, might want in an ideal world, Lady Martingell, is neither here nor there. What we need, in the present political climate, is to be seen to be absolutely neutral while endeavouring to broker a peaceful solution to the Italo-Abyssinian problem. This will be intensely difficult to do should it be learned, as it very rapidly would be, that we are supplying arms and ammunition clandestinely to the Abyssinian Army.'

'But it would have nothing to do with you,' Richard pointed out. 'The arms would be supplied by a German firm, and–' He hesitated.

'Exactly so. They would have been negotiated for, and no doubt would be delivered by, an English citizen. Mrs Elligan is still that, is she not? Also, we have every reason to assume that her friend Carew is also English; it is certainly an English name. I do not think we can permit that. And if, in addition, Mrs Elligan intends to ship the guns in through Kenya, well–'

'Just what do you expect me to do about it?'

'You say you have the means of contacting your wife. I suggest you do so and tell her to forget this whole crazy idea. Or she may well find herself in prison. Along with her friend. And regrettably, Mr Elligan, along with you.'

'Just what do you mean by that?' Richard snapped.

'The lady is your wife. You are a well-known gunrunner. You may claim to be retired but you may find that difficult to prove, especially when you have admitted putting Andrews in touch with Mrs Elligan, business in mind.'

Richard glared at him.

'I'm just trying to paint a complete picture, as it were,' Pemberton said and stood up. 'I'll take my leave. I assume you will be dealing with this matter, Mr Elligan. However, I must make it perfectly clear that if any guns are shipped by your wife through Kenya to Abyssinia, I shall be back with a warrant.' He glanced at Anne. 'Or two. Good day to you, sir. Lady Martingell.'

'The bloody bastard,' Richard exploded when the door had closed. 'He was threatening you!'

'Well, I imagine I'm fairly well remembered as a gunrunner too,' Anne said. 'In the good old days. But there is no way I am going back to gaol.'

'I'll get in touch with Hancock.'

'Who's Hancock?'

'My solicitor. He'll sort this out.'

'I'm not sure that will be a particularly good idea,' Anne said, pouring them each a drink. 'Pemberton is holding all the trumps. You, we, do have a reputation. Sophie is still your wife. You *would* have a problem proving that you have had nothing to do with this transaction. And I imagine your solicitor would tell you that.'

Richard sat down disconsolately. 'So you think I should get hold of Sophie and tell her to forget it? She'd laugh in my face. As for that bastard Carew ... I trusted him. I really did.'

'You need to choose your associates more carefully,' she remarked and sat beside him. 'I think you, we, are in the process of getting a very bad deal. Andrews mentioned a figure of half a million pounds. Your wife is going to obtain that money and swan off into the sunset, leaving us with nothing, and possibly facing a criminal charge. I don't think that is at all fair.'

Richard turned his head to look at her. 'Just what are you suggesting?'

'Do you know Africa?'

'I have never been there.'

'I was born in Africa,' Anne said reminiscently. 'South Africa to be sure, but I know East Africa fairly well. After all, I was a guest of the Mad Mullah for several months. Now that was a hairy experience. And do you know, he never raped me? He had his own strong sense of honour. I was his hostage for James to come through with a delivery. If James had *not* turned up, I think the old rascal had some very interesting plans for me. But of course James turned up. He always did.'

'You sound almost regretful,' Richard commented, a trifle sullenly; he was aware that he was being subtly criticised.

'It was at least exciting,' Anne said.

'Do I gather that you are proposing that we should go to Kenya, attempt to intercept this arms shipment ourselves and make off with as much money as we can?'

'That would seem to be a very sensible solution to our problem. Pemberton has dumped the whole thing in your lap. Stop Sophie from making the delivery or suffer the consequences. He cannot really object if, having failed to persuade her from undertaking the delivery – there is no need for him ever to know that you never even tried – you decide to stop her physically. And the only place that can be done without governmental interference is in Kenya.'

'You are talking about you and me,' Richard pointed out. 'Sophie will have a large force with her.'

'Not so large, if I remember the deliveries from my own youth. On your last delivery how many men did you take?'

'Well ... I was met on the ground by the purchasers. But I had half a dozen of my own people with me. Including Ned Carew,' he said sourly.

'All skilled and determined fighting men, I suppose.'

'They were all unemployed soldiers, if that's what you mean. Who had served under me.'

'What of the other five?'

'Well ... I don't know. I haven't needed them for six years.'

'But you can get hold of them.'

'I imagine so. I have their addresses. But I doubt they'll be interested. They've probably all got jobs by now.'

'I have never met a man who was not interested in making a lot of money.'

'You'll have to tell me exactly what you have in mind.'

'It's very simple,' Anne shrugged. 'As I recall these matters, Sophie will have been paid a certain amount when she agrees to the contract. This is beyond our reach. But the balance will only be paid upon her delivery of the weapons and ammunition. All we need to know is where and when, and we can be on the spot to take over matters for ourselves.'

'Highly risky.'

'It always was a risky business,' Anne remarked.

'Were you planning to come along?'

'Of course. I could do with a bit of excitement.'

'Well ... how do we find out the where and when?'

'You organise our back-up and I will find out where and when ... if you will allow me to pay a visit to Hamburg and give me that card Andrews left with you.'

'Can you do it?' Sophie asked her father.

'I had never expected to see you here again,' Claus said for the second time.

'I am here on business, Papa. I am offering you a lot of money.' Claus surveyed the list some more. 'Mountain guns?'

'You manufacture them.'

'For the German Army.'

'I am sure some can be spared.'

'Not without their permission. I doubt they will give that.'

'Surely they wish to see Mussolini brought back to earth.'

'I think they probably do. But not by arming and equipping Negroes. That is against the Nazi ethic.'

'The Abyssinians are not Negroes, Papa. They are Abyssinians.'

'They have black skins. That is what matters to the Fuehrer.'

Sophie sighed. But she was not going to be defeated now. 'Who do you have to obtain this permission from?'

'Well ... in the first insistence, Colonel von Loeben. He is our gauleiter.'

'Arrange for me to meet this colonel.'

Claus raised his eyebrows. 'You? What can you hope to achieve?'

'Listen, Papa. I am prepared to do a deal with these Nazi friends of yours. You say you are producing guns for the German Army.

How are you being paid?'

'I am paid cash on the barrel for every delivery,' Claus said proudly.

'You mean you are paid in Deutschmarks.'

'Well, of course I am paid in Deutschmarks.'

'So tell me, if you decide to take a holiday in Denmark, can you spend your Deutschmarks? Or change them into kroner?'

'Well, of course not. I would have to obtain permission, and prove that my journey abroad was really necessary.'

'You mean no German can holiday abroad?'

'We are running a very tight exchange control policy at the moment. And why should anyone wish to holiday abroad when there are so many delightful places within the Reich?'

'Absolutely. But what you are really saying is that Germany is short of hard currency. Very short. I do not imagine they would sneeze at a few hundred thousand pounds sterling.'

Claus frowned. 'You will hand over this money to the Government?'

'Your Government, Papa, which you are supporting so loyally.'

'But ... how do I pay my workforce? Where is my profit?'

'Just as you do now. I will propose to this von Loeben that all moneys we receive for this shipment will be paid to the Government, and the Government in turn will pay you the equivalent in Deutschmarks. As you have just said, you only wish to spend your money in Germany, anyway, because it is so beautiful.'

Claus glared at his daughter. But he was interested. 'Half a million pounds sterling,' he said, half to himself.

'Not quite half a million, Papa,' Sophie said. 'I do not intend that *my* share should be converted into Deutschmarks.'

Colonel von Loeben was a precise man who wore a monocle. He was clean shaven and actually not bad looking, and unusually for an important Nazi – with the exception of people like Hitler himself – was dark-haired. He tapped on his blotting paper with one finger as he read the manifest, then looked up at Sophie sitting on the far side of his desk. For this occasion she was as always dressed in the height of fashion, with a huge picture hat drooping over one eye. 'You deal in large numbers, Frau Elligan,' he remarked.

'Are large numbers not more interesting than small ones, Herr Colonel?'

He gazed at her for several seconds, then allowed his eyes to droop to her extremely well-filled bodice. 'I shall have to consider this somewhat strange request,' he said.

'Although I can see nothing against it, at least in principle, at first reading. There are certain aspects of the, shall we say, deal, you are suggesting that will need to be kept confidential. I may give your father permission to export munitions, but in this case I do not wish to know where they are going, or for whom they are destined. And of course, should the matter become public, I will disown any involvement.'

'I understand.'

'Do you also understand that *should* the matter become public, your father may well have to face a charge of exporting arms illegally, and this may involve serious consequences.'

'I am sure my father understands this,' Sophie lied. 'It will be our business to ensure that nothing does go wrong.'

'Of course. Now there is one other small matter. You are asking for my help in making a great deal of money. I think I am entitled to require, shall we say, a sweetener.'

'How much?' Sophie asked.

Von Loeben gave a cold smile. 'I am not interested in a financial arrangement, Frau Elligan. These matters are too easily traced and may well be considered bribery.' Once again he allowed his gaze to drift up and down her body.

Oh, my God, she thought. That had not occurred to her. In the course of her life she had escaped rape by the skin of her teeth on more than one occasion; she had fought Ranatullah the Afghan, resisted Clay Andrews, and killed al-Fadl ... to come to this. But she was committed and her father needed the money. And Clay needed the guns. It would be a simple matter of prostitution.

Von Loeben had been studying her face. Now he pushed back his chair and got up. 'I have a private office behind here,' he said, opening the door behind his desk. 'We shall not be interrupted.'

Sophie drew a long breath, and went to the door.

There was even a bed. No chairs, but a washbasin and a cubicled lavatory. 'Do you often entertain in here?' she asked, surprised and relieved by the evenness of her voice.

'Not as often as I might like,' the colonel said. He closed the door. 'I like my women to be utterly servile. Do you understand me?'

Sophie nodded. He is nothing, she told herself. I will never have to see him again. It will be no more important than having to sit in a dentist's chair for half an hour.

If only she could believe that.

'So strip,' he said. 'Let me see if you are really worth half-a-million pounds.'

Sophie took off her clothes, removing each garment slowly and carefully, playing the coquette, certainly, because she wanted him to come at her and get it over with as rapidly as possible. But he showed no great arousal, although he never took his eyes from her. And when she finally removed her boots and stockings he remarked, 'Quite entrancing. Your skin is so white, where it has not been burned by the sun. You must have spent a great deal of time in the tropics.'

'I have,' she said.

'So come here and let me feel you,' he said.

Sophie stood in front of him, closed her eyes as his hands drifted up and down her legs, round to fondle her buttocks – he made her think of Castelfiardo – and then moved up to her breasts. 'Now kneel,' he commanded. 'And please me.'

Claus von Beinhardt stood up in surprise as his secretary ushered the woman into his office. 'Lady Martingell? But you are...'

'I was in prison, Count,' Anne said. 'But I was discovered to be innocent after all. I do assure you that I am suing the Government for compensation.'

'My dear lady ... do sit down. It is fifteen years since we met.'

'Sixteen,' Anne corrected. 'We met at Buckingham Palace when my husband was knighted in 1919.'

'Of course. But ... well...'

He gazed at the tall, slender, attractive woman with the somewhat hard features. Her complexion still wore the pallor of several years in a cell, but that apart she was most attractive, even with the streaks of grey in her auburn hair. Hair so very like Sophie's, he thought. And she had to be ... in her middle fifties, certainly. 'You are looking well,' he said.

'So are you, my dear Count,' Anne said, not entirely truthfully.

'And what brings you to Hamburg?'

'Business,' Anne said. Claus raised his eyebrows. 'Since my release from prison. I have gone back into business. The only business I know.'

'Ah ... but–' He was utterly confused.

'I am dealing for a man named Clayton Andrews,' Anne said. 'But you know this, I am sure.'

'Ah...' Claus stroked his bald head. 'Clayton Andrews?'

'I didn't really come all this way to play games,' Anne said.

Claus licked his lips. 'I have heard the name.'

'My dear Count, Clay is in the process of buying half a million pounds' worth of arms from your firm.' Claus opened his mouth and then shut it again. 'The transaction,'

Anne went on, 'is being handled by your daughter Sophie, who happens to be married to an old acquaintance of my late husband's, Richard Elligan.'

'They are separated,' Claus muttered.

'Is that so,' Anne remarked. 'However, as far as either Clay or myself know, they are still in business together.'

Claus did some more stroking. 'And they are, as I am sure you know, Count, an extremely devious couple. Clay is concerned. He is concerned that he has never been allowed to meet you.'

'Ah ... I was told by my daughter that Herr Andrews did not wish to come to Germany.'

'Now, why should he not wish to do that?' Anne asked. 'He is engaged in buying a large number of arms from your firm, and he does not wish to come here to your factory and see for himself the manufacture and preparation of these arms? Is that logical?'

'No, it is not logical,' Claus said. 'I am most grateful to you for pointing this out to me, Lady Martingell. What would you like me to do about it?'

'Well,' Anne said. 'It is not for me to advise you, Count. My business, on behalf of Mr Andrews, is to make sure the arms are delivered and in good order. However, it would help if I knew precisely what arrangements Mrs Elligan has so far made.'

'Well...' Claus hesitated and peered at her. 'You can prove that you are working for Herr Andrews?'

Anne shrugged. 'We do not carry documentation to prove that we are gunrunners, if that is what you mean. However...' she opened her handbag and took out the card, placed it on the desk, 'Clay told me to give you this, if necessary.'

Claus picked up the card, studied it, and handed it back. 'I apologise. But you understand–'

'Of course I understand,' Anne said. 'You need to be careful. We all need to be careful. So tell me, when will the shipment be ready?'

'It is ready now. The ship is standing by. I am awaiting clearance from my government.'

Anne frowned. 'This is necessary?'

'Of course. But it will be obtained. Sophie is looking after it.'

'I see. Which route will you take?'

'Well, as you know, Herr Andrews has arranged to take delivery in Kenya.'

'Of course,' Anne said. 'I have told him this is very risky, but he feels there is no other way.'

'Absolutely. But the spot he has chosen, inside the island of Patta, is very sparsely inhabited and has no local authority, so it should be safe enough.'

'And how exactly are the goods being taken to Patta? Your daughter did not specify this to Clay.'

'The route will be through the Mediterranean and the Suez Canal.'

'Will that not be very risky?'

'Not at this time. There is no war declared between Italy and Abyssinia, and even if there were, our ship will be flying the German flag and will be transporting farm implements to Portuguese East Africa. This will satisfy the British, and the Italians would not dare stop a German merchantman on the high seas.'

'I'm sure you're right. However, Clay needs to know the exact delivery date.'

'I am sorry, Lady Martingell. I cannot give you an exact date. I would hope to despatch, as I have said, within a fortnight; the eighteenth September is the date we are aiming for. Then we would hope to be off Patta in another fortnight.'

'The beginning of October,' Anne said, thoughtfully. 'Very good. And then?'

'Well, as I understand it, the goods will be met by Herr Andrews, and then be taken north to Gidole, inside Abyssinia, when the final payment will be made and our interest in the matter ceases.'

'Until the next time,' Anne said, smiling at him.

'I shall look forward to it.'

'Well, then, I will return to England and inform Clay that all is in order, and that he can cease worrying. However...' she tapped her chin with her gloved forefinger, 'it occurs to me that it might be a good idea not to mention to your daughter that I have visited you. I really do not wish her to feel that she is being spied upon. I am sure you understand this?'

'Of course,' Claus said. 'When are you leaving?'

'I shall catch a train tomorrow morning for Rotterdam.'

'Well, then,' Claus said. 'I should be very obliged if you would let me take you out to dinner.'

'The things I do for money, and security, to be sure,' Anne said, soaking in a warm bath.

'Did he ... well–' Richard was embarrassed.

'He wanted everything,' Anne said.

'And you gave him–'

'What he wanted. Oh, it was not so bad. He was inept, and even at his age he was conscience-stricken at cheating on his wife. But I think he felt he was achieving some sort of victory over James; he always hated James.'

'I am sorry you had to suffer that.'

Anne laughed. 'I enjoyed it, Dickie. And you shall not be jealous. He has given us what we need. Now we must be there. You have rounded up your group?' Richard nodded. 'Are they still good men?'

'They are still loyal men, with a financial bonus at the end of it.'

'Well, we must leave immediately. We will sail to Mombasa, announce to the world that we are a big game shooting party, and head north. We have just under a month. But we must be in position by the end of September.'

'The things I do for money,' Sophie said, soaking in a hot bath. 'The bastard,' Ned said. 'But you mean he didn't actually... well–'

'Fuck me? No, no. I think he felt that would be infra dig for a German officer. What he wanted was for me to fellate him.'

'The bastard,' Ned said again.

'Not a difficult business. I'm becoming quite an authority on men's genitalia.'

'He was humiliating you.'

'He thought he was, certainly. But we will have the last laugh. Now, we sail on the eighteenth of September. I must let Clay have that date. I will meet him in Ostend, as arranged, and then we will go on to Hamburg to join the ship. Would you believe that I am quite excited about it?'

'And when you meet Andrews, will you suck him off as well?' Ned asked.

'Ned! You promised not to be jealous.'

'I'm human,' Ned said.

'Well, there is no need to be. Jealous, I mean. Clay isn't into that sort of thing.'

'Nevertheless,' Ned said. 'I'm coming with you.'

The two men stared at each other; the hostility could be felt. 'So there we are,' Sophie said, with determined cheerfulness. 'Everything is ready. All you have to do is pay for the goods, Clay.'

Clay opened his briefcase. 'Here is a certified cheque, payable to Beinhardt and Company, for two hundred and fifty thousand pounds. A further hundred and twenty-five thousand will be paid when the goods are landed in Kenya, and the final hundred and twenty-five thousand on their arrival at Gidole.'

'You mean you are expecting us to accompany the goods into Abyssinia,' Ned said.

'That is up to you,' Clay replied. 'You will have received three-quarters of the full amount at Patta. The remainder will be paid, I promise you. The Abyssinians anticipate a long struggle when war comes, and they will need additional arms. However, if you wish to accompany the shipment to Gidole, neither I nor my associates will have any objection.' He looked from face to face.

'I trust this is satisfactory.'

'I think so,' Sophie said. 'But there is one thing more, is there not?'

Clay opened his briefcase again and took out another cheque. 'A certified cheque, payable to Sophie Elligan, for twenty-five thousand pounds.'

'Thank you.' Sophie folded the cheque and placed it in her handbag. 'I was wondering if you thought I'd forgotten.'

'I never supposed that, Sophie. I know you too well. Will you join me for dinner? And you, Carew.'

'We have a train to catch,' Sophie told him.

'Well, General,' General Graziani said as he stepped down from his command car. 'Is all prepared?'

Edio saluted. 'As prepared as is possible, Signor General.'

'Good, good.' Graziani walked down the ranks of the waiting guard-of-honour. 'They look splendid. And fit. Your effective strength?'

'One thousand nine hundred and fifty, Signor General.'

Graziani nodded, and looked over the rows of machine-guns, the two batteries of mountain artillery, the compound of mules and horses, and raised his eyebrows at the fluttering skirt standing just outside the general's house. 'An old friend, Signor General, who has been spending the summer with me.'

'Hm,' Graziani said, and went to the waiting table and chairs, arranged in the shade of an acacia, and on which there were a bottle of wine and three glasses.

Edio waved Lalia over. 'Signorina Lalia Pastrami,' he introduced.

Graziani kissed Lalia's hand. 'You must find life boring in such desolate surroundings, Signorina.'

'I have been in the desert before, your excellency,' Lalia said. 'With Edio.'

'Yes,' Edio said, not wishing her to go into details of that disaster.

'Of course,' Graziani said, suggesting he might know more about her and her relationship with Edio than he had admitted. 'Well, I should be obliged if you would run along, my dear. General Rometti and I have things to discuss.' Lalia looked at Edio who poured her a glass of wine and then nodded. She took the glass and retreated disconsolately. Edio poured for Graziani and himself as well.

'I have your orders,' Graziani said. 'The invasion commences one week today, the second of October. You will, as instructed, strike for Dildug, take and fortify the town. Further orders will be given you at Dildug. You will destroy any Abyssinian forces that may attempt to resist you. You will receive air support and you may call on additional air strikes should you feel it necessary.'

'Will I have armour?' Edio asked.

'No. The armour is going in further north, from Eritrea. You are the bottom, and weaker, claw of a pincer. But as the main Abyssinian effort will be concentrated in the north, you should not find it difficult. Now, General, I wish you to bear in mind that while the enemy may be inferior in strength, he is a wily and vicious fighter. He knows no mercy to a beaten foe. And his women even less. I wish you to impress this on your men. They cannot surrender with any expectation of being treated in a civilised manner. Even if a party should be cut off and surrounded by superior forces, they must be prepared to fight to the end, or until relieved.'

'I understand, General.'

'By the same token, I do not recommend taking that woman with you,' Graziani added.

'I will ask her what she wishes to do.'

'Well, the decision must be yours.' Graziani drained his glass. 'I must be getting back.' He held out his hand. 'I will wish you good fortune, General, and a great triumph. The avenging of Adowa. Dawn, on the second of October. *Avanti!*'

Invasion

Even the presence of the river did little to alleviate the barrenness of the countryside. It wasn't desert but there was precious little green to be seen, and only the occasional acacia to break the skyline of rolling low hills. At least, Edio thought, it was cooler than it had been a few months ago, even if the early morning sun was broiling out of a cloudless sky and promising greater heat in a few hours.

Lalia sat beside him in the back of the command car, which he intended to use for as long as there was even the semblance of a road. In front of him, at a distance, was an advance guard of lancers, wearing blue tunics over khaki breeches, pennons floating from their spearheads; behind him the column of trucks rolled, mostly filled with petrol and spare ammunition. The guns were mule-drawn, and behind them marched the regiments of infantry, plodding steadily onwards; progress was necessarily slow. 'Do you remember the last time?' Lalia asked.

Edio shuddered. 'I do not wish to.'

'Whatever happened to that ghastly man, Castelfiardo?'

'I believe he is in Somaliland. He is a colonel now.'

'But you are a general.' She kissed his cheek.

'Please,' he protested. 'Not in front of the men.'

One of the horsemen cantered back to him. 'We're at the border, we believe, General.'

Edio snorted. They believed. But that was the trouble with this war and the reason for it. 'Are there people about?'

'We have seen none, sir.'

'Well, keep your eyes open.'

The lancer saluted and trotted off. The column continued to grind and tramp forward. 'How far is it to this place Dildug?' Lalia asked.

'Not far. We will be there by nightfall.'

'Then will I be able to have a bath?' She had bathed last night.

'I am sure you will be able to have a bath,' Edio told her, and took out his binoculars to look left and right. He saw nothing but hills and scrub, but soon another of the lancers came back.

'There are people in front of us, General.'

'Halt the column,' Edio told his deputy, Colonel Lusiardo.

The trucks stopped, and Edio got down. His horse was brought forward, and he mounted. 'Oh, Edio,' Lalia said. 'Please be careful.'

'Shall I deploy, sir?' Lusiardo asked.

'Not until we find out these people's attitude,' Edio said. He walked the horse forward to join the lancers.

'There, General,' said the captain, pointing with a gauntleted finger.

Edio levelled his binoculars. There were perhaps six men, on foot, standing on a hillock overlooking the river, and on the Italians' side of it. They carried rifles although they did not appear to be wearing uniform. Did the Abyssinians wear uniform? 'Let us find out what they want,' he said, and kicked his horse forward. The captain and bugler followed, and then the cavalry, in column of twos, pennons fluttering from their lance heads.

Edio signalled them to halt when they were within fifty yards of the Abyssinians who had hardly moved as they watched the Italian advance. 'Send up Galwar,' Edio commanded.

Galwar was a Somali who spoke Amharic, the main language of the Abyssinians. Now he came forward, riding a mule and looking very anxious. 'Speak to those men,' Edio said. 'Find out what they want.'

Galwar rolled his eyes. He could have told the general what they wanted without engaging in dangerous repartee. But he walked the mule forward and began a shouted conversation. After five minutes he came back. 'They are soldiers of the Emperor, Haile Selassie,' he said. 'They wish to know if you are aware that you are in the Emperor's territory.'

'Tell them that Il Duce, ruler of Italy and the Mediterranean, and of the Horn of Africa, does not recognise this territory as belonging to Haile Selassie,' Edio said. 'Tell him that it is my purpose to advance to the town of Dildug. Tell them that if they attempt to stop us, it will go very hard with them.'

Galwar looked even more apprehensive, but he returned to the foot of the hillock and again began shouting. The Abyssinians listened to what he had to say, then appeared to converse amongst themselves. Edio found he was holding his breath. He sincerely hoped that the advance would not be opposed.

Then, without warning, one of the Abyssinians levelled his rifle and shot Galwar through the head. Galwar fell back out of the saddle and struck the ground heavily; his foot remained caught in the stirrup as the mule reared and galloped off, dragging his body behind it. 'Prepare to fire,' Edio bawled, drawing his revolver as the cavalry drew their carbines from the scabbards. But the Abyssinians had disappeared.

'Follow me.' Edio urged his horse forward

and cantered up the slope, the lancers behind him. At the top he paused in consternation, looking down into the shallow valley beyond. Assembled there were several thousand men, he estimated, and they even had a couple of field guns.

'Fall back,' Edio shouted. 'Fall back. Bugler, sound the recall. Then blow the command to deploy.'

The bugle notes struck across the afternoon, but were almost drowned in the huge roar which arose from beyond the hill. Edio thought of Custer's last stand. But this was on a considerably bigger scale – and he had resources of which Custer had never dreamed. With his cavalry he galloped up to the command car. 'Fetch the telegrapher,' he told Lusiardo. 'Deploy your men to either side of the road,' he told his infantry commanders. 'Dismount your cavalry and have them take up a defensive perimeter,' he told the cavalry captain. 'Send your horses down the column where they will be safe.'

'Shall we get the trucks off the road, your excellency?' asked one of the infantry captains. 'Form a laager?'

'No,' Edio said. That would present an even bigger target to the Abyssinian guns, and besides, once he took the trucks off the road they would have an enormous task getting them back on again.

'Major Cavalli,' he told his battery

commander. 'Sight your guns on that hill, and be ready to fire at anything that shows itself.' Cavalli saluted and hurried off.

'Sir!' The wireless telegrapher stood to attention.

'Telegram to headquarters,' Edio said. 'Have encountered large enemy force ten kilometres south-east of Dildug. Expect imminent attack. Request air support. Rometti. Give them the map reference.' The telegrapher returned back to his truck.

'Oh, Edio,' Lalia squealed. 'Is there going to be a battle?'

'Yes,' Edio said. 'Leave this truck and go to the rear of the column.'

'But Edio, will we not win the battle?'

'We shall win the battle,' Edio assured her, 'but there will be shooting. Now off you go.' She ran along the line of trucks, skirt flying, attracting cheers and catcalls from the deploying infantry.

Edio was pleased. The whole thing had been going very well, and the Abyssinians, while clearly advancing, were doing so very slowly. Now he looked left and right at his men, kneeling or lying amongst the rocks, rifles thrust forward; they had not drawn their bayonets as yet – that would hopefully come later. He checked his own revolver, noted only the slightest trembling of his fingers. They were outnumbered by about four to one, he estimated.

'Look there, General,' Lusiardo said, pointing to the north. Edio levelled his binoculars and saw a flutter of cloth amidst the rocks. 'They are trying to surround us,' Lusiardo said. 'At least on three sides, with the fourth the river. They are trying to trap us, General.'

'They will not succeed,' Edio said.

'Shall I open fire, General?'

'What at?'

Lusiardo gulped; he had not seen action before.

Edio watched the men crawling through the rocks to the north; he estimated there were a couple of hundred of them, nuisance value only. He looked to the south, at the fast-tumbling river, perhaps thirty yards wide. On the far side of the water he could see more movement amongst the hillocks. The Abyssinians intended to enfilade his position. 'Tell Captain Pinar to move two companies round to face the river,' he told Lusiardo. 'But he is not to open fire until I give the order.'

Every momen's delay was precious, giving the planes more time to reach the scene. There was a roar and a whine and a crash, and a shell exploded, actually in the river, sending up a huge plume of water mixed with rocks, but causing no damage whatsoever to the column, although Edio thought he could hear a distant screaming which he imagined was Lalia.

Then there was another whoosh and a bang. This time the shell actually burst on the road, but some hundred yards in front of the column. Again it did no damage to the Italians, but it left a crater in the road which would have to be filled before he could proceed – and speed remained essential. 'Tell Major Cavalli to open fire,' he told Lusiardo. 'He will aim to drop his shells just beyond that hill.'

Lusiardo hurried off, his khaki tunic was stained with sweat. Cavalli's return of fire served its purpose. The noise from beyond the hill grew, and then the entire skyline became filled with Abyssinian soldiers, some armed with rifles, others with spears and swords, which they were waving in the air while they stamped and shouted. 'Barbaric,' Edio muttered. The Senussi had been far more sophisticated in their methods of warfare. But then they had never had the numbers to risk a proper battle.

He signalled the trumpeter to stand beside him and together with Lusiardo they watched the Abyssinians forming into line. 'They are not going to charge?' Lusiardo asked incredulously.

'They are. Tell Cavalli to bring his range down to the hillock top and maintain fire.'

Lusiardo dashed away.

Edio levelled his glasses and saw the first shell drop with perfect accuracy, exploding in the midst of the dense enemy ranks, tossing men to and fro like toys. Again the guns had served their purpose. The Abyssinian host gave another roar and charged down the hill. The trumpeter was fiddling with his instrument and Edio smiled at him. 'There is time,' he said.

The Abyssinians were still half a mile away, running across the uneven ground, disappearing into hollows and reappearing again, some firing their rifles as they ran, others waving their spears. To the north their comrades began to fire into the Italian position, as did those on the south bank of the river. But as Edio had estimated would be the case, their shooting was wild. He was about to give the order to open fire when one of the conscripts lost his nerve and anticipated him. The single shot was followed by several more, and then the entire Italian force opened up.

Edio cursed. Not that it made a lot of difference; his men were armed with repeating rifles and had ample supplies of ammunition, while the enemy were already within range and were being cut to pieces by the chattering machine-guns. But *he* had intended to give the order.

The noise was enormous and the casualties severe on the Abyssinian side. Men fell left and right and none actually reached Edio, standing before his truck at the forefront of the Italian line. One got close enough to hurl a spear which Edio sidestepped before shooting his assailant with his revolver. Then they were fleeing back to the hill. 'Sound the cease fire,' Edio said.

The trumpeter blew, and again, but it was several minutes before the last shot was fired. Then the Abyssinians had retreated up the hill and beyond, leaving a considerable number of mounds, clad in white or brightly coloured kaftans and turbans, sprawled on the road and in the country to the north. 'Casualty report,' Edio told Lusiardo. 'And tell the men they may eat and drink, but where they are.'

'Are we not going to advance?' Lusiardo was astonished.

'Not until we have lunched,' Edio said. He was not the least hungry and he did not suppose many of his men were, but he was still concerned with time.

Lalia arrived. 'Oh, Edio, you said we would win. And we did.' She was highly excited as she stared along the road. 'Are all those men dead?'

'I'm afraid they are, or they soon will be,' Edio said.

Lalia clasped her neck. 'Are you going to help them?'

'No.' His orderly had been pouring and he gave her a glass of wine. 'If we leave our position we may be picked off by sharp-shooters.'

Lusiardo saluted. 'We have four men killed, and thirteen wounded, sir.'

'Seventeen?' Now it was Edio's turn to be astonished. 'They must have been needlessly exposing themselves.'

'The men are very eager to advance,' Lusiardo said.

'We will maintain our position,' Edio said.

'Listen!' Lalia said. 'What is that noise?'

'Aircraft,' Edio said. They all looked up, as did the entire Italian force, to watch the two flights of six planes each swooping low over the hills to the north. 'That is why we are standing fast,' Edio said.

'Oh, Edio,' Lalia squealed. 'You are a genius.'

'Now you may tell the officers to prepare to advance, Lusiardo,' Edio said, 'as soon as the air strike has been completed.'

The biplanes came low over the Italian position, waggling their wings. Lusiardo was just hurrying off to relay the order when the telegrapher came up and saluted. 'Message from headquarters, sir.'

'Yes?'

'The air strike you requested should be with you at any minute.'

Edio nodded. 'For once they are reasonably accurate. Acknowledge.' He levelled his binoculars as the planes soared over the hill to the west.

'There is more, sir.'

Edio turned his head. 'What more?'

'Headquarters said there must be no advance on the enemy position for four hours after the strike.'

Edio frowned. 'Are you sure you received that correctly?'

'Yes, sir.'

'Well, confirm it.'

'It was confirmed immediately, sir. By a further transmission, which reads, repeat, there must be no advance to the enemy position for four hours following the strike. This is a minimum time requirement.'

Lusiardo was scratching his head. 'What is the point in the strike, if we are to allow them time to re-form? Is not haste imperative?'

Edio levelled his glasses. The planes were now dropping their bombs. They could hear the crumps of the explosions, and they could see clouds of dust and rock, and presumably men, rising into the air. Four hours? When at this moment the enemy morale would be shattered?

The planes were turning for another run and again there were a series of explosions. Then the aircraft turned and flew over the Italian positions, again waggling their wings.

Various officers arrived at the command truck staring at the hill. 'When do we advance, General?'

Edio looked at his watch. 'Six o'clock this evening.'

'Six o'clock? But that is—'

'Four hours away,' Edio said. 'Maintain your positions.'

The men were as mystified as himself. There was considerable noise from beyond the hill for some time, but it slowly died, and through his binoculars Edio watched the two flanking parties withdrawing in some haste. With them went the noise, slowly fading into the distance. The temptation at least to go up to the hill and see what lay beyond was enormous, but Edio was a stickler for obeying orders. He watched the hands of his watch slowly perambulating, while Lalia brushed her hair and Lusiardo marched up and down. 'Six o'clock.' Edio summoned his horse.

'Let me come with you?' Lalia asked.

'To look at a lot of dead bodies? Tell the commanders to be prepared to move out,' Edio told Lusiardo. He summoned the trumpeter and the cavalry captain, and the three men walked their horses forward and up the hill. The sun was now very low and it would be dark in half an hour. Dildug would have to wait until tomorrow. But he was acting on direct orders from GHQ.

'What do you expect to see, General?' the captain asked.

'It is better not to expect anything,' Edio said.

They stood on their hilltop and looked down on a scene of devastation. And yet ... there were one or two small craters in the valley floor. But not sufficient to destroy an army. Even more surprisingly, the guns were undamaged ... and yet had not been towed away behind the retreating Abyssinians. And there were certainly casualties; men, and even women, were sprawled on the ground in their hundreds. The most surprising thing of all, however, was that there were no vultures to be seen ... save for one or two lying on the ground, dead. Captain Baldini crossed himself. 'It is as if they were struck down by heaven,' he said.

Edio doubted that heaven had played any part in this catastrophe. He kicked his horse and walked it down the slope. It obeyed him promptly, but when they reached the floor of the valley it checked and whinnied, reluctant to go further. He found his breath suddenly taken away by an unpleasant smell. So the bodies had lain out for four hours, but this was not the smell of decomposing bodies. The trumpeter began to cough. 'My God!' Edio said as the truth dawned on him. 'Back up the hill, quickly.'

They hastily rode back up the slope. 'What can it be, General?' Captain Baldini asked.

'Poison gas,' Edio told him. 'That is why we were told under no circumstances to advance until it had had time to disperse. We will resume our advance tomorrow.'

'I do believe this is hotter than the Sahara,' Sophie said, fanning herself. She sat on the after deck of the *Bremerhaven* and looked at the hills of Yemen to her left, the low coast-line of Sudan to her right.

The Red Sea itself was calm. There was not a breath of wind, and though the steamer was making twelve knots, very little of that wind came sufficiently aft to cool the air. At least the drinks were cold.

'Have you ever been to Kenya?' Ned asked.

'No. Have you?'

He shook his head. 'Another experience to be chalked up. I am just enjoying being on this ship with you.'

'Snap,' Sophie said.

'Tell me this is the last.'

'Won't we be bored?' She squeezed his hand. 'It will be the last. Do you realise that in a couple of months I shall be thirty-five? That is old for a woman.'

'You will never grow old,' he assured her. 'You are too ... too—'

'Febrile?' she smiled.

The captain came down from the bridge to join them; he was their old friend Pfuhl. But today he was looking serious. 'We have just heard on the radio,' he said, 'that the Italians have invaded Ethiopia.'

Both Sophie and Ned sat up. 'They are attacking from both Eritrea and Italian Somaliland, and they are using tanks and airplanes. There is also a rumour that they have used poison gas.'

Sophie clasped her neck and looked at Ned. 'Would we be right in assuming that the Abyssinians are resisting this invasion?' Ned asked.

'Oh, yes, they are fighting as hard as they can, but ... they have no air force to speak of, they have no tanks, and they certainly have no gas.'

'Then they'll still be hungry for our guns,' Ned said.

'Do you think the Italians will try to stop us?' Sophie asked.

'Let us hope not.'

They were tense, went up to the bridge, scoured the sea with their binoculars. In the Red Sea itself they saw only native dhows and a couple of other steamers which had kept them company since the Canal. But when they passed Aden into the Gulf of Aden they were quickly approached by a gunboat flying the Italian flag. 'What are you going to do?' Sophie asked Pfuhl.

'Remind him that I am a German vessel on the high seas,' Pfuhl said.

'Do you think that will stop him if he intends to board?'

'I doubt it,' Ned said. 'But that fellow should.'

For they were also being approached by another warship, and this was a cruiser flying the White Ensign.

'I never supposed a German officer would be happy to see a British warship,' Pfuhl commented. 'But there is a first time for everything.'

The gunboat pulled away, but the cruiser continued to approach. Pfuhl spoke to her by radio claiming to be en route for Beira with the usual 'farming implements'. It was impossible to tell whether or not he was believed, but there was no legitimate reason to stop the *Bremerhaven* and she continued on her way. By now the news bulletins were buzzing, telling of Haile Selassie's appeal to the League of Nations, and of the lead Great Britain was taking in denouncing Italy's aggression, and in proposing sanctions. 'Italy against the world,' Ned commented. 'There's an unlikely pairing.'

'If the world stands firm,' Sophie said, 'Il Duce will have no choice but to pull out and accept the egg on his face. Let's get these guns delivered before he does and the

Abyssinians have no further use for them.'

They rounded Ras Caseyr that night and were in the Indian Ocean proper. The cruiser had remained in sight until dusk, as had the Italian gunboat, but both had disappeared by dawn, as they steered south-east. 'Martingell country,' Sophie observed, having heard so much about the adventures of the great James and Aunt Cecile before the War. 'I feel we are walking back into history.' Ned hugged her.

It was a further four days, steaming as they were at twelve knots, to reach the north-eastern corner of Kenya. There was quite a lot of shipping about, but none seemed curious until the evening of the third day when they were approaching the port of Mogadishu, although staying well off-shore, and the Italian gunboat reappeared. But she had obviously listened to the conversation with the cruiser and did not approach, merely steering on a parallel course. 'He wants to see us past the Italian border,' Pfuhl observed. 'Well, we shall accom-modate him.' Next morning the gunboat was gone and they were looking at a low coastline, lined with mangrove swamps. 'I hope your pilot is around,' Pfuhl observed.

They encountered a fishing fleet whose crews waved and cheered, obviously unused to seeing a steamer so close to shore. 'They'll report all this in Lamu,' Ned suggested.

'By which time we must have the guns ashore, and you will have departed, Captain,' Sophie said.

'Amen,' Pfuhl agreed. 'There is our man.'

The fishing boats were now well astern, but another, single, dhow had appeared in front, flying the Union Jack upside down. Pfuhl altered course and the flag was taken down. Half an hour later they were alongside and, to Sophie's surprise, climbing aboard was Clay.

They embraced, and he even shook hands with Ned and Captain Pfuhl. 'Just like old times,' he commented.

'Let's hope this turns out better,' Sophie remarked.

'It will, but we have to hurry. Hassan here will pilot you in, Captain.'

Hassan and Pfuhl went up to the bridge, and the dhow cast off. 'Why the hurry?' Ned asked. 'Are the Italians in Addis Ababa?'

'Not yet, but they soon will be, unless the League of Nations can stop them. Although we are certainly going to try. No, there is a rumour that there is a big game hunting party in the vicinity.'

'Is that important to us?' Sophie asked.

'It could be. I'm not keen on coincidences. It could just be an Italian-sponsored party.'

'Is there any way they could know we are here?'

'They have agents everywhere. Did you see any warships coming down?'

'Yes,' Ned said. 'We were shadowed by a gunboat for a while. But he didn't interfere with us.'

'We had a British cruiser for protection,' Sophie said.

'But the gunboat will have reported your position and course,' Clay pointed out.

'That can have nothing to do with a hunting party, which must have been organised several weeks ago.'

'We still need to get the guns unloaded and across the border just as rapidly as possible,' Clay insisted.

They joined Pfuhl and Hassan on the bridge as the steamer closed the shore. Hassan spoke no German but the captain understood English. 'You're sure there's enough water?' he asked, staring at the approaching island through his binoculars.

'Round this north end it is deep,' Hassan said.

Slowly the green shore approached and now they could discern that there was a channel leading behind the island. Sophie clutched Ned's arm in sudden apprehension while Clay surveyed the island itself. There was smoke to be seen and the roofs of a village – no doubt the people on shore would also be excited by the appearance of a steamer virtually in their midst, but it was now too late for them to arrange any interference. 'Shit!' Pfuhl muttered, as they rounded the north end of the island steaming dead slow, and were confronted by a narrow mass of sluggish water on which various aquatic plants floated.

'It is deep,' Hassan assured him.

Pfuhl leaned out of the bridge window. 'Prepare to anchor,' he bawled at the mate, who was waiting, equally apprehensive, on the foredeck.

'It will not be necessary,' Hassan said.

Sophie clutched Ned's arm more tightly yet, but the ship continued on its way, while the trees loomed on either side, so close it seemed the branches would brush the funnel. 'We go up there,' Hassan said.

Pfuhl studied the small river that was debouching from their right into the inlet. 'You have got to be crazy,' he commented.

'It will be all right, Captain,' Clay said. 'It is not far now.'

'Starboard two points,' Pfuhl growled, 'then steady as she goes.'

The river was hardly more than fifty yards wide, but it remained deep. Slowly they rounded a bend and came into a broader stretch of water where they saw people and tents and wagons on the bank. 'Eureka,' Clay said.

The anchor was dropped, and lines

carried out from the stern to warp the ship round. It was a matter of toing and froing, and more than once the *Bremerhaven's* keel scraped on the bottom, churning up great puddles of mud and foam. But with the aid of her engine going ahead and then astern in short bursts, and the various warps carried out to the huge trees and then tightened with the ship's winches, she was slowly brought round to face downstream again. 'Whew!' Pfuhl wiped his brow. 'I am exhausted.'

Sophie discovered that she was wet through.

But Clay was as full of energy as ever. 'Let's get these guns ashore,' he said.

Boats were already putting out from the bank and the ship's boats were also put down. They worked all the rest of the day, and into the night. Sophie retired to her bunk and slept through the noise, aware at some stage that Ned had joined her, no less exhausted. But by dawn the last of the crates was ashore; then loading into the wagons commenced, for the journey north.

Clay breakfasted with them on the after deck. 'Our last taste of civilisation – for how long?' Sophie was in a high good humour. She had had a bath, put on clean clothes, and felt ready to take on the world.

'Depends how far you intend to go,' Clay said.

'Oh, we are coming to the border, at least. That is the terms of the delivery, isn't it?'

'Absolutely. But that is not too far. Four hundred and fifty miles. Say a month, if all goes well.'

'And after that?'

'I suggest you simply retrace your way through Kenya to, say, Nairobi and take the train down to Mombasa. The *Bremerhaven* can call for you there, and you will once more be in comfort and safety.'

'Home for Christmas,' Ned suggested.

'With any luck.'

'You owe us some money now,' Sophie remarked.

'The businesswoman as always,' Clay said. From his wallet he took the certified cheque. 'I'm not sure what you are going to do with it here.'

'I'll put it away,' Sophie said, and gave it to the captain for safekeeping. Not only was he an old and trusted employee of the House of Beinhardt, but the cheque was payable to the House and could not be negotiated for anyone else.

'Just be in Mombasa in two months' time,' she said.

'I'll be there,' Pfuhl promised.

Next morning they set out.

It was a considerable caravan, not quite as large in numbers as the one out of

Boujdour, but that was because they were using mule-drawn wagons instead of camels. 'They are going to be able to go all the way?' Sophie asked.

'Certainly to the border. There is a track. After that we shall have to see.' Clay grinned. 'Much will depend on where the Italians have got to.'

The track turned out to be barely discernible and Clay had to send a party ahead to slash their way through the jungle, which in places grew very close. But there were other areas where the trees were scant; these increased as they moved further north and the going became easier. The open spaces were complicated by the presence of both lion and elephant, but these generally kept their distance in view of the size of the caravan. And they helped to provide endless fascination for both Sophie and Ned who had never been in this part of Africa before. In addition to the big game – there were also leopard and cheetah to be seen, not to mention hyena and baboons – there were large herds of various antelope and a huge variety of bird life. 'This place teems,' Ned commented.

'Let's hope it stays this way,' Sophie agreed. 'What about this hunting party?' she asked Clay.

'It's around,' Clay said. 'Hopefully, they won't interfere with us. Perhaps we won't even see them.'

And for three weeks they did not. Then one of the scouts came back to them as they camped for the night. 'There are people in front,' he said.

'How many?' Clay asked.

'I think it is a big number, bwana. I have seen their fire.'

'Do you really think they are there to stop us?' Sophie asked.

'I'm no believer in coincidences,' Clay said.

'So what do you propose to do?' Ned asked. 'Are any of these people of yours any good in a fight?'

'It's what they do best. But it is the guns we must protect.' Clay grinned. 'We don't want a repeat of the last time, eh? So we make camp here, create a perimeter and wait. It will only be for a day or two. If the people in front of us really are a hunting party, they will move on. If they are not, they will stay where they are. In which case we will have to decide whether to try to get round them, which may take a lot of time, or whether to take them on.'

'Three of us,' Ned said.

'And my people,' Clay told him. 'For the time being, let's relax. I am sure we can all do with a rest.'

'I hate to say it,' Ned said that night, 'but

your Yankee boyfriend has a hell of a lot of nerve.'

'Experience,' Sophie said. 'Something we're not short of. But you're not happy.'

'I just hope to hell that *is* a hunting party, and not a British District Commissioner,' Ned said. 'If it is, we're in deep shit.'

'We have been in deep shit before,' she reminded him. 'And we're still here.'

Next morning they were, as Clay had recommended, relaxing over a leisurely breakfast, when Moosah appeared and saluted. 'Any movement?' Clay asked.

'Oh, yes, bwana. Towards us.'

Clay got up, as did Ned. 'How far?'

'Maybe four miles, bwana.'

'But definitely towards us?'

'Yes, bwana.'

'Right. Have your people man the perimeter, six feet between each man. But no one is to shoot unless I do. Understood?'

'Understood, bwana.'

'Check your weapons,' Clay told Ned and Sophie. 'But remember, there is still a chance this *is* a coincidence. If we can get away without shooting, we will do so. If we have to shoot ... well, I guess we'll have to do a complete job.' Another of his grins. 'But you're used to that, I reckon.'

'Yes,' Sophie said. 'If we have to.'

She checked both her revolver and her

rifle. Ned did the same, then with the restlessness of an old soldier he went off to check the perimeter where one of the boxes of machine-guns had been opened and the two weapons inside assembled under Clay's direction. Who now rejoined her. 'Some guy you have there.'

'I know,' Sophie said. 'If it's any good to you, he's coming to respect you, too.'

'Sophie... ' He picked up her hand. 'You know I wish things could have been different between us.'

'Yes,' she said.

'I don't suppose–'

'No,' she said.

'Because of that mix-up with the money? Or because of what happened in the desert. I'm so very sorry about that. But you have to realise that al-Fadl was more than a personal friend and I guess I was outraged at his death. And then, having you, a prisoner, after you had killed some more of my people ... I'm only human.'

'I understand that,' she said.

'Well then, give me a reason.'

'Ned.'

'That–'

'Careful.' She held up her finger.

'You really are going to pretend you're in love with him?'

'I've never been very good at pretending, Clay. Nor, believe it or not, am I promiscuous. I felt a powerful attraction to you when we first met, but I wasn't prepared to commit adultery. If everything had gone according to plan ... I don't know. But nothing went according to plan. So Ned and I were out on our own, with what seemed the whole world against us. Certainly in North Africa.'

'So you settled for adultery anyway.'

'You really are begging for it,' Sophie said.

'Yes. I had found a man I could love.'

He released her hand. 'Supposing–'

'I'm not in the supposing business, Clay. Just let me say that if Ned were to die, from anything save a bullet fired by a certified enemy, the next bullet I fired would be into you.'

He stared at her, an angry flush mounting in his cheeks. 'You really are a–'

'Don't say it, Clay. I know I don't fit into your New England concept of a woman. But then, I'm not a New England woman. I'm just a woman. Who maybe, by the concept of conventional society, should have been born a man. But I wasn't. That doesn't mean I can't be a woman through and through. But also, that I can't fight, or kill, like a man when I have to. You knew that from the moment we met. I like you, I like your ethics, when they're not concentrating on sex. Opposing Fascism is a great business, one we're all going to have to be involved in sooner or later. But don't ask me to give up my man.'

He continued to stare at her for several seconds. Then he said, 'I wish you joy of him,' and got up and walked away.

'They're quite close,' Ned said, kneeling beside her and checking his own weapons. 'Do we leave it all to him?'

'It's his show,' Sophie said.

'Not necessarily,' Ned said. 'The guns are ours, and our responsibility, up till the final payment.'

'Let him do the talking,' Sophie said.

Now the 'hunting party' could be clearly seen, at a distance of about a mile. It was quite large, something like fifty people, Sophie estimated, with a couple of mule-drawn wagons.

She levelled her binoculars, saw that most of them were armed. But only with rifles. If it came to a fight there would be a slaughter. And there were white people over there. Several of them. And a woman, she realised with a start of consternation. A tall, slender woman, with auburn hair tied on the nape of her neck beneath her flat bush hat. 'Holy Hallelujah,' she muttered, and gave the glasses to Ned.

Friends and Enemies

Clay had also been inspecting the hunting party through glasses. Now he came back to Ned and Sophie. 'Looks like someone has been talking out of turn,' he said. 'Now who could that have been, do you suppose?'

Sophie ignored the question: she had her own ideas about the answer. 'What are we going to do?'

'I think they have come to hijack the shipment,' Clay said. 'Obviously we can't let them do that. Nor can we talk our way past them, even supposing that were possible, because then they would hang on our trail and gradually whittle us down. So ... we have to destroy them.'

Sophie swallowed. 'Destroy Major Elligan?' Ned asked. 'And those others? Those are my comrades.'

'Were, surely,' Clay suggested.

'I'm not going to fire on my husband,' Sophie said.

'Then I shall have to ask you to retire, with...' Clay glanced contemptuously at Ned, 'your partner, until we are finished. It should not take long.'

'No,' Ned said. 'Let me talk with them.'

'What about? I've told you, even if they'll let us through, we can't afford to leave them behind us.'

'I'm going to invite them to surrender,' Ned said. 'If I explain to them that they are outgunned, it would be the sensible thing to do.'

'I have no intention of lumbering myself with fifty-odd prisoners,' Clay said.

'You won't have to. The only prisoners we need are Major Elligan and Lady Martingell. For the rest, we'll leave them one rifle and sufficient ammunition to get them back to Nairobi, or wherever they came from. Without Major Elligan to lead them, they won't cause any trouble.'

Clay looked at Sophie. 'I think that's a very sensible idea,' she said.

Clay shrugged. 'You can have a go.'

'I think you should have a white flag,' Sophie said.

Ned nodded and one of his spare shirts was attached to his rifle barrel. Then he stood up and walked through the perimeter into the open. The hunting party was now about 600 yards away and halted as he approached. 'Good morning to you, Major,' Ned called.

'Ned Carew, by God,' Richard said. 'I had not expected ever to see you again, you scoundrel.'

'Nor I you, Major,' Ned said equably. 'But

I guess we're both in the same business. May I ask your intentions?'

'You are carrying an illegal cargo, Carew,' Richard said, advancing in turn to stand clear of his people. Sophie found she was chewing her lip in anxiety. 'And it is our intention to relieve you of it.'

'Major,' Ned said. 'I think you need to be sensible. I have at my back sixty riflemen and two machine-guns. If you attack us, we will cut you to ribbons. I am offering you your lives.'

'Our lives?' Richard snorted.

'Here is my proposal,' Ned said. 'You and your people will hand over your weapons. You may keep one rifle and a supply of ammunition for defence against wild animals and for securing game. Your people will then take themselves off.'

'You are so very generous,' Richard said.

'But you, Major, and Lady Martingell, will accompany us until this cargo has been delivered. Then you too may take yourselves off.'

'You mean you wish Lady Martingell and myself to surrender to you? You must be mad.'

'You will not be hurt or ill-treated,' Ned assured him. 'We just wish to keep you out of mischief for the next fortnight or so.'

'You are a treacherous, wife-stealing bastard,' Richard said. 'Be damned to you.'

He drew his revolver with all the speed Sophie remembered from the old days and fired. Ned went down and Sophie screamed and stood up, only to be thrown down again by Clay as he gave the order to open fire.

It was, as Ned had predicted, a massacre. Caught in the open and having totally underestimated the caravan's firepower, Richard's force was cut to pieces by the machine-guns before they could effectively fire a shot. Richard himself fell while Anne and the other white men took shelter, although at least one of them was hit; the bearers took to their heels, leaving several dead behind them. 'Cease firing,' Clay shouted, and the echoes slowly died away; scattered and terrified birds still wheeled overhead.

'Ned,' Sophie said. 'I must get to him.'

Again Clay restrained her. 'In a minute. You out there,' he shouted. 'Elligan? Can you hear me? Lady Martingell? Come out with your hands up or I will resume firing.' There was a brief hiatus, while Sophie chafed, imagining Ned dead or bleeding to death ... then Anne stepped out from the shelter of the wagons followed by three men. Their hands were high and they had discarded their weapons; two of them were clearly wounded, although Anne had not been hit. 'Just come here, nice and slow,' Clay commanded. 'Okay, Sophie, go get your man. Just don't let any of those four get close to you.'

Anne had already stopped beside Richard. The three others also paused. Clay signalled half a dozen of his men to come forward with him, behind Sophie, who was now running to where Ned lay. 'Ned!' she shouted, kneeling beside him.

He was alive but had been hit in the ribs, at least two of which were clearly broken. 'We must stop the bleeding and bind him up,' Sophie said, and felt his fingers close on hers. 'Oh, Ned!'

'I never thought he'd do that,' Ned whispered.

Sophie tore off his shirt. Clay had signalled for his people to bring up their medical supplies, which included pain-killers. Ned was fed some of these and lapsed into sleep, while Sophie set the ribs as well as she could and then bound him tightly round the waist. When he woke up he was going to be in considerable pain. 'We need a doctor,' she said.

'There is a doctor in Gidole,' Clay said. 'But that is still a few weeks away.'

'A few weeks? Isn't Nairobi closer?'

'Considerably. But the guns have to go to Gidole and so do we. We must do the best we can till then.'

Sophie raised her head, wiping her bloodstained fingers on her skirt. 'We?'

'He's your man, Sophie. I'll help you keep him alive.'

'On your terms. Then I should be eternally grateful.' She stood up, watched Anne Martingell coming towards her.

'Richard needs help,' she said. Her face was ashen.

'He behaved very foolishly, Lady Martingell,' Clay said. 'And dishonourably, firing on a white flag.'

'We never thought you would fire into us,' Anne said. 'He was so confident.'

'As I said, he was foolish.' Clay signalled his assistants, and they went to where Richard lay.

Anne followed. 'And me?'

'You will have to come with us,' Clay said. 'You'll want to stay with Elligan, won't you? And there will be no proper medical aid until we reach Gidole. You three,' he turned to the English ex-soldiers, 'are your comrades dead?'

'Or dying,' one of them said.

'I am sorry for it, but your major caused this to happen. Now I offer you the same terms. A rifle, some ammunition, and a supply of food, and you take yourselves off. Be sure that if you attempt to follow us, I will kill you.'

'And the lady?'

'The lady stays with us. She'll come to no harm.'

'This is a bad business,' said another of them. 'We hadn't counted on fighting a battle.'

'Neither had we,' Clay said. 'You may bury your dead, then be on your way.'

Sophie supervised the loading of Ned into one of the wagons. It was going to be a terribly uncomfortable journey but she intended to see he made it. She supposed she should be hating Clay all over again, but she had known for a long time that he rated the delivery of the guns over any small matters such as life and death and injury; she presumed he included his own life in that determination. By then the dead had been buried and Richard had also been brought in. He had been hit in the left shoulder which was broken, although Clay had bound up the wound as best he could. Like Ned, he had been sedated.

Anne joined her by the wagon. 'We seem destined to follow a very crooked trail,' she said.

'Do you love him?' Sophie asked.

Anne made a moue. 'No. I don't think so. We were lovers, once, but that was a long time ago. Then we quarrelled. Then ... he was good to me these last few years. Did *you* love him?'

'Oh, indeed. Well, perhaps, once upon a time. He was a very romantic figure who was doing what I wanted to do. As a woman, I could only do it with him. Can you understand that?'

'I felt exactly the same about James Martingell. Now...' She looked at Ned, who was moving restlessly, although he was still sedated.

'I love *him*,' Sophie said.

'And when he is dead?'

'He is not going to die,' Sophie said fiercely.

Anne made another moue. 'I was just wondering where your American fits into all this?'

'He is the purchaser of the guns, nothing more.'

'Oh, come now,' Anne said. 'You went off into the desert with him. Richard told me all about it.'

'I went off into the desert with Ned,' Sophie said. 'I think, as you are going to be my guest for the next week or two, we should endeavour to be friends.'

'I just need to know where I stand,' Anne said.

'This place is a dump,' Lalia complained. 'When are we moving on? I thought we were going up to Addis Ababa.' She spent a lot of time nowadays studying maps.

But Edio entirely agreed with her. Dildug was a dump. It was a mosaic of sun-dried brick dominated by a church and a fort. The church reminded him, disagreeably, that he was actually fighting against Christians rather than heathen savages. The fort had cost him two men dead and several wounded to take, even after he had bombarded it with his artillery. What was far more disconcerting was the fact that he was still here after more than a month. Take Dildug, he had been told, and await further orders to advance. But the only orders he had received were: hold your ground.

He knew, of course, from the snippets of news that arrived from the coast, that things were not going according to plan. The Italians were claiming a great victory in the north, but he doubted that victory was any more substantial than his here in the south. And meanwhile, the international reaction had been predictable. Even if the British Foreign Minister, Sir Samuel Hoare, had apparently ruled out the use of force to stop Italy's expansion in Africa, and had even hinted that it might be justified, the latest news was that Hoare might be forced to resign and that the League of Nations was adopting a far more positive view, drawing up a list of economic sanctions to be imposed on Italy if Mussolini did not cease hostilities and withdraw his armies. There was of course only one item which, if sanctioned, could bring Italy to her knees:

oil. She had none of her own, and modern armies depended on oil for movement. As yet oil had not been listed. But if it were ... Edio could well understand Mussolini's reluctance to commit his men further when they might suddenly be left without fuel and thus marooned in an entirely hostile country, with another Adowa a possibility.

Well, Edio thought, aren't we marooned anyway? He had received one supply column from Mogadishu since reaching Dildug, and the column had had to engage in several skirmishes with Abyssinian forces to reach him. The air force had been called in, but the use of gas had been suspended for the moment, as this was causing an ever greater outcry amongst the nations of the League. Dildug was surrounded by cultivated fields, but the residents had all run off and his men were not farmers; the fields were derelict. So he and his men – and his woman – sat, and sweated, and waited. And suffered. He had lost five men to guerrillas since taking the town. Three had disappeared altogether. Two had been found, stripped naked, castrated and with their eyelids cut away, staked out in the sun to die, their eyes pecked out and their vitals torn at by buzzards while they had still lived. Even a hardened soldier like himself had felt sick.

So they had retaliated, caught a few of the

Abyssinians and hanged them. Not for the first time in his life Edio wondered if he was a soldier or an executioner. But for the presence of Lalia, however complaining, he thought he might have gone mad; several of his men, with only captured native women for company – and these were as likely as not to slip a knife between the ribs of the man writhing in ecstacy on top of them even if that also involved a hanging – had already had to be certified as ill when everyone knew they were simply out of their minds.

'There is an aircraft approaching, General.' Lusiardo stood in the doorway of the room Edio had appropriated as his office.

Edio got up and accompanied his second-in-command onto the porch to watch the single biplane coming towards them, and then swooping low over the open land just beyond the town. From its cockpit something white fluttered, then opened into a small parachute. 'Is there no radio?' Lusiardo inquired at large.

'Perhaps it is a secret weapon.' Lalia had joined them.

'Have it picked up,' Edio said. But he remained on the porch as men hurried from the gate to collect the parachute which had by now reached the ground. The plane had turned and flown off again. He was curious. It was a very peculiar way of communicating.

Lusiardo returned, out of breath as usual. 'There is a single package, General,' he said. 'For you.'

It really was nothing more than a weighted envelope. But it was certainly addressed to him and was marked both Urgent and Top Secret. Which presumably was why the message had not been sent through the insecure radio.

'Leave me,' Edio said. Lusiardo saluted. Lalia shrugged and also left. Edio sat at his desk and slit the envelope, took out the sheet of paper inside.

General Rometti, General Graziani had written. *A situation has arisen in your area which must be dealt with immediately. We have been informed that a caravan bearing a large number of guns, both rifles, machine-guns, and field guns, together with their ammunition, is approaching the Abyssinian border from the south, i.e. Kenya. We are informed that its initial destination is the town of Gidole, which is still in Abyssinian hands. This shipment is from the House of Beinhardt, a company with which I understand you have already had contact. It is imperative that this shipment does not reach the Abyssinians. The matter is in your hands. You will use cavalry only, as preservation of our fuel stocks is essential at this time. Under no circumstances will you cross the border into Kenya – it is essential that we maintain good relations with Great Britain. You will therefore aim to intercept the caravan as soon as you are certain it is in Abyssinian territory. If it will assist you in your estimation of the caravan's strength and intentions, I can tell you that it is commanded by an American soldier of fortune named Clayton Andrews. One last thing: it is in the interests of Italy that this mission be carried out in secret, hence this method of conveying your orders. Good fortune. Graziani.*

Edio laid down the letter. Clayton Andrews. A man who had haunted him for too many years. But who had been active again for over a year now. Well, well, he thought. And again with guns from the House of Beinhardt. He wondered if that devilishly attractive woman Sophie Elligan was involved. Lalia had told him all about Sophie and her English lover, Carew. About that unforgettable march across the desert when they had come close to death a dozen times and had still survived thanks to Sophie and Carew's deadly determination. When they had reached Egypt they had given her sufficient money to return to Cyrenaica, and had disappeared. She had not heard from them since. But they had survived. And now ... perhaps this was his opportunity to right a great many personal wrongs.

He studied the letter again. The only direct orders it contained were that the caravan must be captured and that he must use cavalry. That would have made sense even if he had had all the petrol in the world; the country between Dildug and the border, and even more to the west, was singularly lacking in roads, and he had no tracked vehicles. But there was no indication of who should lead the cavalry. His duty, of course, was to remain at Dildug. But Lusiardo was quite capable of commanding here. And obviously, as he had been ordered to detach his cavalry, the brigade's would continue to be a purely defensive role until this mission had been completed. And it would be something to do.

He rang his bell and both Lusiardo and Lalia appeared. 'I have been commanded to undertake a scouting expedition to the southwest,' he said. 'What is our present cavalry strength?'

'We have two hundred and eighteen men and horses available for duty, General,' Lusiardo said.

'Very good. Inform Captain Baldini that he moves out in one hour. One hundred rounds of ammunition per man, two machine-gun sections, rations for three weeks.'

'Yes, sir. Captain Baldini's orders?'

'He will receive them from me on the march.'

Lusiardo goggled at him. Lalia was first to

react. 'You are going yourself?'

'That is what I have been ordered to do,' Edio lied.

'I am to come with you?'

'No,' Edio said. 'It will be an arduous patrol.'

'But...' Lusiardo had recovered. 'Who will command here, General?'

'You will, Lusiardo. You will remain strictly on the defensive until my return.'

Lusiardo gulped; he had not anticipated being left in charge of the brigade. 'And I am to stay too?' Lalia complained. 'In this dump?'

'This dump is better than what is out there,' Edio told her.

'But, Edio, if something were to happen to you—'

'Nothing is going to happen to me,' Edio assured her. 'I shall be back in three weeks.'

'Tomorrow we cross the border,' Clay said, walking beside Sophie, while the wagons creaked and rumbled behind them, and the drivers urged the mules on with cracking whips and loud cries.

'Thank God for that. And then?'

'Another hundred and thirty-odd miles to Gidole.'

'Jesus,' she muttered. 'Over that?' Throughout their march through Kenya the ground had been fairly level. Now she

400

looked at mountains, some of them rising several thousand feet, she was sure, both in front of them and to their right. It reminded her of Afghanistan and Turkestan, save for the heat.

'It'll be rough,' Clay agreed. 'How're the casualties?'

'They're both running a temperature. How long?'

'A fortnight, I'm afraid. We're not doing much more than ten miles a day.'

'And the wagons will make it the whole way?'

'I told you, we have to play it by ear. We'll certainly move them as far as possible. But I am expecting assistance from the north; they know we are coming.'

Sophie went back to the wagons and looked into the back of the medical wagon. Anne had been on sick duty and sat beside the two men. Both were fully conscious and both were in considerable discomfort, but the women had decided to go easy on the analgesics; they did not have all that much. Sophie clambered up. 'Seems we've got up to Abyssinia,' she said.

'A place I have never wanted to visit,' Anne remarked.

'We've been there,' Ned muttered. 'It's not so bad. Bit up and down.' He squeezed Sophie's hand. 'Is that a problem?'

'Not yet.' She dipped a cloth in the bucket

of water and wiped his forehead; he was bathed in sweat, but then so was she.

'How much further?' Richard asked.

Sophie would have found it amusing in any other circumstances that Richard and Ned should be lying side by side, both incapable of movement ... having both tried to kill each other. At least, Richard had tried to kill Ned. She should hate him for that. But as Ned obviously didn't, she couldn't either.

'A fortnight, Clay says.'

Ned grinned. 'We'll be all healed again by then.'

Oh, if that could be true, Sophie thought. Actually, both men were doing quite well, thanks to the modern antibiotics with which Clay had been equipped. But they both had a fever and she wasn't sure the medicines would last another fortnight. While she had no idea what might await them in Gidole. Clay said there was a doctor there, but would he have any medicine? Once again, a disaster? She was determined that would not happen.

Anne walked beside Clay at the head of the caravan. 'When will we cross the border?' she asked.

'We already have.'

She looked left and right. 'How do you know?'

'Knowing is what this war is all about. But I'd say we are now in Abyssinia.'

They walked in silence for a while, then she asked, 'What will you do after the guns are delivered?'

He shrugged. 'Try to make myself useful.'

'Do you mind if I ask you why? I mean, as I understand it, you have a good job and a comfortable lifestyle back in the States. Why do you endure all this discomfort and risk your life, for the sake of–'

'Careful, now.'

'I was going to say, people with whom you cannot possibly have anything in common.'

'That's not altogether true. They're people who are fighting for their right to exist. I happen to agree that they should have that right.'

'Then I apologise. Why is that man gesticulating?'

One of the advance guard was standing on a low hill a few hundred yards in front of the caravan, and waving his arms. 'He is not giving the alarm, that's for sure,' Clay said. 'Would you like to go back to the wagons, just in case?'

'No,' she said. 'I would rather stay here with you.'

He glanced at her in surprise, then shrugged again. They reached the scout who spoke rapidly in Amharic. 'There is water ahead,' Clay said.

'Oh, how splendid. Do you think I could have a bath?'

'I don't see why not. Maybe we all can.'

They reached the waterhole, which fed a small river, just on dusk. The ground had been steadily rising all day and the mules had found the going hard, while always there was the threat of the mountains, now quite close. But by the water there was even a small wood, in strong contrast to the general aridity with which they were surrounded. Camp was pitched and their waterskins were filled. 'I'm for a dip,' Anne said. 'You interested, Sophie?'

'You bet, after we've given the boys a wash down.'

'If you knew how foolish I feel, lying here,' Ned said, as Sophie sponged his body.

'You'll feel better for being clean,' she said. 'How *are* you feeling?'

He grinned. 'As if I've got a knife sticking in my ribs which won't go away. But it's not getting any worse.'

'Only another ten days or so to Gidole,' she reminded him.

Richard was by now able to walk, even if he still had his arm in a sling, and he went down to the stream with Anne for a bathe. Sophie made Ned comfortable and followed, to stand on the bank beside him while Anne disported herself in the water, washing her hair again and again, and soaping her body, again and again. 'She is a remarkably well-preserved woman,' Sophie remarked.

'You mean for her age. I think it is because she has lived an even more adventurous life than you, Sophie.'

'Give me time,' Sophie said. 'Do you realise this is the first time you and I have had a civilised conversation for nearly six years?'

'The night before you left for North Africa,' he said. 'With Ned.'

She sighed. 'I can't say I'm sorry for the way things turned out because that would be a lie. Our marriage was just about done. Did you know that?'

'Men are always reluctant to give up their possessions.'

'Is that how you looked at me, as a possession?'

'I think you will find that is how most men look at their wives, even if you will not often get them to admit it. Don't you think Ned looks on you as a possession?'

Sophie tossed her head. 'Ned and I are partners.'

'But he is the senior partner.'

'If you are trying to irritate me, you are succeeding.' Sophie started to undress. 'Will it embarrass you to watch me bathe?'

'I shall enjoy it. You are still a most lovely woman.'

She dropped her skirt on top of her boots. 'Will you tell me why you are here? You didn't really think you could take over the caravan, did you?'

'I was hoping at least to turn you back.'

'Why?' Naked, she faced him, her body glowing in the slightly chill wind coming down from the mountains.

'Because of a man named Pemberton. Do you remember him?'

'I remember Pemberton.'

'Well...' Richard told her what Pemberton had had to say.

'You mean, when you go home, you are liable to be sent to prison?'

'I am hoping not. If you would provide me with some proof that I did try to stop you. Apart from the bullet wound.'

'I may just do that,' Sophie said. 'Then we're quits, right?'

'Right,' he said. 'What exactly is your relationship with Andrews?'

Sophie looked round and saw Clay coming towards them.

'We don't have a relationship,' she said. 'But same as you, he likes to look.'

She went into the water.

Even watching the women left Ned exhausted. Sophie also retired early, feeling

406

immensely better for being clean. Anne continued to sit on the banks of the stream, wrapped in a towel, enjoying the cool of the evening. Clay sat beside her. They had bathed together earlier and struck a new chord of intimacy. But Sophie had also been there. 'Have you ever had sex with her?' Anne asked.

'Not quite,' he admitted, with a wry grin. 'We were interrupted.'

'But you would like to?'

'Wouldn't any man? She is a lot of woman.'

'Yes,' Anne said thoughtfully. 'One would have thought with that servant of hers so badly wounded—'

'I could take her by force? Sophie isn't really the sort of woman one takes by force. And Carew is not her servant. He is her lover. Didn't Elligan tell you that?'

'Yes,' she said. 'He did. I think you must be a very honourable man, Mr Andrews.'

'You should ask my enemies. Or even Sophie. She doesn't trust me an inch. She reckons I double-crossed her the last time we did business together. That's why she's here, to make sure she gets paid in full.'

'Which will be when?'

'When we reach Gidole.'

'After which she will just fade away? With her lover?'

'I imagine that's her idea.'

'While you, as you said, find something useful to do. I don't suppose you'd care for an assistant?' Clay turned his head sharply. 'So I am probably old enough to be your mother,' Anne said without embarrassment. 'But I don't think that's important. You have had a good look at my body. You won't find a better one – if you can't have Sophie. And I am very capable and experienced, both in the field and in bed. I served my apprenticeship with James Martingell.'

'A man I sincerely regret never having met,' Clay said.

'*Did* you double-cross Sophie?'

'Matters were taken out of my hands.'

'I see. Then you are probably fortunate you never did meet James. He had a habit of killing people who double-crossed him.'

'Touché. But I don't live an easy life, either. You want to think about that.'

'When I return to England...' Anne said, '*if* I return to England, I shall probably be sent back to prison. I don't think I could stand that.' She waited for him to comment, but as he didn't, went on, 'I would be absolutely faithful to you, and as I have said, I am capable of bearing any hardship.'

'And what about Elligan?'

'I think he will have to fend for himself. This whole trip was his idea. I was against it from the beginning. As for suddenly firing on Carew like that–'

'You don't think he was just apeing his mentor, James Martingell?'

'Richard Elligan could never be half the man James was. Do you know that he and Sophie rode off and left James to die in Afghanistan?'

'That's not how Sophie tells it.'

'Well, she would have her own version of events, wouldn't she?'

'I suppose she would,' Clay said thoughtfully.

'So, will you take me on?' Anne asked. 'I want nothing save my keep and the right to be with you and serve you.' She hesitated. 'In every way.'

'Ask me again when we have delivered the guns,' he suggested. She made a moue. 'If that is what you wish. But in the meantime, I think I should at least give you something to consider.' She shrugged the towel from her shoulders and kissed him on the mouth.

The devil, Clay thought, as he walked in front of the caravan the next day; both women were in the medical wagon with their men. Their official men, he thought. He, with his limited sexual experience, had been a complete tyro in the arms of Anne Martingell. Perhaps she *was* what he had wanted, all of these years. All of his life. A woman old enough to be his mother, who could teach him so much, and so enjoyably.

If he could still dream of one day possessing Sophie, he knew she would never be entirely compliant, entirely servile – she was too much her own woman.

Anne Martingell was undoubtedly also her own woman – but she had known how to surrender when it suited her purpose; she had been both mentor and mistress at the same time. And there could be no question that, even at fifty-seven, she had the body and the virility of a woman half that age. James Martingell's woman! That was an attraction, too.

He found himself smiling as he wondered what the folks would say if he turned up back in Connecticut with Anne Martingell at his side. Of course, like most of Connecticut society, they would be impressed by the fact that she was titled. But it would still cut a swathe.

Moosai was waving in front of him again. He signalled the caravan to stop and went forward. 'People,' Moosai said.

Clay climbed the hillock and levelled his binoculars. 'Our people,' Moosai said. He did not need binoculars.

'You're right,' Clay said. 'They've come to make sure we get the goods to Gidole.'

'We must hope so, bwana.'

Clay returned to the caravan. 'Another waterhole?' Anne asked optimistically, thrusting her head out of the back of the wagon.

'Abyssinian soldiers, we think,' Clay said. 'Come to escort us to Gidole.' He told his people to pitch camp, then awaited the arrival of the support. There were only some forty of them, mounted and well-armed. And at their front ... Clay frowned, and felt a sudden constriction of his chest. 'Yusuf?' he asked incredulously. 'Yusuf ben Hashem?'

Yusuf dismounted and came forward to embrace him. 'It is good to see you, old friend.'

'But ... what are you doing here?' Clay asked.

'The same as you, fighting with the Abyssinians. Oh, they are Christians. But they welcome a fighting man with my reputation. And they are fighting the Italians. Perhaps here is our opportunity to avenge ourselves for the catastrophe at Tamanrasset, eh? And when I heard you were also fighting for Haile Selassie, I was delighted. You have the guns?'

'Yes,' Clay said.

'That is splendid. But where did you get them? We have been told that the sources of supply are now very scarce.'

'One can always get guns if one knows where to shop,' Clay said.

'Of course. Now, let us eat, and then resume your march.'

'Italians?'

'We have not seen any, but they have occupied Dildug in force, and who can tell when they may come this way.'

'Then we must hurry,' Clay said. 'Moosai, we will eat now. You'll excuse me, Yusuf.'

He hurried back to the wagons. Of all the catastrophes. Nor was he at all sure what to do. Yusuf was a far older and more loyal friend than Sophie Elligan. He had also obviously been given a command in the Abyssinian Army. But the thought of handing Sophie over to Arab vengeance ... He opened the flap of the medical wagon and clambered in. 'Is all well?' Sophie said.

'No, all is not well,' Clay said. 'Our reinforcements are commanded by Yusuf ben Hashem.'

'Yusuf–' Sophie bit her lip.

'A friend of yours?' Anne asked.

'No exactly.'

'Were you aware that Sheikh al-Fadl was his uncle?' Clay asked. Sophie gulped. 'So,' Clay said, 'it would be safest for everyone if you remained in the wagon until we reach Gidole.'

'But that's another ten days!'

'Can't be helped. If Yusuf finds out you are with the caravan...' It was his turn to gulp, as the back flap was thrown open.

'Shit,' Sophie said and reached for her revolver.

But Clay caught her wrist. She glared at

412

him and tried to pull away. But he would not let go; he had again chosen his side. 'Mrs Elligan,' Yusuf said, with deep satisfaction. His English was surprisingly good.

Sophie stopped trying to free herself. 'Yusuf ben Hashem,' she replied, as calmly as she could.

Beside her Ned tried to sit up but couldn't. 'Well, well,' Yusuf said. 'I had heard there were other Europeans with this caravan. And I wondered ... now I am pleased.' His gaze swept over Anne and Richard but they obviously did not register. Then he looked at Ned. 'And the faithful servant. Wounded, I see.'

'While trying to deliver your guns,' Sophie said.

'That is not my concern,' Yusuf said and looked at Clay. 'I will take the woman – now.'

'Now, hold on a moment,' Clay said. 'Mrs Elligan and I have a business deal to deliver these guns to Gidole.'

'She murdered my uncle,' Yusuf said. 'That is more important than any business deal.'

Clay bit his lip. 'You can't allow this,' Sophie said in a low voice.

'Just what is it between you two?' Anne asked.

'He means to execute me for killing his

uncle,' Sophie said.

'Good lord,' Anne said. Not even the Mad Mullah had threatened to execute her out of hand.

Ned was still trying to sit up. 'I killed the sheikh,' he said.

Yusuf snorted. 'Always the faithful servant. But you are only a servant, Carew. You did what you were told. Put the woman out, Clay.'

'You cannot!' Sophie shouted.

'For God's sake give me a gun,' Ned said.

'You have sixty men here,' Anne reminded Clay. 'He has only forty.–'

'Do you think these men will fight against mine?' Yusuf asked contemptuously. 'They are all brothers, all devoted to the same cause. There is not one of them will deny me my rights.'

'Is that true?' Anne asked Clay.

'I'm afraid it is,' Clay said.

'You...' Sophie could not believe her ears. 'You are going to let him take me? Just like that?'

'There is nothing I can do,' Clay said. 'You killed his uncle. By his law he has the right to kill you in turn. We are fighting a war. I cannot let personal feuds interfere.'

'You bastard,' Ned said. 'You unutterable bastard. When I get my hands on you–'

'I may have to kill you,' Clay said coldly.

Ned turned to Yusuf. 'I killed your uncle,

you dumb ox. I. Me. I shot him.'

'Obeying orders,' Yusuf said. 'Come on, Mrs Elligan. Get down.'

'Oh, my God,' Anne said. 'Oh, my *God!* Richard!'

'What do you wish me to do?' Richard asked. 'Take on the whole Abyssinian army single-handed?'

'And you?' Anne demanded of Clay. 'I thought you were a man. '

'Men have to make decisions,' Clay said. 'I'm sorry, Sophie. I give you my word that the final payment will be sent to your father.'

Sophie stared at him. 'You are an unspeakable cur, Clay Andrews,' she said. 'My mistake was ever to have dealings with you at all.' She looked at Yusuf. 'Am I allowed to say goodbye to my ... servant?'

'No,' Yusuf said. 'We are losing time.'

'Sophie,' Ned said. 'My God, Sophie!'

'Avenge me,' Sophie said. 'When you can.'

She dropped over the tailgate to the ground. The altercation had attracted most of the camp and she was entirely surrounded by the Abyssinians, clearly very interested in what was going to happen. My God, she thought, if I am to be executed as al-Fadl had boasted of executing one of his wives...

'I will spare your sensibilities,' Yusuf told the stricken people in the wagon. He gave orders to his people and Sophie's wrists were bound together in front of her by a long length of line, the other end of which was then secured to Yusuf's saddle. 'I shall be back in an hour,' he said. 'Then we will resume our march.'

He mounted and walked his horse out of the camp towards a low hill to the east. Sophie's arms were jerked and she fell to her knees, but managed to regain her feet and stumble after him. I must not scream, I must not beg, she told herself. No matter what he does to me. She dared not look back because then she would have collapsed into tears. She was close to tears anyway.

Yusuf continued to walk his horse up the slope. The ground was uneven and every so often Sophie fell and had to stagger back to her feet again; her skirt was already torn in several places and she knew the flesh beneath was also cut. But it was worse when Yusuf topped the hill and started down the other side because on the downward slope she fell again and again, and was dragged over the stones and through the bushes. She was being sliced to ribbons.

Then suddenly Yusuf drew rein and dismounted. 'This is far enough, I think,' he said. 'I do not want them to hear your screams.'

Sophie was on her knees, seeing him through a mist of red anger and white tears. He stood above her. 'Oh, you have a great deal of fortitude, Mrs Elligan. But I knew this. Yet you will scream. I am not in a position to execute you as a woman, you see,' he said. 'Therefore I am going to grant you the great privilege of being executed as a man.' He released her wrists. 'Strip.'

Sophie blinked at him. She knew an enormous temptation to go out fighting, hurl herself at him with tooth and claw. But he was a big man and a strong one, and she knew she could not defeat him without a weapon. It would merely be a case of further pain and further humiliation. 'Or would you like me to do it for you?' he asked.

Sophie stood up, staggering a bit, and took off her clothes. He watched her with interest but no great sexual arousal. 'And the boots,' he said.

She had to sit down, on the earth, to do that. While she was taking off the boots he had produced from his saddlebag four small stakes, and the first of these he drove into the ground. 'Come here,' he said.

Sophie drew a deep breath and went to him. 'Lie down,' he commanded. 'On your back.'

She lay down on the hot earth and he secured her right wrist to the stake. Now she could take no more and swung at him with her left hand, nails clawed. But he caught the wrist easily enough. 'A woman of spirit as well as beauty,' he remarked. 'I can break this, Mrs Elligan. Or even cut it off. Do you wish that?'

Sophie subsided, panting. She was beaten. Yusuf released her to drive his second stake into the ground, and to this he secured her left wrist, leaving her quite helpless. She was terribly aware of the sun, now noon high, scorching her naked flesh.

'If you were a man,' Yusuf said, driving his third stake into the ground at the other end of her body, 'I would now castrate you.' He secured her right ankle to the stake. 'But that of course is not possible. Yet you must be mutilated.' He drove in the last stake and secured her left ankle. 'That is the law. So it will have to be your breasts.'

Sophie sucked air into her lungs and then hastily expelled it again, as that only increased his objectives. Yusuf smiled and drew his knife. 'They are marvellous breasts. So large ... our women do not have breasts that large. But there it is. There...' He cupped her right breast in his hand, his knife poised, while Sophie thought wildly, I am going to scream. For all my resolve I am going to scream.

She gazed up, past the man, at a circling vulture. Yusuf looked up too. 'Oh, yes,' he said. 'He can hardly wait to begin his feast. And you will still be alive when he tears at your flesh. There will be others, too. Others...' He suddenly frowned and stood up. Where half an hour previously there had been no vultures at all, now there was a sudden flock of them rising from beyond the next hill, disturbed by something the two humans could not yet see. 'By Allah–' Yusuf began, and spun round to hit the earth with a crash as several shots rang out.

Oh, my Lord! Sophie thought. But if someone had shot Yusuf... 'Help me!' she screamed. 'For God's sake, help me!'

She listened to horses' hooves and a few minutes later was surrounded by Italian lancers, peering at her with a mixture of consternation and delight. 'Help me,' she begged. 'Please!'

Edio himself dismounted to cut her free. 'Fetch a blanket,' he commanded. 'And send up the medical orderly.'

The blanket was produced and Sophie was wrapped in it. Despite the heat, she discovered she was shivering. Edio gave her a cup of wine to drink and the orderly arrived to smear the cuts on her legs and thighs with antiseptic; it burned, but nothing had ever felt so good...

'Sophie Elligan,' Edio remarked. 'You are a great survivor.' Sophie pushed hair from her eyes. 'And this?' Edio nudged Yusuf's body with the toe of his boot.

'I killed his uncle,' Sophie said. 'Sheikh al-Fadl.'

'The unravelling of history,' Edio

remarked. 'And he followed you all this way? However, that is done, is it not. If you are here, signora, your caravan must be close. Ah!' He looked at the hill behind Sophie where some figures had appeared. 'How many men does Andrews command?'

'A great number,' Sophie said. She was grateful to this man for saving her life, as he had saved her virtue five years before, and she felt she owed Clay nothing after the way he had surrendered her to a quite un-thinkable fate, but Ned was down there. 'And he has machine-guns.'

'Ah,' Edio said. 'But then, so do I. And I do not think he has so many men after all. Besides, do not I have a trump card?' He smiled at her.

'It won't do you any good,' Sophie said. 'Why do you think I am here? Clay surrendered me to Yusuf. He isn't likely to allow you to blackmail him by threatening to shoot me.'

Edio considered her for a few moments. 'Then we shall have to overwhelm him by sheer force,' he said. 'That is a treat I have long promised myself.'

Clay got down from the wagon, less to watch Sophie being dragged away behind Yusuf's horse, than to avoid having to look at her husband and lover, much less Anne. If he felt disgusted with what had happened, he still had no doubt that he had had no choice. Sophie had boasted of not being as other women, of having a man's heart inside that enchanting body. She had lived on that scale all of her life. Now she had to die on that scale. It had always been on the cards. While he ... he had been given a job to do and he would do it. He beckoned Moosai. Like everyone else, Moosai was looking unhappy; the members of the caravan had grown very fond of Mrs Elligan on the march north. 'Prepare to move out,' Clay said. 'Sheikh Yusuf will catch us up.'

'Yes, bwana,' Moosai said and gave the necessary orders. Clay went up to the head of the column.

Anne watched him go through the canvas curtain at the back of the wagon. She had been prepared to spend the rest of her life with him, she thought. But was that such a terrible future? He was no more ruthless than James Martingell had been. Or herself, for that matter, when she had had to be. A woman who had killed both her husband and her son. She climbed over the tailgate. 'Where are you going?' Richard demanded.

'Don't you think I'd better find out how *we* stand?' Anne asked.

'Leave your revolver,' Richard said.

Anne frowned at him. 'You're not going to be stupid, are you? She's probably dead by now.'

'Just leave it,' Richard said.

Anne shrugged, drew the revolver, and laid it on the floor of the wagon, then she climbed down and went behind Clay. 'What do you have in mind?' Ned asked. 'One revolver?'

'Two,' Richard said. 'Sophie's is here too.'

'Twelve shots,' Ned said.

'Enough to settle with that bastard.'

'And then?'

Richard shrugged and his mouth twisted with pain from his shoulder. 'At least we'll have avenged Sophie.'

'You do love her, after all,' Ned said.

'Don't you?'

'Give me the other gun,' Ned said.

They gazed at each other in consternation as several shots echoed across the valley.

Anne had just caught Clay up. 'I wish to apologise for what I said back there. I realise there was nothing else you could do.'

Clay glanced at her and was as taken aback as anyone by the shots. 'Fuck it,' he snapped. 'Moosai,' he shouted. 'Get three men up on that ridge and find out who that is.'

Anne caught his arm. 'It can only be the Italians.'

'Yes.' He shrugged himself free and hurried back to the wagons. The caravan had just been preparing to move out. Now he shouted to his people to form their usual perimeter when in danger.

Anne hurried behind him, uncertain what to do, and watched the preparations. It could only be an enemy patrol, surely. But ... two of the men from the ridge were already hurrying back, shouting and gesticulating. 'What are they saying?' Anne asked.

'A squadron of cavalry. Lancers. Maybe two hundred. They have Sophie.'

'You mean she's not dead? Oh, thank God for that.'

'They got Yusuf,' Clay said.

'You value him above Sophie?'

'We have fought together for a long time,' Clay said. He went off to see to the siting of the machine-guns, but before he could do so the afternoon was filled with the drumming of hooves. Over the ridge came the lancers, spearheads lowered, gleaming in the sun beneath the fluttering pennons.

'Fire,' Clay shouted. But the machine-guns had not been emplaced, and already most of his men were retreating; they had never seen death coming at them with such terrifying majesty. 'Stand fast!' Clay bellowed. 'We can hold them. We–' He went down on to his hands and knees.

'What the hell–' Richard painfully crawled to the rear of the wagon to look out.

'I'd say we've been rescued by the wrong

people,' Ned said, watching the Abyssinians running as fast as they could; most were throwing away their weapons in terror.

'Do we fight or surrender?'

'I don't think we have much choice,' Ned said. 'As long as we can get our hands on that bastard Yusuf–'

Anne appeared at the tailgate, supporting Clay with an arm round his waist; her bush tunic was dark with blood. 'Help me get him up.'

'Him?' Ned asked. 'After what he did?'

'He's badly wounded. Help me.'

Richard extended his good hand and with Anne pushing they rolled Clay into the wagon. 'I should blow his brains out,' Ned grumbled and then looked out of the back at the lancers surrounding the wagons.

'Signor Carew,' Edio said. 'It has been a long time. Now, I have something that belongs to you.'

Ned drew a deep breath, uncertain what he was going to see – and watched Sophie dismounting beside the Italian general.

She had dressed herself in her torn clothes and looked like a rag doll – but she was alive. 'Sophie!'

She clambered into the wagon to embrace him. Then looked at where Anne was trying to staunch Clay's bleeding. But Edio had given orders and his medical orderlies now took over, speaking in Italian.

'So this is the famous Mr Andrews,' Edio remarked. 'I have waited a long time for this meeting.'

'He is badly wounded,' Anne said.

'They tell me he will survive,' Edio said.

'So that you can hang him?' Anne demanded.

'Who is this woman?' Edio inquired.

'I am Lady Anne Martingell,' Anne snapped.

'Martingell. Ah! Even more history is unravelled. And you, signor?'

'Major Richard Elligan,' Richard said.

'Ah,' Edio said again, looking at Sophie.

'My husband,' Sophie said.

'But not your lover,' Edio smiled. 'And you are all in this together. I would certainly be within my rights to hang you, here and now.'

Sophie caught her breath and Ned squeezed her hand. 'However,' Edio said, 'from my point of view, this has turned out well. I have captured your guns. And my country has no desire to antagonise either Great Britain or the United States by executing some citizens of those countries. And all three of you...' his gaze swept the men, 'seem to have suffered grievously. Besides, you, Mrs Elligan, and you, Mr Carew, saved the life of my Lalia. That is not something I can ever forget. It is only a few miles to the Kenyan border. I will allow you one wagon and a team of mules, one rifle and some ammunition, and a week's supply of food. Leave Abyssinia and do not ever come back.'

'Touché,' Ned said.

'What do you mean by that?' Edio demanded.

'Merely that it is remarkable how men nearly always think alike.'

'We owe you our lives,' Sophie said. 'I do, certainly.'

The wagon had been turned and equipped, and Anne already sat in the driving seat; she and Sophie would be responsible for the journey back until the men could recover, and that was now unlikely to be until Nairobi. Edio made a deprecating gesture. 'What are beautiful women for but to be succoured?'

'Nonetheless, I am grateful. And for your generosity in allowing us to depart. I wish you to know that. If it ever were to happen–'

Edio shook his head. 'Don't even dream of it. The next time I may not be in a position to be so generous.' He kissed her knuckles. 'Merely to have met you is sufficient reward for anything I have done.'

'There have been some very odd goings-on up-country,' the District Commissioner said. 'First three men stagger in, half-dead,

426

claiming they were set upon by gun-runners...' He paused to gaze at Sophie.

Who looked at Anne. 'How very strange,' Anne commented.

'And now you two ladies arrive, with three wounded men... How are they, by the way?'

'The doctor says they will survive,' Sophie said. 'We shall take them down to the coast as soon as they can be moved.'

'And were you too set upon by gun-runners?'

'No,' Anne said. 'We were after game, and I am afraid inadvertently strayed across the border into Abyssinia, and were set upon by tribesmen. We were fortunate to be rescued by an Italian patrol.'

'An Italian patrol,' the District Commissioner remarked, looking from one to the other. 'I suppose two such charming ladies, blessed with both beauty and brains, have the right to consider the entire world to be composed of fools. However, you may one day discover that there are a few other people who also have brains, if not beauty. May I ask what are your intentions, once your menfolk are sufficiently recovered to travel?'

'We shall go down to Mombasa and take a ship for Europe,' Sophie said.

'I think that is an excellent idea,' the District Commissioner said. 'There is not a shred of evidence that you were doing anything illegal in Kenya, however... I do think you should remove this colony from your list of places to visit in the future. I will wish you good fortune.'

'You are welcome to berths on the *Bremerhaven*,' Sophie told Anne and Richard, when they reached Mombasa. 'And to be dropped off at whatever place you wish.' She grinned. 'You can legitimately claim to have stopped the arms shipment ever reaching Gidole. Even Pemberton must accept that.'

'That is very kind of you,' Anne said. 'We accept.'

'And you, Clay?' They stood on the dockside and watched the steamer nosing its way into the crowded harbour. How good she looked, and on board her there would be baths and clean clothes ... and a certified cheque for a hundred and twenty-five thousand pounds. Once again, not earned. But nobody was going to take that off her, Sophie was determined.

Like all the men Clay still moved stiffly. But he seemed perfectly fit again. 'I think I'll find my own way,' he said.

'Where to?'

'Back to the States. Stockbroking. Maybe I'm getting too old for this kind of life.' He looked at Anne, but she turned away from him. His mouth twisted; he no longer held any appeal for her. 'You want to watch that woman,' he said in a low voice. 'She has both the morals and the venom of a black mamba.'

'I know that,' Sophie said. 'Well I'll wish you good fortune.'

'Sophie ... do you forgive me?'

'No,' Sophie said. 'What you allowed to happen was not something I can ever forgive.'

'I have a notion we'll meet again, you know. There'll be other little wars, needing guns ... although if I ever attempt to do business with you again, I'll need my head examined.'

'If you ever attempt to do business with me again,' Sophie said, 'I shall shoot you on sight.'

'That bastard,' Ned said. 'We should have made him come with us, and then chucked him over the side.' They sat together on the after deck of the *Bremerhaven* as she steamed towards the Horn of Africa.

'He did what he thought he had to do,' Sophie said. 'Just like...' she gestured at the just visible shoreline, 'all those men over there – basically decent men like Edio Rometti – are killing and being killed because they've been told it is what they have to do. I think we want to forget about them. We have each other.' She grinned.

'And a lot of money.'

'And those two?' Ned glanced at Anne and Richard who had just emerged on deck.

'They also have each other,' Sophie said and gave one of her throaty laughs. 'Don't you think they deserve that?'

This Large Print Book for the partially sighted, who cannot read normal print, is published under the auspices of

THE ULVERSCROFT FOUNDATION

THE ULVERSCROFT FOUNDATION

... we hope that you have enjoyed this Large Print Book. Please think for a moment about those people who have worse eyesight problems than you ... and are unable to even read or enjoy Large Print, without great difficulty.

You can help them by sending a donation, large or small to:

**The Ulverscroft Foundation,
1, The Green, Bradgate Road,
Anstey, Leicestershire, LE7 7FU,
England.**
or request a copy of our brochure for more details.

The Foundation will use all your help to assist those people who are handicapped by various sight problems and need special attention.

Thank you very much for your help.